FORTUNES
OF DEATH

SECRETS OF EPHESUS SERIES

Obedient Unto Death
Fortunes of Death
Powers of Death (coming soon)

FORTUNES
OF DEATH

SECRETS OF EPHESUS - BOOK 2

LIISA EYERLY

ST JOSEPH, MISSOURI USA

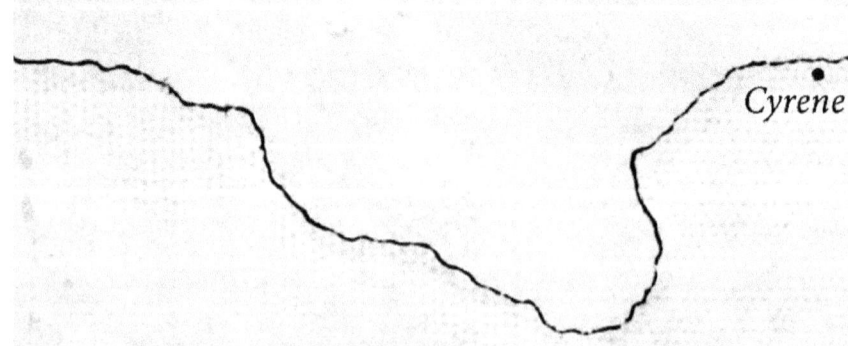

Rome

ITALY

SICILY

MALTA

IONIAN
SEA

GREECE

Corinth

T

MEDITERRA

Cyrene

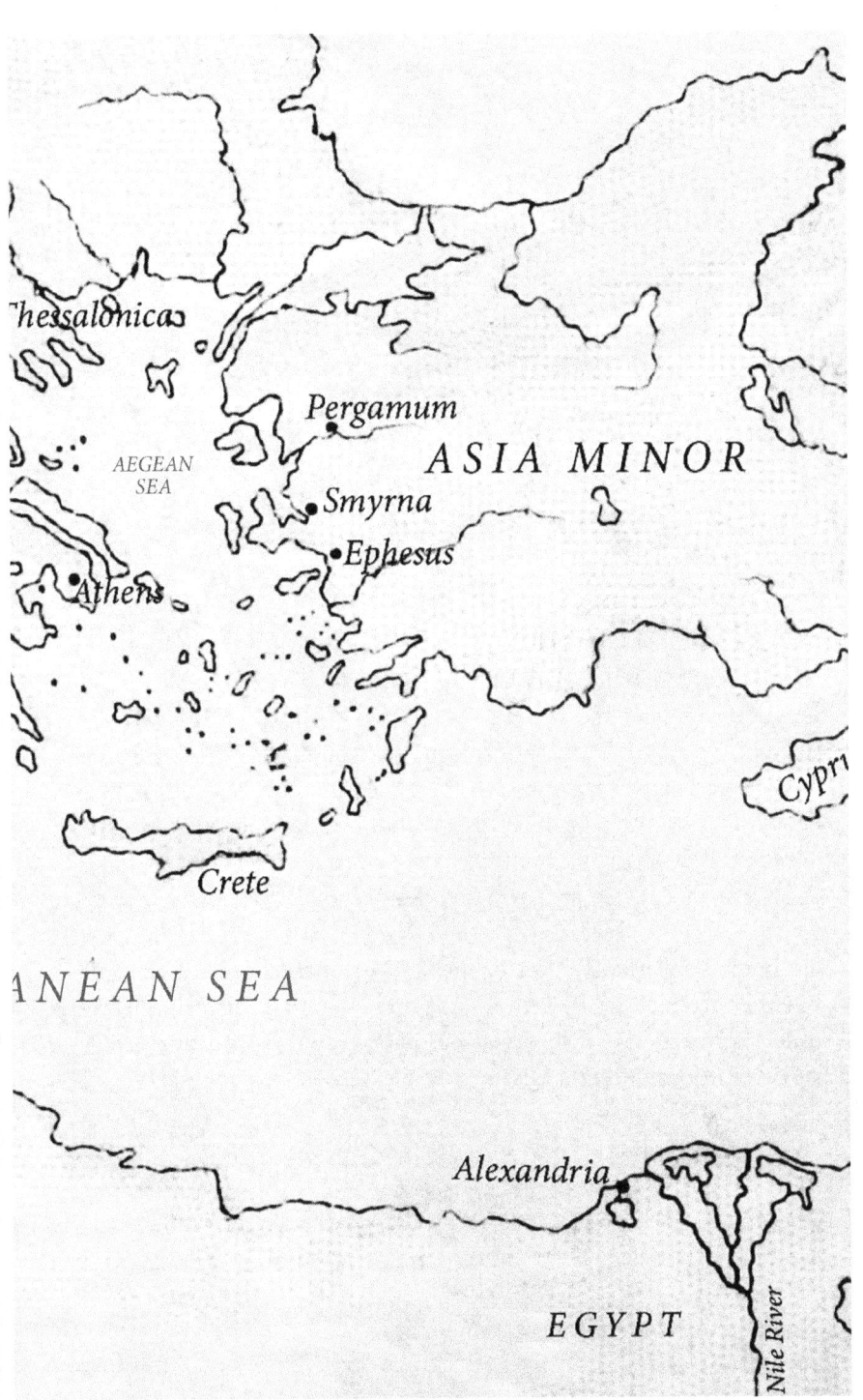

Thessalonica

AEGEAN
SEA

Pergamum

ASIA MINOR

Smyrna

Ephesus

Athens

Crete

Cyprus

ANEAN SEA

Alexandria

EGYPT

Nile River

Editor: Debra L. Butterfield
Cover Design: Tamara Clymer
Cover Image: ID 100619264 © Evgeny Ustyuzhanin | Dreamstime.com
Map Image: ID 18263899 © Pancaketom | Dreamstime.com

CHARACTERS

Sabinus Family

Sabina – daughter and sleuth
Quintus Catius Sabinus – Sabina's father, Roman magistrate titled Eirenarch, Guardian of the Peace
Amisi – Sabina's childhood nurse
Zarmig – father's bodyguard
Felix – family slave
Xeno – Sabina's dead husband

Murder victim's family and household

Dionysius Alexandros Antiochus – wealthy, elite citizen of Ephesus
Ursula – Dionysius's current wife, now widow
Paris – 22-year-old surviving second son from Dionysius' first wife
Diana – 15-year-old daughter from second wife
Titos – Ursula's slave
Ferocianus – slave gladiator
Pelopidas Antiochus – famous grandfather of Dionysius

Suspect's family

Yechiel – architect working for Dionysius on his library
Eunice –Yechiel's wife
Reuben – Eunice's uncle
Benjamin –Yechiel's deceased brother

Sabina's church family

Apollos – bishop of the local church
Apostle John – disciple of Jesus
Portia (Nicia) – friend of Sabina
Horace (Nicia) – Portia's husband

Assorted others

Loukas – Dionysius's banker friend
Agabus – competing architect
Mordax – ex-gladiator, adoptive father to Otho, criminal,
Otho – Paris's friend and Diana's fiancé
Cassandra – fortune teller, pythoness
Gnaeus Gratus – Dionysius's family lawyer
Flavius Fortunus – magistrate of religious observances, Sabina's father's nemesis
Domitian – reigning Roman emperor

VOCABULARY

Adonai: Hebrew word for Lord.

aediles: Roman magistrate responsible for public programs and buildings.

agora: a public open space used for assemblies and markets.

atrium: central court with rooms off of it.

caldarium: a very hot steamy room heated by a hypocaust, an under-floor heating system using tunnels with hot air, heated by a furnace tended by slaves. This was the hottest room in the regular sequence of bathing rooms.

carpentum: a bus or limousine of wealthy Romans. It had four wheels, a wooden arched rooftop, and was comfortable and spacious.

daemon: a supernatural being of a nature between gods and humans.

denarius: Roman coin.

equestrian: second highest social class.

frigidarium: room with a swimming pool filled with cold water used for cold-water baths and swimming.

Hispania: Roman province including Spain and Portugal.

impluvium: open roof with a pool underneath to catch rainwater.

lanista: trainer of gladiators.

litter: open or covered chairs or beds carried by two or more carriers to transport people.

ludus: (plural ludi) a gladiator training school; public games held for the entertainment of the Roman people.

mantle: loose sleeveless cloak or shawl.

manumission: the act of freeing slaves by their owners.

necropolis: cemetery.

nymphaeum: a grotto or shrine dedicated to nymphs. Can incorporate water.

pantomimes: dramatic entertainment in which performers express meaning through gestures accompanied by music.

paterfamilias: male head of the family.

peristyle: a row of columns surrounding a space within a building such as a court or internal garden.

plebian: a commoner.

pulse: an army staple of cooked wheat grains mixed with water, salt, fat, and olive oil or milk.

pythoness: female soothsayer, fortune teller, or conjuror of spirits.

retiarius: gladiator armed with a net and a spear.

sestertius: Roman coin.

stela, stele: a carved or inscribed stone slab or pillar used for commemorative purposes.

stola: traditional female garment corresponding to the togas worn by men.

strigil: curved blade used to scrape sweat and dirt from the skin after exercise.

toga: loose flowing outer garment worn by citizens of ancient Rome.

tunic: sleeveless garment reaching to the knees.

Yeshua: Hebrew name for Jesus.

ONE

S abina's heart raced as she rubbed her thumb over the emblem of the gold coin lying in her palm. The coarse woolen bag lay in the straw where she had dropped it. She sucked in slow shallow breaths easing the tightness in her chest.

"Mistress, are you all right?" Felix, the house slave, panted, having just climbed the steep stairs to the pigeon loft—Sabina's favorite place for respite and her morning prayers.

She blinked, squeezing her fist to hide the coin, and took a slow steadying breath before looking up. "What did the messenger say?"

"He said only to give you the bag."

She nodded, brushing one hand on her tunic, and carefully transferred the coin before she dusted barley chaff off the other. "Bring him to me immediately."

"The street boy…" Felix licked his lips. "I didn't realize you would want…he fled after handing me the bag. I beg your forgiveness, Mistress."

"Find him."

The slave's eyes flared wide, exposing the whites. "It is—"

"Impossible. I know." She let her hands drop, imagining the hun-

11

dreds of children begging in the streets of the teeming metropolis, the third-largest city in Domitian's Roman Empire. The boy would have melded into the crowds of Ephesus, indistinguishable in a filthy lice-infested tunic and bare feet.

"It is not your fault. You may leave me."

Felix bowed. A loud sigh escaped before he scurried off, batting away the flickering shadows of flustered pigeons.

Sabina slumped down on a large grain sack, her mind swirling with foreboding.

Cleopatra, her favorite pet pigeon, pecked at the small bag.

Cheap cloth for a costly coin. A coin she had never thought to see again. She uncurled her fist and read the inscription: Year two, Shekel of Israel. Year two of the Jewish five-year revolt against Rome. It symbolized the rebellion that had ended with Rome decimating Jerusalem, its temple, and over one million Jews across Israel. It didn't matter that they had crushed the uprising twenty-six years ago when she was only two years old or that she was a gentile.

A Christian.

She shivered. The Roman Empire was ruled by Emperor Domitian. If the authorities caught her with this coin, arrest, torture, and execution were assured. How had it found its way back to her?

She pushed an auburn curl from her forehead and plucked the bag from the bird's beak. It was barely light out, and the bird cooed in protest. "Sorry, Cleo, there's no breakfast in that." But something crinkled inside. She tore into the small bag and retrieved a piece of inked papyrus. The script was neat, precise, and brief, *Reuben the weaver. Seventh hour.* She clenched the coin, stopping only when her fingers turned numb. The abruptness of the summons was as disturbing as the cryptic message itself.

The seventh hour of the day gave her seven hours to plan—to plan what?—she was not going. What was she thinking? The anonymous note spelled trouble, danger, and her father would forbid it. Of course, she wasn't going. Her day was full. She was visiting her friend Portia later in the afternoon, much later. She sighed at her prudent decision.

She relaxed her grip, dropped the golden disk and message into the bag, and cinched the drawstring. It was still early. The pigeon keeper hadn't even replaced yesterday's straw. She inhaled the pungent scent of droppings from her father's fifty pigeons.

She moistened her lips and fingered the coin through the cloth. What to do with the coin? Hide it? Throw it away? It was too risky to keep.

Cleo clapped her wings and flew onto Sabina's lap. "No more barley today." The bird flew to her roost, warbling her complaint. Sabina stood and flexed the blood flow back into her fingers.

There was a gamble if she did not answer the summons. Someone needed to return the coin to its owner. How else would she find out who sent it? Did she have a choice? Curiosity had always been her Achilles' heel, drawing her into trouble so many times before. The coin, like a siren, called to her, promising intrigue and excitement. Both were lacking in the monotonous routine of a respectable widow managing her father's house.

Was this a fool's adventure destined to go wrong? It would undoubtedly increase her pagan father's distrust and ire or worse.

The coin could destroy their fragile truce. Or threaten the vital secret protecting Sabina's family and her father's powerful government position.

A position very much in jeopardy should her choice of religion be made public.

The coin's previous owner, Benjamin, had been poisoned, though not because of the coin. She had returned the coin to Yechiel, Benjamin's brother, after they had solved the murder. And yet she was the last person in the world Yechiel would contact.

She shook the bag. The coin's slight weight was real.

There was only one way to answer its mystery. She must ask Yechiel himself.

What did one wear to meet a traitor to Rome?

TWO

Where was he? Sabina tossed aside the scroll she was reading and checked the coin hidden under her mattress for the twentieth time. Felix should have been back hours ago. The Jewish section of Ephesus was only so big. How hard could it be to find one weaver's shop?

Footsteps smacked on the tile floor outside her room. Felix burst into the room, panting and red-faced. "It is not in the Jewish sector, Mistress. The shop is across town. Located among the other city weavers."

The location surprised her. But then, Yechiel was much more adept at espionage than she. Sabina slipped a pale blue linen mantle over her simple white tunic. She would have preferred her long outer cloak, with its secret pocket for her knife and coin purse but wearing wool at the beginning of summer would draw attention. She dug the bag from under her mattress and dropped it inside her money purse. She added her small ivory-handled knife and tied it to her tunic belt. The lump stuck out like a camel's hump. She patted the bulge down as best she could.

Felix frowned. "Your father wouldn't approve."

"We're just going shopping." No, her father wouldn't approve. She thrust a basket into his hands and sailed through the house, past the door guard with Felix muttering behind her.

She turned in the direction of Curetes Street and paused, relishing this façade of freedom. Long gone were her days of unsupervised childhood, where each trip to the market agora had been an adventure into a world respectable patrician women left to servants and slaves.

Her mind turned to memories of her youth when she had scrambled up mountains of rye and barley bags and slid down bales of cotton and papyrus. Hiding behind cages of squawking parrots made her laugh. Her skin still crawled remembering the baskets full of writhing snakes. She rubbed her forearm. She had nightmares of the slave trader's vice-like grip on her arm and his yelp from the prick of the small knife Zarmig, her father's bodyguard, had given her. Were it not for that…

That bruise on her arm had been her undoing. Upon returning home, her father forbade her to leave the house unaccompanied. Her escapades were over.

Sabina felt the crushing isolation of his edict descend like a hammer. Why should he care? He had shown little interest in her in the four years since her mother's death. She was twelve and nearly grown up. Her argument hit the unyielding wall of her childhood nurse, Amisi. Who agreed that Sabina was indeed an eligible young woman. She needed to prepare for a husband, not jeopardize her reputation by running the streets like a stray dog.

Zarmig's worried silence had sealed her fate. But he gave her a bigger knife.

"We turn left here." Felix's directions broke into her memories.

They reached the bustling main street. She patted the small purse avoiding the honed edge of the knife. It appeared her exploits weren't over.

The smokey incense rising from the emperor Domitian's altar filled her nostrils as they passed his temple. Several blocks farther, they skirted the line for the crowded public toilets. She glanced down the side street leading to a popular brothel, busy as usual.

"It's near the market agora." Felix turned onto the weavers' street. "Reuben's shop is one block that way, Mistress." He pointed to the right.

She scanned the crowds and various shops. Yechiel would be easy to spot. She need only look for a man taller than average, thin, and radiating arrogance, pride, and rudeness. He wasn't there. "Wait here until I return." But what if she didn't? What if…no. She couldn't think like that.

Reuben's shop displayed a delightful sign with two upright sheep dancing in colorful swaths of cloth. She fidgeted with the purse, retying it securely under her outer garment. Was she doing the right thing? Why would Yechiel request her help? He would not. It was time to end the mystery. She would hand the coin over and slink home with her father and Amisi none-the-wiser.

Sabina opened the door, walked in, and closed the door. Black enveloped her. She blinked as her eyes adjusted to the dimly lit shop, watching as shadows slowly formed into several racks of modest quality cloth. She bumped into a woman smelling strongly of onions. "I'm sorry."

A short, round-faced man with pudgy arms approached her warily. "May I help you?" The dim light softened but did not conceal two long purple scars, tightening and pulling back each side of his mouth.

Sabina stared at his distorted face. "Umm…" She quickly looked away, hoping he hadn't taken offense at her flustered response. She had expected to greet Yechiel, not explain her mission to a stranger—to return a treacherous gold coin that could get her killed. "Someone recommended your shop," Sabina mumbled.

"Ahh, I know someone. Follow me, please." The man strolled to a curtained doorway.

Sabina stared at the opening, her mouth suddenly dry. She didn't want to move. Was it too late to reconsider the dangers? The risks she had hastily discounted earlier.

She held her breath and remembered she wasn't alone. Felix waited somewhere outside. *Outside* being the critical word.

The man held the curtain aside and gestured her toward him.

She reached for the bulge under her mantel and felt the hard metal of Zarmig's knife—one of his many attempts to keep her safe. Zarmig had issued the warning that the blade was useless as a weapon. He had schooled her in many aspects of self-defense, most included running away, which was still an option. The knife, he stressed, might give a robber or her attacker a surprised pause, but its main benefit was to make sure she didn't pause or freeze in fear. The blade hidden beneath her garment instilled courage.

She let out her breath, deftly loosening the ties of the bag. She had to do this. Had to know what was so great that Yechiel had sent for her. And the coin was a danger to her and her family. Gripping the knife, she passed the man. The curtain dropped closed behind her.

She entered a long narrow atrium that looked in total disarray. Four empty looms stood in no discernable order around the shallow rectangular pool at the center of the atrium. The open roof above the pool slanted inward to spill its rainwater into the household reservoir, providing the business with water for rinsing the jumbled skeins of soaking yarn. Over-filled baskets lined the walls, spilling their billows of wool onto the floor like miniature clouds.

A lone woman sat out of the sun in the shadows at the room's far end. The woman waved her forward, and Sabina approached, withdrawing her hand from inside her money purse.

"*Shalom aleikheim.*" The woman removed her headscarf and smiled shyly. "I am Eunice, Yechiel's wife. You are just as I imagined you."

Sabina squeaked in surprise. "Yechiel's wife?" Eunice nodded, giving Sabina time to process the information. She'd been so sure she'd find Yechiel. The surprise left her mind blank.

Yechiel had spoken of his wife only a few times while investigating his brother's murder. Sabina had a hard time imagining anyone who would put up with Yechiel's stubborn, unyielding, narrow-minded, egotistical ways…but here she was.

"Yechiel?" Sabina glanced around.

"He is not here." The beautiful woman appeared no older than thirty. Her delicate loveliness awed Sabina. She admired the silky black braid falling effortlessly in place over Eunice's shoulder. No matter how much time Sabina spent arranging herself, she came off tousled and casually unkempt. Sabina compared Yechiel's thin disjointed frame next to his petite wife's figure. Remarkably, the pair complemented each other.

"Please sit." Eunice indicated a stool beside hers. "Thank you for coming."

Sabina sat, releasing a sigh. "My curiosity got the best of me."

"I was counting on that." Eunice smiled. "And perhaps the added lure of intrigue?"

Sabina raised an eyebrow. "Perhaps."

"Would you like some pomegranate juice?"

Sabina nodded. "Thank you."

The storefront's sounds filtered in from the other side of the curtain, but no one intruded.

Eunice filled two goblets from a ceramic jug on a table next to her with hands that trembled.

Sabina adjusted her initial observation. Eunice appeared calm, but she held a nervous tension in check under the surface. Her smooth honey complexion was unnaturally pale compared to the native coloring of her hands.

Eunice replaced the jug on the narrow wooden table and handed Sabina a goblet. Each woman silently sipped the tangy juice.

"First, I ask your forgiveness for putting you in danger. It is a risk I had no right to ask."

"It was my choice to come." She could not blame Eunice for a danger Sabina had dismissed after a few minutes of thought.

"My husband is in trouble," Eunice said.

What trouble? Why her? Why were they meeting here? Because none of the answers would fully explain Eunice's request, she said. "I don't understand why Yechiel would ask for me."

Eunice's face turned from the palest peach to bright pink.

"Ahh." Sabina set her drink aside. "He does not know I'm here."

Eunice clasped her hands. "Please, do not judge me a disobedient wife."

"I am not in a position to judge others' disobedience." Sabina had struggled her entire life to follow the rules and proper etiquette and had failed miserably. "My shortcomings are myriad."

"Do not belittle your strengths." Eunice's face turned serious. "If not for your cleverness and insight, Yechiel's brother's murderer would have escaped."

"Yechiel told you that?"

"It was easy to surmise from what he didn't say." Eunice's smile lit up her eyes.

"It's just that I barely know Yechiel, and *know* is a great exaggeration. After solving Benjamin's murder, we did not expect to meet each other again. Not to mention the risk of death for whoever is caught carrying the coin." She shook her head.

Eunice's eyelashes fluttered. "I meant no threat. You are courageous to have come. The coin carries no obligation to help us, but I had hoped you might make some inquiries on Yechiel's behalf. Perhaps investigate."

Investigate what? Why hadn't Yechiel asked her?

As if reading Sabina's thoughts, Eunice continued, "My husband fights for the righteous causes of others, but he can be extremely stubborn where his safety is concerned. He would never have agreed to involve you."

"Has Yechiel been accused of wrongful actions?"

Eunice shook her head. "Yechiel designed a library for a rich man who died yesterday. We Jews cannot be too careful when the Romans look for conspiracies everywhere."

The coin hidden in her bag was Jewish gold minted to support the Israelite rebellion. And a coinage that could expose a secret Jewish brotherhood committed to a resurgent uprising. A brotherhood, Sabina believed, Yechiel would kill to protect. "It is not that I would not help, but…I don't know what you think I can do."

"My uncle Reuben offered this meeting space away from the local gossips." Eunice gestured to the looms. "I lead a sheltered life. I do not leave my home except to attend synagogue, visit family, and shop in our local Jewish neighborhood. But even within our close family, there can be resentment and jealousy. I do not need access to the outside world to recognize plotting. No matter what Yechiel says, I do not imagine the danger."

"You do not strike me as fanciful."

Eunice inclined her head. "No, if you ask anyone, they will say that Yechiel married me for my level head and good sense. We also love each other very much. I could not live if something happened to him."

"I'm flattered that you think I'm courageous, but I'm not belittling my skills. I'm honest about them. While solving the murder, I endangered my father's magisterial position and my family's wealth and status. I was nearly arrested. I don't think those are skills you want."

"Realistic and sensible as well."

"Not everyone would agree. Eunice, I came here to return the coin. And to see why someone had sent it to me. I don't know how I can help. And Yechiel has not been accused of anything."

"Yechiel has shared events of recent days," Eunice said quietly, "and though he says there was nothing suspicious to worry about and he is in no danger, I believe my husband lies to me only because he is deceiving himself. The authorities are calling it a horrible accident for now, but I know the Romans will need to place blame. Who better than a Jew?"

"I am sure someone within your community could help you. Someone more qualified."

Eunice dropped her head. When she looked up, her lips formed a polite smile. "Yes, of course, I have a large family. I should have tried them first."

"I believe you've misplaced your hope." Sabina put her cup down. "I'm sorry."

"Do not apologize. I had no right to ask you."

Sabina stood. Eunice's charitable assurance did little to comfort Sabina. Against any good sense, she sympathized with the plea of this charming woman. And, as always, the nosy part of her muzzled her internal warnings to leave as fast as possible. "Perhaps I could listen to the gossip. Be ears on the outside. It's not a lot."

Eunice leapt up. "It gives me much. It gives me hope." She clapped her hands together. "I will not apologize for wasting your time. I am delighted to meet the extraordinary woman who risked so much to hunt down Benjamin's killer."

"Extraordinary?" Sabina raised her eyebrows.

"Yechiel may have said impertinent, but I know what he meant." Eunice squeezed Sabina's hands gently and then released them. "I am grateful you came."

Sabina handed her the coin bag. "You will need this."

"It is best if we wish to keep you out of trouble." Eunice shook her head wryly, placing the bag on her chair.

Sabina walked to the door and then turned to Eunice. "Most gentile women are not as impertinent as I."

"Then I thank God you are not like most women, Eunice said, her tone somber.

Sabina coughed softly. Not like most women was exactly her problem.

She walked home, ignoring Felix's curious looks. The less he knew, the less he could report to her father.

She would do as she promised but had little hope she'd hear any news of a Jewish architect. She understood Eunice's dilemma. Her cloistered life left her few options. Sabina may well be her only choice.

Eunice's world was so different from her own. Full of supportive family members, an obstinate but devoted husband, and the surety that she belonged and was loved. Just because God hadn't granted Sabina even one of those blessings, didn't mean she envied Eunice's situation exactly. But her morning prayers, asking for a chance at love, were becoming less optimistic.

Even God couldn't fix her most significant hurdle, her dead suitors.

She couldn't repair her reputation as a cursed woman or the resulting absence of marriage proposals. She drew in a long quivering breath. Except Marcus, who had defied the superstition. She pushed thoughts of him away. It was becoming easier with each day.

THREE

Sabina followed a slave through the atrium of the large sprawling villa. Sounds from the nearby harbor and warehouses disappeared as they entered the cool of Portia's private garden. They stopped by a bush sculpted into a leaping dolphin, its leafy image mirrored in the crystal water of a reflecting pool.

"Mistress." The slave bowed, announcing their presence.

Portia lay with her face buried in the couch. Her hennaed locks were tousled and strewn across the cushions. "I said I didn't want to be disturbed." The words emerged with a muffled sob.

"Portia?" Sabina stepped away from the shrub.

Portia sat up, wiping the back of her hand across her wet cheeks. "Oh, Sabina, I didn't think you would get here so quickly." The black sackcloth of mourning hung limply on her willowy figure. "Thank you for coming."

Sabina stiffened in alarm. The sixteen-year age difference between the two women was usually indistinguishable, but today, Portia looked every one of her forty-four years. Over the years Sabina had known her, she had never seen the stylish older woman without her ivory face cream, tastefully kohled eyes, and glistening rouged lips. Today the reddest part of Portia's face was her nose.

Sabina rushed to her and knelt. "Has something happened to Horace? I would have come immediately had I known." Had Portia's gregarious husband succumbed to his yearly dangerous trading ventures that left Portia running the business alone for months, worrying about her husband, bandits, deadly storms, disease, injury, and deceitful trading partners?

"It's not Horace. Just this week, he sent news and a package ahead of his caravan's arrival." Portia sniffled.

Relief washed over Sabina. "The congregation has been praying for his safe return."

"Thank you. It could be worse. I thank God he is not a merchant sailor and I am spared the torment of shipwrecks and drowning."

Sabina glanced down at her hands and didn't move.

Portia stopped speaking, then gasped. "Oh, Sabina. I am so thoughtless. You still miss Marcus?"

Did she miss him? Is that what the hollow feeling was each time she thought of him? Or selfishly because he was likely her last chance for a husband and children? "It's been months since he sailed back to Rome. He's probably married and starting a family by now. I'm happy for him." She tried to sound lighthearted, but it wouldn't fool Portia.

"It is still a loss." Portia patted the cushion beside her. "Come sit. It is hard to see God's goodness when we are hurting."

"I'll be fine. I'd just rather not talk about him." Sabina slid her sandals off and curled up next to Portia.

"Have you found news of your sisters? You said you were beginning to search."

Sabina shook her head. Another failure. "I don't know where to start. In the twenty years since Mother died, any clues to the location of the newborns have vanished. Amisi said she gave one infant to a family traveling through Ephesus, so I am concentrating on the older two who may live here." And who probably didn't survive. "I can't help but think how different...how happy my life would have been if they'd been part of it...if only father..."

"Sabina, if you pursue the search for your sisters, remember it is a path to the future, not into the past. Satan uses our pain and bitterness chaining us to old injustices."

"It's hard to let go of the hurt."

"It sounds contradictory, but to find peace we must fight, giving thanks to God for His goodness."

"Which means to stop feeling sorry for myself."

"It's not easy."

Sabina wasn't sure she wanted to let go. She sighed and leaned in. "But discussing my problems isn't why you asked me here. Tell me, why are you grieving?"

Portia covered her mouth, constraining a sob. "I have received news of the death of a dear friend, Dionysius Antiochus."

Sabina gasped. "The Dionysius? He's dead? What happened?"

Portia's head dropped. Muted sobs alternated with hiccups. "I shouldn't have burdened you. I'm a mess."

"I'm glad you asked me to come." Sabina wrapped Portia in her arms and held her. "I am just surprised. I didn't realize you were friends. He was one of our city's most..."

Portia's wet nose sniffled across Sabina's ear before pulling away. "Notorious citizens, I know."

"I was going to say prominent. The citizens of Ephesus enthusiastically follow every one of his scandalous exploits, but like all gossip, separating truth from fiction wasn't easy."

"You're too kind. Dio was never one for subtleties. His money and sexual liaisons were renowned throughout Ephesus, perhaps throughout the empire. He didn't flaunt them, but he didn't hide them either."

Sabina bit her lip to keep from blushing. "It is hard to disregard the stories."

"Hard even for me, and I loved him deeply."

"You never spoke of him." Sabina tried to imagine Portia loving or even befriending the man Sabina knew only by his roguish reputation. Portia held the respected position of deaconess in Sabina's church. Portia had converted to the faith as an adult and was a devoted leader. Her reputation was unblemished. Sabina tried to emulate Portia's good, faithful, and loving example.

"You could say Dio and I were friends from birth. Our families trace their allegiance to each other back generations. We were born only hours apart and spent more time together than most siblings. Somewhere amongst the great aunts and distant cousins, we were related." Portia swiped her finger over her cheeks. "Mostly he was a friend."

"I'm sorry." Sabina hugged Portia tightly.

After a minute, Portia sat back. "He always reminded me he was older, irresistible, and indestructible." Portia sniffed and began crying again. "Those were about the only things we agreed on."

Sabina waited until her friend dried her eyes and blew her nose. "Not indestructible."

Portia sniffled and nodded. "I miss him already. Many friendships face storms. Ours hit rocks but never sank."

"Then you have memories to cherish."

"Many." Portia clapped her hands, and the servant who had escorted Sabina appeared. "Bring some wine, figs, and roasted almonds." She turned back to Sabina. "I haven't eaten all day. But you are cheering me up already. Just talking about Dio brings him back, his life spilling over because nothing could contain him."

"Memories are gifts. That is a terrible part of death, and how fast we forget characteristics we cherished most in a person." Sabina thought of the childhood memories she clung to of her mother.

"Dio was not one to be forgotten. He was not afraid of death but refused to be irrelevant after death. Leaving a worthy legacy had become an obsession of late. He commissioned a library to rival Alexandria's. A monumental achievement that would guarantee the Dionysius Antiochus family name would be honored for centuries."

Tentacles of coincidence wrapped around Sabina's heart. What had Eunice said? A man Yechiel was designing a library for died. "A library?"

"To immortalize himself as a benefactor of the city. It is a magnificent civic gift to the people of Ephesus."

"It's extremely generous." A rich man Eunice had quoted. "How did he die?"

"That is what makes his death even more tragic. The entryway arch

26

of the library accidentally collapsed. He was crushed."

Sabina gasped. "How awful."

What had Eunice said? *They're calling it a horrible accident for now.* Sabina felt a twinge in her stomach. Could it be a coincidence? Zarmig didn't believe in coincidences. Sabina couldn't count the times he'd said that most troubles began with a reputed coincidence. "What caused the collapse?"

Portia closed her eyes as if blocking out the nightmarish image. "I don't know. The rumors are that the stones broke every bone below his neck. The slaves who lifted the blocks from his body found Dio with his eyes open, his handsome face untouched."

Sabina shuddered. "Who is the architect?" She held her breath.

"A man named Agabus. He has designed and built many monuments and buildings in Ephesus."

"Agabus?" Sabina exhaled a deep, audible huff. Apparently, coincidences did happen. "Are you sure it wasn't Yechiel?"

"I remember the name Agabus because he built that gaudy monstrosity of a nymphaeum near the market agora. It takes an unimaginable lack of talent to destroy the meditative relaxation of a fountain." Portia's forehead creased in thought. "Why does the name Yechiel sound familiar?"

"I worked with Yechiel to solve Benjamin's murder. They were brothers."

Portia tapped her upper lip with a fingernail. "Also, an architect, correct?"

Sabina nodded.

A frown flickered across Portia's face. "What a strange coincidence."

"Yes, odd." Sabina's stomach fluttered.

Portia pursed her lips. Her natural beauty radiated through puffy eyes and tear-streaked cheeks. "I confess I asked you here for more than your company today. I have a favor."

Sabina self-consciously tucked an errant curl back into place. "Of course."

"Dio lays in state at his family home. I must visit. With Horace gone, I can't bear to go alone…would you accompany me?"

"I didn't know Dionysius."

"Nor does half of the town who will be calling on the family. And I have a gift to deliver to his daughter. Dio requested it during Horace's previous trading venture, and it arrived in Horace's package. Dio spoiled his children terribly."

"How many children does he have?"

"Two living. The eldest son died. Paris is his son from his first wife, and Diana, a daughter from his second marriage. I must remind myself she is fifteen, a woman now." Portia sighed, shaking her head. "Dio and Ursula, his third wife…widow, had no children." Portia sniffed. "I confess I'm a coward. I can't bear meeting Ursula alone."

"Comforting the bereaved is difficult."

"That's not the problem." Portia drew a deep breath, straightening her shoulders as if weighed by a huge burden. "Ursula has always suspected Dio's friendship with me was more than what it was."

Sabina raised an eyebrow. "But you are married."

Portia gave Sabina a cynical half-smile. "Married women were a challenge to Dio, not a deterrent. After all of Dio's affairs, I can't blame Ursula. But I was never one of his conquests. Once, when we were thirteen, Dio tried, but his seduction was half-hearted, and we both knew it. Our shared passion was learning, and knowledge was our mutual love. Once I married Horace, Dio came to respect him, even though Horace was well below Dio's social status, and worse, Horace had to work to earn a living."

Sabina looked around the luxurious home that hosted her Christian congregation as a church and place of ministry. Horace had walls removed between two rooms to accommodate the growing flock of believers. A three-storied marble colonnade encircled three distinctive interior gardens. A fountain in the distance splashed as it sprayed its cooling mists throughout its outdoor sanctuary. All possible because of Horace and Portia's import and export of eastern silks and trade items. Portia had married below her social status but not below her economic station.

"Ursula can be erratic in the best of times, and I have no idea what to expect with Dio's death. Grieving? Tantrums? Threats?"

"She sounds lovely."

Portia rose. "Don't underestimate her. She can be bewitching. So much so that Dio divorced his second wife to marry her."

"I heard he seduced Ursula away from his best friend." Sabina wiped a rivulet of sweat from her brow. The noonday sun overpowered the shady arbor plants, and the reflecting pool offered no cooling fountain mist.

"I wish I could say don't believe everything you hear, but Dio did what Dio wanted, and nothing deterred him. The old Dio, at least."

"The old Dio?"

"Dio had never cared what others thought of him. But he had decided his reputation and legacy needed enhancing."

"Noble acts? He doesn't sound like a God-fearer?"

"Dio? No." Portia's voice carried an intense sorrow. "We often debated religion. I'd share my Christian beliefs, and he would laugh at them. He did his best to demolish my reasoning, sometimes bringing me to tears. His logic was piercing. But logic leaves gaps, and he'd bring more questions the next visit. More than once, I went to the church elders, Apollos, and even John to get answers."

"Our John?"

"Who better to respond than an apostle taught by Jesus?" Portia said. "Dio mocked all religions, not just Christianity. When I first confessed Christ as my God, I expected him to disappear like my other friends. Either embarrassed or afraid to associate with me."

"Did he abandon you?" Sabina asked.

Portia's eyes welled with tears. "No, he alone defended me. He applauded my rebellious nonconformity. His highest praise. He was a complex man." Portia wiped her eyes and smiled. "Our life choices were incompatible, yet our friendship survived, even thrived on our disagreements. Dio and I were blessed with tutors who molded and encouraged our curious and questioning natures. Many tutors are mere childcare."

"A rare friend indeed." Few of Sabina's friends would sympathize if they knew she practiced Christianity.

"Dio was fascinated by our God until I explained how a holy God differed from the Roman, Greek, and Egyptian gods he knew. He took

29

particular offense to our God demanding moral perfection from His followers. The irrationality of God requiring the impossible and then condemning humans for not attaining it. You shall be holy, for I, the LORD your God am holy."

"I can see where his life choices would make that mandate challenging."

Portia snorted. "He said just because I was a paragon of virtue didn't mean everyone had to follow my moral code."

"You do set a high standard." A standard Sabina routinely failed to emulate but so appreciated.

"Compared to Dio I may look exemplary, but not when tested against God's standard of holiness." Portia reached for a fig and took a bite. "During that visit, his wine goblet had leaked onto this white tunic. We discovered a small crack. Before I could apologize, he flung the vessel, shattering it against the wall."

"Was he angry at his ruined tunic?"

Portia shrugged. "No, Dio had a temper. But he smugly pointed out that it only takes one tiny transgression, like the goblet's crack, and he and I instantly become the same…defective, imperfect, and worthless."

"So at least he recognized that if God expects perfection, every cracked vessel must be thrown away."

Portia sighed. "Dio took great pleasure throwing my words back at me. If one transgression or sin is intolerable, my life of sacrificial living and charitable works and his hedonistic pleasures and indulgences all come to the same end. Hopelessly unacceptable."

Sabina sympathized with Dio's defiance. "No one wants to acknowledge they are failing. Did you tell him that our God loves broken vessels?"

"Failure wasn't a problem as long as he set the rules." Portia drew in a long breath that quivered. "If he didn't break his own standards, why would he need God's love or forgiveness? Dio was a flame that tested and strengthened my faith." She closed her eyes briefly as if cementing the memory before resuming. "I shall miss our heated exchanges."

Sabina rolled her eyes in skepticism, then noted Portia's sincerity. "Honestly, I can't imagine anyone enjoying debates," Sabina said with conviction. She did not enjoy sparring with her father, Zarmig, or

Amisi, which is what seemed to be happening all the time.

"Nor could Horace. Can you imagine Horace arguing politics, Plato, Aristotle, or the latest astronomical discovery? He would go to bed rolling his eyes, as Dio pounded his rebuttals into the table late into the night." A smile formed then flitted quickly away. "Horace will be as heartbroken as I."

"God blessed you with a friend who shared your passions."

Portia sniffed and dabbed a napkin under her nose. "Dio and I delved into the great mysteries of life. His library will be a fitting testament to his quest for answers." Portia reached for a second fig, then put it back. She paused, tipping her head. "I'm certain Agabus was the name Dio mentioned as the building's architect."

Relief washed through Sabina. Agabus, not Yechiel. "It is easy to forget a name." Perhaps she could help Portia and Yechiel. With one simple visit, she'd confirm that the architect wasn't Yechiel, alleviate Eunice's worry, and fulfill her friendship duty to Portia. "I'd be happy to accompany you."

Portia smiled sheepishly. "Tomorrow morning?"

"Into Ursula's den, we go."

"Thank you." Portia tipped her head back and rubbed her neck. She sighed, rolling her shoulders to relax. But Sabina did not relax. A tingling of fear nagged at her. If Agabus was not the architect and if one of Ephesus's most influential and powerful families accused Yechiel of Dionysius's death, Eunice did not imagine the trouble brewing for her husband. Yechiel would need help.

FOUR

Sabina reclined among the pillows, stabilizing her and Portia against the jostling of the litter carriers. "Does Dionysius's family know you're Christian?"

"No. Dio would not have given Ursula that weapon to use against me. They are a household devoted to the old ways and would be shocked that anyone would insult the gods and bring down their wrath."

"Especially Artemis." The battle between the protector goddess of Ephesus and Christianity fueled her father's opposition to her faith. Why his wife and only daughter had joined a religious sect inviting arrest and execution infuriated and baffled him. Were it not for his deathbed oath to her mother, Sabina might well be worshiping the goddess.

"Yes." Portia straightened her shimmering yellow linen stola, adjusting it over her pale green tunic. "I see no reason for the topic to come up. Ursula would probably call Magistrate Flavius Fortunus to arrest me on the spot."

Sabina shuddered at the mention of her father's political and personal nemesis—a man devoted to destroying her father and whoever got in the way of his revenge. Cautiously, she had observed Flavius Fortunus's influence grow as the magistrate of religious matters. He monitored the observance of the god's festivals and sacrifices, excluding the God of the new Christian cult. The Christian blasphemers were to be located and killed.

The four litter carriers stopped their conveyance. Portia drew the curtains aside and Sabina stared out at a massive home nearly the size of a country villa with a broad staircase leading to an ornate portico with marble pillars depicting life-size muses.

A man of average height descended the stairs.

"That's Loukas Rhodius," Portia whispered into Sabina's ear. "Dio's friend and financial advisor. Dio trusted him completely with his finances. The house of Dionysius Alexandros Antiochus would not be as rich were it not for Loukas's financial genius. He has funded several of Horace's riskier ventures. He is rumored to be Ursula's lover."

"And Dionysius trusted him?"

"With his finances."

Sabina watched Loukas duck into a litter waiting at the bottom of the stairs. "Surely, Ursula wouldn't be entertaining a lover. Her husband just died."

"The rich make up their own rules."

"You're rich," Sabina said.

Portia wiggled a finger at Sabina. "Not that kind of rich. Perhaps it is just gossip. Dio didn't talk about his love life with me."

"If Ursula was having an affair, why was she jealous of your friendship with Dio?"

"If Ursula had heard half the arguments Dio and I engaged in, she would know I was no competition for his affections. Dio directed his skewering wit at religion, Christianity in particular, and me."

"Yet, you enjoyed it?"

"Not being skewered, but it was intellectually exhilarating. So, yes."

What would it be like to discuss with a give and take, given a chance to defend or explain one's beliefs and ideas with friends and family? Sabina would never describe conversations with her father as enjoyable. She couldn't even describe them as conversations because that required a two-way exchange. Her father spoke, and she listened and obeyed...most of the time.

She didn't want to dwell on the other times.

"Ursula is unpredictable. I'm never sure what to do, like the winds of Boreas and Notus—winter and summer. Her volatility was one of the qualities Dio loved. He said she kept life exciting."

"She sounds exhausting," Sabina said as a litter bearer helped them alight.

Portia nodded. "It's Diana I've come to see. I'm hoping you can divert Ursula. She loves to talk about the latest hairstyles."

"Then we'll have nothing to talk about. I'm constantly behind on the latest styles." No matter how hard Amisi tried to interest her, she never found the time, spending it instead with her plants, gardening, and raising pigeons. Amisi informed her that performing slave tasks would not attract a husband.

"You'll come up with something," Portia said distractedly. "Try perfumes."

Sabina scrunched her nose. "Seriously?"

"Don't worry. She'll probably refuse to speak to either of us." Holding Sabina's hand, Portia led the way to the columned semi-circular porch and mounted the short flight of stairs.

Two attendants swung open the brass-inlaid double doors. Portia stopped on the top step, Sabina next to her. A beautiful woman, tall and slender like Portia, stood inside the entryway, silently observing them from the shadows, a physical do not trespass sign.

Portia squeezed Sabina's hand and whispered. "The lioness in her lair."

Ursula's long straight hair was the same color as her floor-length black tunic and matching stola. Both hair and clothing fell loosely over cream-colored arms gleaming in the murky entryway. Her white makeup did not conceal the dark circles under her sunken and sorrowful eyes. Even so she was stunningly gorgeous.

The woman raised her chin and took several steps, stopping in the doorway. "Portia," she said, her eyes narrowing.

Portia eyed the woman warily. "Ursula, I'm so sorry about Dio."

Ursula raised her precisely arched kohl-blackened eyebrows. "I suppose Dio would have wanted you here."

"Thank you," Portia answered modestly.

"However. Dio's not ready to be viewed." Ursula choked back a small sob. "The embalmer needs more time. Dio's body was mangled. No bone below his neck remained unbroken, from his sandaled feet to the rings on his fingers. Were it not for his face, he would have been unrecognizable."

"I heard. I can't envision a death that violent." Portia stepped forward as if to offer comfort. Ursula stiffened, and Portia stepped back.

"The architect said he died instantly." Ursula patted her eyes with a cloth. "Thankfully."

Sabina started at her statement. "Architect? Did he witness the accident?"

Ursula stared at Sabina as if seeing her for the first time. "Dio was alone."

"I'm remiss." Portia reached out and grabbed Sabina's hand, pulling her tightly to her side as if offering protection. "May I introduce my dear friend Sabina?"

Ursula's eyebrows raised again as she scrutinized Sabina, starting at her braided hair and finishing with the copper chains embellishing Sabina's sandals. Ursula tapped a finger on her frowning lips, obviously unimpressed.

"I'm sorry for your loss," Sabina said. "I didn't know your husband, but I…"

"Everyone knew of him, and Dio knew everyone…everyone who mattered." She whirled around, leaving Portia and Sabina standing on the porch, hesitant and unsure of what to do. The two attendants bowed after Ursula but left the door open.

Portia glanced at the opening then shrugged and gestured for Sabina to follow. "She can only ask us to leave."

A wave of cedar, myrrh, cinnamon, and a potent perfume she couldn't identify assaulted Sabina as she passed from the entryway into a large atrium. She held her arm up, covering her nose but not before the pungent odors had penetrated her nostrils and worked their way behind her eyes with a throbbing stab.

Slaves bustled past carrying assorted containers on trays, small jars inset with colorful stones, large glass bottles stopped with corks, and small inlaid wooden boxes. Water sloshed from pitchers carried in and out of a room to the right side of the atrium. Sabina took shallow breaths, hoping to hold off a headache.

Ursula stopped and gestured toward the closed door. "I sent for a makeup artist living in Smyrna. He is from Egypt and learned secret potions for preserving the body. The love of my life will be presented as magnificent in death as he was in life. I am sparing no expense to restore and rebuild his body for presentation. Dio will travel to the underworld like the Adonis he was when alive."

They wove their way through small groups of people, Dionysius's relatives, clients perhaps, local officials, or friends. A group whispering in the corner avoided eye contact with Ursula as she passed.

"They descend like vultures." Ursula did not lower her voice. "Your arrival gives me an escape from their simpering condolences. As if anyone cares how I feel. No one gives the third wife the respect, attention, or consideration I deserve."

"The funeral is usually about the deceased," Portia said under her breath. If Ursula heard she didn't react.

Relieved when they left the atrium and preservation balms, Sabina trailed behind as they passed an archway opening to the outside. Sabina sucked the fresh air into her lungs and rubbed her temples.

Portia turned back. "Are you all right?"

"I'll be fine." Sabina waved her forward, hoping she would be. She took several deep breaths before catching up.

They stopped at an alcove furnished with a small marble-topped table surrounded by two low-backed cushioned couches. The table had a messy assortment of notes and letters. Sabina assumed condolences.

"Of course, the color black completely washes me out." Ursula dropped onto one couch. "Sit."

Portia glanced nervously between the couches and chose the one farthest from her hostess. Sabina drew a cleansing breath and eased down next to Ursula, closing her eyes momentarily to let a wave of dull pain ease.

"Sabina." Ursula sounded almost friendly with a note of curiosity.

Sabina opened one eye and then the other.

Ursula observed her unblinkingly and tapped a pale, pink-painted nail against her lips. "I've heard about you."

Sabina frowned. "Me? I don't think so."

"How many friends does Portia have who apprehend villainous murderers?"

Sabina shifted under Ursula's unwavering stare. "It was my father who arrested the murderer."

Ursula raised an eyebrow. "Ah, Magistrate Catius Sabinus, Eirenarch of Ephesus," she purred. "I know him well."

Sabina kept her expression neutral. "Yes, well…he arrested the killer." Sabina knew she could never explain her desperate assignment to exonerate the bishop of her Christian church of murdering Yechiel's brother. Or relate how her father had arrested her bishop intending to execute him. Revealing the investigation details into a religion outlawed by their emperor would endanger her fellow believers, Portia, and her father.

"No. Dio said you solved the murder." Ursula tipped her head toward Portia. "And he would know."

Sabina shot her friend an exasperated look. "Portia."

Portia shifted uneasily on the edge of her chair. "I shared a few details with a trusted friend."

"Don't worry, Sabina, your titillating exploits are safe with me." Ursula tucked a finger under Sabina's chin and turned her head to each side. "I pictured you…thin. Don't spies need to sneak around squeezing into private spaces?"

Sabina pulled back, feeling her face warm. "I don't sneak…."

"Dio said you risked your life to spy on that filthy cult of Christ worshippers. Bringing one of those murderous heathens to justice."

"That's not what I said, Ursula," Portia said.

Ursula ignored Portia and grabbed Sabina's hand. "I want to hear all the delicious details."

"Perhaps, at a more appropriate time," Portia said, her irritation obvious. "I was hoping to give my condolences to Diana and Paris."

Ursula pursed her lips as if making an immense decision. Then sighed. "Another day then. Promise me." She squeezed Sabina's hand until Sabina nodded. "I don't know where the absent son and heir is. He should be attending to his father during these last hours. Diana is in the garden, daydreaming and leaving me to worry about the formalities. I haven't slept in two nights."

"It must have been a terrible shock," Sabina said.

Ursula stared at her lap. A small hiccup escaped. "It has been difficult, but Dio's death was not a surprise. I was told he was going to die."

"You knew the wall would collapse, killing him?" Sabina covered her mouth.

"Not how he would die or the date. Just that Dio would die within the year."

"When were you told this?" Portia leaned forward, her voice strained.

"A year ago." Ursula dabbed her eyes with the small cloth, although Sabina could see no tears.

Portia's hands clasped together, her fingers turning white. "I don't understand. If someone warned you about this, why didn't someone stop it? Dio said nothing to me."

"Why would he tell you?" Ursula sounded annoyed.

"Who issued this death threat?" Sabina asked.

"It was not a threat," Ursula chided. "Cassandra is a pythoness. She has the power of divination, the gift of prophecy."

"A fortune-teller?" Sabina was not surprised. Trusting in divination was a common belief and a benefit of worshipping a pantheon of gods who interacted through spirit daemons to advise mortals.

Ursula narrowed her eyes. "Fortune-teller is a vulgar term. Even the emperor seeks guidance from the gods, be it through direct contact with an oracle, a prophet, a priest, or a gifted seer with the spirit of a powerful daemon guiding her."

"Did Dio believe Cassandra communicated through this daemon?" The precision of Cassandra's prediction surprised Sabina. Communications from the heavens were answerd with yes or no. Give the gods a choice, and they would answer good or bad, stay or go, attack this week or next, invest or put your money in a bank. Predicting the future with a specific event that could prove very wrong wasn't done.

"I believed her," Ursula said. "But Dio always had to have proof."

And the proof was his death.

"Dio took me to see the oracle in Claros once." Ursula gave an exaggerated shiver. "I was afraid to enter the cave. Dio wasn't. He had fasted and prayed to Apollo. Dio remained celibate the entire week prior, which was a miracle in itself. He wouldn't tell me what he asked her, but shortly after our trip, he divorced Diana's mother, and we were married."

Sabina looked at Portia who raised her eyebrows and mouthed *their own rules.*

"I was told your husband wasn't religious," Sabina said.

Ursula smiled as if remembering a private moment. "True, I don't believe it was a genuine religious experience. More of a show to convince me that our union was the will of the gods." She flashed her wedding ring. "It worked. If for no other reason than I was impressed with his commitment to courting."

"What exactly did Cassandra predict?" Sabina asked.

"That I would be a widow within the year. I told Dio. He laughed, but later, he started asking me questions about Cassandra. Who was she? Who else had their fortunes read? Had any of her fortunes come true?"

"What did you tell him?" Portia asked.

"To go ask her himself. It took two months, but eventually, he did. That's when this whole obsession with his immortal legacy began."

"Building his library," Portia said.

"I believe he settled on a ludus, a gladiator training school. It doesn't matter." Ursula sounded bored.

It did matter. If Dionysius died in a ludus, then Yechiel wasn't connected to the death of this rich man.

Portia looked confused. "Dio told me he'd decided on a library."

"He changed his mind several times." Ursula yawned. "I could only listen to Dio's boring details of architecture, marble finishes, and construction mechanics for so long without falling asleep. Now it doesn't matter. He's dead, and the accident is being investigated. Something suspicious." The lines of grief etching her face deepened.

Suspicious? Ludus or library? Sabina wanted to report back to Eunice that her fears were unfounded. That Yechiel, the Jew, had nothing to worry about.

"I'm sure it's nothing." Ursula sighed. "The inspectors have a duty, but it puts a pall over Dio's death. An unsettling unpleasantness."

Sabina felt pressure mount behind her eyes. "Did the inspectors question the fortune-teller? Have you spoken to Cassandra since your husband's death?"

"Yes. It's more important than ever now that Paris will be head of the family and managing the family fortunes. I need any insight I can get now that my future depends on the youngest infantile, hapless son."

Portia tilted her head toward Sabina. "Dio's eldest son was groomed to take over but died from a fever five years ago. Paris was seventeen at the time. Everyone assumed that Paris would have time to mature into the role."

"It's a heavy responsibility for such a young man," Sabina said.

"He's had five years," Ursula snorted. "Paris showed no interest in managing the family assets."

"Perhaps he will seek your guidance now," Sabina said.

Ursula laughed cynically. "Everyone knows Dio didn't marry me for my household or money management skills. No one will ask my opinion." She waved any objections away. "I wouldn't care except that Paris's financial skills are no better than my own. I at least acknowledge it. I pray Artemis takes pity on my and Diana's future and that Paris follows Loukas's counsel, as Dio did."

"If Dio thought he was going to die, surely, he made accommodations for you and Diana in his will," Portia said.

Ursula drew in a ragged breath. "There are rumors Dio was planning to divorce me."

"Dio didn't tell me your marriage was ending." Portia's voice rose with surprise.

"Why would he share that with you?" Ursula bristled.

41

Portia flushed a little and examined her fingernails. "He wouldn't, of course."

Ursula raised an eyebrow. "I heard the whisperings of the servants. Paris heard the same rumors. That little jackal plans to take me to court and have me thrown out of Dio's will."

"But you weren't divorced. You're still his wife…his widow," Sabina pointed out. "Paris can't go to court based on gossip."

"It isn't all gossip. I also had a tiny mishap a year ago when I realized my marriage was ending," Ursula said. "I got angry."

"That would be natural," Sabina said.

"She attacked him with a knife." Portia smoothed an imaginary wrinkle from her mantle.

Sabina looked questioningly at Portia, who had experience with married life. "Not so natural."

Ursula shrugged. "If Dio hadn't been so clumsy wrestling the knife away, he wouldn't have gotten hurt. The servants bandaged the wounds before he lost much blood." Ursula drummed her fingers. "No one believes I'd actually kill my husband. Except Paris. He's using my little outburst as a pretext to remove me from the will."

Sabina looked at Portia and then back to Ursula. "Paris may have a case." Sabina could understand divorce as retribution for Ursula's attack.

"I was upset at losing my husband. Any court or magistrate would sympathize with that. And Dio forgave me. It took a while for his manly pride to heal."

"And his wounds," Portia whispered under her breath.

"Did he forgive you? Did anyone hear who could repute Paris's divorce claims?" Sabina asked.

"You are a nosy one, aren't you?"

"No." Sabina stiffened and leaned away from Ursula. "I was just curious." And now suffering the consequences.

"I see a curious spy. Like your father. Why are you here?" Ursula narrowed her eyes.

"I'm here because Portia needed a friend to accompany her." Sabina blinked and looked to Portia for help.

Ursula's expression grew sober, and Sabina felt the woman's gaze drilling into her. "No, that's not your only reason. A certain Eirenarch taught me that everyone has hidden agendas and secrets. Was the architect present? Did the inspectors question the fortune-teller? Why should that matter to you?"

Portia mouthed, *I told you not to underestimate her.*

Ursula tucked her legs under her and curled up on the couch. "I just had a brilliant idea. I will hire you to prove to the court that I loved my husband, that I was an adoring and devoted wife, and that I was devastated by his death. I will testify that I am heartbroken over that unfortunate dinner accident. And you will gather evidence to support me."

"Evidence? From where? From who?" Sabina sputtered.

"You can spy on my family and friends or investigate them, if you prefer that word, and record the statements that will counter Paris's lies."

"You just admitted attacking your husband." First, Eunice pleaded with her to help Yechiel, and now Ursula. How had she gotten herself into this? "You are mistaken. I'm not a spy or an informer. My previous investigation was an accident."

Ursula looked puzzled. "Portia told Dio it was murder."

Sabina took a deep breath. "I meant it was an accident that I solved the murder."

"That's not true," Portia disagreed. "Without your investigative skills, your father would have executed an innocent man. You saved his life."

Sabina huffed. "You're on my side, remember."

Ursula clasped her hands and said in a theatrical tone. "I'm not asking you to solve a murder. I need evidence that convinces a magistrate that I loved my husband. Just ask a few people questions. How hard can that be?"

"I'm not sure a woman is the best choice to find your proof." Sabina floundered, grasping for excuses.

"Exactly the opposite is true. Men pay little attention to what they let slip around us simple-minded women," Ursula said.

"And women complain and gossip incessantly to other women," Portia added.

Sabina glared at Portia. "You're not helping."

"You are the perfect choice." Ursula brushed her hands together as if wiping all of Sabina's arguments away. "I can tell you like a challenge, adventure, and danger." Ursula's grin was nothing short of a smirk.

"I don't like any of those things." Ursula wasn't giving her time to think, to pray, or to back out. A jitter of alarm replaced her headache. "I can't just start questioning your family."

"You're right. We need an excuse that isn't too blatant," Ursula said.

"We…I'm not doing this."

Ursula chewed on a fingernail ignoring the refusal. "We will say you are helping Dio's devoted and adoring widow to write a family tribute, a memorial. You know how to write, don't you?"

"Yes, but…my father would never agree to this." Sabina had the perfect excuse.

"Years ago, your father, with whom I spent a wickedly sensuous summer, taught me not to let anything get in the way of what we want. You'll think of something brilliant just like your father."

"Ursula, please stop. I am not my father." She was nothing like her father. Sabina tasted the bitterness on her tongue. Her buried anger rose at thoughts of her father's curt uncaring statements, his callous disregard for life…especially the lives of her sisters. Since deciding to look for them, finding excuses to leave the house was hard enough. She didn't have time for Ursula's scheme.

Ursula leaned forward and gripped Sabina's hands in hers. "Help me build a convincing defense to keep me in the will, and you can get your questions answered. The name of the architect and what the authorities learned from Cassandra the fortune teller."

Yechiel may not be involved at all…or he might be the prime suspect, as Eunice feared. Ursula had just opened the door to the answer. Sabina might uncover something she could share with Eunice, information that she would never have access to if Sabina said no. Unlike finding Benjamin's murderer, she would not have to risk her life skulking outside the city after dark, scale walls to escape being arrested, or pose as a slave to infiltrate a murderer's home. All Ursula wanted her to do was ask a few questions.

"I have no idea where or when I would start." Was she seriously considering doing this?

Ursula smiled again, that seductive glint in her eye. "Why not today?"

"Sabina," Portia said gravely shaking her head.

Sabina took a moment before answering. "I will agree to talk to your family. That's all." For some undiscernible reason, her headache was gone.

An unreadable emotion flitted across Ursula's face, ending in a self-satisfied smile. Ursula's emotions may rule her actions, but a sharp and manipulative mind appeared to lurk behind her passions. Sabina needed to handle this widow very carefully.

"Family and friends. Start with Loukas. Paris will strike him first."

"Loukas? Why?" Sabina asked.

"He's my lover. I'll inform him of our plan."

Sabina shot a panicked glance at Portia. What had she agreed to do?

FIVE

Sabina and Portia stared at each other. "Lover?" Sabina stuttered. "Not malicious rumors, then?"

"It's still malicious, even if it's true," Ursula covered her mouth to hide a yawn.

"You can't mean...I mean your husband just died." It wasn't as if Sabina wasn't aware of loveless marriages formed for political or monetary benefits. But even arranged marriages followed some ethical etiquette, if only for appearance's sake. Flaunting her lover before Dionysius was buried was shocking.

"I am aware that adultery is breaking the emperor's dictatorial marriage code. As if banishing his wife to some deserted island made him the perfect husband. The facts are that I cannot be unfaithful to a dead man." Ursula's grin held no humor. "Losing Dio has been devastating. Loukas is willing to provide support and compassion to a poor widow."

"Poor widows act devastated," Portia said.

"Don't worry. I shall play my role. I'm not going to hand Paris any more arrows. He will have nothing to testify to except a kind friend visited his grieving stepmother and advised her through this difficult time."

Sabina had never mastered the female wiles of charm, vulnerability, and distress that Ursula expertly employed to excuse her behavior. Amisi had attempted to fill in Sabina's lack of womanly survival skills—witty banter, flattery, and seduction. When Sabina expressed little interest and even less aptitude, the lessons floundered.

Portia rose abruptly, unable to hide her disgust. "I need to deliver this gift to Diana."

"She's in her garden. She rarely leaves it." Ursula uncurled her legs and smoothed her tunic out. "I told Dio she's a teenager who should be socializing with friends. She's too young to lock herself away like a vestal virgin."

"Diana and her father were close." Portia glared at Ursula. "Some people need time to grieve."

"What would you know of grieving? It wasn't your husband who died." Ursula's nostrils flared, and the two women locked gazes in uncomfortable silence.

Sabina pushed up from the cushion. "We should be going."

"This nearly slipped my mind." Ursula plucked a small papyrus roll off the marble table. "A note Dio addressed to you." She handed Portia the roll with her name inscribed on the outside.

Portia ran her finger over the ragged edge of broken wax. "It's been opened."

"Yes, well…" Ursula shrugged, her smile untroubled, but her eyes locked on the unrolled papyrus. "I honestly think he forgot to include the message."

Portia unrolled it. "I look forward to our next debate. Your thief…" Portia's voice faded away, her lips pinched tight. She turned it over, looking for more. Then eyed Ursula suspiciously.

"There was nothing more." Ursula insisted. "Is it a private code between…?"

Sabina could almost see Ursula biting back the word *lovers*.

"It is a private…joke." Portia's fingers shook.

"You aren't laughing." Ursula nudged closer.

"May I see it?" Sabina asked.

Portia's face tightened, and she handed Sabina the letter.

Sabina flipped it, scrutinizing each side, and gave it back, shaking her head. "He signed it, Your thief on the cross."

"He's making fun of me." Portia clenched her fist, sucking in a short gulp. "His last message to me is a cruel taunt."

"Not an endearment?" Ursula clucked. "Too bad."

Portia drew in a deep breath and then released it slowly. "It's time to leave. I have Diana's gift to deliver."

Ursula pointed. "The celestial garden is to the left before you get to the atrium. Through the archway, past the waterfall and fishponds."

Leaving, Sabina bumped into a slave delivering a cup of wine.

"Ah, Titos, you read my mind." They left Ursula sipping wine with a sly smile.

"Can you hold a grudge against the dead?" Portia's voice blazed with an emotion Sabina had never heard from her—reproach, censure, blame.

"To be fair," Sabina noted, "Dionysius didn't know it would be his last communication with you."

Portia crumpled the note as they walked. "And God doesn't condone grudges. Can you find Diana and let her know I'm here? I need a minute to calm down."

"Of course." Sabina rarely saw Portia shaken and trembling. Sabina squeezed Portia's hand.

Sabina understood why the garden had been named celestial. Twelve evenly spaced statues of the zodiac stood, three on each of the garden portico's four sides. She passed the gods' vibrantly painted marble busts, Ares, Hades, and Poseidon, corresponding with the zodiac symbols carved in their corresponding pillars, a ram, a scorpion, and two fish.

As Sabina neared the fishponds, a nude marble Aphrodite rose from the highest tier of a three-tiered fountain, its gurgling waterfall flowing from a handheld shell into a string of two fishponds. Gardens filled with lush vegetation and flowers surrounded the ponds.

Two men walked toward her under the garden's bordering colonnade. Both were affluently dressed men who appeared to be in their twenties or early thirties. The lithe blond, smooth-shaven with refined Adonis-like features shook his head at something the larger man said. His muscled companion sported a narrow black beard accentuating a square jawline, a raw and unrefined handsomeness. Neither noticed her nor moved aside as they conversed. She deftly skipped behind a portico column as they passed.

The blond gestured exuberantly. "I tell you, the gods delivered the best gladiator in the empire into our laps. Ferocianus will be the jewel of our gladiator training school."

"Truly, we are lucky. He must have cost your father an exorbitant amount."

The blond's answer was muffled as the men strolled away. Before exiting the garden, the dark-haired man's head turned to a young woman standing in the garden smiling at him. He nodded toward her and strolled out under the archway.

Sabina stepped from behind the column and approached the young woman. "Are you Diana?"

The young woman jumped, jerking her gaze away from the empty walkway. "Oh?" Her cheeks turned a splotchy rust color. "You startled me. Yes, I'm Diana." Diana plopped onto a stone bench and snatched a wax tablet and stylus, lowering her head shyly as if focusing on writing.

"I'm sorry. I thought you saw me." What age had Portia said Diana was, fifteen or sixteen? She was petite and not overly beautiful, with dull brown hair pulled back, accentuating a relatively flat face. But she had a clear ivory complexion and lively sparkling eyes. "I see you are intent on your work. Or is it pleasure?"

"Composing poetry is usually enjoyable, but not today," the young woman said gravely, displeasure flitting across her face.

"I'm a friend of Portia's. She sent me ahead while she...visits with your stepmother."

Diana put her stylus and tablet down and swiped a wisp of hair from her eyes. "Would you like to sit?" She moved aside on the small bench.

"I'll stand, thank you. I'm enjoying your garden." A two-foot-long stem crowned with an orange-red swirl of downward-facing flowers drew her eye. "The imperial flower. It's one of my favorites."

"Were you a friend of my father?"

Sabina turned from the blooms. "I'm afraid I never met him. I am so sorry he's gone."

"This poem is for him. I am going to read it at his funeral."

"What a thoughtful tribute. I'm sorry I disturbed you."

"No, I was distracted before you arrived." The spotty blush returned. "My brother, Paris, was here earlier."

Sabina could see a slight resemblance to the slender blond man she had passed. Her brother was the more attractive of the siblings.

"Ahh, Diana." A composed Portia swept into the garden, arms extended. "My dear, I'm so sorry about your father. How are you?"

Diana stood and embraced Portia.

"It's been difficult to focus. I'm preoccupied. Luckily, I have Paris." Diana sniffed and sat on the end of her bench, allowing room for Portia next to her. "Even Ursula has been nice."

Sabina couldn't help but compare the difference to when her mother had died. Portia had been there during her mother's last child birthing, but because Portia was Christian, Sabina's father had forbidden her in their home after his wife died. Sabina had navigated the sudden death of her mother alone. A fussy Amisi and battle-scarred Zarmig had tried to help, but it was talking to God that had provided her comfort and healing.

Portia stroked Diana's hand. "I have a gift." Portia held the package she had carried with her from the litter. "It's from your father."

Diana blanched, her eyes widening. "My father, but…"

"He commissioned it before he died," Portia quickly explained. "He gave Horace a special order before the last caravan departed. The shipment just arrived."

Diana hesitated, fingering the strings on the package. Breathing in deeply, she pulled the tie, opened the box, and took out a folded square of the most beautiful sky-blue silk Sabina had seen. "It's my favorite color." Diana blinked rapidly.

Portia took a corner and held it to Diana's face. "It will set off your beautiful eyes."

"Thank you. Father felt obligated to buy me presents."

Portia frowned. "I'm sure he wanted to. He loved you very much."

"Of course." Diana set the cloth aside and fingered the edge of the tablet. "I am glad you came. Would you review my poem when I'm done? It's for father's funeral."

"I'd love to read it." Portia glanced at the discarded silk slipping off the bench and puddling on the ground.

"I've rewritten it a hundred times. I can't find the right words. It's making my stomach hurt. But Ursula said I have time. It will take days to arrange the funeral procession and the cremation."

"Diana takes her work very seriously," Portia explained taking Diana's hand. "Remember, your father took joy in creating as much as the final work."

"I'm glad he can't hear it." Diana pulled her hand away and crossed her arms.

"What a strange thing to say," Portia said.

"I'm sure it will bring others as much pleasure as it would have your father," Sabina said in sympathy.

Diana picked up the tablet and hugged it to her chest. "Usually, when I write, the outside world disappears. Since he died, I can't seem to get anything right."

"Give yourself time," Portia said softly.

"There are so many questions." Diana shook her head. "The authorities spoke to Paris this morning. He's head of the family now."

"What questions?" Portia asked.

"They are investigating Father's accident. It's so upsetting I didn't believe it." Her voice broke. "But Otho confirmed it."

"Otho?" Sabina and Portia said in unison.

"My frien—my brother's friend." Diana lowered her gaze. "The authorities said the accident is suspicious."

That word again. Sabina swallowed hard. "Suspicious how?"

Diana shrugged. "They said something about cheap construction materials. Paris told them about the architect."

Sabina stiffened. "What about the architect?"

"Father complained that he was impossible to work with. The architect refused to come to our house. He made Father come to him." Diana lowered her voice conspiratorially. "So arrogant."

Arrogant. Strong-willed? Could there be another architect like Ye-chiel? "Yet your father kept him as the head architect?"

"Father said he admired the man's vision. Not many people could sway my father. He did. Father gave him the honor of designing and building the legacy project and was repaid with betrayal."

"Betrayal? What have the authorities found?" Perhaps something Sabina could report to Eunice.

"Nothing. They are speculating at this point. The magistrate wanted us to know it is a priority." Diana's lip quivered. "Father was a prominent citizen."

"Do you know the architect's name?" Sabina asked.

"No." Diana shook her head.

"Agabus?" Portia interjected.

A bee circled Diana. She swatted it away. "Is Agabus a Jewish name? Paris said it was a good thing he didn't come to the house because he was Jewish or worse—a Christian. He might have harmed us."

Sabina choked. "I doubt a Christian would do that."

Diana's face puckered in concern. "You mustn't defend them. Emperor Domitian said Christians are guilty of perversions against the gods. They insult Artemis."

"It is true they don't worship Artemis," Sabina forced her voice to remain neutral. "But Domitian is…exaggerating."

"Oh, but he's not. Father agreed that anyone who worships a cruci-fied criminal as a god is unstable."

Portia slapped her thighs and bolted up. "I have heard enough from your father for one day." She picked up the silk fabric and folded it back on the bench. "I have to go. Remember, you can call on me if you need anything." She kissed Diana on each cheek.

When Portia and Sabina were in the litter, Sabina looked uncertain-ly at a pale Portia. "You told me Dio was the one friend who accepted your Christianity, who didn't condemn you."

"I said he didn't abandon me. I didn't say he didn't mock my faith."

"What do you think he meant by his note?"

"Oh, I know what he meant." Portia's voice took on a steely tone.

"Remember when I told you Dio was incredulous that any God would demand perfect obedience? And that we are accountable for every act of rebellion."

"Yes, but why call himself a thief?"

"In my rebuttal, I told Dio about the two thieves crucified beside Jesus. The first thief mocked Jesus's death, denying it as payment for his sins. The second thief believed in Jesus's divinity and asked Jesus to remember him in God's kingdom."

"I remember Jesus told the second thief that day he would be with Him in paradise."

"Yes, the second thief accepted Jesus's death as payment for his flawed and imperfect life."

"Which thief was Dio?"

Portia snorted as tears pooled, glistening in her eyes. "Without a doubt, the first. Dio couldn't understand why our God needed to die. Or how a dying God could save anyone. Defiant to the end. Dio said he would pay his debts himself." She broke off, her body shaking. "I'm so angry that stupid note is my last memory of him. And even after death, he got the final say. It's so Dio." She leaned back in the pillows letting the tears trickle unheeded.

Sabina squeezed Portia's hand but stayed silent, wanting to do more but afraid she'd say the wrong thing. Now was not the time to question her about Ursula. And if Dionysius's accident had been preventable? Was the architect to blame? Was Yechiel the architect? Agabus was not a Jewish name.

She had to alert Eunice that her fears were very real.

SIX

Sabina paced her bedroom floor. There was no reason to be nervous. She had done what she had promised Eunice. Now she could only wait. A hesitant knock on her door jolted her like an earth tremor. She threw open the double doors. Felix waited outside. She gestured him into the room and slammed the doors behind him.

Felix cleared his throat. "The weaver received a reply to your message. Eunice will meet you in an hour at the same location."

Sabina hugged herself. "Did anyone see you or follow you from our house?"

"No, Mistress. I was careful and slipped away without anyone seeing me."

"Excellent. Now I have to manage the same feat."

"You cannot go alone." Felix's eyes darted to the door. "No, no. The master and Amisi directed me to keep you away from…" Felix stopped.

"Trouble, excitement, anything interesting. I'm not a child." Sabina willed her frustration not to show. But she knew her age was not the issue, even grandmothers of rank and status required chaperons wherever they went. But she wasn't aware of a grandmother investigating a murder.

"Amisi will punish me if I let you go alone." The slave's right eye ticked with nervous tension.

Amisi could cause trouble for both Felix and her. It didn't help that her childhood nurse did it out of love. Sabina adjusted the belt of her stola and patted the floor-length linen mantle.

"Someone will notice if you are gone again. And then Amisi will start asking you questions. This way I will be back before anyone knows I'm missing."

"This will not turn out well." Felix's lips trembled uttering a prayer of protection to Zeus.

She wasn't sure if it was for him or her. "I will be safe with Eunice." She slipped out the door. "No one will find out."

Sabina paused to allow her eyes to adjust to the dim interior of Reuben's shop. It was unoccupied, and Reuben beckoned her through the curtain and into the back atrium. The impluvium pool was empty of all but water. The washed yarn hung, drying on racks and waiting to be spun. The atrium was deserted as well.

"You will wait. My niece will arrive soon."

"Of course."

The door to the shop squeaked open and clicked closed. A moment later, Eunice pushed through the curtain, her movements graceful even in her haste toward Sabina.

"You have information? So soon? Were you not the same woman I spoke to yesterday, doubting your abilities? Never doubt again." The words tumbled from Eunice in a rush.

"I visited the home of Dionysius Antiochus this morning."

"Who is Dionysius?"

"I believe he is the man who hired Yechiel to design his library. The man who died."

"Come, come sit." Eunice led her to a bench beside the pool. She swept off a small puddle. "Yechiel never told me his name. You are sure?"

"Even in our city of two hundred and fifty thousand, there cannot be two different Jewish architects, designing two different libraries that collapsed at the same time, crushing their patrons to death."

Eunice's hand flew to her mouth. "That is how he died? How horrible. His poor family."

"No one mentioned Yechiel's name, but the authorities are investigating. They do not think it was an accident."

"Then they are not blaming Yechiel for this man's death. That is good news." Eunice nodded eagerly.

"Dionysius was a prominent citizen. Extremely wealthy. They will want to know the facts. Everyone involved in the building will be questioned, including Yechiel."

"But now we know. Yechiel will have the facts ready for them."

"Eunice, did Yechiel tell you he had argued with Dionysius?"

"Yechiel kept his work separate. He shared information about the death of the library's patron, which was unusual and one of the reasons I became worried."

"The authorities are looking into inferior construction."

"What lies are you telling my wife?" A familiar masculine voice boomed from the doorway, and Sabina and Eunice jumped up in unison. Sabina stood frozen in place.

"Yechiel! You are not at work?" Eunice ran toward the tall man striding into the room.

"And you are not at home." His eyes hardened, and his jaw clenched as he pointed at Sabina. "What is she doing here?"

"Yechiel!" Eunice grabbed his arms. "Not only is Sabina taking a risk to help you, but she is also my guest."

Yechiel's gaze softened when he looked at his wife, but he removed her hands from his arm. "She has no business here."

"I asked her here. We need help, and you wouldn't listen to me," Eunice pleaded.

"We will not argue in front of strangers."

"I'm not exactly a stranger," Sabina mumbled under her breath.

Yechiel quelled her with a cold stare. "You are inventing conspiracies."

Eunice huffed, unable to hide her frustration. "Sabina has information about a man named Dionysius Antiochus."

Yechiel's attention snapped to his wife. His eyes narrowed.

"It is as I thought." Eunice grabbed his hand and continued. "The authorities are investigating his death."

"Your employer?" Sabina verified.

Yechiel nodded.

"They don't believe it was an accident," Sabina said. "They are looking into inferior construction. Buildings do collapse."

"Not mine," Yechiel growled. "Unlike the structures of my esteemed colleague Agabus."

"Do you remember the insula that collapsed last year?" Eunice's voice caught. "…killing three families, sleeping children. It was horrible. For Yechiel, mistakes are unforgivable. Which is why I know he isn't to blame for this death."

Sabina tilted her head. "I've heard his name. You and Agabus work together?"

"On this project," Yechiel said. "I had no choice."

Sabina asked, "Is there something Agabus did that—"

"The man is incompetent. Not a murderer." Yechiel's voice lowered menacingly. "And neither am I."

"Yechiel." Eunice drew his attention without raising her voice. "Where are your manners? Sabina's not accusing you."

"Spreading rumors that my buildings are substandard is damage enough."

"But Dionysius did die under your wall," Sabina said.

"You know nothing about construction," Yechiel scoffed. "The archway that supported the grand entrance into the library collapsed. My plans and construction were not to blame."

"Well, something went wrong." Sabina didn't mean to sound accusatory.

"And I will find out what. I wasn't there." Yechiel rubbed his forehead. "Even so, if a carpenter or stonemason made an error that morning…"

Eunice placed a calming hand on Yechiel's arm and turned to Sabina. "Roman law allows us to worship and serve God one day a week."

Sabina envied the luxury of worshipping without fear of being arrested, something she had never known.

"We do not take Rome's concession for granted," Eunice replied as if reading her mind.

"Were you together at your synagogue?" Sabina asked.

"I was ill that morning and was not with Yechiel."

Sabina turned to Yechiel. "Was Dionysius accepting of your six-day work schedule?" So different from worshiping on state holidays and venerating the Roman gods with weeks of entertainment, festivals, and parades.

"Dio viewed it as disloyal to him by not working my full seven days." Yechiel lowered his brows, frowning. "He asked what my God gave me in return for my obedience."

Eunice added. "We do not worship our God for what we get from him. We worship so He can draw us closer to His will. We delight in His commandments."

"He demanded I make up the days, completing the project in an unrealistic time frame." Yechiel shrugged.

"Risking a safe building." Sabina imagined the pressure on Yechiel.

"Needless to say, we argued." Yechiel reached for Eunice's hand. "Dio dispensed with construction principles the same way he did any rules that he didn't like. But even the great Dio could not discard the laws of physics, and I refused to compromise the integrity of my buildings."

"Perhaps Dionysius dying on the Sabbath was not an accident." Sabina studied Yechiel's unyielding face. "Who knew you would not be supervising that day?"

Yechiel's glare nearly burnt through her. "Every worker knows I don't work on the Sabbath. Does that narrow it down for you?"

Eunice squeezed Yechiel's hand. "We need to find out what happened. Otherwise, the authorities will be the ones inventing conspiracies. We need facts to refute their charges."

"There won't be any charges. I have my drawings. They are perfect."

"The magistrates might disagree," Sabina said. "You would be wise to examine this archway."

"I see your bossy nature has not changed." Yechiel glared at her. "I was on my way to inspect the site when my wife went missing."

Eunice blushed.

"I can join you now," Sabina said.

"Women are not allowed...."

"Yechiel, please." Eunice pleaded. "This is not the time for religious exclusions. You worked with Sabina to find Benjamin's killer. You can break the rules and work with her once more to save yourself and our family. You must prove this accident wasn't your fault."

Yechiel rocked from foot to foot. The first hint of worry Sabina had seen. Which meant he wasn't an idiot.

In her experience, the laws of physics were not a defense that would win when pitted against a sobbing widow and fatherless children. Yechiel's arguments with his employer confirmed what Diana had told her, placing him under suspicion for no other reason than that. His innocence depended on what they found in the wreckage.

SEVEN

"How far to the construction site?" Sabina panted as she jogged to keep up with Yechiel.

"Not far."

A dribble of sweat tickled her neck. Thankfully the distance to the worksite wasn't far.

They mounted the four steps to the veranda adjoining the library's entryway. "I tried to enter yesterday," Yechiel said. "The site was already roped off. Guards refused to allow anyone in."

They slipped under the rope. Yechiel stood speechless while scanning the chaos before them. Even in its demolished state, the grand entrance loomed impressively. Two enormous marble cubes anchored the base of the arch's intact side pillars. Smaller yet still huge blocks of matching creamy-white stone were fitted together, rising at least twenty feet high. On the marble floor between the pillars, she counted fourteen narrower identically shaped blocks jumbled atop each other like tossed dice, some displaying cracks or chipped corners.

"There's no mortar," Sabina noted. "Is that why they fell?"

"Mortar is not needed." Yechiel's passion for his job was unmistakable as he pointed away from the tumbled broken blocks to one large wedge-shaped stone, conspicuously undamaged. "Once we place that keystone at the top of the arch, it locks the other stones securely in place, stabilizing the arch."

"It's massive." Sabina looked at the keystone and then at the sky twenty feet above her head. "How do you get it up there."

"It is mechanical. I'm not sure you would understand."

Sabina clenched her jaw and drew a deep breath. "If you think—"

"Fine." Yechiel cut her off, pointing to a machine near the destruction. "We lift the blocks with a crane using a winch and pulley system."

"Why wasn't the keystone already in place?"

Yechiel glared at her. "Now you sound like Dionysius. He demanded I set the keystone as soon as possible. But it takes time to construct the supports that hold the surrounding stones during construction." Yechiel pointed to a cracked wooden plank lying among the marble. "That beam bridges the two columns. We fit smaller wooden pieces onto the beam to brace the stones. The system temporarily supports the suspended blocks."

Splintered timbers mixed among the stones littering an area with a dark stain that someone had tried to wash away. She shuddered.

"Normally, I would have supervised, but as I said, it was Shabbat. I left early on Friday and didn't work Saturday. Always impatient, Dionysius wouldn't wait until I returned on Sunday, so Agabus filled in. Always pushing to move on to the next stage."

"The authorities will be checking to see if corners were cut."

"Not me, although that's how Agabus increases profits. He promises three-story insulas for the price of a two-story. His clients see silver denarii flying through the air and landing in their bank accounts. He neglects to tell these greedy landlords that without the costly foundations and necessary support their building will collapse at the first minor earthquake."

"Was Dionysius greedy?"

Yechiel shrugged. "Not greedy, but impatient. He thought he knew enough about building design to modify designs, substitute materials, or alter work schedules. Our arguments frequently became heated."

"And Agabus?"

"If Dio wanted something done yesterday, Agabus would happily abandon every safety procedure to accommodate him. I made sure that didn't happen. Agabus wasn't pleased, but he wasn't in charge."

"Except for placing the keystone." The shattered bracing testified to that.

"Even Agabus's rudimentary building standards would have averted this massive accident."

How horrible Dionysius's last seconds of terror, hearing the wooden arch supports snap and give way. The half-circle of stones overhead would have had nothing to hold them in place. She imagined the sturdy beams toppling, a panicked scream cut off as a thudding wedge of marble brushed by his arm, followed by a hailstorm of half-ton stones. No time to escape. Lying unconscious as cracks sprouted like a giant root system, the tendrils spreading across the marble floor, followed by a creaking and groaning until the dust floated down in silence.

"It would have taken hours to move the blocks and retrieve the body," Yechiel said.

"Do you see anything out of the ordinary?"

Yechiel's laugh startled her with its bitterness. "Besides complete destruction of my library?"

Sabina ignored his rudeness. "We should inspect the arch supports. Several smaller timbers are splintered and broken. Perhaps one gave way." Sabina picked up a cracked piece. "Ouch." She pulled a sliver from her finger and sucked at the oozing blood.

Yechiel picked up another piece. "This could have been shattered by the blocks falling on them. It's impossible to tell." He examined and tossed aside several more supports. "These prove nothing. What do you expect to find?"

"I don't know. You're the architect. Something that doesn't look right?"

"Nothing looks right. This is a nightmare. It wouldn't just collapse."

"Then something caused it." Sabina walked to the column where a pile of rope, marble, and splintered wood lay. "The last pieces landed here." Sabina knelt and started digging through the mess. "Next we can survey the outside and see if anything there triggered the collapse."

"This is a waste of time." Yechiel watched her with his arms crossed.

Sabina pointed to a section of wood. "This is shattered, and there's a rope tied to it." She grunted, lifting the timber a fraction off the ground, then dropped it.

Yechiel frowned, walked over to the piece of timber, bent down, and ran his thumb over the knot. "It could be a piece of the main brace or another of the shorter supports. It's impossible to tell."

Sabina lifted the knotted rope snaking toward the machine with its pulleys and ropes. She turned to Yechiel. "It ends at the crane."

"We use the crane to lift the wooden braces into place. But the rope shouldn't have been left tied to the beam once it was in place." Yechiel frowned "We also use the crane and winch to pull the supports down after stabilizing the arch."

"The magistrates have seen what we have and would realize this."

Yechiel's hands opened and closed several times. "Agabus and the crew were finishing the bracing when I left on Friday. If Agabus was hurrying and didn't take time to untie the rope, he's guilty of severe incompetence."

"Deadly incompetence." Sabina lifted the rope letting it run through her fingers as she trudged to the crane. "Could Dionysius have tripped on the rope, accidentally pulling out a brace?"

"Dismantling the supports would be impossible without turning the winch. The supports are tightly wedged, bearing the weight of the stones."

"But if someone turned the handle?" She reached out, touching the crank. "Would it take mechanical skill or much strength to use the winch? Could a woman do it?" She waited for his laugh.

Yechiel grunted as if seriously pondering her question. "It is a simple mechanical concept, which you appear to grasp." He waved at the destruction around them. "The beams dislodge quickly. But the execution to release at an exact moment would be challenging even for an architect."

"But if someone understood the mechanics, they wouldn't have to be an expert in construction, an engineer, or an architect?"

"It is possible."

Sabina heaved a deep breath. "Hopefully, the investigators will come to the same conclusion. Because right now, you appear to be one of the few people with the knowledge and motive to have caused this tragedy."

A heavyset man with a pudgy face and fleshy bowed legs shuffled toward them, head down. He looked up, surprise on his face. "What are you doing here?"

"Agabus." Yechiel's voice was half whisper and half growl. "I'm inspecting the damage on my project."

"Ah." Agabus's lips curled as if trying to hide a smug smile and failed. "You didn't get your letter?"

"What letter?" Yechiel flipped his hand as if batting an annoying insect away.

"This is no longer your project." Agabus fumbled in the folds of his tunic, opened a leather pouch attached to his belt, and retrieved a piece of parchment. "Signed and dated by our esteemed employer and patron, Dionysius Antiochus, before he died. I assumed he informed you."

Yechiel grabbed the parchment. He rapidly scanned the document. "These are instructions for building a ludus." Yechiel flipped the letter over, and his grip slackened. "There's no explanation. Where did you get this?"

Ursula had mentioned a ludus, a gladiator training school. Had she known about this letter? Had Paris? His conversation about purchasing a prized gladiator would suggest Dionysius had shared his change of building plans with his son.

Agabus snatched the papyrus sheet. "It was delivered to my house the morning of the accident. I was at work discovering Dionysius's body. And right here…" Agabus pointed to the last line, his thick finger jabbing at the letter. "it says Paullus Agabus, head architect."

"Dionysius said nothing about this to me." Yechiel's brows drew together.

"It's obvious he was tired of arguing with you. I understand Dionysius's family applauded his change of mind, especially reinstating me as the lead architect. You'll be following my orders if you're still around."

"What's that supposed to mean?"

"The family wasn't pleased with your performance. And the authorities are looking at all possibilities. An inferior building design or perhaps something more…intentional." Agabus smirked.

Intentional? Sabina looked at the beam knotted to the rope. The authorities were looking into the same possibilities she had. But intentional didn't mean Yechiel was a suspect. The family hadn't even mentioned him until after the authorities began asking questions.

"There was nothing wrong with my plans or the construction. Ask Dionysius…" Yechiel trailed off.

"It couldn't have been your charming personality." Agabus puffed out his lips. "From now on, when you're at work, I insist you show me the respect a head architect deserves. You will give me the deference you didn't give Dionysius. Luckily this building can be renovated without too much demolition and without hiring extra labor."

Yechiel clenched his fists as he glared at Agabus. "A head with no brains."

"There see, that's why Dionysius demoted you, and the next time you threaten—"

"You wouldn't dare fire me," Yechiel said.

Agabus opened his mouth, closed it, then turned to leave.

Sabina stepped in front of Agabus. He couldn't leave. He was first on the scene and a co-worker who didn't like Yechiel. She needed more information like how well he got along with Dionysius. "Could you tell me about finding the body?"

Agabus stared at her as if she'd just dropped from the sky, then turned to Yechiel. "Who is she?"

"I'm a friend of Ursula, Dionysius's wife."

"Why is this woman with you?" Agabus snapped at Yechiel.

"She's not," Yechiel growled.

"We happened to arrive at the same time." Sabina stepped forward. "I am writing a memorial tribute for Dionysius."

"Is this a joke?" Agabus asked Yechiel.

"Apparently not," Yechiel stared at her with a bored expression on his face.

"Do you even know how to write?" Agabus sneered. "You're a woman."

"So is Dionysius's widow." Sabina was beginning to understand Yechiel's dislike for this man. "And she expects your cooperation." She wasn't exactly stretching the truth. Ursula hadn't excluded talking to business associates. "Can you tell me about that morning? Who found the body?" She hoped her irritation didn't show.

Agabus eyed her rudely as if examining a bug. "What's that got to do with writing his memorial? Never mind." Agabus mumbled something about Ursula being an irrational female. "There's nothing much to tell. It was early, just getting light enough to work. The building crew was straggling in when we heard a scream and a crash. I got to him first." Agabus grunted and waved toward the patch of discolored marble between a stack of blocks. "His eyes were open when I found him. Thought he was alive from the bloody bubbles on his lips. But if he was, he didn't last. Which was a good thing."

A good thing? Sabina shuddered once more and looked at the blood stains.

"There was nothing we could do except move the blocks off the body. It took time. Didn't want to tear him up more than he already was."

"That's directly under the arch?" Sabina looked up. "He hadn't tried to escape?"

Agabus grimaced. "Once those blocks gave way, I'm surprised he had time to scream. Site is closed." He pointed toward the roped off area. "A bad omen to begin construction until Dio's returned and remains at home. We don't want his ghost haunting the ludus."

Sabina didn't believe in ghosts but most people did and took precautions. Could Agabus be worried that the angry ghost of a murdered Dionysius would seek revenge? "Was anyone else around at the time?"

"A slave guards the materials during the night. But they aren't stored near here. He admitted he'd fallen asleep, but he woke when the rest of us arrived. He was gone before the collapse."

"Did he report anything prior to you arriving?"

"Nothing was stolen if that's what you're suggesting." Agabus shifted his eyes away from her.

"I meant did he talk to Dionysius? Could he have accidentally bumped into something like the winch handle?"

Agabus's lips pressed tightly in a frown before answering. "I told you he was asleep. Best to leave him out of this. The only thing I can think of is that one of the arch's wooden supports shattered. Maybe a defective piece of wood," Agabus offered.

Yechiel grunted. "I inspected each support."

"You aren't perfect, Yechiel." Agabus said in a high-pitched wheeze.

Yechiel turned on Agabus. "Dionysius wanted that arch finished. You were rushing the job and to save time you didn't untie the rope."

"What rope? I don't know what you're talking about." Agabus puffed out his lips and sucked them in again. Sabina and Yechiel looked at each other.

"You're lying." Yechiel spat. "It was your responsibility to inspect the site before going home that night."

"Why don't you take your accusation to Dionysius?" Agabus's face was turning red. "Oh, that's right. You can't." His voice shook. "Until I declare this building stable, no one's allowed here. I've got major modifications to make if its footprint is going to accommodate Dionysius's ludus. It's going to take a lot of ingenuity."

"Where are you going to get that?" Yechiel asked.

Agabus gestured rudely to Yechiel. "Get out of my building."

Yechiel didn't move. The two men faced off.

Agabus looked away first. "You can't intimidate your way out of this one, Yechiel." He turned and picked his way through the chaotic scene.

Yechiel's gaze followed Agabus long after he disappeared.

"Do you believe him?" Sabina asked. "We only have his word that he hadn't tied the rope to the beam. He found the body, and he would have known how to use the winch. He could have turned the winch, collapsed the arch, and ran back joining the others to appear like he'd just arrived at work."

"That's an absurd theory," Yechiel scoffed. "Agabus can't run. He waddles."

"How could he not know that the rope was tied to the beam?"

Yechiel focused on her. "Unfortunately, he wouldn't know evidence if he stood watching the murderer tie the rope and turn the winch handle."

"I need to talk to him again."

"You?"

"Agabus seemed a bit annoyed with you."

"But you're just a woman." Yechiel's mouth twitched.

Did he just smile? No. Maybe?

Yechiel disappeared around the corner. Sabina needed to find Agabus. He was her only chance to learn the details surrounding Dionysius's death. She couldn't ask the investigating magistrates. And then there was the letter. Did Agabus have anything to do with the sudden change of building plans the day before the accident? Or, more likely, the murder? She definitely needed to quiz the new head architect.

EIGHT

S plintered debris crunched under Sabina's sandals as she passed between the two partial pillars of standing marble and entered the library, or maybe a ludus after the funeral. She bent and removed a marble shard from her sandal. The crunching noise continued. Baffled, she locked eyes with Agabus tramping toward her, a giant hammer swinging at his side. She swallowed and forced herself not to retreat.

"Get out of here." He pointed the hammer at her and then to a crack running the length of an interior wall. "It's not safe. The walls need to be stabilized before people can wander in, satisfying their morbid curiosity."

She forced a casual lightness in her tone. "I need an expert opinion on what caused the collapse."

"For Dionysius's tribute?" he asked skeptically.

"It is the cause of his demise."

Agabus puffed out his cheeks, releasing the air in a wheeze. "The inspectors asked me about the cause. I told them what I told you, a defective brace."

"You didn't find the rope suspicious?"

"Yechiel can accuse me all he wants, but no one knows what caused the collapse." Agabus's face flushed as he pounded the hammer into his opposite palm. "And when did someone not untying a rope become a crime."

71

"Someone?" She didn't want him defensive, but Agabus's denial sounded more like a confession. She had too many questions. "Did Dionysius usually come to the building site that early?"

"He was here a lot. Too much, according to Yechiel. I figured he'd come to watch us set the keystone." Agabus raised his chin. "It's a bit of a milestone. Then the authorities found the note on Dionysius's body."

"A note?" Sabina's heart skipped. "What note? What did it say?"

Agabus took his time. "What kind of memorial are you writing again?"

"The kind that needs details about Ursula's husband's legacy project."

"Hmm." Agabus clamped his lips together.

He didn't believe her. She wanted to pry the answer out of his mouth. Instead, she asked calmly, "You didn't mention a note before."

"The inspector asked me not to say anything, but I suppose Ursula will tell you. Women can't keep secrets. The writing was blurred and soaked in Dionysius's blood, almost unreadable." Agabus grimaced. "But they deciphered a few details requesting a meeting that morning."

"You said the blood made it unreadable?"

"Almost. Not the important parts, the library, and Yechiel's signature."

"Why would Yechiel arrange a meeting on the day of his religious observance?"

"We only have Yechiel's word on that. The inspector agreed a crowded gathering sounded like the perfect alibi for someone who wanted to slip away unnoticed." Agabus licked his lips. "I told the inspector something like this was going to happen."

"A murder?" Sabina blinked rapidly.

"Well, not a murder." The muscles along Agabus's jawline flexed. "But Dio and Yechiel argued about everything. That's what I told the inspector. Yechiel would introduce new construction techniques or design changes, claiming we needed better material or additional workers, money that cut into our profits. Dionysius insisted on approving the changes and dared to add a few suggestions of his own."

"I'm guessing Yechiel didn't welcome the intrusion."

"Welcome?" Agabus's voice rose. "Yechiel believes he is the only one with worthy ideas. Me? I do whatever the customer asks, no matter how idiotic. That's how it's done."

"But not Yechiel?"

"Like Vulcan's anvil, the sparks flew every time they met." Agabus smacked his hammer into his fleshy palm, warming up to the topic. "Once, Yechiel ordered Dionysius out of his own library. I mention it only to illustrate how rudely Yechiel treated Dionysius."

"I understand." Sabina understood only too well how disagreeable Yechiel could be and how that reputation wouldn't help him. "But why would Yechiel kill his employer?"

"It's not a secret the two couldn't stand each other. Maybe an argument went too far. Or Dio finally fired Yechiel in his letter."

"But Yechiel didn't receive a letter. He had no idea Dionysius had changed his mind."

"We only have Yechiel's word on that as well." He pointed the hammerhead at her. "I'm guessing our egotistical Yechiel wouldn't let Dionysius ruin his career."

Sabina stepped back. Agabus's interview with the inspector would have successfully pointed the finger of guilt at Yechiel—and away from himself. What was Agabus hiding? "Dionysius's daughter told me her father's original plan was to build a ludus with you as the head architect."

"His original and final plan." Agabus gazed steadily at her.

"When did the library come in?"

"Dio said Yechiel's designs inspired him. And Yechiel refused to build a ludus. Some nonsense about his Jewish faith forbidding work on a building dedicated to celebrating and worshipping false gods."

Sabina knew the argument well. Christians debated the same issue. If she offered the required pinch of incense to Zeus upon entering a gymnasium or arena, was that worshipping a pagan god? Many Christians agreed with the Jews that it was.

"I admit Yechiel's library had a certain grandeur, but I wouldn't call it inspiring." Agabus shrugged. "I was surprised when Dio chose it because he was promoting his reputation as a wealthy benefactor of our city. The impact of his gift weighed heavily in his consideration. An influential seat for Paris on the city council depended on the council's measure of appreciation. Of course, the more extravagant his spending, the wealthier the suitors for his daughter."

"And the library accomplished these goals?" Sabina asked.

"None of them. It was the ludus that profited Ephesus and Dionysius the most." Agabus sighed, his agitation settling into head-shaking acquiescence. "But the client gets what he wants. And Dionysius's name would be immortalized on either building, chiseled into the marble pillars. But..."

"But?"

"Most people can't read. What good are books to the city of Ephesus? How much acclaim can he gather pandering to a few educated elites?"

"Yet, Dionysius agreed on the library. With Yechiel taking over your role, I imagine you were more than surprised. Maybe angry?"

Agabus fastened a wary gaze on Sabina. "Is that what Yechiel told you?"

"It's just that Yechiel is..." Sabina searched through several unflattering terms before choosing the one she had experienced the most. "An extremely stubborn man. I can imagine working with him would be difficult."

"You have no idea. Yechiel's the smartest, most creative, and most knowledgeable man on the project. Just ask him."

Hostility laced Agabus's comments. But was it enough to frame Yechiel for murder?

"Dionysius thought Yechiel and I worked as equal partners. However, I had to step in to keep the project on schedule. I assure you, I was very much in control from the beginning to end."

She wondered if Yechiel knew that. "And now, the project is all yours. Congratulations." Sabina hoped she sounded sincere.

"Yes, yes." Agabus nodded with enthusiasm. "And Dionysius's name will be chiseled into the pillars of the ludus, immortalizing his legacy."

"With your name carved beneath, cementing your future and career as well."

Agabus eyed her guardedly. Had she overdone the flattery?

He spoke slower, his tone muted. "True, but I don't need the recognition."

Sabina held her tongue. Every living, breathing Roman craved recognition, and Agabus was definitely breathing.

He continued. "My name is on numerous notable and prominent structures in Ephesus. Specifically, the nymphaeum, the fountain dedicated to our illustrious former governor. You may have seen it near the market agora."

"Yes, I've seen it. It is—large." Sabina forced a smile.

"Thank you."

A swarm of giggling women surrounded by their slaves erupted through the library's broken archway. "Is this where Dionysius died?"

"Out! Out!" Agabus brandished his hammer for real this time. "You too." He pointed the hammerhead at Sabina and gestured toward the group of retreating women. "You're interfering in my work."

Sabina stopped outside the roped-off area and brushed a coating of marble dust from the hem of her mantle and sandals and shook a pebble loose from between her toes. She would put on different footwear the next time she questioned him.

Agabus had made serious accusations, but if he had proof beyond his antagonism, he hadn't shared it. And for all his slander, Agabus hadn't criticized Yechiel's expertise. His jealousy unwittingly acknowledged that Yechiel was best qualified as the lead architect. His integrity and high standards drew a contrast to Agabus's mediocrity, and no one likes their shortcomings pointed out. Unfortunately, Yechiel's rude and insolent behavior made him a perfect target. Eunice's desperation was understandable.

Strolling home, she imagined Dionysius's last seconds as the arch collapsed. Agabus said he had heard him scream. Did Dionysius have any warning? Did he see his murderer, or was it just a horrible accident? She shivered. She was sure Agabus was diverting suspicion away from his ineptitude. Could he be hiding something more? And had that something led to Dionysius's death?

Sabina appeared to be the only one on Yechiel's side. Putting her head down, she trudged up the hill to her house with Ursula's voice echoing *You'll think of something brilliant, just like your father.* At the moment, she could think of nothing brilliant.

75

NINE

Sabina padded into the dining room, yawning from a fitful night of restless sleep. She froze in surprise at seeing her father at home eating breakfast. Mid-morning was always reserved for meeting with clients in his office. She stopped at the threshold.

She had been avoiding him the last five months, after Benjamin's murder investigation prompted another revelation, one she struggled to comprehend. After Sabina's birth, her father had exercised his paternal right of refusal, rejecting and refusing to acknowledge three of his children at birth. He had ordered the newborns to be discarded outside the city walls and left to die from exposure. He directed the midwife to tell his wife the babies had been stillborn.

Sabina knew a son was paramount and necessary to consolidate their wealth and family name, and the three girls born after her could be legitimate liabilities. She also knew her father had destroyed a life with shared laughter, sibling squabbles, and someone to cuddle with when storms raged.

Her father did not make decisions based on omens, signs, and portents, but he did for the sake of his ego. The curse linked to his second daughter's red facial stain would have been a convenient excuse to rid himself of an embarrassment. The curled foot of his third daughter was another unacceptable deformity. And the fourth child, having survived the death of her mother had been a burden for a grieving widower. Knowing his actions were not considered contemptable by Roman authorities—discarding inconvenient or unwanted babies was lawful—did nothing to lessen Sabina's condemnation and judgment. And longing.

Her father's secret had been kept for twenty years, and Amisi had begged her not to confront her father with her discovery. It would only cause trouble. So, she hadn't. But she could not forgive him even after Amisi confessed that strangers had saved each baby. God did not hold grudges, but she did. Her mother had died when she was eight years old. Raised as an only child with a neglectful and indifferent father and no extended family, she imagined remaking her life with the loving relationship of a sibling.

Amisi had also begged her not to search for information about her sisters. It would infuriate her father if he found out, and it was an impossible task that would only lead to despair. Sabina disagreed. Unfortunately, Amisi had been right. There was hopelessly little information to go on.

Sabina stayed away from her father whenever possible and had only the minimal conversation necessary for two people living in the same house. Mainly he gave orders, and she followed them. He hadn't noticed her snubbing him.

He wouldn't care if he had.

She scowled and spun around to leave.

"Where were you yesterday?" Her father's question stopped her. Slowly she turned to look at him. He popped a quail egg into his mouth. "Amisi said you are keeping strange hours again. Not attending to your household duties."

Not a caring fatherly inquiry. She hadn't had one of those in twenty years. "Someone close to Portia died. I've been consoling her."

"Another death in your church?" He put down his knife. "Do not tell me you are involved."

"What? No. I didn't even know the man."

"You didn't know the man, yet you spent all day at Portia's."

"Well, not all day," Sabina hedged. She had no way of knowing at what point Amisi had noticed her absence, and Sabina would be confined to the house if she got caught lying to her father. How much did she need to reveal to keep her agreement with Ursula confidential? An arrangement her father would abruptly terminate. "I accompanied Portia when she visited the deceased's family."

"The family of Dionysius Antiochus." Sabina's father wiped his mouth with his napkin.

He knew.

Sabina threw her hands up. "You had me followed?" Her father hadn't achieved his reputation for keeping the peace and apprehending criminals and escaped slaves alone. His network of informers was legendary. He had eyes and ears everywhere. People called them rats, believing that her father gleaned his information from the sewer rats that infested every public and private building in Ephesus.

He shook his head and folded his napkin deliberately. "Why would I waste time tracking my wayward daughter? Do you think anyone cares where you buy fish? My people were observing the mourners who came and went from Dionysius's house. When they reported seeing my daughter mingling with the visitors, I don't know why, but I was surprised." He drummed his fingers on the table as he frowned at her.

Disturbing her father took some doing, and his irritation gave her a measure of satisfaction. But her triumph evaporated as his steely glare chiseled into her. "Why were you there?"

She lifted her chin and took a slow breath, thankful she had told him the truth—well partial truth. "I accompanied Portia because her husband is traveling. Why were you watching the house?" Did she need to ask? Roman society trafficked in knowledge, and spies often discovered illicit information that could be bartered to save your life or family fortune or cause a rival to lose theirs.

"Dionysius was one of Ephesus's most distinguished citizens." His mouth compressed as if repudiating his statement.

"You disliked him?"

"There are principles a Roman abides by, self-control, discipline, devotion to family and empire. Dionysius Antiochus had none of those. However, my like or dislike is irrelevant. We take an interest in our wealthy and influential citizens and their deaths. The investigating magistrates have questions."

Sabina fought a sudden surge of anger at her father—criticizing Dionysius for a lack of family devotion. Dionysius hadn't abandoned his newborn children outside the city walls. Dio hadn't used his right as *Pater Familia* to expose Diana or Paris to the ravages of nature and wild animals. Dionysius hadn't lied to his wife, saying his children were stillborn.

Dionysius had apparently loved his children. She bit her lip so hard she tasted the tang of blood to keep from retorting. How dare her father judge the man.

If he noticed her reaction, he ignored it. "You will stay away from that family."

What about the pact she'd made with Ursula and the danger to Yechiel she'd learned about? "The family graciously invited me to return anytime."

"The city council has ordered an investigation into the death. You will not go back."

Other magistrates had been speaking to her father. Why involve his law enforcement unless they'd suspected murder? "I heard Dionysius's death was a terrible accident. What caused the authorities to think differently?"

Her father glared at her. "What are you after, Sabina?"

She changed subjects abruptly away from Yechiel. "Ursula asked if I might help her with a small task. She requested I return. She's a persuasive woman and difficult to turn down."

Her father worked his jaw back and forth. "You don't want to get mixed up with Ursula. She could crush you with her little finger."

"When I mentioned you wouldn't approve, Ursula told me you knew each other."

Her father's cynical laugh surprised her. "Of course, she did. Her not-so-subtle attempt at coercing you. What is this small task?"

"She asked me to gather information for Dionysius's memorial."

"You? Why you?"

Did she dare tell him that someone admired her investigative skills and believed she could accomplish things a man couldn't? He'd never believe her. "I don't know."

"No, you wouldn't, and whatever reason Ursula gave you would be a lie." Cynicism permeated his words, furthering her suspicion that Ursula had manipulated her into a situation more complex than simply clearing her reputation.

Her father's bodyguard and secretary, Zarmig, tramped into the room. "Did I hear the name Dionysius Antiochus?" His cheery intrusion was anything but accidental. Nor did he just happen to overhear. He was her father's extra hands and extra set of ears. Or ear, to be exact, owing to Zarmig's left ear having been cut off as a child caught spying on her father's army encampment. He owed his right ear and his life to her father.

"The enchantress, Ursula, has ensnared Sabina," her father said.

"Like father like—" Zarmig stopped abruptly when her father shot him a commanding look. The latitude of honesty shared between her father and his former slave sometimes crossed the line between master and servant. "As your father said, you should be wary. Did you meet any of the other family members?" His laidback tone didn't fool her.

"His daughter, Diana," she answered cautiously.

"We heard a rumor that Dionysius had received a death threat," her father said.

"I wouldn't know. I just met them." Sabina shook her head, confused. First, he calls her into the room. Now he shares news with her... No, she knew better than that. He was gathering intelligence. "It's not like they laid out their family intrigues to a stranger."

"Hmm, then he wasn't forewarned," her father said.

Forewarned was different. She knew something her father didn't, another small victory. "If you mean the fortune teller, it wasn't a death threat."

"No family intrigues, huh?" Zarmig glanced meaningfully at her father, communicating a private message. Sabina sensed more than she saw.

"What?" she asked.

"Perhaps one more visit," her father said to Zarmig as if she wasn't in the room.

"What happened to never return? And be wary." Now she was wary.

"I stand by my advice to watch your back. Ursula is not to be trusted," Zarmig said. "Your father learned the—"

"Shut up, Zarmig."

Sabina gaped, looking from one man to the other. "You want me to spy on Dio's family?"

"No one said anything about spying." Zarmig's mouth twitched. That was exactly what they meant.

"Ursula invited you to gather information. Did she forbid you from sharing your findings?" her father asked.

"It didn't come up," Sabina answered.

"Well, there we are." Zarmig clapped his hands. "You can make Ursula and your father happy at the same time. An unlikely occurrence."

"Enough," her father rumbled a warning to Zarmig. "I have no interest except in protecting our illustrious citizens from deceitful people."

Sabina cleared her throat. "Are you protecting Ursula, or is she the deceitful one?"

Her father stabbed his knife through a hunk of cheese on his plate. "The point is that if you were to fall victim to any devious individual, it would complicate matters."

"In other words, watch your back. That family is not all it seems." Zarmig raised an eyebrow in emphasis.

"What if I don't want to go back?"

"I'm not in the mood for games, Sabina," her father thundered.

"Unless it's with Ursula." Zarmig's mouth twitched.

Her father gripped his knife and hurled it, sticking it vibrating into a chairback inches from where Zarmig stood. "You go too far."

Zarmig blinked but didn't move. The two men locked stares.

Sabina had never seen her father react to Zarmig's barbs with more than a stinging rebuke. Seeing the confrontation alarmed her. She stepped between them. "Ursula confessed to having attempted to kill Dionysius during a dinner party. Do you think I'm in danger?"

Zarmig dropped his gaze first. He turned to Sabina. "We don't know. Just be careful. Ask a few questions, that's all Ursula asked you to do."

Ursula had asked a bit more than that, but Sabina wasn't about to confess to her ill-advised agreement with the woman. Her father chose the perfect word—ensnared.

"I will check into Ursula's previous incident. I believe there had been rumors at the time." Her father went back to eating as if nothing had transpired. "She will go to great lengths to protect what is hers. I'm not sure where she would stop."

"A message arrived this morning." Zarmig handed her a small parchment roll she had not noticed him carrying. "For you."

Someone had broken the seal. Sabina looked at her father. She unrolled it and read an invitation from Ursula, summoning her that afternoon. Her fingers shook as she rolled it up. Her father and Zarmig's words did nothing to calm her. Had she made a serious mistake agreeing to Ursula's request to spy on Dionysius's family? She followed Zarmig from the room, clutching the invitation.

She was to spy on Ursula and not for Ursula.

"Father must believe I have some talents if I'm to be a double spy."

Zarmig snorted, followed by a shrug. "We will review a few surveillance procedures I taught you as a child. They are for your safety."

She took that as a yes. "I've not seen Father upset by your jabs before."

"I should have known better today."

"Today?"

"Your father received news this morning that he lost a small fortune on one of his investments. He will recover, but no more needling for a while."

"What investment?"

"Do you remember several months ago when he entertained a merchant from Rome? The merchant's business reputation was exceptional, taking calculated risks that impressed your father, who does not suffer fools."

"Marcus…his name was Marcus." Sabina felt her chest tighten.

Zarmig nodded. "He'd just arrived from Alexandria with a cargo of India cloth, selling it in Ephesus for twice what he'd paid even after significant taxes."

Sabina smiled faintly. "I informed him it was the naturalist, Pliny, who named it cotton. Amisi nearly died from embarrassment. Women are to use their intelligence for flattering potential suitors, not humiliating them."

"Wise counsel. Most men are not as enlightened as I am. They find educated women incomprehensible. I believe they are just odd."

Sabina rolled her eyes. "Amisi couldn't get too upset, because during our next dinner he spoke almost exclusively to me. We enjoyed a heathy discussion on Pliny's travels and writings on the geography and biology of North Africa."

"I believe that was the dinner he convinced your father to finance a cargo of wool to be transported and sold in Rome for a hefty profit."

"An ill-advised investment. What happened?"

"That is what the investors wanted to know when the ship didn't arrive in Ostia's harbor. The Roman navy initiated an inquiry, and the report arrived today. Some cargo washed up on the beach of some island, suggesting that the ship and cargo sank. A storm or pirates sank it."

Sabina's voice shook. Pray for a shipwreck. Pirates took prisoners for one reason, and drowning was better than the short, brutal life of a pirate galley slave. "They recovered nothing?" No one? The apostle Paul had survived three shipwrecks. "Surely there is hope."

"Yes, hope. The carpets were insured, but not for what your father paid. And the fortune he expected is gone."

"Carpets?" She didn't care about carpets.

"Armenian woolen carpets. It took Marcus years to put the trade deal together—a rare business opportunity to export an even rarer commodity to Rome, or so he said. Your father is in a foul mood with the cargo at the bottom of the sea and the crew dead."

Sabina nodded listlessly. She had worked to banish the memory of Marcus's bantering smile, calloused fingers caressing her cheek, and his kiss. Would his death make forgetting any easier?

Zarmig looked at her, his expression changing to understanding. "Ah. You liked him."

She lowered her eyes, partly to hide her tears. "We had a private dinner one night." And he asked me to marry him and sail away to Rome. She would have fallen in love with him, if they'd had more time. Marcus had foolishly risked more than pirates and storms. He had risked loving a woman, now four times cursed.

TEN

"Come this way, please." A slave ushered Sabina through Dionysius's large vestibule.

Ursula strolled toward them. The dark eye circles from the other day were less visible. She must have had a decent night's sleep, or her slave applied thicker makeup.

"The master is lying in wait in the atrium." The slave bowed.

Sabina frowned. "Lying-in-wait?"

"Lying-in-state, you idiot." Ursula slapped the slave, dismissing him. She turned to Sabina. "The embalmer performed a miracle stuffing Dio's body with straw soaked in honey. Ingenious. Come see." Ursula sailed into the atrium, her floor-length black stola of finely woven linen still unbelted as befitted her mourning but cut to flow stylishly around her, unlike the limp sack of mourning she'd worn during Sabina's first visit. Was that only yesterday?

Dionysius was displayed on an elaborately carved gilded couch, wearing a pristine white toga and crowned with a laurel wreath. Mourners paying their respects crowded around the corpse. Few of the visitors shed tears. But that was the job of the professional mourners who would earn a substantial fee during the funeral procession through town.

A hazy smoke from burning cedar incense hung in the air. Traces of yesterday's perfumes and spices lingered, prickling her nostrils. Sabina sneezed, bracing for the resulting headache that, thankfully, didn't strike.

"Come closer." Ursula waved her over.

The gory details of Dionysius's death would have reached every corner of the province by now. And if there was one thing the Romans loved, it was gore. But the onlookers would be disappointed. Dionysius's stuffed body hidden beneath the many folds of his toga, looked fit, vibrant, and too young to be dead. Ursula casually described preserving Dio's crushed torso and mangled limbs as if showing off a newly refurbished chair.

Sabina shuddered. Had the realization of her husband's death not sunk in? Perhaps her flippancy was a result of shock or not wanting to contemplate dying? Daily life conveniently distracted most from confronting their mortality. Sabina gazed at the corpse. Until it couldn't be ignored. "You opted not to use a death mask for Dionysius."

"I couldn't bear to hide his gorgeous face." Ursula pressed her lips together. "I pretend he's sleeping. The makeup artist nearly brought him back to life. Don't you think his skin tone looks natural?"

Sabina nodded politely. The talented makeup artist had recreated Dionysius in realistic color. Still, nothing—not even his hair meticulously oiled and perfumed could hide the odor of death—could disguise the unnatural rigidity of his face. The coin for his boat ride across the river Styx into Hades rested between grimacing lips, expressing his final seconds of horror. A flute player wafted a mournful melody from a stool in the corner.

How many of these people knew Dionysius only by reputation? Were they aware of the devoted father and loyal friend hidden behind the self-indulgent public persona? Or was the witty, selfish, womanizing man the real Dionysius, skillfully playing the role of husband and father?

Ursula's discourse shifted to the open-doored cabinets surrounding the couch. She solemnly gestured to the wax death masks of Dionysius's father, grandfather, and the older ancestors of the Dionysius Antiochus family. "I think he looks like his great-grandfather, Pelopidas

Antiochus, don't you?" Ursula pointed to an oversized mask cabinet, ornately decorated with a lion insignia on the top and labeled First Germanica Legion. "Pelopidas established the family dynasty by dying in the battle of Long Bridges over eighty years ago. A German spear struck him in the throat while he defended his general, Aulus Caecina. The emperor Tiberius honored Pelopidas posthumously. We don't talk about the legion's unfortunate downfall."

Ursula paused and stared at Dio. Her impassive expression gave no clues as to her current state of mind, feelings, or scheming. Sabina followed her as they sailed by several people attempting to offer their condolences. Ursula flicked her wrist as if swatting flies. The onlookers melted away out of respect for her mourning or perhaps her temperamental outbursts.

Sabina followed her out of the crowded atrium, past the curtained alcove where she had entertained Sabina and Portia. The conversations and clatter of the public viewing faded to a muffled hum. They passed through a private garden and entered a second smaller atrium. Ursula stopped outside a room with a solid door. She slid the door aside and gestured Sabina in.

"It's nice to meet you, Sabina," a man reclining on a couch raised a goblet in greeting.

Sabina's mouth dropped open. She stared mutely at Loukas Rhodius, Dio's banker, investor, friend, and Ursula's lover. Preoccupied by Dionysius she had let her guard down, exactly what her father warned her not to do. Alarm bells on full alert her gaze flicked between the two. She clamped her mouth shut.

"I told you she'd come." Ursula pushed past Sabina sliding the door closed. She slunk down on the couch, curling up beside Loukas.

"Who could resist you, my sweet." Loukas took one of Ursula's hands and nibbled at her fingertips.

Ursula pulled her hand away. "Sit," she ordered Sabina, pointing to an adjoining couch at a right angle to the couple. Loukas poured wine from a pitcher into two glass goblets on a small table laden with a plate of figs and small honey cakes. Ursula snatched a goblet.

"Is this wise?" Sabina mumbled. The atrium was brimming with people. When had Loukas arrived?

"Wise? Loukas must be here. How else can I keep track of Paris's scheming?"

Sabina studied the closed door, more concerned with what Ursula was plotting and the ambush she had just walked into.

"It's only natural Sabina is suspicious," Loukas chided. "Just like her father, she's cautious."

"She's nothing like her father." Ursula slapped his hand playfully, nearly spilling his wine then flashed a tight smile at Sabina. "I said sit."

Sabina paused, bunching a fistful of her mantal. Why, she groaned inwardly, had she agreed to Ursula's proposal? Because Eunice believed she could save Yechiel. If that was possible—under no circumstances—could she allow herself to be distracted again. Sighing loudly, she plopped on the couch. "Perhaps you should explain your relationship…the one you intend on denying to the authorities."

"I didn't ask you to prove we weren't lovers. I asked you to prove that I loved my husband. The two are not incompatible."

Loukas filled and offered a third glass toward Sabina. She took and sipped, savoring the bite and aroma of the spiced wine.

"What about being faithful to him?" Sabina asked.

"We may need to modify the definition of faithful." Ursula sipped her wine slowly. "I stayed with Dio while he took lovers. How much more faithful could I be?"

"Compared to Dio's numerous affairs, you would be a vestal virgin, my sweet." Loukas kissed her cheek. "Dio was a flawed husband. Unfortunately you will be judged against the pinnacle of virtue and faithfulness, Caesar's wife."

"Livia's been dead over eighty years and we still can't rid ourselves of that sanctimonious cow." Ursula snatched her hand from Loukas. "By the gods, I hate her."

Loukas's hands made a protective motion. "Do not speak ill of the dead. Remember, Caesar and Livia are now gods."

"Don't patronize me, Loukas." Ursula slammed her glass down, splashing drops of wine onto Sabina and Loukas.

Loukas passed Sabina a napkin and she dabbed at the wine speckles on her tunic.

"It is your devotion to Dio that matters," Loukas tutted. "It is why you asked Sabina here."

Sabina worked not to roll her eyes in disbelief.

Ursula uncurled her legs and turned a full smile on Sabina. "And she has already begun gathering the evidence to prove my love and commitment. I've informed the family that you're helping me write Dio's tribute." She squeezed Sabina's arm, her voice warm and affectionate.

Sabina shivered.

The winds of Boreas and Notus, describing Ursula's moods, took on new meaning. Unpredictable and dangerous.

Ursula offered her cup to Loukas to fill. "You can start by reporting what Diana told you."

There was a moment of startled silence before Sabina replied. "Reporting?"

"Surely she told you something I can use against Paris in court."

"I barely met her. We discussed the poem she was writing for her father's funeral. She seemed concerned that it wouldn't be good enough."

"That's Diana. Nothing is ever good enough for her. What do you call it, darling?"

"Perfectionism," Loukas said.

"It's the only trait she inherited from Dio." Ursula nodded. "She's dutiful, shy, not particularly attractive, and devoted to her father. I finished a distant second in Dio's affections. How can I say wearisome without appearing spiteful?"

"I'm not sure you can." Loukas lifted the wine pitcher toward Sabina. "Refill?" She shook her head. "Figs?" He offered as if he were the host.

"No, thank you," Sabina said.

"I have no children of my own. Contrary to what Paris says, I feel an obligation as a stepmother and a protectiveness for Diana. She has never yelled, shrieked, or harbored the vengefulness of a normal adolescent toward me."

"You expected that?" Sabina asked in surprise.

"When Dio divorced Diana's mother to marry me, her mother committed suicide."

"Oh." Sabina choked on her sip of wine. Pity for the young Diana flooded her. "That is hardly something she'd share upon meeting a stranger."

"Of course not," Ursula said. "Which is why I'm telling you. Diana retreated after her mother's death. And I was sympathetic. I said nothing disparaging about her, so she should have nothing bad to say about me."

"Does she believe you loved her father?" Sabina asked. Paris's accusations of money grabbing could be shared by his half-sister.

"Diana lives in a romantic fantasy. She's not experienced enough to realize love is either comedy or tragedy. She's more sheltered than most girls her age, but you can trust what she says. I don't think the poor thing knows how to lie."

"She appeared preoccupied when I met her. I assumed it was because of her brother's friend," Sabina said.

"Otho," Ursula's voice held disgust. "Her fiancé."

"What!" Sabina sputtered, surprised by this change of circumstance. "She said nothing about a fiancé?"

Ursula shrugged. "Diana told us Otho proposed again yesterday. Paris granted consent to the marriage. It is a total disaster."

Sabina must have looked confused because Loukas explained. "Dio had refused permission for the union. It was the only thing he'd ever denied Diana. With Dio dead, she is getting what she wanted."

Ursula looked away. "She doesn't know what she wants."

"Fifteen is old enough to marry," Sabina said. Several of her friends had married younger.

"It's not her age Dio objected to, it's Otho. It is one thing for members of that family to work for us, quite another to lower ourselves to marry them. No matter how in lust you are." Ursula licked her bottom lip; her eyes glittered as her hand caressed Loukas's arm. A man could be easily seduced by this woman.

"Otho's adoptive father is Titus Mordax." Loukas said the name as if Sabina should recognize it. "The famous gladiator."

Baffled, Sabina raised her shoulders.

Ursula slid off her slippers and wiggled her toes. "Twenty years ago at the Artemesian festival, Mordax defeated six gladiators in a row. Impressed with his ruthless brutality, the emperor Titus rewarded him with his freedom. He's quite renowned."

Loukas shifted his body, settling back against the couch. "When Dio first announced the different options for his legacy, he came to me for advice. We discussed the costs and benefits of various projects. The library and ludus ended at the top of his list. I recommended the ludus even though the startup costs were greater than the library, but once the ludus was operational, it would have generated income the library couldn't."

"Was money an issue?" Sabina said.

"Not for Dio. But as his financial advisor I recommended he consider it. I also advised against hiring Mordax."

"But Dio always had to have the best." Ursula patted her lips with a napkin. "And Mordax had that reputation. I told Dio he couldn't climb in bed with that viper and not get bit."

"He went against both of your recommendations." Why? She tried not to sound suspicious. "Would you have profited from the ludus's success?"

"It's what I do. Invest." Loukas nodded. "Dio's money would buy the best slaves as fighters, combined with Mordax's skill at training the gladiators and managing the ludus. It had the potential to make a handsome profit."

"When the project changed to the library, Agabus lost the honor and tribute for designing one of the largest building projects in Ephesus." Sabina calculated. "And Mordax lost a status job with a large salary." She didn't add that Loukas also lost out on a lucrative investment. "I imagine both men were distraught."

Loukas sighed. "Dio was negotiating wages with Mordax but hadn't signed a contract. All financial and other arrangements stopped once Dio decided on the library. I'm sure both men are pleased that Dio changed back to his initial plan," Loukas pointed out.

Ursula leaned into Loukas and squeezed his arm. "I told you she was perfect. Can't you see her conniving mind turning over suspects and motives?" Her tone mirrored her smug expression. "You will find someone to blame for Dio's death, leaving me as the poor, misunderstood widow." She pouted and fluttered her lashes.

Sabina gaped at Ursula, trying to decide if conniving was an insult or a compliment. Conniving had good meanings. Didn't it? Devious, cunning, and scheming came to mind. She landed on shrewd as the best of the lot. "Mordax must have been more than pleased when he received Dionysius's letter announcing the change?"

Ursula grumbled. "Mordax and Paris have had their heads together all day. One reason Loukas is here is to protect Dio's investments. Loukas isn't a lawyer, but he has extensive experience with…what do you call it, darling?"

"Joint business partnerships. For over ten years Dio has trusted my skillful management of his finances and investments. I assured Ursula the family fortune is safe and well cared for."

Well-cared for or skillfully taken over? How much control did Loukas have over the money with Dionysius gone? Portia said that Dionysius trusted Loukas. Ursula ran her bare foot up and down Loukas's leg. How good of a character judge was the dead man?

"Safe until Paris takes over." Ursula sniffed. "He's more interested in his chariot races than overseeing the family's welfare."

"Give him time." Loukas massaged Ursula's feet. "What family doesn't have an indulged child or two?" Loukas turned to Sabina. "Dio failed miserably to teach and discipline his children. But Paris is not that different from other sons of wealthy patricians, and Dio could afford to indulge his children, so no harm done."

"No harm?" Ursula pulled away from him. "Paris is trying to get me thrown out of the will and out on the street."

"You said your husband was going to ask for a divorce." Sabina pointed out. "Wouldn't that have been the same outcome?"

"Dio didn't get the chance. It's your job to make sure Paris doesn't either. Find out what he plans to say against me in court."

"Perhaps your husband would have changed his mind had he lived," Sabina said.

"Cassandra said that was one possibility if Dio's fortune had changed," Ursula's voice softened.

"Cassandra the fortune teller?" Sabina spoke her thought out loud. "Fortune telling is illegal."

Ursula shrugged. "Which is why her patrons guard her identity. You can't see her without a recommendation from a trusted client. Even we patricians aren't guaranteed meeting with her."

"Are all her patrons wealthy?" Sabina asked.

"Yes, but money has nothing to do with it. Cassandra has a gift. She wants to help people. She charges only one sestera. Of course, I pay her much more for her advice."

"You find her advice helpful?"

"Ursula got more help than she bargained for." Loukas raised his glass in a mock toast.

"I didn't expect to be told I would be a widow in a year. Dio didn't laugh at me quite so hard after that."

"You said he wasn't one of her clients?"

"He thought Cassandra was stealing my money. He said frauds like her ask prying questions pretending to read your future when what they're reading is your reaction. Dio said my dramatic expressions would reveal my life story in two minutes."

"You can understand his skepticism." Sabina certainly could.

"Cassandra isn't like that. She didn't need to ask me anything. She just knew. She's gifted with the sight and power of the oracle. Her guiding daemon unveils the secrets of the spirit realm to her."

"So, this guiding daemon told you Dio would die?"

"Not the first time I went to her. I returned after the unfortunate dinner incident."

"Where you tried to kill your husband?" Sabina failed to keep the cynicism from her tone.

Ursula wagged her finger at Sabina. "I told you I just wanted him to know I loved him. I needed to hear he still cared. I was jealous."

"You were drunk," Loukas said.

"A tiny bit." Ursula shrugged. "Anyway, I wanted to ask Cassandra if

Dio would leave me. He was drifting away. I knew he had a lover and I wanted Cassandra to tell me her name."

"Instead, she told you he was going to die," Sabina said. "Why did Dionysius see her if he thought she was a fraud?"

"I'd say Dio was skeptical but curious," Loukas said.

"He had ridiculed the spirits and meddling gods his entire life. But he began questioning acquaintances who'd gone to her, and everyone told him the same thing. Her predictions come true." Ursula stretched and held out her glass. Loukas filled it.

"Why didn't he take measures to protect himself?"

"When he finally spoke to her, Cassandra told him the same thing she'd told me. You cannot avoid your fate." Ursula chided Sabina. "Besides, Cassandra did not know the time or nature of his death."

"Did Dio believe her?" Sabina asked.

Ursula put the cup to her mouth but didn't drink and set it down. "He changed after seeing her. That's when he began designing his legacy building. He became consumed with plans and architects. I rarely saw him. But when Dio came to my bed, he was different. He acted as if…I began to hope that he was falling in love with me again. I was going to ask Cassandra, but Dio died before I got a chance."

Ursula was Dionysius's link to Cassandra's deadly prophecy. Did that mean anything? Could Ursula and Cassandra have conspired to murder Dio, concealing their plot inside a prophecy? Cassandra's predicted timing of Dionysius's death left Ursula a wealthy widow instead of a disinherited divorcee. It freed her to pursue her affair with Loukas. The fortune-teller's reputation could have benefited from Dionysius's death as well. Were more rich clients flocking to her?

Sabina looked back and forth between the two. Was she being drawn into the collusion? "Did Cassandra tell you to hire me?"

"That was my idea." Ursula grabbed Sabina's hand. "But Cassandra could help you if you need advice."

Sabina shook her head and gently tugged her hand free. "I don't think so." The warnings from the church elders and readings from the scriptures book of Second Kings flashed through her mind. He practiced soothsaying and divination and appointed mediums and persons who used spirit guides. He did much that was evil from ADONAI's perspective, thus provoking Him to anger.

"I will arrange a visit. It will be late in the day. She never meets clients in the morning," Ursula announced as if Sabina hadn't spoken. "If Cassandra agrees to see you, you have no choice." Ursula snuggled against Loukas. "I will beat Paris at his own scheme."

The doors to the small room slammed open, and the blond man she'd seen the other day leaving the garden burst into the room, his face mottled red with rage. "I should have known you'd be sneaking your lover into our house for a tryst, while my father is barely cold."

Loukas untangled himself from Ursula, set his glass of wine down, and gracefully rose from the couch. "I don't sneak into people's homes. Your stepmother has serious financial decisions to make. Your father's death is no time to discard prudent planning."

"She," Paris pointed at Ursula, "has never been prudent."

"Have you met Sabina? She's the woman compiling your father's tribute." Loukas's calming voice held the tone of an admonishing parent as he pointed out the third person at the supposed tryst.

"No." Paris blinked as if confused. He didn't look at Loukas.

"Sabina, may I introduce Paris, Dionysius's son and heir? Paris, this is Sabina, a friend of your father."

Sabina smiled. It was not the time to correct Loukas.

Paris nodded, saying nothing.

"Paris, you are welcome to join us," Ursula interjected. "As the new master of the house, I would advise it. Our business with Sabina is concluded." She nodded toward the door.

Sabina rose, gladly taking the cue to flee the tension in the room, like water pressing against a dam ready to burst.

"I'm busy," Paris stuttered. "Otho and I have plans."

"Perhaps you can spare a few minutes to discuss your father's legacy with Sabina." Ursula stopped Sabina's escape. "We wouldn't want to leave out Dio's son in the tribute."

"I don't know," Paris muttered, sounding unenthused with the options.

"I'm sure many duties are clamoring for your attention." Sabina stood at the door. "I don't want to waste your valuable time. We can talk while we walk." How much pressure was Paris under with Dio's large estate suddenly his responsibility. And navigating under a torrent of emotion. First his father's sudden death and now confronting a united Ursula and Loukas.

Paris lingered as if unwilling to abandon his argument. Then as if realizing his outraged advantage was gone, he left the room without glancing back. Sabina followed.

"I couldn't stay with them...with her." Paris's words came out in a rush. "It's difficult to concentrate when I think Father's dead and she's still alive."

"You have a lot to think about." She struggled to keep up with his long stride.

"It is overwhelming. Too much to learn for one person."

Sabina understood why he hadn't accepted Loukas's offered help. "I am sorry about your father."

He jerked to a stop and faced her. "Even now, it's not real. I thought I was having a nightmare when my steward woke me and said father was dead." He choked out a whisper. "I couldn't move."

"Shock can do that."

"My first reaction was guilt."

"Guilt?" She tried not to sound shocked. "For your father's death?"

"It will be good to tell someone." Paris nodded. "Keeping the secret has been unbearable."

Had she just completed Ursula's assignment? Surely, solving Dionysius's murder couldn't be as easy as one simple confession? Could it? "I'd be happy to help."

ELEVEN

S abina walked beside Paris as he headed toward the atrium. "The night before he died, Father had asked me to visit the building site with him the next morning. He said he wanted to show me something special. I agreed to go, but when he knocked on my door that morning, I was tired and fell back asleep. I thought we would talk later that afternoon." Paris choked back a sob. "I can't help but think that if I'd been with him," his voice quivered. "I could have pushed him out of the way or yelled a warning."

"Or the arch could have fallen on you." Sabina touched his arm. Not the confession she had anticipated. But heartbreaking to hear.

Paris shook his head. "True, but…I will carry the guilt of never knowing if I had been there would he still be alive. I can't forget the image of retrieving his body from the wreckage. His bones…" He gulped, shuddering at the memory.

"It's a terrible time for your family."

"Not for Ursula." Paris stopped abruptly and spun to face Sabina, his voice suddenly sharp. "You should know Father intended to divorce her before she and Loukas bled away his fortune. Father ran out of time, so now it's up to me."

"Spoken like a dedicated son." The mourners and gawkers were

97

gone when they entered the atrium. So many questions were flying through her mind. She couldn't waste this chance to get answers. "Your father's legacy project will be expensive."

Paris lifted both eyebrows in surprise. "Money is not an issue." He raised his nose in the air. "My father shall have the grandest legacy imaginable. He wanted his name remembered for eternity, and I will see his wish completed. I won't let Ursula stand in the way."

"Would Ursula stop Dionysius's memorial?"

"Ursula siphoned money from Father all the time. You know she divorced her first husband because he wasn't rich enough. Father realized too late that she married him for his money. That is why she won't get one more drachma of Antiochus money." Paris increased his pace, clearly in a hurry to meet his friend.

Sabina skipped to catch up. Was money the reason Dionysius wanted to divorce Ursula? Had Ursula blamed the troubled marriage on Dionysius's infidelity when the fault lay in her greed? "People can be unreasonable when it comes to money."

"As I said, this isn't about money. Our family honor is at stake. I really am busy today." They passed the entrance leading to the gardens Sabina had visited yesterday.

"Of course." She eyed the front door. She had time for two more questions. "Do you know why your father changed his mind and decided to build the ludus at the last minute?"

"It may seem that way, but he never really committed to the library. The ludus was his first love from the time he overheard Otho and me discussing a rumor that Ferocianus, a prized gladiator, might come up for sale."

"Ferocianus?" Sabina asked.

"They named him after the greatest gladiator to fight in Rome's colosseum. This young Ferocianus's skill is unmatched. He's undefeated, with years of victories ahead of him," Paris's voice increased in fervor. We had a once-in-a-lifetime chance. "Whoever could afford him would reap thousands in return. At the same time, Father had begun considering options for his legacy. Everything fell into place once Otho's father, Mordax, agreed to be his trainer. It was a match designed by the gods."

"Mordax, the famous gladiator?" Sabina frowned, remembering Ursula's warning of getting bit by a viper.

"Yes. Mordax worked as a lanista training gladiators at small schools, but competing with Rome for good talent is difficult. Father realized the opportunity. With his money backing a larger ludus, Ferocianus as our star, and Mordax as a trainer, Father's legacy would reap money, fame, and eternal accolades from all Ephesus."

"You introduced him to Mordax?"

"I did, and Father sold Mordax on the idea. After that, Mordax, Father, and Agabus drew the plans."

"When your father decided to build the library instead, you must have been disappointed?"

Paris waved her off. "Of course. I tried to change his mind. I couldn't see how Father would get more glory from a room full of books. But it was Father's legacy. And his choice, not mine."

"Was Mordax angry after your father abandoned the ludus?"

Paris shrugged. "Wouldn't you be? Mordax tried talking sense into Father, but he wouldn't listen to reason. We all thought he'd abandoned the ludus until his letters arrived."

"Letters?"

"He wrote to Agabus ordering him to begin alterations for the ludus and to Mordax, offering him the position as lanista in charge of managing the ludus."

"Were you surprised by that?"

"I admit it came suddenly. Father included me in all major decisions, but I had no idea he'd written to Agabus and Mordax. He must have sent the letters the night before he died."

"He hadn't hinted that he'd decided to build the ludus?" Sabina slowed to a stop, wanting to prolong their conversation.

Paris halted. "I've been thinking about that. After Ferocianus went up for auction, I found a bill of sale in Father's office."

"Ferocianus would have been the first step to a successful ludus?"

Paris nodded. "I believe Father intended to tell me that morning that he had decided to build the ludus. If I had only known. Unfortunately, his passion for his legacy led to tedious lectures detailing measurements, types of marble, and other things. You can imagine why I wasn't excited to listen to a physics lesson before the sun was up."

"Did Agabus say anything about the ludus when he delivered the news of the accident?"

"He didn't know at the time. Agabus's letter was delivered after he'd left for work that morning. Honestly, I went into shock after hearing about the accident." Paris took a slow breath. "It wasn't until Mordax showed up later wielding Father's job offer that I realized the news Father had planned to share with me. I'm sorry but talking about this is difficult for me." He closed his eyes and bowed his head.

"I understand." But she needed more information. "I'm curious to know what changed your father's mind about the library."

Paris shuddered as if he'd forgotten Sabina was there. "Perhaps common sense prevailed, and he remembered the glories the ludus and its gladiators would provide." Paris shrugged. "You could ask Mordax or Agabus. Father may have confided in them."

Sabina lifted her chin, considering. "Agabus appeared as surprised as you. Will you be involved in managing the ludus after it's completed?"

"I…maybe," Paris mumbled. "It is my money, my family's investment, but we have a few details to finalize." He shrugged and started walking.

They were almost to the door, so Sabina rushed her question.

"Are you switching architects?"

"Father already did. He'd had enough frustration with Yechiel, complaining about him constantly. And now to discover he may have murdered my father. The authorities found a note in father's tunic. It confirms that Yechiel set up a meeting that morning."

"That is hardly proof of murder." Unfortunately, it was the only evidence, and it pointed to Yechiel. Sabina could squeeze in one more question before Paris left; she stopped walking. He kept moving.

She skipped to catch up.

"At the very least, Yechiel caused the collapse due to his incompetence. I will haul him into court and charge him with murder if the authorities don't. After we bury Father, of course."

Sabina lowered her gaze. "Of course." She wouldn't win Paris's confidence by defending Yechiel. And Yechiel wasn't helping his cause by insisting he didn't need defended. The door slave opened the door ahead of them. She rushed her last question. "What were your father's other lectures about?"

Paris stopped, startled. "What lectures?"

"The other things you didn't want to be lectured about the morning of his death." She had crossed into personal territory, but she'd leverage every second of their time together until he quit answering. Paris said he wanted someone to talk to. It might as well be her.

"Oh, that. It seems so petty now. I realize now he was trying to be a good father by reminding me I had responsibilities as the future heir to one of Ephesus's oldest and wealthiest families. I didn't want to hear his counsel again." Paris closed his eyes briefly as if blocking tears. "Now, I wish he were here to ask advice."

"Loving fathers have given children unwelcome guidance since the beginning of time." Hers hadn't cared enough to offer counsel. Even regarding her calamitous decision to marry Xeno.

"I don't know how I'll manage without him. We didn't share many interests, but when my older brother died, Father and I became close."

"He sounds like a wonderful father."

Paris nodded just as they reached the front door. "I don't mean to be rude, but I must go." Paris looked around expectantly. "Otho said he would meet me, but he must have meant at the circus track. The red team's horses beat the blue, green, and white teams at last week's race. I'm wagering their winning streak will end today." He jangled a small purse under his belt. "I can't miss the opening race."

"If you'd like to share more about your father's…"

"I doubt if there will be time. The funeral is in…" He scrunched his face. "It is in a few days. As the head of the family, I will write my own eulogy. I won't need your help." Paris sprinted out of sight.

She looked back to where Loukas and Ursula were closeted, planning a defense or scheming to get Dionysius's fortune. Before confronting the pair again, she needed more than Paris's accusations. It would be helpful to speak to Diana and follow up on her allegations of Yechiel. Hopefully Diana could share insights into her father's relationships.

If she could remember the way to Diana's garden, she might casually bump into her.

She strolled to the garden, where a quick look revealed no Diana, lurking slaves, or servants. The celestial fountains beckoned within Diana's solitary garden. The gloomy funeral activities inside the home contrasted with this inviting space full of life, fresh air, and sunshine. She understood why the mourning Diana isolated herself here. The granite bench where Diana sat yesterday was deserted.

A potted vine with unfamiliar white flowers caught her attention. She wandered over, surprised she hadn't noticed it on her first visit. Leaning in she examined the tiny thorns spiking from the woody vine that entwined the ebony lattice trellis. The mosaic walkway's black and white theme continued with these snowy blooms. She sniffed. Heavenly.

She had a little time to wait. If Diana didn't turn up shortly, she could come back tomorrow. Paris mentioned funeral preparations, which meant Diana could be sequestered, determined to finish her father's poem. She'd wait ten minutes longer and then leave. Perhaps, asking for a slip of the plant on her way out. She imagined it growing outside her bedroom door—a delightful scent to wake to.

A woman's giggle tinkled amid the gurgling fountains. The laugh repeated from behind the shrubbery in a far corner of the garden. Sabina followed the sound.

Diana and a young man Sabina recognized as Paris's missing companion, Otho, were clinging to each other, kissing, and unaware they had company.

"Ahem," she cleared her throat.

Diana jumped back, pulling Otho's hand away from her breast. "What are you doing here?"

"Who in the name of Zeus are you?" Otho glared at Sabina as he pulled Diana towards him, much too close for propriety's sake.

Sabina looked for a chaperone, nurse, slave, or anyone. But the three of them were alone.

Diana's engagement shouldn't mean propriety was abandoned. Amisi's nonstop lectures stressed that a woman's reputation must be spotless. Her future depended on it. Did the naïve Diana have no one safeguarding her?

TWELVE

Sabina took a step back. "I'm sorry to intrude. I didn't realize anyone was in the garden." Especially when you're hidden in the bushes.

Diana's face blushed the same unattractive spotty wine color of the day before. "Did Ursula ask you to spy on us?"

"What? No." Sabina shook her head, sure her face showed surprise. "I'm gathering material for your father's memorial, at your stepmother's request, but she doesn't know I'm here with you."

Otho snorted.

"We have nothing to hide." Diana jutted out her chin and pulled away from Otho. "We were discussing wedding arrangements."

"Diana, I'm not accusing anyone, nor do I think you have done anything wrong."

"Oh." Diana averted her eyes as she adjusted her tunic. "I'm sorry. I was rude." Her mouth, puffy and chafed from Otho's kisses pressed with a shy smile. "This is Otho."

"Your brother's friend." Sabina nodded to Otho.

"Diana's fiancé." Otho's arm tightened possessively around Diana's shoulder.

"Yes, Ursula shared the good news." Sabina forced a smile.

"Did Ursula also tell you she is against our marriage?" Diana asked. "She sided with Father."

"She said your father had not granted permission for your union."

"It doesn't matter since Paris signed the marriage agreement," Otho said. "We're getting married."

"Not right away," Diana quickly added. "After the appropriate mourning time has passed."

Otho curled his lip and scoffed. "Even dead, your father keeps us apart."

Diana winced. "Father said the adopted son of a slave wasn't good enough for me."

"Former slave." Otho gritted his teeth.

Diana bobbed her head. "We were going to run away. Otho was planning the details when Father died. He couldn't keep us apart."

"I'm sure your father believed he was doing what was best for you." Sabina looked sideways at the glaring Otho, whose muscular build reminded her of a gladiator.

"I don't want Father's idea of what is best. I know what makes me happy." Diana gripped Otho's hand. "I have found perfect love."

Sabina remembered Ursula's assessment of Diana's innocent and romanticized world. "Diana, no one has a perfect life. Or a perfect love." Sabina risked glancing at the hulking Otho.

"You sound like Father. He said he and I strove for perfection but were fated for disappointment. I proved him wrong."

Otho lifted her hand and kissed her knuckles. She beamed.

"It sounds like he loved you very much."

"Father said I was the only perfect thing in his life." Diana scowled. "He didn't know what love meant. But I can trust Otho's love."

"For eternity," Otho said.

Sabina frowned. "I'm confused. Didn't you just say how much you meant to your father?" Hadn't Portia and Ursula recounted Dionysius's love for his daughter? And hers for him?

"Father didn't understand that love cannot survive lies." Diana clamped her lips as if defying the dead Dionysius.

"What lies?" Sabina asked.

"It doesn't matter. Her father is dead," Otho growled at Sabina. "And people need to leave us alone."

Diana nodded. "Ursula is trying to keep us apart so she and Loukas can steal Father's fortune."

"How do you know this?" Sabina had questioned Loukas's control over the family finances. And Paris had voiced the same accusation.

Diana lowered her voice. "I overheard Loukas telling Ursula that they needed to move Ursula's money before the will was read. Paris said they are lovers as well as swindlers."

"I'm sure your father's will safeguards your inheritance." Unless Loukas had drawn up Dionysius's will. "And Ursula must have money of her own. Her dowry."

"I don't think so." Diana shook her head vigorously. "Ursula was always begging Father for money. Rumors are her previous divorce left her bankrupt. Loukas and Ursula secret themselves together every time Loukas comes to the house." Diana's eyes narrowed. "Ursula made an appointment for me to see a fortune teller. I shall ask her about Ursula stealing our family money."

Otho squeezed Diana's hand. "Mordax won't let you and Paris get cheated." His mouth hardened into a straight line. "Paris's best protection was making Mordax his business partner. Mordax now has a stake in ensuring Paris and Diana's inheritance is safe."

"Paris said he hadn't finalized the business details," Sabina said.

"They're drawn up. Paris has to sign," Otho said.

Diana stiffened and her brows furrowed. "Paris doesn't have to sign. He has to fulfill Father's legacy."

"That's what I meant. Your father wanted a ludus. Paris will sign the contract honoring his wishes." Otho patted Diana's hand. "That's what everyone wants."

Diana faced Sabina. "Paris won't allow anyone to cancel the ludus a second time."

Otho nodded. "An eternity of gladiatorial contests bringing glory and tribute to your father. Smarter than wasting your fortune on a tomb of molding old poems and legal speeches no one cares about," Otho said.

Diana bristled, pulling away from Otho. "Are you saying poetry is a waste?"

"Not yours. I love your poetry." Otho tugged her back toward him.

Diana stiffened and pulled away. "Don't say what you don't mean." She turned toward Sabina as if answering an unasked question. "I will not tolerate flattery of inferior work, especially my own. I am striving to write the perfect poem. And someday, I will."

"Diana," Otho soothed. "Don't be angry with me. You know I am an athlete, not a scholar who sits reading Homer. I know about chariot racing, gladiators, bull and bear fights. You must be patient in teaching me these loftier thoughts. You promised poetry would cleanse my mind and body." He stroked her cheek with his finger.

"Poetry is transforming," Diana whispered, leaning into his caress. "It has the power to conquer all of man's primitive urges."

"I only meant that building the ludus benefits both families."

"And our marriage." Diana fluttered her eyelashes. Her eyes glistened, vibrant and beautiful. They transformed her face.

Otho nodded. "A benefit your father would have had to accept after we were married."

"True love won't wait," Diana said, curling against Otho and placing a hand on his formidable chest.

Sabina left Otho nibbling on Diana's neck, wondering what he meant when he said Paris had to sign. And if he had signed the contract with Mordax, why did Paris deny it?

The day was well advanced when Sabina walked home. She agreed with Yechiel and Eunice's insistence on his innocence, but she'd found no proof to clear him.

But the deeper she dug into Dionysius's family, the more motives there were to investigate. Which meant possibly someone she had spoken to had murdered Dionysius.

Had Yechiel met Mordax while discussing the library? Did Agabus always give the customer what he wanted, or was he entangled in Dionysius's change of mind? Then there was Dionysius's relationship with Diana. What had caused her detachment? Her distrust? Was it his rejection of Otho or something else?

She plotted her next steps. Agabus said work on the ludus would begin after the funeral. When Yechiel went to the work site, he would find that Agabus hadn't been lying about Dionysius's change of plans. But she could alert him now to what she had discovered, giving him time to prepare his defense.

She went to bed with more questions than when she had awoken that morning.

THIRTEEN

A hum of pounding and hammering greeted Sabina as she neared the construction site. The tomblike quiet from two days ago was gone. A red-faced overseer gestured, yelling orders at two lounging slaves. She side-stepped someone pushing a cart smelling of chalky fresh plaster. Plaster dust swirled in the air, coating the steps, patio, and workers.

Mounting the marble steps, she coughed, and waved a hand in front of her face.

Men shuffled in and out of the damaged building, giving her disapproving looks but no one demanded she leave, too busy to care about her or that a man had died where they tramped. The rusty patio stain marking Dionysius's crushing last breath was gone. Someone had separated the fallen archway's marble blocks into two piles on the side. Not an easy task. Yechiel had said each block weighed over seven hundred pounds. The larger pile consisted of cracked and chipped marble wedge-shaped blocks. The undamaged mound held fewer pieces, including the smooth, glistening white marble keystone.

The pulley sat where she and Yechiel had seen it, unmoved four days after Dionysius's accident or murder, as the pulley's rope suggested. Evidence that pointed to Yechiel once the inspectors had discovered it.

Yechiel was nowhere in sight. But two older men, heads together, squatted over a large roll of papyrus spread at their feet. Agabus's wiry silver hair looked like a fitted helmet as he jabbed at the roll, shaking his head. "I'm telling you it can't be done."

Absorbed in their conversation, neither man noticed her until she tripped on a brick and nearly fell into them.

"Excuse me." She caught her balance before stepping on the papyrus.

Agabus scowled, his knees creaking as he rose. "What are you doing here?"

Looking for Yechiel, but she could not admit that to Agabus. Dionysius's memorial biographer would have no reason to speak to the architect of the now-abandoned library project. "Umm…" Sabina mumbled, looking at the drawing on the papyrus at her feet.

"Leave. I already answered your questions." He turned his back on her.

"The ludus…that's why I'm here. Ursula wanted Dionysius's new memorial mentioned…in his funeral commemoration…that I'm writing." A jolt of guilt hit her. When had she become so proficient at lying? Then again, Ursula had given her permission to interview anyone who could help the widow's cause. And Sabina wouldn't know who could help until she questioned them.

Agabus raised his palms in impatience. "There it is." He waved his hand toward the plans. "Now leave."

"It's important to Ursula that I add a few details." Sabina nodded toward the drawing. "She wants everyone to know about your spectacular building."

Agabus grunted, but his face relaxed almost into a smile. "Mordax and I were working out a few misunderstandings."

"Titus Mordax, the gladiator?" Sabina turned to the other man. His arms and legs were gnarled with hardened old muscles and scars from his past. "I have heard of your amazing career."

Mordax stood, his bored gaze brushed past her. The flattery she had used to sway Agabus fell flat. "Get her out of here," he addressed Agabus.

She had walked all the way here and wouldn't be rebuffed that easily. She cleared her throat. "I spoke to your son, Otho, yesterday. He described the impressive ludus you are undertaking."

"Impressive? Ha!" Mordax glared at Agabus, his laugh held no humor. "I told you once, and I'm not telling you again. I need a bigger arena."

"You don't understand." Agabus scratched his head and stared at the plans, both dismissing her without a word.

Sabina took three strides backward. Being ignored had a positive side. She wouldn't disrupt their discussion or stop the flow of information.

"You don't understand gladiators need space to train, you idiot." Mordax's rude gesture flicked over the plans open at his feet. "This is garbage." He punched his finger into Agabus's chest.

"It isn't my fault that the foundation has already been laid. I cannot move the walls." Agabus sputtered.

"Then tear them down. Gladiators can't fight in a library. I need spectator seating for three thousand."

"The cost would be prohibitive. We already have added expenses for building supplies to restore the arch." Agabus puffed out his cheeks and pointed a shaking finger at the drawing and the inked rings surrounding the open arena. "I have included seating for one thousand. This isn't Rome."

"We need to be better than Rome if we are to compete with Domitian's Ludus Magnus for the best combatants, the best slaves, and the best trainers. I don't care how much it costs."

"You aren't the one making that decision. I will speak to Paris about my additional fees to alter the design again."

"Paris." Mordax spat on the ground. "Knows nothing about training fighters. I'm the lanista. I will make that decision, not him."

Sabina stifled a gasp. Was this one of the details Paris hadn't yet worked out?

"Perhaps we can take out the vendor booths and shops ringing the outside." Agabus indicated the drawing's small rectangular chambers with doorways facing the outside.

"First, you cut my audience profits by two-thirds, and now you want me to lose rent from the merchants. You are cheating me, and I will slice something besides your fees." Mordax rubbed his crotch. The threat drained the color from Agabus's face.

Agabus raised his hands. "You can't threaten me. I'm the head architect."

"For now," Mordax growled. "I might rehire the one that planned the library."

"If we had started with my original plans we wouldn't have a problem," Agabus whined.

"It's not my problem."

"I'm getting a headache." Agabus rubbed his temples.

"I don't mean to interrupt," Sabina interrupted.

Both men's heads snapped around. Mordax glared at her.

"You're still here?" Agabus stepped toward Sabina.

Mordax glared at her, then turned to Agabus. "Get rid of this."

Agabus paused. "Ursula asked her to chronicle Dio's accomplishments."

"This is his accomplishment." Mordax swung his arm encompassing the destruction.

"Yes, I understand." She adjusted her mantle. "But Ursula is very interested in where his legacy will go from here. And who might direct it now."

"That would be me," Agabus said.

"Not necessarily." Mordax was obviously enjoying tormenting Agabus.

"Have you met Yechiel? The one you might rehire?" Sabina asked.

"Right after Dio decided to build the first ludus, he introduced us. I remember Dio saying the man was arrogant and demanding." He turned and leveled an ugly smile at Agabus. "But a gifted architect."

"Before I go." Sabina had no intention of leaving. "When did Dionysius first tell you he'd changed his mind on the library and wanted to reinstate the ludus plans and your contracts?"

"We found out in his letters." Agabus answered sounding relieved to change the subject. "I had already arrived at work and didn't get my letter until I returned home later. Mordax was home when his letter arrived—"

"Shut up. I can answer for myself." Mordax paused, cracking his knuckles.

"My letter was delivered that morning. I went to Dionysius's house as soon as I read it. Agabus had already been there and announced that

Dio was dead. First I'd heard he died."

"Had Dionysius spoken to either of you or hinted that he was thinking about changing his mind?" Sabina asked.

"The letter was his first communication with me since he scrapped the first ludus," Mordax said without hesitation.

"Our letters were identical." Agabus nodded. "The instructions were short and explicit. Construction on the ludus was to begin immediately. Dionysius wanted to discuss construction plans and redirect the money from the library project. As previously agreed, I was to be the head architect in charge of the building and construction, and Mordax the lanista, in charge of training the gladiators."

"Dio put up the money, but he didn't know how to run a training facility or what it needed to succeed. He wanted his legacy done right." Mordax pounded his chest in a gladiatorial salute. "And it will be."

She was relying on their testimony of their movements and the sequence of events. Unlike Yechiel, neither appeared shocked by Dionysius's change of plans. They had returned to work as if plans for the library had never existed.

Agabus grabbed her arm like a buffer. "And my plans exceeded all of Dio's expectations. My building was perfect."

"And now it isn't." Mordax stepped on the plans and ground his boot into them. "We're no better off than if you'd designed a dung heap." He scraped his foot as if wiping off animal waste.

Agabus screeched, dropping Sabina's arm. He yanked the plans out from under Mordax's foot and brushed off the dirt. "Dionysius ordered these plans, and it's his family's money...not yours...paying for it," Agabus said with a flash of bluster. "I am honored to build it for them."

"There'd be no ludus if it wasn't for me." Mordax's low growl was more intimidating than Agabus's yelling.

"Paris told me it was Dionysius's idea to build the ludus," Sabina said.

"Dionysius heard Otho complaining to Paris about traveling to Rome to replenish our performers. The procurement takes two months if we we're lucky enough to outbid the emperor for top entertainers. That's why he contacted me to partner with him."

"Partners?" Paris stated Mordax was hired as a trainer, management at best.

"Dionysius knew nothing about training fighters. The local slave markets are overflowing with men captured throughout the empire. But we need quality, trained men to maximize our investment." Mordax smiled grimly. "A maggot, Publius, runs a ludus in Athens. His gladiators have brief careers."

"Lucky for you that Dionysius overheard that conversation," Sabina noted.

Mordax pounded Agabus on the back. "The gods bless those who grab luck by the balls."

"And fortunate for you that Dionysius changed his mind," Sabina said.

Unblinking, Mordax locked her with a deadly stare. "The rich and mighty Dionysius is getting the legacy he desired. Every time a fighter's blood drenches the arena's sand. Win or lose, live or die…Dio's name will be acclaimed."

"Compare that to reading a book." Agabus bobbed his head.

Sabina felt the rising tension. Now might be a good time to leave. She broke from Mordax's glare. "Speaking of the library…where is Yechiel?" Sabina asked as casually as she could. She hadn't seen him among any of the workers.

"Escaping Ephesus, if he's smart." Agabus rolled up the building plans. "The authorities were here this morning looking for him."

"For Yechiel?" She watched Agabus slip the drawings into a leather tube.

"They're charging him with the murder of Dionysius Antiochus." Agabus didn't try to hide his smirk.

She went rigid. Eunice had been right. And Sabina's meager evidence wouldn't convince anyone Yechiel wasn't the chief suspect. Did he know the authorities were looking for him? Had he already been arrested?

She watched as the two men disappeared in opposite directions. Their mutual antagonism might provide clues and deserve more scrutiny. She could imagine either one grimly turning the murderous winch. But why? Dionysius had just handed them the opportunity of a lifetime. So why had Agabus become defensive when she had pressed him on the details of finding the body? And Mordax had silenced Agabus when including Mordax's role in the morning's events.

Men shoveled broken marble and shattered pieces of wooden braces into a cart. One untied a rope and tossed it at the foot of the pulley. Men hammered, plastered, and chiseled, transforming the murder scene and erasing evidence.

She didn't have time for indecision. Yechiel didn't have time. She would follow up on the one loose thread within reach, Agabus's alibi. Where had he been When Dionysius died? Was the tied rope left accidentally or intentionally? When did Dionysius decide to cancel the library and had head architect Agabus anything to do with that?

FOURTEEN

Sabina meandered home from the construction site, sorting through the conflicting statements from the workers she'd questioned. Out of dozens of men, only two agreed to speak to a woman. She should have known they would expect something in return. Quick on her feet, she managed to extract a kernel of information and escape unmolested while the men argued. One insisted Agabus had arrived after the work crew had found the body, the other was positive Agabus had been tugging at a chunk of marble when he and the others had rushed to the scene. Both statements contradicted Agabus's version of arriving with his workers. Eyewitness accounts were notorious for tiny discrepancies. This one was significant.

She plunked on a bench beside her favorite fountain and rested her head in her hands.

It wasn't just the workers' conflicting accounts that complicated matters. When she couldn't find the man who guarded the building materials, they told her Agabus had fired him. Suspicious timing? The man deserved to lose his job after falling asleep. But Agabus hadn't sounded concerned when he mentioned it and had even downplayed the negligence. Then there was Mordax—Paris's new business partner—according to Mordax. Was he giving the orders for Dionysius's legacy building.

A loud, insistent drumming jarred her from her thoughts. She jumped up, unaware dozens of people drawn by the commotion had gathered around the fountain. A boy of eight or nine bumped into her, breaking her concentration. Instantly, she felt for the small pouch tied to her belt, her fingers brushing against the boy's as she reached her small monthly allowance first. She clutched it, releasing a sign of relief. Within seconds the child had ducked and disappeared into the churning crowd filling the square.

Pickpockets flocked to public events where spectators were distracted. Some worked in cooperation with the entertainers, splitting their stolen loot. The authorities received hundreds of complaints from tourists during the festivals, but the guilty were rarely caught.

To her right, an imperial troupe of dancing mime artists was drumming up customers for the night's performance in the amphitheater. The lead pantomimus, his face hidden behind a woman's mask, swooped and twirled with exaggerated movements acting out Persephone innocently picking flowers before her abduction into the underworld. The tragic myth, sung by a trio and accompanied by two flute players and a drummer, increased in volume and tempo as the pantomimus exchanged masks—becoming her abductor, Hades.

Amused, Sabina wanted to stay and watch, but she had a real-life tragedy to solve. She refocused her thoughts. The authorities would have seen the pulley's rope attached to the splintered support and realized that the arch hadn't fallen under its own weight. They would be looking for suspects after reaching that conclusion.

Someone had intentionally destabilized the arch, turning thousands of pounds of marble into a murder weapon.

Sabina pushed her way through the crowds, gripping her purse strings.

She knew why the authorities had pointed the finger at Yechiel. Even without the incriminating note found on Dio's crushed body, Yechiel was the likely suspect. Who else but the two architects had the mechanical knowledge to destabilize the arch at its weakest point? The builders followed his directives. Agabus denied knowledge of the rope and of disobeying Yechiel's orders. His co-workers and Dionysius's family reported volatile interactions with his employer, which was at odds with the relationship Yechiel described.

What evidence did Yechiel have to support that he hadn't written a note to lure his client to the site? Did he know something he hadn't shared with her?

She needed to understand his relationship with Dio and the other family members. Did he know the authorities wanted him for murder? There were questions she needed to ask Yechiel. But would she get the chance?

Her father was in his office, at his desk, head down and turning a pen between his fingers. She spun around, backtracking before he saw her. She had avoided him since her visit to Dionysius's home yesterday, not because she didn't want to talk to him—which she didn't—but because he would ask for a report. And she hadn't decided what to confide to him. One thing she knew, she had to keep her involvement with Yechiel a secret.

"You're home late." Her father's voice stopped her.

She turned around slowly. "Good afternoon, sir."

"I expected you this morning."

She shuffled forward. "I was following up on information. I thought you'd want a full report."

Her father tented his hands under his chin, pursing his lips as he scrutinized her. "I did not direct you to follow up."

"You asked for news on Ursula."

Her father started to protest, then stopped. His past or lingering feelings for Ursula were a complication. Sabina didn't know if her father would welcome suspicions of Ursula's involvement in her husband's murder or if he'd feel obligated to protect her. How would he react to proof that her new lover and family financier, Loukas, had a motive to remove his rival?

Her father growled. "I expected news about Dionysius's entire family."

"I also questioned Agabus, the architect in charge of Dionysius's ludus project."

Her father shook his head as if he already knew. Which he probably did. "You are testing my patience. It was a mistake listening to Zarmig when he advised your involvement."

"It was a logical inquiry. Dionysius sent two letters before he died. One to Agabus and one to the man Dionysius hired to run the ludus."

"There is no need for your involvement. The inspectors have discovered Dionysius's killer. He was the head architect who was fired when Dionysius changed plans. I believe you know him."

Sabina's pulse raced. She forced her voice to maintain its regular cadence. "Yechiel." He had mistakenly believed his innocence was indisputable. Instead, he turned out to be the perfect scapegoat.

"You aren't surprised?" Her father's face remained impassive, but he did not blink as he scrutinized her.

"Agabus, the other architect, accused him." She knew that and much more she couldn't tell him. After she had caught Benjamin's murderer, her father erased all evidence of Sabina's association with Yechiel. There was to be no further contact to prevent any suspicions leading back to Sabina, her church, or her father. However, no one had told Eunice. And Sabina was again embroiled in murder with the surly architect. This time without her father's knowledge or permission.

"What proof do you have?" she asked, taking a deep breath.

"The inspectors have not determined exactly how or why the murder occurred, or they aren't saying." Her father eyed her closely. "But he and Dionysius had a falling out after a quarrelsome relationship. When Yechiel discovered he was losing his job, he sent Dionysius a note to meet him at the building site before anyone else arrived. He devised the collapse that killed his employer, then fled to his synagogue, hoping to establish an alibi."

"Losing a building project is hardly proof."

"The man has disappeared, escaped. I will find him."

Her stomach tightened. "You always do." Fled? Oh, Yechiel. What are you doing?

Her father tapped his pen on the desk. "Did Dio's family mention the Jewish architect?"

Sabina bit her lip. How much could she tell her father without harming Yechiel's cause? How much did he already know? "Paris, Dionysius's son, mentioned that Yechiel and his father had disagreements while working on the library, and Diana believed Yechiel had betrayed her father. But she had no proof. I found Agabus a likely suspect."

"While interfering where you weren't allowed?"

Sabina forced herself to meet his gaze. "Agabus accused Yechiel of stealing the project from him. Jealousy oozed from his every word."

"Jealousy is not a conclusive motive," her father quipped.

"Dionysius could have found out Agabus was lying about construction costs." Sabina clasped her hands.

"Did Agabus admit to stealing from his employer?"

"Of course not." Yechiel had accused him, but she couldn't tell her father that either.

"Inflating construction costs is standard practice."

"Agabus was at the site the morning of the murder. He said he arrived after the arch collapsed with the rest of the workers, but two co-workers disputed Agabus's timing. It would be worth finding out if he is lying." She pictured the rope tied to the wooden support, a rope she believed Agabus had tied on purpose, preparing the murder weapon.

"Agabus would need a motive."

"He is now the head architect."

Her father brushed his hands together as if dusting her off. "If that's all you've found, it appears you are done. You may go."

"Done?"

"Your information has confirmed my suspicion of the murderer."

She felt a hot flash of panic. It couldn't be Yechiel. "There was a second letter to Dionysius's contractor."

Her father waved her off. "I have work to do. If you wish to play spy, do so with your own time."

Sabina bristled, play spy? What had she been doing for her father if not playing spy? "Mordax described his ludus arrangement as a partnership. No one in the family had used that term. And Dionysius had previously canceled the first ludus project under Mordax. Perhaps there had been a disagreement between Mordax and Dionysius."

"Who is this Mordax?"

"Titus Mordax, the famous gladiator."

Her father snapped to attention. His hands clenched, flexed, and clenched again. "I knew Dionysius cared nothing for decency, but to partner with a man like Titus Mordax lands him in the sewers of Ephesus."

"Ursula was not happy with his choice. She called Mordax a snake."

"The man has no morals. Mordax will do anything to advance his interests. Nothing is sacred. Even a traitor, a weasel, has an allegiance to their new masters, not Mordax."

Her father rarely reacted so vehemently. Was this an opportunity to turn his attention away from Yechiel? If her father directed the investigation toward Mordax, that might give her and Yechiel time to gather the evidence needed to keep him out of jail, if he wasn't already captured. Yechiel's belief in justice wouldn't shield him.

Sabina stepped closer. "You know Yechiel to be a man of moral and honorable character. If Mordax is guilty, I could question the family members…"

Her father shot up, slamming his hands on the table before him. "You will not go within a mile of Titus Mordax. You are forbidden to contact the family again. Is that understood?"

"What has he done?"

His eyes flashed, and she felt the heat of his stare. "His crimes are legendary, and he has eluded prosecution for years. He chooses his victims based on opportunity, random chance, a rumbling in his bowels. We watch and try to predict his movements, but we think as humans. Mordax acts as a beast. It is a rare man who believes no truth is higher than himself. Mordax is one."

"Diana is engaged to Mordax's son, Otho. Dionysius forbade the engagement. Otho admitted wanting Dionysius gone from their lives and showed no remorse for his death."

"The offspring of a scorpion stings with the same venom. Mordax gaining access to one of the great houses of Ephesus would be disastrous for us."

"Not to mention Diana."

Her father's jaw flexed. He paced as he processed her news. "I could see Mordax murdering Dionysius if he opposed the family fortunes falling into Otho's clutches."

"Perhaps someone should warn Dionysius's family," she raised her hands, offering.

"I said your role is over. If you value your freedom, you will stay away from that family and Mordax." His voice was low and menacing.

What of Eunice, Yechiel, and Diana? She couldn't give up. "Ursula won't be happy. I am helping her with a delicate matter."

"She will survive without you." Her father shook his head. "Your collaboration with Ursula stops now. Had I known she was consorting with a criminal of his class, I would never have sent you there. You are lucky Mordax didn't discover you are my daughter. The man is dangerous, and where money is involved, ruthless."

She pressed again. "According to Loukas, a great deal of money is at stake. He said Mordax could make a fortune, and Paris hasn't demonstrated to be a reliable manager of the family money."

He turned around slowly, his face hard, his hands clasped behind him. "Loukas is correct about the earnings. Emperor Domitian saw the potential wealth of the ludi in his empire and seized the gladiatorial schools in Rome. All the city's ludi and their income are under his authority."

"Paris is young and inexperienced. If he puts Mordax in charge, I don't believe Paris can control him. This morning Mordax spoke as if he held the building's purse strings. He even threatened to fire Agabus."

"If Mordax has slithered into Dionysius's family's personal and business affairs, this might signal his end."

"Sir, what about Diana and Otho? Shouldn't I warn her?"

Her father raised an eyebrow. "There are consequences to inviting a snake into her bed. I am not going to tell you again. Do not go near that house. Mordax doesn't realize that I have found out about his dealings. Nothing must tip him off. Perhaps this time..." Her father's voice trailed off as he spun and left the room.

"Don't you mean the dealings your play spy found out about?" Sabina said to no one. Her head swam with indecision. Diana was innocently enthralled with her new love, unaware of the possible snare closing around her, the disaster looming in the young woman's future. Would she listen to a warning? Sabina doubted it.

And there was Eunice and Yechiel. If Yechiel was running, it would take a miracle to escape her father and his network of informants around Ephesus, spies at the docks, on city walls, inns, and watering stops.

"Mistress." Felix bustled into the room and handed Sabina a note. "This just arrived."

Sabina broke the seal and unrolled the short note with a crude map drawn in the corner. *Cassandra third floor, third door on the left. Tonight, 13th hour. Be well, Ursula*

The fortune teller.

Sabina's heart raced. Her father'd ordered her arrangement with Ursula to end, and she wasn't to go near Dionysius's home, but he said nothing about the fortune teller. Could she ignore the person who had predicted Dio's death? Who had predicted his murder? Cassandra might know more than she had told Ursula. Perhaps even what or who had led to Dionysius's death. Sabina hadn't been interested when Ursula had first suggested a meeting, but with Yechiel running for his life, she couldn't ignore a possible life-saving clue. This summons she would accept.

FIFTEEN

Sabina unrolled Ursula's drawing showing Cassandra's location. Ursula said her husband had changed after speaking to the fortune teller, and Ursula had arranged their meeting. If Ursula had orchestrated Dionysius's murder, she could have conspired with Cassandra. Predicting his death a year earlier provided an ingenious cover. And since it came true, the fortune teller's reputation would have grown.

Was she walking into another of Ursula's traps?

Sabina followed Ursula's map into an unfamiliar section of the city. The wide streets bustled with storefront merchants beckoning wildly with alluring sales. She sidled around a crowd of seven or eight beggars who had staked out an alleyway. An adult female shoved two children, four or five years old, into Sabina's path. Round eyes framed with long lashes stared at her from thin faces as the children shook their wooden plates.

Her father forbade almsgiving when she shopped with his money, but the small bag of coins she carried today was hers. She knew better than to open the bag in front of the adults. She slipped the bag's tie loose. Feeling for the largest copper coin, she deftly plucked it out, spun around, tossed it into the plate, then sped away before the others accosted her.

The horse-drawn carts clattering along channels ground into ancient paving stones slowed to an occasional donkey. The shops dwindled, turning into blocks of rundown insulas. Her steps rhythmically crunched on crumbling plaster and loose mortar falling from buildings. A baby wailed in one of the buildings. In another, a muffled argument started and abruptly ended.

Eventually, the street narrowed to a concrete-lined lane barely wide enough for her and a woman wearing a tattered tunic pushing a food cart. Sabina stepped into a doorway, allowing the woman to pass. She sniffed barley porridge steaming in one of the two kettles, the bland odor of turnip mash in the other. A cheap hot meal since most tenants couldn't afford a brazier or oven.

Intent on studying the map, she barely jumped aside as a bucket of slop showered inches from her head, splattering a reeking concoction across her sandals. She dared to glance up as a wooden bucket disappeared from a third-story window. She said a heartfelt prayer of thanks that the foul human waste hadn't drenched her. Rainwater usually washed the neighborhood refuse out to sea. Unfortunately, it hadn't rained in over two weeks. Sabina wrapped her scarf over her nose and held her breath until she had no choice but to suck in another.

She imagined Ursula and the other noble patrons' delighted squeals partaking in a daring adventure entering the squalid bowels of the city—a titillating entertainment for the patricians but not for those living in this decaying poverty.

She was close. She checked her map, noting the sun's height just above the next-door insula. She needed to hurry. There would be no illuminating street torches after dark.

Movement ahead caught her attention. Three men appeared from a side alley a block ahead. It wasn't beggars assaulting people in these neighborhoods. Ursula had warned her to take a chaperone. Sabina would have brought Felix if she had had that option. Her father's orders terminating her investigation prevented a bodyguard—a bodyguard who would report her movements to her father.

One man silently sauntered toward her, and the others walked behind him on the narrow street. Were they politely giving her room to pass? Or were they cutting off her path of escape? Her steps slowed.

She scanned the enclosed space. Her breath turned to rapid pants.

She stopped walking and fumbled for the small knife, trying to ignore Zarmig's warning. If you need a blade, it's already too late.

A rat skittered across her foot. She shrieked.

They were getting closer.

She spun in a circle, her heart pounding. Did she remember the way back?

She glanced at the map, now crumpled in her shaking hand, and realized she was standing next to the insula marked on the drawing. An open stairway rose to her right. She darted inside and sprinted up the first flight of stairs. She paused at the landing, listening for pursuers. Gravelly footsteps stopped at the ground floor opening. Motionless, Sabina held her breath. She looked at the stairs and the dead-end hallway. She had nowhere to run.

There was no movement outside. "Follow her," a high-pitched voice ordered.

"You go after her," a man said.

"Not alone, I'm not," the first man grumbled.

"You afraid of one woman?" taunted another man in response.

"Nah, one witch." Their footfalls moved on. Sabina's squeak of relief echoed off the end of the dark passage.

She climbed the second flight. The doorway's light diminished the higher she rose on the splintered and open risers, fading from a weathered gray to dark charcoal in the windowless shaft. She reached the third floor, the pressure of darkness closing around her. She could not get caught here after dark.

For tenants who could afford privacy, curtained doorways lined the shadowy hallway. The first doorway she passed had none. She peeked into the shadows of a windowless room lit by a crack in the outside wall. Four woven reed sleeping mats lay wall to wall, barely fitting in the tiny enclosure. Three small children, not more than five years old, lay cuddled together, asleep under a thread-bare sheet. The warm summer air wouldn't replace blankets or a brazier for warmth when fall arrived. Their parents would be working or begging. Three pottery cups, a bowl, a plate, and a chamber pot, were arranged neatly in a corner.

Sabina continued to a thin, brightly striped curtain hanging over the third door on the right.

"Come in," a female voice beckoned her from the other side.

The room behind the curtain seemed larger than the one she had just passed. And a second curtained doorway near the back suggested Cassandra's living quarters included another space that offered some privacy.

Sabina breathed in the minty odor of sage, tracing it to a wisp of smoke rising from a small incense burner in a corner. A woman sat behind a small table. Her body was shrouded in multiple layers of clothing, a tunic, a thread bare stola, and two shawls. One with tassels swathed her shoulders and arms, revealing young supple hands with no spots or wrinkles. The other covered her head, a fringe of brown hair framed the half of her face that was visible. A translucent gray veil hid the lower half of her face, revealing little but the movement of her lips. Her eyes glittered in the small flame from the table's oil lamp, but the fire reflected in her gaze didn't illuminate their color. She radiated mystery just as Ursula had described.

"I am Cassandra. Sit." She motioned Sabina toward a stool on the other side of the table.

Sabina pulled the stool, its legs scraping against the floor, and sat. "I'm Sabina."

"I know who you are and why you have come."

Sabina narrowed her eyes. "Your spirit told you?"

Cassandra's girlish giggle clashed with the veiled secrecy surrounding her. She tipped her head as if aware of something under the table, then wrinkled her nose. "No, Ursula told me when she asked for my help."

"Oh." Sabina crossed her ankles. She could do nothing to lessen the disgusting odor on her sandals.

Cassandra smiled. "Your body radiates skepticism. I could feel it before you entered my room. It is often the case with Christians… at first." She lowered her head and reached for an ebony box.

Sabina stared at the fortune teller for a startled minute. How did Cassandra know she was a Christian? Did Ursula suspect? Had she told Cassandra? Who else would have revealed her secret to this woman? "I don't mean to ridicule—"

Cassandra shook her head, her eyes crinkling in a frown. "Because I value Ursula's patronage, I agreed to meet you."

"Ursula said you predicted her husband's murder."

"I did, but aren't you curious about your love life, children, and health?" Cassandra raised her palm to face Sabina and closed her eyes. "I sense a man."

Sabina fidgeted. "My God warns that no one knows the future."

Cassandra blinked, threw her head back, and laughed. "As you wish. The wayfaring man will disrupt your life, not mine."

"There is no man..." Cassandra's vague insinuation could be anyone. After all, what man isn't disruptive? But Cassandra was wrong. Sabina's wayfaring man was dead and could no longer disrupt her life.

"Perhaps you will change your mind. Dionysius also doubted." Cassandra shrugged, placing the black box on the table. "My spirit daemon revealed Dio's death, not his murder, but you already know that." She met Sabina's gaze with a hooded stare.

"He didn't believe in your powers...your daemon?"

Cassandra nodded. "The same spirit you don't believe in, but for different reasons. Dionysius's cynical mind was closed to anything he couldn't see, touch, or prove. He blocked any reality he couldn't identify, including the spirit world that guides me."

"Yet he came to you, and you agreed to read his future."

"Even in my seclusion, I had heard of Dionysius's reputation." Cassandra stroked the ebony box. "I was curious."

"Dionysius's family said he changed after meeting you."

"He changed, but not because of me. I sensed a tremendous struggle growing within him."

Sabina forced her skepticism from her voice. "Perhaps Dionysius struggled with your prediction of his dying within the year."

"Dionysius did not reveal the nature of his battle, nor did my daemon." Cassandra looked deep into Sabina's eyes. "What would you do if you knew the hour of your death?"

Sabina bit her bottom lip. "After hearing Dionysius's fortune, I asked myself that. I would do something to make my final hours meaningful."

"The Buddha calls it karma. In Egypt, the deceased man's heart is weighed against the feather of truth." Cassandra stared at her a moment, then said quietly, "Christians call it acts of repentance. I don't know whether Dio believed my daemon's prediction, but when confronted with his mortality he understood he had limited time to balance the goddess Justitia's scales of justice."

"So, he commissioned a library." Sabina frowned. "Or a ludus. My friend said Dionysius wanted people to remember him."

"Your friend spoke correctly. What Dio didn't understand was that memorializing earthly achievements lasts only until the mortals who remember us die."

"To ensure that doesn't happen. Dionysius's heirs will engrave his name on every stone entrance of the ludus and announce his generosity at each gladiatorial match."

Cassandra smiled sadly. "He bragged of this glorious achievement as if it could make up for his past, but the Fates will not be cheated so easily. Call it what you like. He could not rewrite his past."

"If he was focused on his past, did he mention anyone specific? A debt? Revenge? Did he need to correct a more recent wrong?"

"Dionysius had many questions. Did his life have meaning? Was he just a compilation of his pleasures, power, and possessions? He, like all of us, wanted to know if he mattered. He understood death was too late to seek answers."

"Did he believe you could help him balance the scales?"

Cassandra shrugged. "Perhaps my spirit guided him on his path of inquiry. He returned to me three more times. Each time asking if his future had changed. I don't know if he expected it to, but his destiny did not alter. Ursula would be a widow within the year. She was entangled in his death."

Entangled? Because she was his wife or his murderer? "Ursula said you didn't predict how Dionysius would die. Were you surprised?"

"The many faces of death do not surprise me. I have heard some Christians do not believe they are going to die. Is that what you believe?"

"No...well, maybe." Was Cassandra avoiding answering, or were her questions sincere? Cassandra stared at her as if waiting for an explanation. "Jesus is returning to take His children to paradise to live eternally with Him. It makes no difference whether I am alive or have died when He comes for me."

Cassandra's fingers tightened on the box. "What if Jesus comes before you balance Justitia's scales? Like Dio, I see Christians furiously working on good deeds to outweigh the evil. Helping the poor to benefit themselves."

Sabina stopped herself from looking at the sparseness surrounding her. The woman knew poverty that Sabina couldn't imagine. "They help the poor, not themselves. The cross is where Jesus paid for my evil deeds. There are none left to put on God's scales of justice."

Cassandra narrowed her eyes as if testing Sabina's sincerity, then shook her head, cackling. "The door to Dio's future was closing, but he found no easy Christian escape."

Sabina bristled, her father's disparaging remarks flooding her memory. Your faith is foolish, simple-minded, and irrational. She took a deep breath and held it, brushing Cassandra's ridicule aside and focusing on why she had come. "Did Dionysius mention anyone who wished him harm? Someone who wanted him dead?"

"Your answers exist with Dionysius in the spirit world." Cassandra reached across the table. "Come, I will see if your futures cross."

Sabina tucked her elbows tight and curled her fingers into a fist. The spirit world fights over the souls of men and women, and she would not enter their realm. Sabina leaned forward with her hands in her lap. "He mentioned no one, no person or event that troubled him during any of his four visits?"

With a mysterious smile, Cassandra pulled her hands back. "No, during the first visit, he chatted cheerfully as if the news of his death entertained him. On the second visit, he returned defiant and smug in the armor of his denial. Humans have an amazing ability to dismiss anything, even their conscience, if it conflicts with their chosen reality."

Cassandra's answers were non-answers. Infuriating. Was she hiding information? Perhaps her involvement in the murder? But she had not cast blame away from herself either. She had not mentioned Dionysius's disagreements with Yechiel. "He revealed nothing to you about a dispute or falling out?"

Cassandra tipped her head, her mouth puckering in amusement. "People come to me for revelations, not the other way around. Even so, people cannot hide their emotions. At the third reading, a wall of sweat surrounded him. He reeked of struggle and conflict."

"Conflict over what?"

"Perhaps his life choices. My spirit did not reveal it, but something or someone had disturbed him."

Sabina ran through Dio's life after hearing about his fortune. "When was the third visit?"

"He boasted that he'd just laid the foundation for his grand achievement."

"The beginning of the library had no shortage of disturbances." And it wasn't just Yechiel. He had demoted Agabus. Mordax maintained he had amiably bowed out when Dio abandoned the ludus, but Mordax's recent threats against Agabus told another story. And what about Paris? Did Dio express disappointment in his son? A rebellious Diana might have caused turmoil. Ursula said Dio planned to divorce her. A third failed marriage would be upsetting. Dionysius had many life choices to re-evaluate.

"And his last visit? Was anything different?"

"He arrived for the fourth visit a week before he died, no longer anxious. He asked, and I confirmed his death as before. I cannot say he believed me, but he did not dismiss me either. I thought it strange that he asked nothing more and left resigned, content even." Cassandra shook her head. "My spirit has spoken no more of Dionysius."

"I wonder if he'd made peace with dying."

Cassandra shrugged. "Dio wanted to be a hero. But the gods have no patience with such arrogance. One snip and the Fates end our lives. Yet we continue to think we matter."

Cassandra had shared nothing specific. Her reflections on Dionysius could be explained by his life events. If she was hiding information or lying, Sabina had no way of knowing. It appeared Cassandra wasn't going to be of help.

The room had no windows to judge the lengthening shadows of evening. She had lost track of time. "If you remember anything else that would shed light on the murder, please let me know." Sabina pushed her stool back. "I have to go."

"You brought money."

Sabina nodded. "Of course, I will pay you."

"My spirit whispers revelations of you and your traveler."

Sabina shook her head. "I don't need my fortune told." Sabina remembered another warning. There must not be found among you anyone who is a diviner, a soothsayer, an enchanter, a sorcerer, a spell-caster, a consulter of ghosts or spirits, or a necromancer. For whoever does these things is detestable to ADONAI.

Sabina jerked the purse from her belt containing the month's alloca-tion from her father. It wasn't much, but she hoped it covered her fee. "How much do I owe you?" She looked at the oil in the lamp. The tiny flame sputtered. "It's getting late."

"You have time." Cassandra caressed the box. "I would dishonor the spirit if I took money without an equal exchange." Cassandra turned the ebony box over, and a jumble of small bones squared off like de-formed dice clattered upon the table. She counted eight, each with strange markings carved on its sides.

"I don't believe in divination."

Cassandra cackled softly. "Many things exist that people don't be-lieve in." She picked up a bone and stroked it. She positioned it on the table and then added the remaining bones forming a circle. "You of all faiths should believe in the powers of the spirits. The spirit followers of your God wield even more power than my daemon."

"Our angels minister to us," Sabina said, surprised by Cassandra's knowledge. "We are cautioned to trust only in the revelations and writ-ings of our God. Not unknown spirits, oracles, or those who read the stars or bones."

"My spirit whispers it is not an accident that you sought me," Cassandra responded as if Sabina had not spoken. Her voice lowered to a gravelly throaty demand. She stared at Sabina, her eyes unfocused as she moved the bones absentmindedly. Sabina shivered, chilled by Cassandra's change of tone and the breeze that somehow stirred the windowless room. Cassandra cupped a bone. Her fist turned white. She opened her fingers and dumped a palm full of white granules onto the table.

Disintegrated bone.

The three thugs afraid to enter the witch's insula began to make sense. Trembling, Sabina placed the small bag of coins on the table. "Please, take this."

Cassandra grabbed her wrist. She froze as Cassandra's grip tightened, her fingernails cutting into Sabina's wrist. Cassandra's head flung backward, her eyes rolled up, and a gravelly voice gurgled from her throat. "Dionysius's curse shall crush her bones."

"Let go," Sabina screamed, her breath visible in the sudden chill in the air. She jerked her hand, breaking Cassandra's hold, and shot up knocking the stool over.

Cassandra's head slumped forward. Her body jerked in tiny fits of movement. Slowly, she looked up, her eyes wary, refocusing on Sabina. The left side of her veil had slipped to the side. With trembling fingers, she fumbled to reattach the clip. Instead, it clattered to the floor. She stood up, looking for the clip. The loose scarf hung limply to one side, exposing Cassandra's face.

Sabina gawked, then looked away. Too late to hide her shock.

Staring at Sabina, Cassandra's face hardened. She scratched at the cloth, ripping the scarf as her quivering fingers dislodged a second clip holding the other side. Ignoring the clips, Cassandra threw her arm over the sizeable red stain covering her face's lower half. "Leave me," she screamed, her voice once more that of a distraught young woman. "Go." She pointed to the door with one hand, the other hiding her face. Cassandra spun around and disappeared behind the curtain at the back of the room.

Sabina's heart raced. Fear demanded she leave, but a turmoil tearing her life apart kept her rooted in place, unable to move. Amisi said she had abandoned the first newborn in a public plaza where an old woman had taken her—a baby with a facial disfigurement.

Looking up at the motionless curtain, she doubted Cassandra had left or that she had anywhere to go. Sabina bit her lip to keep her teeth from chattering. If she stayed, apologizing for her rudeness, would she embarrass Cassandra more? The lamp oil had burnt down to a greasy sheen, and night was coming. She must return home.

She had many questions for Amisi.

The children down the hall were awake when she passed their room. An older boy, maybe seven or eight, tore pieces of bread from a loaf, sharing them with the children jumping eagerly around him.

She felt the sting of Cassandra's scratches on her wrist. Looking down, she still clutched the money bag. She motioned the boy over and handed him the bag, knowing her father would call her foolish, simple-minded, and irrational if she were required to explain why she had given away her monthly allowance.

Was she like Dio? Furiously doing good acts hoping to outweigh her bad. Helping the poor to benefit herself? No, she had already received the gift of eternal life. There was nothing more she could do to benefit herself. She recited Jesus's directive. "'For I was hungry and you gave me food, I was thirsty and you gave me something to drink, I was a stranger and you made me your guest, I needed clothes and you provided them, I was sick and you took care of me, I was in prison and you visited me.' The King will say to them, 'Yes! I tell you that whenever you did these things for one of the least important of these brothers of mine, you did them for me!'"

Fortunately, when she arrived home, her father was dining out. Unfortunately, Amisi wasn't home either. After meticulously performing her daytime duties, supervising the slaves and servants, planning meals, and overseeing household chores, Amisi would disappear for hours at night. But day or night, she never neglected her primary responsibility—Sabina. Amisi's controlling and bossy oversight of Sabina's clothing, hair, food, sleep, health, and various other womanly tasks usually drained Sabina. Still, after an exhausting day, she missed Amisi's attentive pampering. Sabina rummaged in her chest, pulled out a sleeping shift, undressed herself, and collapsed on the bed. Tomorrow would have to be soon enough to interrogate Amisi over the details of the births of her sisters. One in particular.

She fell asleep praying for Yechiel and Eunice's safety, Horace's safe return, Portia, Amisi, Zarmig, and her sisters, wherever they were, and for the poor and hungry in Ephesus. And though every ounce of her didn't want to, she made herself pray for her father.

She fell into a restless sleep haunted by a disturbing voice: Dionysius's curse shall crush her bones.

Whose bones?

SIXTEEN

She arrived early for breakfast, but her father was already strolling out the door. She ran, cutting him off. "Have you found Yechiel?"

"Not yet. He has friends willing to risk arrest by hiding him. We are switching our focus to searching outside the city walls. He is a fool to think he can escape." Her father adjusted the folds of his formal woolen toga, pulling a section over his knee-length tunic. Formal attire he wore to court and council meetings. He would not be hunting Yechiel today.

"Have you found more evidence against him?"

His expression hardened. "If Yechiel can explain the note found on the body, it may help his defense."

She hadn't known about the note the last time she spoke to Yechiel. Had he arranged a meeting with Dionysius that morning? Did he know the authorities had found it? "What if he didn't write the note?"

"Until we ask Yechiel, he remains our prime suspect."

"Have you questioned Agabus? Did you ask him why he fired the night watchman? And what about Titus Mordax? You said he's a suspect."

Her father's hands opened and closed several times. "Remember your place, Sabina."

She knew she should stop. "I know. It's just that those people are suspicious."

"Now you are saying I don't know how to do my job. You are taking liberties with the freedoms I allow you." Her father whirled on her. "Your meddling may have already put Mordax on alert."

She mumbled under her breath. "If I hadn't meddled, you would know nothing of Mordax's involvement."

Her father's face hardened. "We have one murder suspect, and you are no longer involved. Do not test me, Sabina, or the independence I allow you will end without another warning." A servant opened the door, and her father strode out.

She sat listless, stirring a bowl of morning pulse, cooked wheat with water, olive oil, and salt. A staple from her father's army days that he retained a taste for. She should not have tested his patience. He could rescind her liberty for no reason. Her investigation into her sister's whereabouts would stop if she were locked in her bedroom for the next month or year. He could stop her worshipping, visiting Portia, everything she valued. She would not let him provoke her again.

Without finishing, she wiped her lips with a napkin and went to find Amisi.

She recognized her nurse's backside sticking out from a wooden dish cabinet. "I found her, Amisi."

Amisi mumbled from inside a cabinet she was organizing. "Am I supposed to know who you are talking about?"

"I think," Sabina raised her voice, almost unable to voice the words because they sounded impossible. "I found one of my sisters."

Amisi lurched, slamming her head into an upper shelf and rattling a newly purchased stack of red pottery bowls. "Ouch." She eased back, rubbed her head, and turned, her face hard and set in a scowl. "Your sisters are dead." She bent and pulled a glossy plate from a crate on the floor.

"You do not know that." Sabina stamped her foot, refusing to be dismissed. "You're the one who defied Father, giving them a chance at survival."

Amisi turned, her face impossible to read. "Don't ever say that I disobeyed my master. He said to dispose of the babies. I carried out the task. I did no wrong."

"He did. And then hid it from Mother." The task? How could ending a human life hide behind such an innocent word?

"The law gives him the right. He gave them life. He can take it away. Remember that."

"It is God who creates life. Exposing them is the same as child sacrifice."

"I did not say he was right. Like your mother, you are wasting time wishing, hoping, and searching. I thought you had stopped this foolishness. I curse Apollos for putting this idea in your head. It will bring us nothing but trouble and sorrow."

"It was your information that I remembered. Father wouldn't accept her because of the red stain on her face. When Cassandra's scarf dropped, I saw her face. The stain covered most of her lower face, just like you said. It was a dark reddish-purple."

"If a child survived, she is no longer your sister. You cannot rewrite the past." Amisi's words mimicked Portia's.

"I, too, thought it impossible to find a child from over twenty years ago, and then I met her. She is a pythoness, a teller of fortunes."

Amisi rolled her eyes. "You believe you have found a person only three people knew existed, someone you have never seen? Hundreds, maybe thousands of babies are marked for death by the gods. The first marked woman you meet, you believe, is your sister?"

Amisi made her think. Slowly and with less enthusiasm, Sabina continued. "Cassandra looks to be close to my age, and if you saw her, you could identify the stain. You're gifted; you must remember her face."

Amisi cackled. "You are forever telling me magic does not exist. It was twenty-six years ago when I took the first squalling babe from your mother's womb and left her naked in the plaza square. You think I would remember her puckered face, nearly as red as her mark?" Amisi raised her hands and made a pagan hex sign.

Sabina did believe in Amisi's powers. Her nurse's gift of second sight had thwarted many of Sabina's childhood plans. And Amisi's potions and medicinal brews cured headaches, stomach ills, and fevers. She just didn't believe it was magic. "You said you watched until an old woman picked her up. What did the old woman look like?"

"Like me, old, decrepit, hunched-backed."

Sabina smiled. "You aren't any of those." Sabina watched the spry nurse bustling back and forth as she finished unpacking the crate and storing the fashionable pottery.

Amisi stopped. "This Cassandra, teller of fortunes, did she ask for money?"

"It's how she makes a living. But she didn't take any—yet." Sabina wasn't ready to explain the reason for that.

"My magic is simple. I see into the hearts of people, their cravings, and twisted desires. The secrets of plants and spells, passed to me by my mother, turning evil into good or, when necessary, good into evil. I know how imposters prey on the gullible and most fortune tellers are professional thieves. What web of lies did this teller of fortunes spin for you?"

"We didn't talk about me." Although Cassandra had tried.

"Actors make a living by pretending to be someone they are not. She will conjure a fortune for you, a marriage, children, fame. All the things you desire."

"I don't want fortune and fame."

"Your mother heard the crying of her third child and realized your father had lied. She searched for her until she died of a broken heart."

"Mother died from loss of blood giving birth to her fourth daughter."

Amisi gripped Sabina's arms. "Do people know you are searching for your sisters?"

"Not many."

"Cassandra could have overheard that your father has money and begun to scheme. Did someone you know speak to her?"

Ursula flashed into Sabina's mind. "You're wrong. She doesn't know she is my sister."

"What kind of a fortune teller wouldn't know her sister? You are not thinking. What did she ask you? For your patronage? To live here? You should never have gone to her."

"She asked for nothing. Why are you so suspicious?"

"Why aren't you? Where are your prying questions and that irritating logic you torment me with? A true seer, or a fraud, she would not ask for something during your initial visit. First, she must convince you she has a higher power at her bidding. Maybe someone dead communicates with her. Were you asking to speak to your mother? That I could understand."

"No." Sabina was horrified.

Amisi sighed. "When did she tell you to return?"

"She asked me to leave." Amisi would think Cassandra's trance or whatever had happened was an act. And looking back, perhaps it was—but. "I plan to see her again."

"Of course, because she hasn't taken your money yet. She is skilled, this one. You believe it is your idea to go back."

"She's not…"

Amisi's nostrils flared. "What if she is your sister?" Sabina cringed as Amisi pointed an accusing finger at her. "What then? You may long for the past, but your father cannot know who she is. He could erase her life with a swipe of his pen."

"He has no reason to. He doesn't know…"

Amisi's jaw set, and her gaze drilled into Sabina. "Your father does not need reason. You spoke to her because she is involved in the murder of a rich and powerful man."

Sabina's mouth opened to question. "How did you know?"

Amisi rolled her eyes. "I listen. How else can I protect you? Would your father allow this association to defile his name and reputation? She is more repulsive now than as the cursed innocent he abandoned."

"You are speaking as if she is the child he exposed."

"I am speaking of your fantasy. Your desire for a sister. Do you think I do not know of your loneliness? Your solution to a family is a husband, not adopting the first woman you see with a facial curse."

"A husband?" Anger boiled up in Sabina. "It is I who am cursed, not Cassandra. Perhaps she should avoid me, so she doesn't die unexpectedly joining my four suitors."

"Only three fell under your curse. Your Marcus did not marry his betrothed."

"Because he is dead. Drowned or murdered by pirates." Sabina shook her head, biting back painful feelings Zarmig had stirred up.

"I have heard different whisperings. There are things…"

"About Marcus?" Sabina wanted to reach out and shake her. "What have you heard?"

Amisi's expression stiffened. "It is only a rumor. I healed one of the harbor master's dock workers last night. Sailors talk. Marcus was seen. Maybe a month ago. North in Dalmatia, across the sea from Italy."

"On a pirate ship." A half-hysterical thought flashed through Sabina's mind. Marcus's hands manacled to a pirate oar, bones protruding from blistered flesh, his back muscles shredded by the whip and cane. "A slave?"

Amisi shook her head. "No. Walking free."

"Does Father know?"

Amisi snorted. "It is a riddle that Marcus's investors are zealous to solve. How could a storm or pirates destroy their costly venture, yet the ship's owner survives? Where did their money go?"

"Do they believe Marcus swindled his investors? Does Father?"

"Time will tell. The good news is Marcus did not return to Rome to marry."

"How can you say that? If Marcus had gotten married, he would not be in trouble now."

"I am pointing out that all is not lost." Amisi's lips quirked into a tiny smile before she could hide it.

"You are hopeless. You believe Cassandra is a fraud yet ignore that Marcus may also be. What do you know about him besides that he sailed away and is never coming back?"

"I know he asked you to marry him. And what do you know of this fortune teller? Nothing."

"That doesn't mean she isn't my sister. Please come see her."

"Do you believe this woman of mystery will welcome two strangers poking into her private life? Fortune telling is illegal. She leads a life banned by the emperor," Amisi said without apology. "Like the Christians, she must be wary."

The invitation-only appointments, the safeguarded location, the veils, and the secrecy came to mind. "Wanting privacy isn't a crime." Sabina persisted.

"It is, if she's a criminal, swindling the rich, stealing from the powerful, getting paid to lie to the trusting."

Sabina crossed her arms, refusing to look away. "I may be gullible and naïve, but we could learn more about her, ask where she was born. If she has parents, we'll know she isn't my sister. If you see her, speak to her. Then I can know for sure."

"Your sisters were never meant to be. Their fate isn't yours to know."

"What harm can this do?" Sabina took a deep breath. She could order Amisi to go, and Amisi would obey. But she couldn't order Amisi to tell her the truth. "Please."

"I promise nothing." Amisi pressed her lips together.

Sabina drew a deep breath, barely daring to ask anything more. "Except not to tell father. You are right. He cannot know. I don't want to put Cassandra in danger."

"You have already done that, Sabina." Amisi sighed, her distress evident, and left the room.

Amisi was right. If Cassandra knew who Sabina was and used the information to extort or blackmail them, her father would make sure the fortune teller wasn't a problem, no matter who she was.

Sabina needed to be extremely careful with future inquiries.

SEVENTEEN

Sabina waited until Amisi was in the kitchen scolding Cook for the herbs used for today's lamb dinner and demonstrating the correct amount of mint that Cook would add. She tiptoed past her father and the ever-observant Zarmig, in her father's office. The slaves and servants were busy with their duties. She deftly picked up her shopping basket and breezed by the door guard.

Heading down the hill, Sabina turned at the second insula. Would anyone think of following her to the market agora? She dropped her basket. Picking it up, she glanced back. No one from the household followed her. A precaution Zarmig had taught her mother and Sabina as a child. He had drilled them on the basics of evasion, concealment, and half-truths, sprinkled with an ounce of self-defense, all to hide their Christian faith.

Sabina had become even more cautious after Benjamin's murder. Flavius Fortunus, Ephesus's highest-ranking religious magistrate and relentless enemy of her father and Christians, had raided Portia's house and nearly caught her. Flavius had searched for anything to discredit her father. Discovering an unlawful Christian assembly in Portia's house would have been commendable, but catching Sabina worshipping there would have been invaluable and fatal for Eirenarch Catius Sabinus and family.

She melded into the anonymity of shoppers wandering in and out of open stalls and shops. She stopped two more times.

Flavius Fortunus was only one of the powerful enemies her father had acquired after the emperor appointed him the Imperial Eirenarch of Ephesus. His duties involved influential contacts in Rome, connections many in Ephesus envied and feared. Many in Ephesus would breathe easier should her father lose his life or, second best, his job of enforcing Roman peace and order.

Sabina's family hadn't survived in this cut-throat world for decades without considerable precautions to keep dangerous information hidden from their enemies.

Or each other.

Sabina doubled back, stopping at a shop to try on a pair of shoes. Nothing suspicious.

She methodically wound her way through neighborhoods of the weaving district ending at the door of Reuben's woolen shop.

The familiar dim interior greeted her. The shop wasn't empty. A whiff of potent garlic stopped her from bumping into a dark shadow of a woman wearing a long-sleeved black garment and head covering hiding all but her face and hands. Another woman, wearing the same attire, stood by her. Sabina's lightweight linen stola and delicately embroidered mantle covered her head and shoulders but bared her arms below her elbow. She made a note to acquire some everyday common clothing when investigating unaccompanied.

The women pursed their lips, displaying disapproval or suspicion.

Eunice's stocky uncle did not acknowledge Sabina. Instead, he walked over to the women. "I am afraid I have nothing of that color. Come back next week. We should have a new batch of wool dyed by then." Smiling, he led the women to the door, holding it open for them. "Shalom aleikheim." The Hebrew words Eunice had greeted her with when they first met.

Squinting in the bright outdoor light, the two women responded, "Aleikheim shalom." And turned back, staring over their shoulders at Sabina. Or was that her anxious imagination?

Her mouth went dry. Surely, not even her father's cunning could plant spies within this tightly closed Jewish community.

Reuben silently watched the women leave, perhaps to make sure they were not coming back or to recover from her unannounced appearance. After several seconds passed, he closed the door. He whirled around, his eyebrows drawn together, and his smile turned to a scowl. "Why are you here?"

"I have a message for Eunice. I didn't know how else to reach her."

"You coming here endangers her." His curt rebuff tugged at the scarred tissue of his lips, half of his mouth unmoving, rigidly held in place by callused flesh.

She stepped back, his emotion like a hostile slap. Hostile or fearful? She was rapidly second-guessing her visit. "Eunice asked for information about Yechiel."

He thrust out his hand. "Give me your message, then leave."

"I didn't write anything down." She stammered. "I didn't think that would be wise. I could tell you."

"Or you can tell me." Eunice peered out from the curtained backroom doorway.

Reuben groaned. "Go then." He shooed Sabina toward Eunice. "Quickly, she doesn't have much time."

Eunice held the curtain aside, and Sabina ducked into the atrium. The spindles, bundles of wool, and looms lay scattered in the same disorganized clutter around the water-filled impluvium. What was different was the person at the end of the atrium.

Yechiel stood when she entered.

If Reuben's face had been unwelcoming, Yechiel's was combative.

Sabina steeled herself. "The magistrates are looking for you."

Yechiel strode toward her, his long stride reaching her swiftly. "That news has circulated Ephesus twice now. You are not needed here."

"Yechiel, stop." Eunice stepped between them, reaching up and putting a hand on her husband's chest.

"Sabina has risked much to come here. We are nearly friendless, and this is how you thank her?" She pulled her hand back and faced

Sabina. "We are both under much strain. Excuse him."

"You don't need to apologize for me. I am sorry." Yechiel sounded sincere. "But you jeopardize my freedom by reporting useless gossip."

"Freedom?" And then Sabina saw that it was not just bundles of wool lying nearby, but two bags, one with a folded dark gray tunic laying half in, half out. "You are packing."

"He must leave, Sabina. We cannot risk the authorities arresting him."

"Running away will make him look guilty."

"I am innocent." Yechiel laughed bitterly. "Matters more far-reaching than the death of one man are at stake. I cannot risk being caught."

Sabina thought of the coin, the brotherhood that guarded it, and the movement that sought freedom from Roman rule. A rebellion that would get them all killed as traitors. "You can flee. But they will find you. My father tracks down fugitives and runaway slaves and no one escapes him."

"We have no choice." Eunice picked up the full bag and tied it shut. Sabina noticed the tears threatening to spill from her eyes. "Unless someone finds Dio's killer, Yechiel will be convicted for the murder. He'll be tortured and killed. We cannot risk that. Have you…?"

"I am still investigating." Sabina wanted to offer a glint of hope, but she had nothing to argue against the scenario Eunice described. "If I can get more information from Yechiel, there is a chance."

"We don't have time for this." Yechiel reached down and punched a tunic into the bottom of the second bag. "We delay for Reuben to bring food." His strained features tightened as he looked toward the door.

"You can talk to Sabina until my uncle returns," Eunice pleaded.

Yechiel dropped the bag. "What have you heard…that I don't already know?"

"Dio's life was a mess."

Yeichiel grunted. "I said something I *didn't* know."

"His wife confessed to having an affair with his friend and personal banker. His daughter is in love and was distraught over a marriage proposal Dio rejected. Dio's son, Paris, spends most days at the circus chariot races, with little concern for taking over family responsibilities, and Dio's legacy is now in the hands of Agabus." Before Yechiel could interrupt, she hurriedly added. "And Titus Mordax."

"I met the infamous gladiator. Dio consulted with him on the first ludus. I was not impressed."

"Now he is fully involved. My father has been following Mordax's criminal activity for years. He is shrewd, but most of his crimes have been among the lower-class plebians. He hasn't managed to break into big money, the upper-class, or senatorial families. With Dio's money backing him and the ludus under his control, the authorities are alarmed."

"This does not concern me." Yechiel nervously stroked his chin.

"It might. Agabus and Mordax had much to lose when Dio chose you to build the library. Something made him change his mind. You were working with him. You sent him the note to meet."

"What note?" Yechiel looked perplexed.

"The note requesting he meet you that morning."

"I wrote no note."

"It is evidence against you bearing your signature."

"I sent a message the week before. The note would be old."

"You must tell my father." She spoke more sharply than she intended. Yechiel slammed his hand against the wall. "Did you not listen? They have no evidence against me yet seek my arrest."

"You are accused of regularly fighting with Dionysius."

"Arguing, yes." Yechiel's jaw tightened. "To finish the library early, Dio was willing to allow Agabus's substandard work. I told him no."

"And he fired you." It wasn't hard to imagine.

"No. We had an understanding. We respected how far we could push each other. I had no motive for murder."

Eunice stepped forward, putting her hand on Yechiel's arm. "You said Dio was asking you questions in his last weeks. Strange questions that you shared with me."

Yechiel shook his head and moved away from Sabina. "It makes no difference now. He's dead."

"What did he ask you?" Sabina's tone was steady, calming both her frustration and his. Why did he fight against her help?

"Nothing that would lead to his death. He wanted to know why I didn't cheat him as Agabus was continually trying to do. Dio asked if I was afraid of him or of getting fired."

"And?"

"I told him I do not choose what is right and just because of a man. I obey and fear God.

"ADONAI is in his holy temple. ADONAI, his throne is in heaven. His eyes see and test humankind. ADONAI tests the righteous; but he hates the wicked and the lover of violence. For ADONAI is righteous."

Sabina looked at Yechiel expectantly. "And?"

"I quoted my scripture. I told you it wouldn't help," he said.

"Perhaps he was asking because of Agabus? If Dionysius knew he was a thief, perhaps he planned to fire him. Agabus would know how to collapse the arch. And he nearly confessed to preparing the winch. He had the means."

"You met Agabus. He is a pompous ass, dishonest, and an incompetent architect, but I cannot imagine him devising anything as precise as murder."

"Perhaps it was an act of passion, not precision." Sabina's exasperation rose as Yechiel paced, seeming to ignore her efforts to defend him.

"Do not discount Agabus." Eunice's words carried urgency. "Your talent threatened him. He disparaged your designs. You said he was always trying to get you to cut corners or look away when he did." She turned to Sabina. "Yechiel's uncompromising sense of right and wrong offends people."

"If Dionysius threatened to fire Agabus and…" Sabina acted out turning the winch, "it would have only taken seconds. Agabus is vain and highly motivated to keep his job."

"If Dio promoted Agabus to head architect," Yechiel sounded dubious, "he had no motive to kill Dionysius."

"You were a thorn in his conscience. That is motive," Eunice said.

But not one that could be proven. There had to be another clue. "Did Dionysius speak to you about his family? Or mention visiting a fortune teller?"

"One time he professed love for his wife, but except for Dio's questions, we spoke only of work. It was Agabus who told me the project began because a fortune teller foretold Dio's death." Muffled noises filtered in from the storefront. "Reuben has returned with food for the journey." Yechiel's voice broke at the end. He reached for Eunice, and they clung to each other.

Sabina watched as Yechiel pulled away while Eunice hung on, her tears flowing. Sabina followed Yechiel's gaze as it settled on his wife's stomach. The petite woman with slender hips had a barely noticeable bump under her clothing. He stroked the back of his hand against her cheek. "Yahweh shall preserve you from all evil."

Eunice leaned into his hand. "He shall preserve your soul."

Sabina blushed. "I should go."

"As should I." Yechiel cupped Eunice's cheeks. "Dio had one redeeming principle. He professed a committed love for his wife. And I profess my undying love for you." Yechiel pulled Eunice into his arms and kissed her passionately, then abruptly broke away. He hefted a bag over each shoulder. "Reuben," he shouted. "Where are my provisions?"

Reuben passed through the curtains empty-handed. Yechiel opened his mouth and then closed it immediately. Two uniformed guards and Zarmig followed Reuben into the atrium.

Yechiel turned white as he leveled a deadly glower at Sabina.

"Zarmig?" Sabina took a step back, shaking her head. "How?"

Eunice looked from Sabina to Zarmig and back again with a confused look. "You know him?"

"These are her father's guards." Yechiel's voice was as hard as iron.

Sabina glared at Zarmig, barely able to breathe. What had she done?

Eunice blanched, stifling a sob with her hand. "You betrayed us."

"No…I didn't mean to." Mortified, Sabina could barely string words together as she stared at her fatal mistake, his head peeking out between the curtains. Without looking at her, he disappeared, jerking the curtains closed.

"Felix stayed with you until you lost him at the shoe stall," Zarmig said with a hint of a mentor's approval.

"He didn't need to follow me. He was the one who first found the shop." She didn't think she could feel any worse until she looked at the quaking Eunice.

One guard bound Yechiel's wrists. The other announced, "Yechiel ben Jonah, you are charged with the murder of Dionysius Antiochus and attempting to flee, evading the right and true justice of our supreme emperor Domitian."

She cringed at the clanking chains as Zarmig locked the iron rings around Yechiel's hands and neck on her father's orders.

The guards pried Eunice's fingernails from her husband's cloak as they dragged him away. "I'm sorry," she choked. The guilt written in her wide eyes and quivering chin tore at Sabina. Eunice blamed her own disobedience for leading the guards to their hiding place. Eunice believed she had betrayed her husband by asking for Sabina's help. His arrest wasn't Eunice's fault.

The guilt belonged solely to Sabina.

Sobbing, Eunice collapsed on the floor, wrapping her arms around her stomach.

Every emotional fiber of Sabina demanded she offer comfort and solace. Reason shouted failure, blame, and guilt. Sabina mouthed *Please forgive me,* and left Eunice to Reuben's ministrations.

Numbly she followed Zarmig and his prisoner from the room. Would she ever learn? Her father always won.

EIGHTEEN

Sabina stomped to Dionysius's home in a haze of fury. She had to do something, anything, even if it couldn't undo her horrible mistake. Yechiel's last statement about loving his wife ignited questions about Ursula and Dio's conflicting views of their relationship—a clue she could follow up on.

Grinding her teeth, she silently raged at Zarmig and her father. But the worst blame she heaped on herself for leading Zarmig to Yechiel. Yechiel's devastating accusation hammered at her every step. Guilt burned in her stomach. After her first feeble excuse of I didn't know, Sabina had quit pleading innocence. If she were Yechiel and Eunice, she wouldn't believe her either.

Her pride had caused the fatal error that could cost Yechiel his life. All because she thought she could outwit her father, the spymaster, and his pawn, weasel, puppet, and lapdog Zarmig. She unclenched her fists, flinching as stinging sparks flowed through numb fingers. When had Zarmig turned from friend to traitor?

She was being irrational. Zarmig dutifully completed his assignment, and it was unfair to expect anything else. She could not afford emotions to interfere with finding Dionysius's killer and freeing Yechiel.

If her father and Zarmig had a job to do, so did she.

Surprised, she stopped outside Dionysius's house. She had been so lost in thought she didn't remember getting there. She counted to ten, then another ten, and another, taking slow, soothing breaths. What was her plan of action? Her strategy to elicit confessions?

The street outside the villa was quiet. A single groom rested near a carriage, but no line of mourners going into the villa or curious bystanders greeted her. The door opened, and Ursula, with Loukas at her arm, descended the front steps looking like any wealthy married couple attending an afternoon outing.

Diana scurried out behind them, then stopped when she noticed Sabina. "Oh, Sabina, I didn't know you were coming with us."

"Coming where?" Sabina asked.

"We're going to see Ferocianus's first exhibition fight."

"Paris's gladiator?" Sabina recognized the name.

Ursula lifted her brows. "Our gladiator, apparently. Paris insists the family fortunes depend on this Ferocianus. We will see if his skills are as good as advertised. And if not, how vulnerable our bank accounts are."

"I didn't know about the exhibition." A noise turned Sabina's attention toward the house. A slave exited, struggling to close the door. He juggled several cumbersome five-foot-long poles with ostrich feather fans mounted on one end. He dropped a fan, picked it up as another fell, and finally managed to slide the fluttering plumes into the carriage.

"I'd hoped to ask you some questions." Sabina turned to Ursula.

"Then you should come with us," Diana said. "Paris is meeting us at the exhibition."

"Yes, join us. There is room." Ursula smiled like a spider waiting for a fly. "We can catch up. Titos." Ursula snapped her fingers at the flustered slave to assist her and Loukas into the covered carriage.

Sabina tried not to stare at the lovers. What was the truth about Dio's marriage and Loukas's relationship with the family?

Sabina peeked inside. She had never ridden in a carpentum. This one could transport six people, but the fans and cushions took up much of the space. Diana waggled her fingers for Sabina to join.

Loukas settled next to Ursula. "Mordax is making a spectacle of his new star. It should be interesting."

"Mordax will be there?" Sabina stepped back.

She did not doubt her father's threat to lock her in the house for months if he caught her anywhere near Mordax. She viewed the criminal as a sleeping cobra that her father wanted to keep that way. Surprised by an enemy, Mordax could once again slither away, or worse. Snakes had fangs. Her father's warning left no doubt he would do whatever was necessary to protect Mordax's future prosecution from Sabina's meddling. She shook her head in frustration. "Thank you, but I'm not a fan of gladiator fights."

Ursula poked her head out of the carriage. "As you wish. But this may be our last chance to speak. I heard your father wasn't happy with our arrangement."

Sabina wasn't overjoyed with her father either and couldn't hide her frustration. "No, he wasn't."

"Men always think they know best." Ursula squeezed Loukas's arm.

Diana leaned down and offered her hand. "We don't want to miss the opening fight."

Sabina set her mouth in a grim smile as she grabbed Diana's hand and climbed into the carriage, confident she would easily blend in with the theater's twenty-four thousand spectators.

Her father would never know.

Titos ambled up beside the driver. With the crack of a whip, they jerked forward.

The straw seat cushions barely buffered the carriage's shaking and jarring as the wooden wheels rattled within grooves worn into the marble paving. Progress was plodding as the carriage settled into a rhythm of bumps and jolts. Titos yelled at those ahead to clear the way. The carriage driver's whip snapped, followed by a yelp.

Sabina watched as they passed push carts, pedestrians, and sightseers. Their pace sped up as they neared the theater carved into the side of Mount Panayirdag. The last time she'd attended a play there, she'd returned home covered in dust. Hopefully, the construction of additional seating would be completed. People were flocking to Ephesus and the building could barely keep up.

She braced for the carriage to stop then snapped her head around as they sailed past the theater's entry. In a reckless moment of rebellion, she hadn't considered that a single gladiatorial exhibition wouldn't justify reserving the large theater without festival revelers to fill it. Her chance at the colossal theater providing plenty of cover died when the carriage passed Harbor Street and turned onto a narrow side-street.

They stopped and disembarked in front of a school gymnasium. A buzz of voices vibrated from inside the building. She guessed the school rented their student wrestling and gymnastic arena for outsider events such as gladiatorial exhibitions.

Sabina waited with Ursula, Loukas, and Diana in the entrance's alcove while Titos and the driver attended to the carriage. A swell of muffled cheering drew her attention—a small but enthusiastic venue. Loukas asked around for the event manager.

Ursula glared at a man coming toward them. Sabina's heart constricted as he neared. Her day was not going well. Mordax's scarred arms and knotted leg muscles extended from under a short tunic. His grizzled face needed a shave. His jaw jutted in determination as he pounded toward them.

She'd been there five minutes and was already defying her father's orders.

She slouched behind Diana, frantically searching for a place to hide, remembering his threat if he found her anywhere near the ex-gladiator turned criminal thug, turned shady business partner. The alcove had nowhere to hide. Had she just ruined years of her father's undercover work to arrest Mordax? Your meddling may have alerted Mordax. She slid next to a vine-covered trellis, hoping to blend into the greenery.

Mordax, followed by Otho, barreled past her paying her no attention as they halted in front of Ursula.

Sabina nearly collapsed in relief.

Mordax eyed Otho's fiancée up and down. Ruddy spots mottled Diana's face as she stared at the ground.

Otho tried to catch Diana's eye, but she looked away.

Mordax bowed to Ursula. "I am late in offering my condolences for the loss of your husband."

Ursula raised her chin and sniffed dismissively. "I hadn't noticed."

Mordax frowned but continued. "Dionysius was a man of character. I mourn the loss of our partnership. Tragedy struck before we got to work together. I shall miss your husband's business insights, but I assure you the ludus is in competent hands and shall not suffer."

"In Paris's hands." Ursula sounded aloof and superior.

Mordax's face tightened into a feral smile. "Paris's, yes, of course."

"And yours." Ursula twisted the end of her mantle, her knuckles white.

"Isn't that why you are here, to celebrate the beginning of a successful partnership?" Mordax stood straighter. "I guarantee a spirited afternoon of entertainment. I have reserved special seats. Otho will join you and can explain—"

"That won't be necessary. We can find our seats." Ursula waved her entourage forward.

Mordax blocked her path with his arm. "Otho would like to accompany his fiancée."

Ursula's nostrils flared as she glared at his arm, her voice turning to iron. "Paris was tasked with informing you that Diana has changed her mind and wishes to call off the engagement."

Loukas moved forward.

Slowly, Mordax lowered his arm.

Sabina's eyes widened in surprise. Had she heard correctly? She looked to Diana for confirmation. Were these not the two she'd witnessed passionately entwined only two days ago?

Diana, who had ducked behind Loukas, continued staring at the ground.

Sabina held her breath, not daring to add anything to an already tense situation. When did this happen? What was Diana's reason?

"Paris mentioned something," Mordax growled. "But he did not explain. Otho deserves to speak to Diana."

"Otho deserves nothing from Diana. My stepdaughter gave her answer." Ursula's voice trembled in anger or fear. "You will let us pass. This conversation is over."

"No." Otho pushed forward to stand by his father and closer to Diana. "Diana, I love you."

Diana looked up. "Do you? That is not what I was told." Diana pressed her lips together and folded her arms.

"Whatever your stepmother told you wasn't true." Otho pointed his finger at Ursula, his voice a low snarl. "She is lying." Otho moved toward Diana.

Loukas stepped forward, blocking his way. Otho, a much larger and stronger man, could have flung Loukas aside, but he stopped at Diana's frightened shriek.

Ursula's raised her chin, seething through gritted teeth. "I won't be called a liar by a cockroach who isn't worth my time to step on."

Otho spat at Ursula's feet but stepped back, never taking his eyes from Diana. "Ursula has poisoned you against me."

Diana wrinkled her nose. "It wasn't her." Her head dropped, and her voice lost much of its earlier conviction. "You say you love me. You say you love my poetry, but you don't. Just like Father, who said he loved my poems but lied. I cannot trust what you say."

Sabina shifted, trying to make sense of Diana's reasoning for breaking her engagement. A thorn from the trellis poked her. She stifled an ouch, not wanting to draw attention.

"The poem? Your poem?" Otho's tone rose in frustration, mimicking the expression on his face. "You're breaking our engagement because I didn't understand your poem? That's all this is?"

"That's all?" Diana's voice was calm with a surprising razor edge. "You make it sound like my poetry isn't important. You never took me seriously. I'm grateful you served a purpose, but it's over."

"You're grateful!" Otho's voice exploded. His face turned purplish red.

"Otho." Mordax lowered his brows and put a calming hand on his son's arm. "The exhibition match is starting. You can speak sense into the girl later."

"I will remind you that my husband agreed to share a business partnership. His daughter wasn't part of the arrangement." Ursula's hand sliced through the air. "Diana's made her decision."

Mordax's eyes flashed and hardened. "Diana is too immature to decide something this important. Young brides get nervous, and Paris signed the union," Mordax said with a note of finality.

Loukas cleared his throat. "Dio's seal was destroyed when he died. Until Dio's will is publicly read, Paris has no authority to sign legal agreements, including a marriage contract."

Otho pointed to Diana. "My fiancée signed the contract. Aediles witnessed our official pledges."

Ursula stood rigid. Her hands gripped in front of her. "How convenient that she wasn't too immature when she signed your pledge."

Mordax's heavy brows lowered even farther. His rumble edged with anger. "The contract is binding, with or without your family seal. The courts will hold you to it."

Panting, Titos ran up with the ostrich fan poles clanking together and spitting a feather out of his mouth.

"We are late for the exhibition." Ursula didn't acknowledge Mordax's threat. She signaled Titos they were leaving and that he should lead the way.

Turning in a circle, obviously unsure of which direction to go, Titos set off away from the men causing his mistress distress.

Ursula grabbed Diana's hand and stalked after Titos. "Take note, Diana. The earth is littered with creatures unable to rise above their boorish behavior."

Sabina lowered her head and slunk past Mordax and Otho. Their attention remained fixed on Diana. She held her breath until she caught up to the others, releasing a deep huff.

After two false turns, one ending in a dressing room full of naked wrestlers, Ursula spun around and screeched. "Where is this ill-advised exhibition?"

After asking directions, Titos and the small assemblage stumbled into an open courtyard surrounded by a covered arcade with raised wooden benches. Sabina stiffened and lurched to a stop. Could her day get any worse? She estimated five hundred people packed the modest setting. Mordax's publicity had filled every seat.

Titos led them to a roped-off awning shading four empty chairs in the front and center of the spectator benches. Diana grabbed her hand and pulled her forward. "You can sit in Otho's chair." The crowd's din quieted to a titter of speculation as the honored guests sat down.

Sabina averted her face, drew her mantle farther down over her hair, and prayed no one recognized her.

A young boy stood alert, waiting to serve their private viewing tent. Several wine pitchers, cups, and bowls filled with figs and nuts covered a small table. Titos elbowed the boy away, positioned himself beside the table, poured a cup of wine, and offered it to Ursula.

"Thank the gods." Ursula grabbed the cup, took a long swig, and spit the wine out. "The sour stench of Mordax persists." She took another drink and swallowed. "Dio must have lost his mind to sign a contract with that barbarian. He can't even dress in a proper toga."

"Father must have had some reason to become business partners with Mordax. He complimented father's business insight," Diana said.

Ursula squealed, shaking her head at Diana. "Mordax was mocking us under that thick brow of his. Everyone knew your father's talents didn't extend to business or finance. That's why he hired Loukas."

Loukas's expression grew sober. "If only he had taken my advice on choosing his business partner."

Ursula sniffed. "Now Paris invites Otho to suck even more blood. I blame Dio for allowing Paris to be dragged into the gutters of Ephesus."

"Paris didn't need to be dragged," Loukas said. "He took advantage of Dio's patience."

"Father said exploring life's pleasures was good for Paris." Diana sounded defensive.

"Titos, the heat is oppressive," Ursula complained, and Titos rushed to flourish a large feathered fan. "Dio hoped the law, the military, science, or the arts would inspire Paris—not gambling."

Grunting and wheezing, an overweight man clambered down from a higher bench, waving an unsteady hand at their group. "You! I recognize you," he yelled, falling when he reached the bottom bench, forcing Titos to jump out of the way. Obviously drunk, Agabus staggered to his feet and rounded on Sabina. "It's all your fault."

Titos stopped fanning.

The crowd grew silent, all eyes drawn to Sabina—the center of the drama. Sabina felt the blood drain from her face. She had nowhere to hide. Agabus swayed on his feet. "If you hadn't interfered…I'd still be…" Agabus turned to the crowd and bellowed. "I didn't do it."

"Remove this drunkard," Ursula ordered, and two attendants rushed forward, grabbing Agabus and hauling him away, screaming, "She lied."

"I recognized him." Diana fanned herself with her hand breathlessly.

"He's the architect Paris fired." Ursula grabbed her wine cup and drank, then signaled for Titos to refill it.

Sabina let out a breath. Her hands began to shake. "I'll have a small glass of wine now."

Titos handed her a large filled goblet.

"Was he blaming Sabina for being fired?" Diana asked.

"I didn't know he had been." Sabina sipped the wine and looked at Ursula. "Why was he fired?"

"Zarmig questioned Paris. He wanted to know if Paris knew that Agabus lied about his whereabouts when Dio was murdered. I don't know how Zarmig knew, but Paris fired Agabus shortly after. Your father continues to watch him."

"My father?" Sabina sputtered a panicked denial. "Why do you say that?"

Ursula pointed to a large man with unnaturally black hair cut just below his chin, glaring at Sabina four rows back in the stands. The hairs on her arms and the back of her neck rose in sync with the blaring trumpet that cut Ursula off and drew the crowd's attention to the arena. The stands erupted with cheers and shouts, breaking through the alarm bells ringing in her brain. She thought she heard the name Ferocianus. The crowd's screams faded to a buzz as her vision tunneled in, blocking out all but one black-haired man.

Zarmig's unblinking glare met her. His grimace communicated the full measure of his disappointment. He had repeated one rule in his lecture on a successful investigation, blend in, stay unnoticed, be invisible. She turned away, sagging down in her chair. Her father would use this catastrophe to question her sleuthing capabilities.

NINETEEN

Several large Nubian slaves pounding huge drums followed a trumpeter in a procession around the courtyard. During the last booming crash, Mordax jogged into the center of the improvised arena wearing a leather breastplate over his tunic and brandishing the weapons of a retiarius gladiator: a three-pronged spear and a large fishing net. He pumped his fist in the air. The crowd screamed their approval, chanting, "Mordax, Mordax, Mordax."

At least Zarmig was no longer scowling at Sabina. He must have been ordered not to cause a scene by hauling her home. Not yet, anyway. Zarmig's gaze didn't waver as he appraised the ex-gladiator.

Mordax walked back and forth before the audience, shaking his trident and stirring the crowd into a frenzy.

"He was the best retiarius gladiator Ephesus ever produced," Loukas yelled over the commotion. "The emperor Titus was so impressed with Mordax's ruthless skill ensnaring his opponents with his net that he freed him."

"Shut up, Loukas." Ursula slammed her glass down, splashing wine on the table.

Mordax advanced on a drum player who had traded his drum for a wooden sword. The drum player rushed toward Mordax, brandishing the sword. Mordax twirled his net above his head, squatted, and somersaulted away from the fake attack. The crowd roared as Mordax flipped onto his feet, avoiding another swipe of the wooden sword. The acrobatic prowess of the battle-scarred older man astonished Sabina. Whipping his net in the air, he slipped it over the drum player, tangling his arms, and with one jerk, sent the man and his sword rolling onto the ground. Mordax leaped as if piercing the man's neck with the trident's fatal jab. The audience cheered and clapped. With his act finished, Mordax bowed, and the crowd began throwing stems containing clusters of small white flowers surrounded by lacy leaves.

Sabina recognized the plant immediately and sucked in a breath. Dozens of foot-long branches littered the arena floor. "Hemlock. Deadly."

"Reportedly, his favorite plant," Loukas yelled over the noise.

Mordax picked up one of the flowers thrown at him, kissed it, and reached out as if presenting it to Ursula, then whipped it away. He waved the crowd to silence. It took several minutes while the musicians ran out and gathered the flowers.

Ursula looked up sharply and took a deep breath to compose herself. "He certainly knows how to manipulate a crowd." She turned. "I see the wayward son is gracing us with his presence." Ursula raised a glass to greet Paris.

Paris stormed to their table. "By Pollux, Diana! What did you say to Mordax? He was furious, barely able to calm down enough to introduce the games." Spectators near them turned to listen.

"Don't yell," Diana scolded. "You were supposed to have told Otho the engagement is off."

"I did, but they're not accepting it on my word." Paris held out a gold bracelet. His face twitched as if considering a dozen appeals, and he gave up. "Otho said he's sorry about the misunderstanding. He wants you to have this as a symbol of his undying love. It's studded with rose quartz, your favorite."

"Now he's buying my love?" Diana slapped Paris's hand, and the bangle dropped, thudding on the wooden platform. "I don't want his gifts."

"Otho said he loves your poetry," Paris pleaded.

Diana shook her head incredulously. "He admitted he didn't understand anything I wrote." She kicked at the bracelet with her toe. "He's like Father, selfishly giving gifts for his own gratification."

"It's not wrong to take pleasure in doing nice things for people." Ursula massaged the sprinkling of rubies decorating her neck. "I appreciated your father's generosity."

"We aren't talking about Father." Paris glared at his stepmother. "Diana needs to apologize to Otho."

"Absolutely not," Ursula and Diana said in unison.

"Dio wasn't perfect." Ursula's voice cracked. "But he was better than most fathers. His gifts were symbols of his love."

Diana grimaced. "Am I supposed to admire Father because his flaws weren't as bad as others? Whose measure is that? His? He ridiculed me. I was devastated. He said he tried. Well, he didn't try hard enough."

Ursula looked perplexed. "I can't imagine your father ridiculing anything about you."

Diana straightened her back and moved away from Ursula. "I was six years old when Mother died. Father was all I had left. I worshiped him. When I showed him the poem I wrote. Perfect, he said, and he wanted to share it with you." Diana looked at Ursula. "I was so excited. I hid, waiting to see your reaction."

"Nine years ago," Ursula stammered. "I don't remember a poem."

"Apparently, the poem wasn't memorable. You both laughed at it—laughed at me. I cried alone in my room for days."

Ursula broke in, reaching for Diana's hand. "I'm sure we were just amused at your childish sentiments." She stopped at Diana's glare.

"I wrote about my mother's death."

"Oh." Ursula settled her hand in her lap and cleared her throat. "One mistake shouldn't poison a relationship. It doesn't mean he didn't love you."

Sabina understood Diana's vulnerability. She remembered the pain and confusion when her mother died and her father withdrew into his grief. "It must have devastated you."

Diana nodded. "I worked striving to earn his love and respect. Eventually, I realized it was impossible. It didn't matter how hard I worked. I could never know if he loved me."

"Your father expected excellence in himself, not others." Ursula signaled for Titos to pass a bowl of dates. She bit into one, shaking her head.

"Like a stone dropped on winter's first glaze of ice, his betrayal shattered my life, my trust."

"Honestly, Diana. Real life isn't a poem," Paris said.

"If my poetry bores you, Paris, you can leave." Diana stood, raising her voice. Onlookers around them stared. She sat, her voice quieter but just as emphatic. "True love is perfect. There are consequences when you betray someone. I told Father I hated him."

"When did you tell him that?" Sabina asked. Portia described Dionysius's devotion to his daughter. Was this the emotional turmoil that Cassandra sensed?

"I said it when he forbade my marriage to Otho." Diana steeled her shoulders and raised her chin, staring at Paris defiantly. "I was so angry. I told him I'd never forget how he'd laughed at me. I told him I'd never forgive him." Diana tossed her head.

Sabina traded a glance with Ursula and then addressed Diana. "That is a harsh judgment," she said, brushing aside her own unforgiveness.

Dionysius did love his daughter and wasn't aware he'd hurt her, unlike Sabina's father, who didn't care whom he hurt and who had earned her severe judgment. Sabina prayed every night for her sisters but rarely for her father.

Ursula clasped her hands. "Now that you see Otho for who he is, shouldn't you be grateful that your father protected you from an unwise marriage?"

"A month before Father died, he boasted that our noble, aristocratic family would be revered because of his contribution to the empire. Father didn't refuse Otho out of love for me," Diana said. "Otho embarrassed him."

"Then why aren't you marrying Otho?" Paris butted in. "If you hated Father, why punish Otho? You love him."

"I loved him," Diana said quietly and unassumingly. "He's no longer a part of my life."

"Well, he still loves you. He wants to marry you." Paris bent and picked up the bangle. "This isn't cheap."

Diana rolled her eyes. "It's not just the poem." Her voice was raw with sarcasm. "It's what people do."

"Were you listening to gossip about his prostitutes…his gambling?" Paris's voice rose in exasperation. "That is what men do. You will grow to accept that."

Diana's mouth dropped open, and her eyes grew wide. "Harlots?"

"Exaggerated rumors. You'll understand once you're married."

"It's not about harlots. Otho lied about wanting my money, my dowry."

"Your dowry?" Paris squealed. "He doesn't want…he doesn't need your dowry. His family is going into business with me. He'll have plenty of money. Who told you that lie?"

Ursula smiled, holding up her hands. "Certainly not me."

Diana glared at him. "Cassandra doesn't lie. She said a man with false intentions coveted my inheritance."

"The fortune teller?" Paris clenched his fists. "She clearly meant Loukas—and Ursula—as I warned you."

Ursula's eyes blazed. "That is ridiculous! Loukas has done nothing but increase your family's fortunes. You should be grateful, you little weasel."

Paris started toward Ursula, but Diana caught his hand. "Ursula arranged the meeting with Cassandra. Why would she do that if Cassandra were going to condemn her and Loukas?"

Ursula could have paid Cassandra for a false prophecy. If Cassandra sowed doubts about Otho at Ursula's request, could she have done the same with Dio's readings?

Diana's eyes narrowed. "Cassandra said a young man. Loukas is old. I'm writing a new poem, Betrayal of Innocence."

Paris groaned and rolled his eyes.

Diana glared at him. "Go home!"

"I can't. I'm the co-host of the games." Paris pushed himself off the wall and spun the bracelet around his finger but didn't offer it again. "Everyone isn't like Father. Give Otho a chance. Let him defend himself."

Ursula moved between Diana and Paris. "You will not force her into marrying that man. Dio was correct that Otho doesn't have the breeding or honor. He can't even wait until after the funeral to force his way into her bed. Your duty is to your sister. I'm ordering you to break the contract."

Paris paled. "No one breaks contracts with Mordax."

"Find a way. It's time you put your responsibility for your family above yourself." Ursula met Paris's glare, and the two remained locked in a power struggle until Paris looked away.

"They are waiting for me to announce Ferocianus." He whirled around and strode away.

Titos sidled up to his mistress and refilled her glass of wine.

Ursula sighed. "Titos, I shall miss you when you're freed." Her voice sounded tired.

"Perhaps I will stay with you," Titos cooed, picking up one of the larger ostrich feather fans.

"He could do worse than remaining your pet," Loukas said with a note of testiness.

Ursula gave Loukas a small smile and extended her hand to him. He kissed it, and all seemingly returned to normal.

Loukas caught Sabina staring at him and raised his glass to her in a mock toast. Was he the person to shed light on Ursula and Dionysius's marriage? The swoosh of Titos's fan stirred a curl loose from her braid. It had been an exhausting day. "Are you giving Titos his freedom?"

Ursula shook her head. "Dio is. Upon his death, he willed the household slaves to be granted their freedom…manumission. Dio relished grand gestures."

Diana pursed her lips but said nothing.

Paris appeared in the arena. The crowd stirred, jostling each other, impatient for the main attraction. He raised a speaking horn. "In honor of the life and death of my father, Dionysius Antiochus, I want to introduce our citizens of the great capital of Asia Minor to a mighty fighter, a killer extraordinaire, a Dacian soldier who slew fifteen brave and honorable Roman infantrymen in battle. Ferocianus!"

The crowd booed and jeered. A side door slid open, and a man bound in chains with his head hanging down stumbled out, led into the arena by two men dressed in Roman infantry uniforms and looking suspiciously like the earlier drummers.

Paris raised the horn again. "He was captured and brought to his knees by our Seventh Claudia Legion in the battle of Tapae." The crowd screamed their approval and thunderously stomped the wooden bleachers until Sabina thought they would crack.

Paris yelled into the speaking horn. Sabina could barely hear above the roar. "And now, this lowly slave has sworn to fight until death for the honor of our emperor and your enjoyment. Today I introduce to you the famous Ferocianus." Paris walked around the arena, his arms sweeping up and down, fueling the crowd's cheers until he exited through the side door.

Ferocianus lifted his head, bared his teeth, and growled at the crowd. The audience quieted as he struggled against his chains, swinging a loose end and knocking one guard to his knees. The crowd booed. The other guard raised his wooden spear. Ferocianus flung his arms out in one sweeping motion, breaking his chains, as shattered links flew off his body.

The crowd gasped.

The lone guard and newly liberated gladiator circled each other, and the audience grew silent. Ferocianus reached down and picked up a longer length of chain. The other guard clambered up and joined his partner. Together, they closed in on Ferocianus. The crowd began chanting the battle name, "Tapae."

"Amusing stunt," Ursula sighed. "I saw that same chain trick in Miletus last year."

"It never gets old," Loukas added.

Ferocianus and his guards enacted a brief battle that ended decisively, with both guards cowering at the gladiators' feet, begging for mercy. Ferocianus, courting the spectators, bestowed clemency with a nod to the crowd as if including them in his fateful decision.

The delighted crowd responded, cheering, "Ferocianus" over and over.

Loukas smiled and lifted a pitcher toward Ursula. "It appears the Antiochus estate includes a celebrity. Would anyone like more wine?" Loukas poured wine into a goblet. Sabina shook her head.

Diana took the offered cup and whispered to Sabina. "He wrote me a letter."

"Otho?" Sabina raised an eyebrow. "When?"

"No, Father. The week before he died, after I told him I hated him and never wanted to speak to him."

Her shaking had stopped. "What did it say?" The letter could hold a clue to understanding who had killed him.

Diana crossed her arms. "I didn't read it."

Before Sabina could reply, Ursula signaled they were leaving.

Diana wouldn't be the first person who let their emotions dictate their actions. Sabina didn't want to think that Dionysius's refusal had ignited a fury intense enough to commit murder.

Ursula walked beside Diana. The older woman's awkward attempts at reconciliation were rebuffed. Ursula continued her efforts as they exited the arena.

Loukas fell in beside Sabina. "Ursula appears indifferent at times, but she loves Diana. I believe the grief of not having children is why Ursula sometimes appears uncaring."

Sabina blinked, knowing full well the emotions of being childless. When a woman's role was to birth children and produce heirs to continue the family legacy, Ursula's barren heartache was something Sabina understood. Embarrassment enveloped her each time she thought of her desperate marriage to Xeno. A marriage that she'd hoped and prayed would end with a babe in her arms. Instead, her arms ended up doubly empty, with Xeno dying on their wedding night and all hope of being a wife and mother extinguished—until Marcus.

She couldn't be distracted by thoughts of Marcus. Later, she must face the fact that she had almost committed the same mistake. Agreeing to marry a man she barely knew—a man who swindled her father out of a small fortune.

"Your father is investigating Dionysius's death." Ursula looked back, and Loukas motioned for her to continue ahead.

"Not just my father." Loukas would not know that the authorities had arrested Yechiel for the murder.

"There are rumors suggesting Ursula had a reason to kill her husband."

A blush warmed Sabina's cheeks. "Ursula told us about your affair. Why are you telling me this?"

"Ursula said your father listens to you."

Sabina stifled a scornful laugh. "Don't believe everything you hear."

"That is my point. There is a crucial detail Ursula left out. Your father should know we were not lovers before Dio died. We had nothing to do with Dio's death."

"You could tell him."

Loukas shook his head. "Ursula believes the world views her as more attractive, desirable, and loved, with men competing over her. I am not in a position to dispute her."

"I'm not sure my father would believe me."

"I love Ursula. I loved her long before she met and married Dio. His death was my chance at true happiness."

Sabina stopped walking. Did Loukas admit to ridding himself of a rival? "Jealousy is a strong motive."

Loukas slowed, allowing her to catch up. "I'm not confessing to murder. Jealousy was not a trait Dionysius or I bore. He, because he had everything he wanted, me because I accepted I never would."

"That's a terrible defense."

Loukas laughed, but it was a sad laugh. "Is that what I'm doing? Defending my actions?"

"Ursula said Dionysius was having an affair and would divorce her."

"Now we get to the difficult part. Dio was not having an affair, and for some reason—which he didn't explain to me—shortly before he died, he had changed his mind about divorcing her. Dio told me he wanted this marriage to work." Loukas placed a silencing finger on his lips.

"You haven't told Ursula?"

Loukas shook his head. "Ursula believed Dio preferred a younger woman. I did not dissuade her. That is my confession. As long as she believes getting older makes her undesirable, she needs me. Once Ursula realizes she is more beautiful now than when she was younger… well, I am petrified."

"That you will lose her."

Loukas nodded. "Ursula cannot know I told you."

Sabina tried to imagine Ursula as insecure, frightened of losing Dionysius and the security of his wealth. "If she was afraid of being thrown aside. Would she have killed Dio?" She blurted out.

He paused. "Ursula is unpredictable, passionate, and impulsive but capable of murder?" Sabina barely heard him murmur. "I desperately hope not."

Loukas gamboled up with Ursula and Diana. Sabina strolled behind a fan-juggling Titos, trying to observe the three people in front of her through the wavering ostrich feathers and having no luck.

Diana's hurt and distrust distorted her view of love and the people around her. She had dismissed Otho by saying he served his purpose. Was this the fickleness of youth? Or was this reserved young woman capable of turning her distrust and unforgiveness into revenge? A revenge that enlisted her suitor to settle a childhood hurt, a hurt that had grown into a sickness eating away at her life? Had Otho been a means to an end? Dismissed after serving his purpose. It was challenging to imagine Otho as an unwitting pawn in a murder scheme. But who wasn't susceptible when chasing their heart's desire—a rich wife?

What purpose did Otho serve? Sabina's curiosity filed that question away.

She would deliver Loukas's confession to her father without pointing out it confirmed Ursula's motive to murder her husband. Was Loukas's declaration his way to direct suspicion away from himself? Away from the man who hadn't disclosed where he was the morning his rival was murdered.

That detail was something she would point out to her father.

TWENTY

armig didn't accost and drag Sabina home after the exhibition, as she expected. She declined Ursula's carriage ride home. It would be a long walk, but she needed to make the most of her remaining hours of freedom. Once her father found out she had connected with Mordax again, she had no idea what he would do, but she needed to plan for the worst, a plan that included a stop in the fortune teller's neighborhood—perhaps her last opportunity to find the truth.

Cassandra was a vital link to the murder, and also a suspect, though Sabina didn't want to think it. She wouldn't have turned the winch handle, but Ursula could have enlisted Cassandra into her scheme, even paid her to forecast Dionysius's death—he couldn't divorce her once he was dead. Then Ursula could point to the prediction as a cover. And a trustworthy fortune teller could make a comfortable living—both plausible motives.

She reviewed Cassandra's evasive answers. She said she sensed Dionysius's inner conflict when the library project began but hadn't given any details to identify the incident or person causing his turmoil. It could be Agabus, Mordax, Paris, Diana, or Yechiel by his admission. The week before Dionysius died, his worries appeared to have vanished. Had he come to his senses about constructing the ludus as Agabus said? Had he given in to Diana's wish to marry Otho? Had he decided not to divorce Ursula? Or to divorce her? Cassandra knew more than she was sharing.

The last visit had ended badly, and as much as she fought it, Amisi's arguments against Cassandra being her sister made sense. She was determined not to let her emotions influence her, but that didn't prohibit probing into Cassandra's past.

If Cassandra spoke to her.

She jingled the silver denarii she had tossed into a small coin purse that morning. Since becoming a widow, she had saved a small amount of her meager allowance. After giving most of it away on the last visit, she hoped what was left would entice Cassandra to speak to her. Perhaps Cassandra still wanted to tell her fortune.

Picturing Ursula's map, she set off.

No ruffian thugs barred her way when she turned onto the narrow street. Instead, several gaunt-faced children ran ahead of her, waving sticks and laughing at the game they played.

She entered Cassandra's insula and climbed the stairs. Reaching the top, Cassandra's voice floated down the narrow hallway. "Welcome, Sabina." Sabina's step faltered. Perhaps Cassandra had heard her mounting the steps. Perhaps not.

She passed the barren room. The children weren't there.

She flipped Cassandra's curtain aside.

"Come in." Cassandra beckoned, dressed precisely as before, her face scarf securely in place, and gestured for her to sit. "You came for your fortune." Her voice held no reproach for Sabina's previous offensive behavior.

"I hoped you would see me again." Sabina shifted uncomfortably.

"That was not our choice to make. The spirit said our destinies were intertwined." Cassandra's voice rang with confidence that Sabina had returned at the daemon's summoning.

"Like Ursula and Dionysius?"

"Mysterious bonds of jealousy exist between lovers, husbands, and wives."

"But they don't usually lead to murder."

"You might be surprised." Cassandra's stare was penetrating.

"I need facts." Not poetic recitations. "Was Ursula's jealousy a motive to murder her husband?"

"You would have to ask her. I already shared what I know." Cassandra stroked the box containing the bones. "But there was something I recalled about Dio's final vision."

Sabina's pulse quickened.

"My daemon's first three communications were potent, clear, and unfaltering. During the last one, I struggled to see through the distortion as if something were blocking the message."

"You said he had changed. Could that have caused the blocking?"

"Perhaps. I have held the hands of hundreds of supplicants. Touch is the bridge between my daemon's spirit and the physical world. His fingers cling to mine even now." Cassandra sounded troubled. "I have not retained a presence this long after death. I feel the crushing of bones, but there is only silence as he grips my hands."

Sabina was unable to hide her disappointment. "Everyone knows he was crushed to death." It must be easy for desperate people to interpret Cassandra's words to fit their longings.

"It shows how desperately Dio wants to stay here. Whatever choice he made will follow him to his grave. Right or wrong, he cannot avoid the final accounting of his deeds on the scales of justice. No one can."

Sabina began to interrupt.

Cassandra held up a finger. "I know. Unless you are a Christian. I heard your apostle John preaching in the agora."

Sabina nodded. "If we acknowledge our sins, God will forgive and purify us from all wrongdoing. Jesus the Messiah has mercy on us."

"Mercy?" Cassandra's cynicism rang out. "My suffering tells me no god offers mercy. Why would I believe your Christ's promises?"

"Because you believe in justice. Because human hearts long for freedom from condemnation and peace. Christ alone has the power to remove evil from the scale of justice."

Cassandra's bitter laugh was like a slap. "You preach what Dio wanted, a life without guilt. Everyone knows the gods do not excuse wrongs. They punish. Justice is what Dio sought to avoid. And it may have caused his death."

"God does judge, and our evil actions must be paid for. The problem is imperfect humans have nothing to offer as payment but sinful confessions."

Cassandra tapped the ebony box with a fingertip. "Many scholars, priests, and philosophers lecture in the agora where John spoke. I hear students of Plato, the priests of Buddha, Ra and Isis, the sophists—none need to convince me I am not righteous enough for God. I know. I can only labor to be better to ease the pain, sickness, and suffering in my next life and the next. That is true justice."

"Christ suffered the punishment for us once and for all...out of love."

"A perfect but impossible solution. Gods do not care about human troubles." Cassandra adjusted a shawl on her shoulder and fidgeted with the ebony box of bones. "We are born to suffer, then die, and the cycle begins again. That is the way of the world."

"You are right. God's divine wisdom is not the way of this world."

"I will ponder your God of love. It is an appealing thought." Her rigid posture eased as she settled back. "One irrefutable truth is that Dio is now beyond your God's love and mercy."

"And I am no closer to finding out who killed him." Sabina sighed at her failure...multiple failures. The veiled woman before her looked at her expectantly. Amisi was right. There was no way to know if Cassandra was one of her lost sisters. She would leave before she wasted any more time. Before she invested more of her heart. "I should go."

Cassandra narrowed her eyes. "You did not come to discuss Dio's afterlife...nor to find his killer."

"That is not true."

"I do not need my daemon to see that something troubles your heart."

Amisi's warning blared in her mind. She shoved it aside. "I would like to know about you, your life."

"My life is irrelevant."

"I brought money." Sabina untied the coin bag from her belt.

Cassandra laughed. "You think money will help you understand life. Dionysius's, mine, or your own?"

Sabina laid her bag of coins on the table between them. "Is this enough?" Was Amisi correct that Cassandra only wanted Sabina's money? This was all she had.

Cassandra shook her head. "The spirit does not share my future with me."

"I'd like to know about your past."

"Which past?"

Sabina shook off her confusion. "I am curious how you became a teller of fortunes?"

"Why do you care when you lack faith in my powers?" Cassandra leaned forward as if challenging Sabina to contradict her.

Cassandra's accusation was not entirely true. She didn't know where Cassandra's powers came from, natural insights or unnatural spirits, but they weren't all tricks and deceptions.

"Does it matter what I believe?" Sabina opened the bag's drawstring and began to shake. Four coins fell, one at a time, next to the ebony box. "You are human. Where were you born? Where did you learn your...talents?"

Cassandra grabbed her wrist and snatched the bag. She scooped up the two silver denarii and the two brass sestertii that had dropped, slipped them into the bag, and drew the string closed. She tucked it under the table. "An old woman found me after my mother threw me out, a newborn—she reminded me often—that no one wanted."

A shiver raised the hairs on Sabina's arm. "An old woman with a humped back?" She recalled Amisi's details about the woman who rescued her sister.

Cassandra's eyes widened, a reaction barely perceptible in the dim lamplight. "She suffered from stiff joints and aching bones like anyone who leads a hard life. The old woman was a seer. I was twelve when the spirit chose me. I prophesied her fate, and she died the next week."

"You foretold her death?"

"She was my first." Cassandra stared at Sabina, challenging her skepticism. Cassandra opened the ebony box and dumped the bones on the table. She picked one up and distractedly rubbed it between her fingers as she spoke. Sliding them into position, she arranged the bones in a precise circle as she had the previous visit. "These were her rooms, and I was her slave. When she died, I took her name. I also took her customers. I read the fortunes of fat patrons living in huge villas and luxurious palaces." It wasn't a complaint. Sabina heard resilience, even pride, in her voice. "Do not pity me. I have a home while hundreds on the streets starve or barely survive on free bread."

If Cassandra was her sister, how could she tell her she had been born one of those patrons in a wealthy home? "Did the old woman care about you…love you?" Sabina hoped Cassandra hadn't been lonely and isolated as a child.

Cassandra shrugged. "She rarely beat me, and at three years old, I became useful. I carried water up the stairs and emptied her slop bucket. I was an obedient slave. In return, she provided this." Her lips curled in a half-smile as she looked about the tiny space. "Not all people are meant to have a mother's love. The spirits grant husbands, family, and friendship. These I will never have because of the curse." She pointed to her veiled face.

There were many superstitions involving curses. The emperor outlawed hexes and spells, but people still paid sorcerers huge sums to cast them. Should she confess that she, too, suffered under a curse? The rumors that Marcus had not died had given her a reprieve. She couldn't be blamed for the fourth death of a betrothed, but the curse making her a marriage pariah remained. Would any good come from her revelation? Shared pain wouldn't change the fact that her father had abandoned a daughter he considered cursed.

Sabina looked around the sparsely furnished room. With no money, authority, or influence to help Cassandra, she needed to slow down and think this through. Amisi had been right when she asked Sabina what she hoped to accomplish. "You are free to choose a different life."

"Freedom is something the privileged wrongly believe is possible. I am under no such illusion. My spirit master's rule is total and unyielding. We are all slaves to our fate controlled by desires, love, fear, hate, anger, comfort, sex, jealousy, pleasure, or power."

"What was Dionysus's? Pleasure? Wealth?"

"Dio feared failure. But he acknowledged his taskmaster. Most people believe they are their own rulers. What controls you, Sabina?"

Or who? "God's Spirit leads me. It is a spirit of freedom, not of slavery. You have only to ask Christ into your life to share an inheritance of mercy and grace now and for eternity."

Cassandra smiled, her expression heartbreaking. "My freedom ended at birth." Cassandra adjusted the scarf, hiding her face. She swept the bones aside into a jumbled pile. "The bones provide an illusion of mystery. The old woman needed props. I do not use them. My visions are powerful gifts. They are my destiny."

Was it fear of what God would ask Cassandra to give up that was keeping her in bondage? "Do not be afraid to ask God to change your fate. The church—you're not alone."

Cassandra's face turned stony. "Is that why you came? To save my enslaved and lost soul?"

"No...I mean, that wasn't my intent. I have questions."

"Your ignorance is stunning." Cassandra voiced a harsh rebuke. "No one refuses a daemon spirit. They are jealous and vindictive." Cassandra picked up one bone and ran her thumb over its carved surface. "You paid generously for my life's story. I hope I earned my fee."

Cassandra picked up the bones one by one and gently dropped them into their box. She forcefully slammed the lid and set the box aside. "We should begin if you wish to leave before dark."

"Begin what?" Sabina's prying was over. Cassandra's expression was shuttered, her openness gone—the time of sharing had passed.

"I can offer you nothing more until I read your fortune. The spirit is awake. If there are answers to your questions...." Cassandra drifted off.

Was it Sabina's imagination, or had a chill stirred the warm air?

Cassandra slid the ebony box behind the oil lamp. "You must remove your ring. Earth elements block the spirits. I need unobstructed contact."

Sabina looked at her ring. What was she doing? She was taking a risk, opening her mind to an evil and very real spirit. A spirit that had enslaved Cassandra. Portia would be horrified and scold her mightily. Apollos would quake at her reckless disregard for her soul. But how else could she find out if she had a living sister? And Yechiel's life depended on what Cassandra could tell her. She needed information. So had Dionysius—and he was dead. Cassandra's hands beckoned.

Sabina slipped off her ring.

Cassandra nodded in approval. "At first, Dio refused to remove his ring. He said he never took it off. Men cling to money, gold, and silver, craving the fleeting powers they can touch. Christians understand true power resides in the unseen principalities that rule the heavens."

Sabina shuddered as a chilling sweat broke over her skin. Could she pray for protection while doing what God had forbidden? She tensed.

The lamp flickered wildly as if a breeze blew through the still room. Cassandra riveted her gaze on Sabina. Sabina's arms shook as she slowly offered herself to Cassandra's spirit.

Please, God, protect your disobedient servant.

She didn't know what she had expected, but Cassandra's pale skin was warm and smooth, not the rough, dried skin of the lower classes. The fortune teller's fingers tightened around Sabina's hands with a forceful and surprisingly strong grip. Bending forward, Cassandra bent one of Sabina's hands, positioning it palm-down on the table. Cradling the other, she traced each line of Sabina's palm with the nail of her index finger. She moved to Sabina's thumb, pressing her fingernail into Sabina's skin, and ended by caressing the pad of the thumb with a gentle circular massage. She repeated the motion on each finger, releasing the small finger's pressure. She put the hand down and repeated the process with the other hand. When finished, she grasped both hands at once and gently lifted them even with her shoulders.

She closed her eyes. Her head lolled to one side and then to the other. Her head began to roll, rotating in a circle, dipping forward, around, and back, her grip increasing with each orbit. The blood squeezed from Sabina's fingers, they began to prickle.

Cassandra started to hum, and the undulating vibration reverberated up Sabina's arms, neck, and face. A throbbing echoed in her ears. A warning?

Sabina tensed, pulling at Cassandra's grip, but the teller of fortunes clutched tighter and raised the volume of the chant. Sabina shook her head, attempting to block the pounding, pulsating sound. Her fingers numbed.

Abruptly, Cassandra's humming and head rolling stopped. She let out a guttural cry. Her eyes flew open as she thrust Sabina's hands from her. She stared unblinkingly. "Who are you?" Cassandra's melodic voice turned raspy.

Sabina shifted in her seat and pulled her hands into her lap. "I told you, I'm helping Ursula find answers to Dio's death."

"That is not why you are here. I can tell you nothing." She shot from her chair and pointed to the door. "You must leave."

Sabina stared, "But my fortune?"

Cassandra's entire body trembled. "Deceiver. Liar. Death follows you." Her voice grew louder and more insistent as she stepped away from Sabina. "Go. Never come back."

Sabina stood, her throat dry, her mouth parched. "What did you see?"

Cassandra stared at her, eyes unfocused as if Sabina wasn't there. She said in a hollow voice not directed at Sabina. "Nothing. The spirit has blinded me." She stalked around the table toward Sabina, her shawl falling from her shoulder. She went to grab Sabina's arm, then jolted away as if afraid to touch her. Instead, she gestured wildly and screamed, "Leave."

Sabina snatched her ring and stumbled from the room.

Cassandra pulled at the curtain, tearing the cloth. Behind it, a knocked-over stool clattered to the floor, followed by the barely perceptible whisp of the back curtain being swept aside.

Sabina's legs shook. She braced herself against the hallway wall to steady herself and stared at the drawn curtain. Again?

What had just happened? Her hands trembled so much she dropped her ring twice before finally slipping it on. She was the one who had been reluctant to have her future told. She was the one who should have pulled away.

Deceiver. Liar. She hadn't lied. But she hadn't been entirely truthful either. But *death follows you* seemed a bit dramatic.

Cassandra's daemon said their destinies intermingled, then refused to show how. Cassandra said the daemon did not reveal her future. If their futures were linked, could that mean their pasts were also? Would the daemon be unable or unwilling to disclose the fate of sisters?

She was giving Cassandra's daemon much more credit than it deserved.

She pushed off the wall, startled at the effort it took. Starting down the stairs, she tripped as her foot, feeling weighted and clumsy, missed a riser. She grabbed the sidewall and wobbled, trying to shake off an engulfing wave of exhaustion. When she reached street level, she labored to breathe. The long walk home seemed interminable as she sucked in air with every slogging step.

The scriptures prohibited any interaction with the occult, and Portia would be upset, but she desperately needed advice about what had just transpired. She didn't have the stamina to worry about that now. She wasn't sure she would make it home.

Felix caught her as she stumbled through the front door. He yelled for Amisi just as Sabina collapsed.

Amisi helped Sabina into bed, her face creased with worry. Sabina fell asleep, her nostrils stinging from the acrid vinegar of one of Amisi's potions.

TWENTY-ONE

She half expected to be locked inside her room when she awoke. Sleep had banished the strange exhaustion of yesterday, but the potion's odor remained. She sniffed her bedclothes. Her hair. Her bedding. Everything reeked of it.

Amisi bustled into the room. "You are lucky you aren't dead," she lectured.

"I didn't need one of your potions. I was tired. That's all."

"Hmm." Amisi lifted Sabina's wrist and felt her pulsing blood. "That is not all. But there is no lasting damage. The potion restarted your heart."

"Restarted my heart?" Sabina jumped from her bed.

"Your heart was slowing. A powerful spell that, with prayers to Isis, I stopped."

"Spell?" Her sluggishness had disappeared with a good night's sleep. In the daylight, the word *spell* sounded ridiculous.

"You made someone very angry." Amisi pursed her lips.

That didn't sound so ridiculous. She had made several enemies while investigating Dionysius's murder. Agabus was the most obvious. She didn't want to consider who or what was the most recent. Sabina ran her finger through her hair and immediately wished she hadn't. Newly released vinegar swirled out. She shut her eyes, blocking its burn. "I stink."

"You are welcome." Amisi picked up a small vial from the bedside table and placed it outside the door.

"Your mother would be most unhappy if I let you die."

"Then, thank you." Sabina sighed at her well-meaning nurse. Sabina knew her mother disapproved of Amisi's mystical practices, but now was not the time to argue.

She was sure her lethargic walk home from Cassandra's was due to the emotional upheaval of her day. Starting with leading Zarmig to Yechiel and his subsequent arrest. Her father's threat she did not heed when she had walked into the arena and made herself a spectacle, jeopardizing his investigation into Mordax and endangering herself. To be accurate, Agabus should get some of the blame.

She glanced at the bedroom door, half expecting her father to burst through, bellowing her sentence of solitary confinement. How ironic to be allowed unfettered freedom as a child and now, as an adult woman, married and widowed, to be bound by a man's rules and society's disciplines. Women were often banished or locked up for life, and no one complained. Few considered it unjust.

Christ's followers preached a different world of equality and respect, where there is neither Jew nor Gentile, neither slave nor freeman, neither male nor female, for in union with the Messiah Jesus, you are all one. She tried to imagine a world where God's love and justice ruled, not man's shifting, self-serving rules. One man—her father—ruled her world.

And she had disobeyed.

Amisi helped her disrobe. "You need a bath." She scrunched her nose, unable to hide a quick smile.

"Fortunately, Portia invited me to meet her at the baths today." A perfect excuse to forestall her home confinement.

Amisi opened the trunk and removed a yellow linen tunic and pale blue stola. She wrapped Sabina's breasts in a lengthy cloth, helped her into the tunic, and pinned the shoulders of the stola together before sitting her down to comb and style Sabina's hair.

"Don't spend too much time. I'll have my hair washed and perfumed at the baths. I visited Cassandra yesterday."

Amisi stopped combing. Her moment of good humor gone. "That was who tried to kill you."

"It wasn't her. Nothing tried to kill me."

"She is not what you think. Your mother died searching for a dream. I will not let it happen to you."

"Searching for her children didn't kill her." Sabina didn't want to get into a power struggle with her slave. What should be a simple order was never simple with Amisi. Sabina had learned as a child that if she forced Amisi to do something she didn't want to, Sabina would pay the price. One way or another, Amisi had established the rules of their relationship. In return for Amisi's unquestioning devotion, love, and selfless service to her mistress, she claimed a certain independence. Unfortunately, Amisi's self-determination asserted itself at the most inconvenient times. "I won't stop until I know who Cassandra is." She didn't bother clarifying that Cassandra had no intention of seeing her ever again. "I will stop if you go with me. One time. That's all I ask."

Amisi began combing as if she hadn't heard. "I have many things to do this morning."

"You don't want me to go alone, do you?" Sabina kept her voice level as if coaxing one of her pigeons. "We could go this afternoon." Sabina peeked at the door. If her father didn't stop all her plans.

"Quit turning your head. You are ruining my braid," Amisi tugged at the braid, forcing Sabina's head straight. "Zarmig is waiting for you in the dining room."

"Zarmig? Why isn't he at Father's office?" Sabina knew why. She turned her head, glancing at Amisi. Amisi tightened the braid, jerking Sabina's head forward.

"I told him I would deliver his message. But no, he said I cannot be trusted."

"He didn't say that."

"No, but I knew what he meant." Amisi sniffed.

The feud between Zarmig and Amisi had begun after her mother's death. Each was charged with protecting Sabina from herself but employed different strategies. Her father was forced into the role of unwilling arbitrator and often let the battle rage, sometimes confining her to the safety of Amisi's feminine activities. At other times, he gave in to Zarmig's lessons on self-reliance and preparedness.

She was still furious at Zarmig for Yechiel's capture and didn't want to speak to him. She would gain nothing by defending the exhibition disaster but couldn't avoid him forever.

Dressed and styled, Sabina marched out with a deep breath. The closer she got to the dining room, the slower her steps. Zarmig's back met her. "You wanted to see me?"

He turned slowly, his frown so intense his eyebrows almost touched. "I thought you didn't like gladiator fights."

She braced herself. "I didn't enjoy it."

"Yet you seem to enjoy disobeying your father's direct decree to stay away from them."

"It wasn't intentional…well, part of it was…but I didn't know Mordax would be there…well, I did know, but I didn't think he would know I was there. And Agabus surprised me completely."

"Enough." Zarmig waved her to silence. "You aren't appreciating the possible deadly consequence of your misadventure."

"I understand it better than you. It's my…" She paused. What relationship did she have with Yechiel? She didn't know. "It's my friend who is going to die."

"And you thought you'd help Yechiel by doing what? Announcing to the world that…"

"No." Sabina took a deep breath. "But I am gathering information. I found out Paris fired Agabus when you informed him about Agabus's lying."

Zarmig raised his eyebrows and nodded. "After you told me about the inconsistent testimonies of Agabus's whereabouts the morning of the murder, I located the night guard. He was boarding a ship to Rhodes with a full purse given to him by Agabus."

"Bribed to hide Agabus's part in the murder? Did you arrest the guard?"

"No."

"What about Agabus?"

"What happens to Agabus will be up to Paris."

"I don't understand." Sabina shook her head questioningly.

"Agabus had been stealing supplies from Dionysius, selling them, then repurchasing them. Standard practice, according to Agabus. Paris disagreed."

"Dionysius could have found out. That gives Agabus a motive to kill Dionysius."

"Agabus was delivering payment to the night watchman. His partner in crime was his alibi when the arch collapsed. Neither man was with Dio or near him." The big man crossed his arms. "Your information uncovered a thief, not a murderer."

"Then Yechiel is still the main suspect."

"Unless you have other evidence."

Sabina sighed. Her hands were shaking. "I have leads, but I don't know if they go anywhere. Diana wants out of her marriage arrangement, and Otho and Mordax are fighting it. Loukas claims that Dio loved his wife and didn't plan to divorce her. And Cassandra...." She gulped. What did Zarmig know of Cassandra or her possible link to Sabina? Amisi's warning returned. You have already put her in danger.

"Cassandra?" Zarmig asked.

Sabina assessed each word before she spoke. "The fortune teller who predicted Dio's death said he had made a decision shortly before he died. It could have something to do with his death. Or not. I need more information to clear Yechiel."

"I would advise against any more theatrics. They don't end well for you. I will speak to your father when he returns tonight, informing him of yesterday's fiasco."

Sabina perked up, cocking her head. "Tonight?" Zarmig hadn't reported her last night. Nor this morning. Could this be a peace offering? Was he allowing her one more day of freedom? One more chance to help Yechiel before he reported Sabina's disaster. Even if she read too much into Zarmig's significant delay, she needed to take advantage of it.

"I'd also advise you to switch perfumes." Zarmig plugged his nose.

∝

Sabina was thrilled to receive Portia's invitation. She'd intended to meet and share her discoveries with Portia earlier. Somehow, events had kept them apart, and it had been four days since they'd last spoken. Sabina's head spun as she tried to put her discoveries in order. Portia would be the perfect person to fit the pieces together, if they fit at all.

They had decided to meet at Sabina's favorite bathhouse near the luxurious villas built one upon the other up the side of Mount Bulbuldag. Sabina preferred the intimacy of this privately owned bath over the popular municipal public bath with its theater, library, and gymnasium sprawling over several blocks near the harbor.

Sabina and Portia's litters arrived simultaneously and dropped them off at the side door reserved for women next to the colonnaded main entry. The grand entrance would be busy during the expanded hours of afternoon and evening set aside for men. Climbing roses grew in a riotous tangle of red, yellow, and white blooms, arching over the small door, their fragrance saturating the air but not enough to keep Portia from discreetly covering her nose as Sabina approached.

Promising to pay Portia back, Sabina explained her grim financial status. Portia waved her offer aside. "I will gladly help you get rid of that ghastly salve. What has Amisi been plying you with?"

"A potion to restart my heart." Sabina rolled her eyes. "It's one reason why I need your counsel."

Portia paid their entry fee of four bronze denarii and additional monies for towels, oils, and refreshments. Two slave women escorted Sabina and Portia to the changing room, undressed them, and led them into the heated tepidarium. Lying, stomach down, on massage tables, Sabina relaxed, delicious heat radiating from the stone table. Soothing harp music drifted in from the pool area.

She rested her head on folded arms. The kneading hands of the slave rubbed olive oil into her skin. "I went back to Dionysius's house."

Portia rolled on her side. "To spy on Ursula's family members?"

"I'm not spying on them. I am interviewing them."

"Hmm, so you believe that Ursula is innocent? That she loved Dio?"

"I'm working on that. I thought jealousy would motivate the lovers to want Dionysius out of their lives. But Loukas claims he and Ursula weren't lovers at the time."

Portia snorted. "The master manipulator, Ursula, is at the top of my guilty list."

"Dionysius could still have been jealous of her and Loukas." Sabina sighed as the tension from the last few days melted away.

"I can't imagine Dio being jealous of Loukas."

"That's what Loukas said. But I suspect he is lying. If Dionysius believed the gossip about an affair, he wouldn't have to be jealous. How would Ursula react if Dio's wounded pride demanded a divorce?"

Portia rolled back to her stomach. "She already admitted to stabbing him. Asking you to investigate could be a ploy to get sympathy from your father."

"That's true." Sabina pondered Portia's allegation while the attendants scraped her back with the edge of a metal strigil, removing excess oil, dead skin, accumulated sweat, or grime. Sabina rolled onto her back while the slave repeated the process. She sat up and ran her hand over her smooth skin. Sitting on a bench next to Portia, she could almost feel any remaining oil absorbing into her skin in the room's warm air.

"Father told me not to trust Ursula. But she is providing access to the information I need to fill the gaps in Dionysius's life before his murder. Important resolutions he made, perhaps deciding to divorce Ursula. And people he had arguments with, besides Yechiel."

"I'm not going to be much help, I'm afraid. As I told you, I saw little of Dio, and when I did, we didn't discuss his private life. He wanted to discuss ideas, the latest scientific discoveries, old and new philosophies..." Portia halted, tears welling. "Oh, Sabina, I miss him." Portia put her hands to her cheeks, and her voice cracked. "In my dreams, he's the rebellious nine-year-old who convinced me to sneak a ride on his father's stallion. I was paralyzed with fear when the beast reared up, hurtling both of us into the air. Dio slammed against the stable wall. I thought he had died. He woke from the coma with a smile, having survived the exploit with a broken arm and me…" She pulled back a lock of hair, revealing a scar. "But reminiscences aren't what you need."

A woman arrived carrying a platter piled with figs, pears, and plums. Another offered a tray with three narrow pitchers and two cups. "We have fruit, pomegranate juice, white wine, and chilled mint tea."

"I'll take tea," Portia pointed to the tray.

"For me also." Sabina sniffed the tangy liquid in her cup. "When I spoke to Cassandra, she said Dionysius was struggling with a decision."

"You saw Ursula's fortune-teller?" Portia lowered her cup and sat straighter.

"Twice." Sabina braced for the rebuke.

Portia lowered her voice almost to a whisper. "God gives us rules for our protection. Sabina, there is danger in opening yourself to demons of the occult." She shook her head. "We are not struggling against human beings, but against the rulers, authorities, and cosmic powers governing this darkness, against the spiritual forces of evil in the heavenly realm."

"I was careful." Was she? What about her eagerness to learn what Cassandra knew about the murder? She clenched her fists, recalling the grip of Cassandra's hands and her voice's soothing vibration. "I did pray for God's protection."

Portia pinched her lips together before sighing. "Then your prayers were answered. You don't just learn witchcraft. You practice it. You give yourself over to those dominions. They are powerful spirits."

"Cassandra admitted she is bound to them. But she is different. She does not issue curses and uses her power to help people."

"Then you are both deceived. No one uses the darkness. The father of lies uses us to carry out his hate and chaos."

Sabina bristled at Portia's criticism. "I had to go. Yechiel's life is at stake. And something happened the first visit." Sabina took a deep breath and leaned forward. "I think Cassandra might be my sister."

Portia's face went still. After a minute, she asked. "Why do you think that?"

"Cassandra doesn't know where she's from. An old woman, a fortune-teller, rescued her after she was abandoned."

Portia pinched her lips together again. "Hundreds, perhaps thousands of babies, are thrown out to die. The chance that she is whom you hope is not promising."

"That's not all. My sister was born with a stain covering half her face. The veil covering the lower half of Cassandra's face slipped, and I saw a mark from her cheek to her jaw. It matched Amisi's description of the baby's stain."

"Your sister was barely out of the womb when Amisi saw her. How could she possibly remember twenty-six years later? It hasn't been long since you learned about your father's actions. It would be understandable if you—"

"Amisi said I wanted a sister so badly I'd invented one."

"I don't believe that. But you did say you would be happy if you found your sister, that your life would be different."

"It's a bit more complicated than I imagined. Cassandra got upset when she could not see my future. She said her daemon had blinded her, and she threw me out."

"Darkness cannot exist in the light of truth." Portia's posture relaxed a little. "You tested God by putting yourself at grave risk."

Sabina bowed her head, weighing the truth of Portia's rebuke. Her reasons for jeopardizing herself appeared less and less wise. "I wanted to help her. I told her peace and freedom are possible when led by the Spirit of God."

"Choosing what she believes is the first step in changing her life." Portia gently squeezed Sabina's arm. "You also have a choice, peace and freedom versus bitterness and anger."

"My father?" Sabina raised her head, noting the worry lining Portia's face. She wasn't reprimanding her. She was worried. A rush of affection confirmed her love for this woman who cared so much for her.

The two women strolled into the caldarium. The furnaces blasting under the floor heated the air to sweltering, and steam rose from the tub water. Sabina nodded to the round tub. "You can go first."

Portia sunk into the tub, reclining against the sloping backrest and releasing a deep sigh.

"I have to see Cassandra again."

"Argh." Portia lurched up, her voice serious. "You are obstinate."

"A good trait. Right?"

"And if she is not who you think she is?" Portia's voice held the same warning but with a note of resignation. She slipped down into the water.

"If Cassandra is my sister, Amisi will know." Sabina voiced a confidence that appeared less and less warranted. Whomever Cassandra was, the last person she wanted to see was Sabina. She finished drinking her tea.

Portia rose from the tub, her face a sheen of sweat, her rosy-red body matching her red hennaed hair escaping its pins and tumbling onto her shoulders. She signaled the attendant for help stepping from the tub. "Your turn. I'll meet you in the frigidarium."

Sabina passed her empty cup to the attendant and climbed into the soaking tub, sucking in her breath as she sunk chin-deep into the near-scorching water. She motioned for the attendant to wash her hair. The woman unbraided her hair and kneaded the soap through her tresses, finishing with a rinse of the establishment's signature rose fragrance. Ten minutes later, she climbed from the tub. The attendant toweled her body dry, then her hair.

She joined Portia and a dozen other women enjoying the rectangular open-air pool. Five were giggling with heads together, several floated on their backs, and two swam from one side to another.

Portia and Sabina sat on the side of the pool, splashing their feet in the water, allowing the caldarium's heat to radiate from their bodies. "Dionysius changed in his final days. Why? What prompted the switch from the library to the ludus? Was he upset at Ursula or at losing Diana?"

"Why would he be afraid of losing Diana?" Portia asked.

They slid into the refreshingly cold water. Sabina shivered as chill bumps popped out on her skin.

"So much has happened I forgot to mention Diana was getting married."

"What!" Portia shot up from the water. "She said nothing about a wedding when we spoke to her."

The group of women stared at them.

Sabina lowered her voice. "She wasn't engaged at that time. Events evolved rapidly."

"How rapidly?"

"Now she's not getting married. Dionysius had forbidden the suit of Otho, the son of his new business partner. After his father died, Paris signed the contract." Sabina filled in the confrontation with Otho and Mordax at the gladiatorial exhibition.

Portia sunk back into the water. "First, she demanded to marry Otho. Then, she announced she was ending the engagement, by saying Otho had served his purpose." Sabina swam to the steps of the pool. Portia followed her.

"What are you implying?" Portia's voice echoed off the walls. She clamped her mouth shut.

"I don't want to believe Otho's purpose was to murder her father, but the timing of the engagement and the abrupt ending is awkward."

"You can't mean that," Portia said gravely. "Young love is awkward and erratic. She loved her father."

Had Portia's love for Diana blinded her to Diana's resentment toward Dionysius? "Diana harbored a deep animosity toward him. It began with her mother's suicide. Dionysius's rejection of Otho a month ago drove her anger into the open."

"I don't understand. As a child, she spent as much time as she could around him. Dio loved her. He would have been devastated if he knew."

"She accused him of only loving himself and said her times with him were desperate attempts to win his love."

"Dio did love himself. He also loved his daughter. Finding out she had rejected him would have killed him."

"Someone else took care of that," Sabina said.

"I haven't had much sympathy for Dio lately, but if he and Diana were estranged, it might explain his antagonistic behavior."

"Diana's hurt was real. So was her anger."

"Her memories of him would be what mattered most to him. He said Diana was the one pure thing in his life that made up for his bad choices. If she rebuffed his love, he must accept that his good wasn't enough."

"And admit that he couldn't meet his ideals."

"Let alone those of a perfect God. His last words to me were that he hated the Christian God."

"Because no one wants to be told, even by God, how to live our best lives."

Portia choked back a sob, her lips quivering. "We never spoke again. It breaks my heart that Dio and I didn't have time to reconcile and that our lifetime friendship ended without a hug and a kiss."

They climbed out of the pool. The attendants held out dry, heated towels to warm them. They lounged on a bench, nibbling fruit and filling their cups with chilled pomegranate juice.

Portia lifted her cup to her lips but didn't drink. "Are you seeing Ursula today?"

Sabina thought of all the questions she needed answered in the small window of freedom she had left. "I had hoped to go there after visiting Cassandra." Which may be a very short stop.

"Diana requested help with her poem. And I would like to speak to her about these latest events."

"And you need a bodyguard?" Sabina smiled. "We can meet at Ursula's after the mid-day lunch."

"I'm not sure a bodyguard would stop Ursula." Portia didn't smile.

They strolled back to the dressing room. Before helping them dress, the attendants anointed each with scented oil. Portia picked musky cinnamon and Sabina the rose to match her hair.

Portia drew a deep breath. "A more pleasing choice than vinegar."

They exited, squinting into the blazingly bright late morning sun. "Thank you for this morning," Sabina said, kissing and hugging Portia. "I needed this relaxation, but more importantly, someone to share my findings."

Portia squeezed her hand. "Thank you for listening to me about Dio. I hope you find who killed him."

"My father arrested Yechiel for the murder. I led Zarmig there inadvertently."

"Inadvertently?"

"That's another story. The inspectors had found a note on Dionysius's body with circumstantial evidence pointing to Yechiel. I went to warn him, and Zarmig followed me. Yechiel was caught planning an escape."

"Running and hiding from your father doesn't sound like an innocent man. Are you sure he's not guilty?"

"I am. He is a God-fearing man, and he would never murder someone—who didn't deserve it," she added, remembering the underground Jewish rebellion she suspected Yechiel would kill to protect.

"I would ask you not to visit the fortune teller if I thought you'd listen."

Sabina only smiled.

"Then I will be on my knees in prayer until I see you safe this afternoon."

The women hugged again and stepped into their waiting litters, closing the curtains.

TWENTY-TWO

Sabina climbed the familiar stairs. Amisi followed, stopping to look behind her every few steps. Sabina waved at her from the first-floor landing. "Dawdling will only prolong the visit."

Amisi pinched her lips together but caught up to her on the second floor. Reaching the third floor, they passed the empty room where the children had been. The building groaned, then settled into an unnerving silence. Sabina stopped at the torn colored curtain.

"Cassandra?" Sabina expected to hear the fortune teller's acknowledgment before she announced herself, but silence greeted them. "Cassandra, it's Sabina. I'm sorry I didn't make an appointment." Nothing.

"She is not here." Amisi huffed in relief. "We cannot stay. We don't know how long she will be gone. Days?"

"She has nowhere to go. We can wait."

Amisi opened her mouth to protest, but Sabina raised a finger for quiet. She shook her head and squinted down the dark hallway. Something felt different from her previous visits. She tugged at the curtain and peeked inside. The oil lamp had burned out, and the small front room was lit only by a sliver of daylight gleaming behind the back curtain. She allowed her eyes to adjust to the gloom. Empty.

The incense had burned out. The odors of the insula had invaded the room, decay, rat excrement, human sweat. Sabina stepped into the room.

"You told me she was a private person. You are trespassing," Amisi hissed from the hallway.

Sabina sucked in her breath and edged farther into the room. Her gaze darted around the space, peering into the murky haze. Yes, Cassandra would know Sabina had been here. Somehow, she would know.

The table sat askew, and Cassandra's stool lay on its side. The bleached bones and their ebony box lay strewn across the floor. A scratching sound sent her whirling around.

Amisi had crept into the room. She looked at the scattered bones. Her eyes grew wide. "We should not be here."

Would someone have dared to rob the witch? Sabina walked to the side of the table where Cassandra had sat. She felt under the tabletop. A small built-in nook held a cloth bag. She pulled out the bag she had given Cassandra. Sabina jiggled the coin bag, feeling the coins' familiar weight and sound. She looked at the back curtain.

Amisi shook her head. Her nostrils flared, her tightly clamped lips losing color.

Sabina dropped the bag of coins.

It took one step to reach the curtain and one second to jerk it aside.

Sunlight from a tiny window flooded the back room. Cassandra lay on her back, her neck twisted at an impossible angle. Her face was exposed, and her eyes were wide open, staring but not seeing. A pool of blood encircled her head. A thin mattress had soaked up some of the blood her hair and tunic could not absorb. Her head scarf hung from a nail on the wall. Shattered glass bottles, a fractured clay cup, and broken pottery littered the floor under an empty shelf.

Sabinas's throat muscles tighten. She couldn't move.

Amisi bumped into her. "What is it?" She shrieked.

Sabina swallowed and opened her mouth, but nothing came out. She staggered into the room, her trembling legs giving out as she crumpled beside the body. Who would have done this? The local thugs? An unhappy customer?

And then another thought pierced her. Had she led her father to Cassandra as she had Yechiel? Had he found out she suspected Cassandra was her sister? How badly would her father have wanted to permanently rid himself of a child he couldn't bear to acknowledge? Enough to kill? He'd intended the baby girl to die years ago, after all. Where grief should have been, there was only a hollow numbness. What had she done?

Amisi hissed into her ear. "Get up, now. We must leave."

"But I—"

"No buts." Amisi clawed at her arm. "The killer could still be in this lice-infested hovel."

"Look at her. Do you see her face? Why would someone—"

"You are babbling. I see a dead woman, her neck broken, and blood. I see nothing but danger. I don't know why I let you talk me into this. Now get up." Amisi tugged at Sabina's arm, tearing her mantle loose from her shoulders. "For the sake of your God and mine. We have to go. Now!"

Sabina rose, the stupor of yesterday returning. Her voice was faint, barely audible. "Is she the baby you remember? Is she my sister?"

Amisi pulled at Sabina's hand. "The killer…"

Sabina stared at the pattern of blood that had pooled on the floor. She reached down and felt the dried outer edge. "The killer is gone."

"What if your father finds out?" Amisi wailed.

"I have to tell him." Maybe accuse him, but first… "We came here for a reason." Sabina tugged her mantle from Amisi's clutches and knelt again beside Cassandra. "I won't leave until you view her face."

Amisi rocked back and forth, kneading a fistful of fabric from her tunic. "He does not want us here. We must go."

"Father?"

"No." Amisi's face was white. "The spirit."

"Look at her. Look at Cassandra."

Amisi shivered and stepped around Sabina. Sabina plucked at Cassandra's shawl tangled around her shoulders and neck, pulling it aside. She exposed bruises on her neck and the birth stain on her cheek trailing down her jaw.

Amisi's rapid breathing drew closer. "I see. Now we go." The panicked squeal pierced Sabina's ear.

There was nothing Sabina could do for Cassandra. It was silly, but she straightened the loose shawl, its tassels trailed in blood, arranging it in place. She spread it, covering Cassandra's arms as if tucking in a child for the night. A flash of color on the lifeless wrist caught her eye. A bracelet woven in colored thread peaked from beneath Cassandra's shawl. She lifted Cassandra's hand and fingered the band.

Amisi gasped behind her. "What are you doing? Leave her."

Sabina tugged. The thread tightened. Cassandra's arm rose as Sabina wrenched until the circlet broke free. Cassandra's arm thudded to the floor. Sabina balled the broken fibers tightly in her fist as she rose.

"Ayii, stealing from the dead," Amisi shrieked. "Her ghost will haunt you."

A chill wafted through the room, dropping the temperature despite the sun beating outside. Sabina shivered. "No, her daemon will."

Amisi's eyes pleaded as she half-shoved, half-pulled Sabina toward the door.

Sabina forced herself to move. Staggering forward, with Amisi stepping on her heels, she passed the table and overturned stool. She took a last look at the scattered bones, leaving them to reveal Cassandra's fate.

Sabina put her hand on the jumpy Amisi. "Father must be alerted. It's a murder."

"Your father can't know we were here." Amisi's gaze skittered to a young woman sitting on a stoop across the street nursing a baby. The woman watched, her neck stretching toward them. "We should never have come here."

"I will send an anonymous note. Father won't find out," she said, with a lingering thought that he may already know. Had she been followed on a previous visit? Had she caused Cassandra's death? She didn't want to think her father would kill an innocent person. Except for abandoning her sisters, she had always believed he was honorable. He carried out his magisterial duties with ruthless honesty and integrity, values she had witnessed in few others. How could he have discovered Cassandra might be his daughter? Sabina had just found her two days ago.

Amisi's eyes were wide, her face still pale. "We need to go home before someone discovers the body and us."

"I can't go home yet. Portia is meeting me at Dionysius's house, and I'm sure Cassandra's murder is tied to that family." Once Zarmig told her father she had encountered Mordax the day before, any chance to speak to the family would be over.

Amisi sighed and leaped in relief when Sabina ordered her home.

Sabina's racing heart slowed as she left the run-down neighborhood. Her cheeks bore the salt of dried tears she hadn't realized she'd shed. She had kept her emotions harnessed, her mind clear, afraid if she didn't, she'd miss clues at the murder scene. Did that make her heartless? Was she more like her father than she wanted to admit? No. Her grief would break through after she found Cassandra's killer.

The walk to Dionysius's allowed her to review what she'd seen. Cassandra's room, clothing, and her body. Had the killer left clues to his violent act? She said *he* acted because she couldn't imagine a woman had the strength to strangle and break Casandra's neck, especially if she had fought back. The blood was a sign of a struggle. Someone desperately wanted Cassandra dead, and she was convinced that Cassandra's and Dionysius's murders were connected.

She needed to find out how.

TWENTY-THREE

I was getting worried," Portia greeted Sabina as she arrived at Dionysius's home.

"I'd wish I could say you had no need, but…" Sabina choked, trying to voice the horror she had just encountered. "Cassandra is dead."

Portia stared at her blankly.

Sabina repeated. "Cassandra is…"

"I heard," Portia's breath came in gasps. "Did you…were you…what if you…"

"I'm unharmed, frightened, and more determined than ever to investigate Dio's family."

"You think one of them might have killed her?" Portia's voice rose in surprise.

"I have no proof. She was dead when Amisi and I arrived. Somebody broke her neck."

Portia gasped and wrapped Sabina tightly in a hug. "I said prayers for your spiritual safety. I did not imagine you were in physical danger."

"Your prayers covered both. Thank you." She shivered, remembering the ominous cold in Cassandra's rooms. "May I send one of your litter bearers to my father with a note? There's no need to tell him who sent it."

"Why don't you want him to know you found the body?" Portia questioned with concern.

"I will tell him, eventually."

"A murderer roams the streets. You are being reckless," Portia chided.

"Oh, look," Sabina nudged Portia motioning with her head across the street and changing the subject. "That is Otho."

He leaned against the wall of the house. His gaze nailed to an upper balcony at the far end of Dionysius's villa. Sabina followed his gaze and caught the movement of someone on the balcony with Diana's mousy brown hair.

Loukas opened the door. "I've been demoted to door slave." He smiled and ushered them into the atrium, where the household slaves lined up before Ursula.

Ursula patrolled like a Roman general ordering a disorganized unit of conscripted soldiers. She directed the higher-ranking slaves, wearing white cotton tunics, to the front of the chaotic line and a lowly kitchen worker, a child of six or seven in brown wool, to the end. She caught sight of her visitors and pointed at Sabina. "Stay here. I'm doing Paris's work for him again."

Portia gestured toward the garden. "I'm here to see Diana."

Ursula glared. "You can wait with Loukas." Ursula waved to an alcove where Loukas had retired, a bored look on his face.

Portia's nostrils flared as she sucked her breath in but moved to sit beside him.

Sabina sat on Loukas's other side and whispered. "Are you aware Otho is outside?"

Loukas nodded. "Ursula has forbidden Otho to enter the house until after the funeral. She can't ban Paris's new business partner forever, but even Paris seems to understand now is not the time for Otho's over-zealous courting. Poor Diana's been hiding in her room after Otho grabbed her hand this morning and wouldn't release her until I threatened him."

"An unpleasant scene," Sabina said.

Portia leaned over. "I heard she called off the engagement."

Loukas grunted. "Otho is unwilling to let her go. I can't tell if he's following his father's orders or if it's a crude display of his affections. He produced a poem given to him by Diana a month ago. She declared her undying devotion, love, and fidelity. A young girl's idealistic drivel." Loukas flicked his hand dismissively.

"Mordax will use it to reinforce his claim on the marriage contract," Sabina said.

"Most likely," Loukas said. "In the meantime, Otho pines away outside with the tenacity of a boa constrictor. Ursula's afraid his fervent resolve may win Diana back."

"If I can speak to her," Portia leaned over. "Perhaps I can dissuade her. Diana asked me to help her with writing her father's poem."

Loukas frowned and stretched out his legs, crossing his ankles. "After her outburst at the exhibition, I'm surprised she's still writing one. Work to keep her spitefulness from being the chief entertainment at the burial."

"Ursula looks occupied." Portia rose and whispered to Sabina. "We can slip away."

"I believe Ursula wanted to speak to Sabina." Loukas straightened, planting his feet on the floor.

Sabina looked pleadingly at her friend. Portia sighed and sat down.

A man Sabina didn't recognize wore an official toga with a thin border of purple. He was reading from a large scroll. "If any person wishes to continue working here as a freedman, you may petition Titos. Titos has refused his freedom and will be promoted within the ranks of the household to Ursula's private secretary."

"Gnaeus Gratus," Loukas answered the question on Sabina's face. "Dio's lawyer is executing the decrees of the will. Upon Dionysius's death, all household slaves will be set free."

"Manumission," Portia repeated.

Loukas nodded.

Gnaeus continued. "Compensation based on the value of your past and future service is non-negotiable." Titos hefted a large pile of cloth onto the floor next to a jumble of new sandals. He pulled out a tunic, held it up, discerned its size, and began distributing tunics to each household slave. "You are entitled to one new tunic, a pair of sandals, one week's worth of bread, and a generous week's wages of seven silver denarii."

Paris stormed past Loukas, tripping on his outstretched legs. He turned and glared at the Loukas. "What is this?"

"Ursula left messages for you the last three days that you needed to distribute the slaves' new clothing before the funeral procession," Loukas said.

"You had no right to proceed without me." Paris turned to Gnaeus. "I am head of this household, not her." Paris glared at Ursula. "This is my responsibility."

"You're right." Ursula stepped back with a flip of her wrist. "Please take over the supervision duties. Titos has pages of positions that need filling immediately. If you want to eat, I advise putting a cook at the top of your search priorities."

"Do not advise me." Paris glared at Ursula, his face turning dark. "I order everyone back to their duties. I will deal with this matter later."

Gnaeus cleared his throat. "I'm sorry, sir. We cannot wait. Every freed or retained slave is required to participate in the funeral procession tomorrow. I must file the tax documents today."

"Freed? Today?" Paris's eyebrows drew together. "I don't understand."

The lawyer flourished to the scroll. "Your father has followed the customary tradition of manumission. He entrusted his last will and testament to me, and I am supervising."

"You may continue then, as long it is you and not her," Paris glowered at Ursula. "I have other work to do. I don't have time to deal with this, this…" Paris waved his arms at three slaves, tossing sandals about as they sized up the leather closest to their foot length.

"If I might detain you one moment. We appear to be short one slave," Gnaeus pointed to a line on his ledger.

Paris glared at the lawyer. "I'm sure whoever it is must be hiding somewhere to get out of doing work. They'll turn up when they get hungry."

"You would know." Ursula's catlike smile brushed over Paris.

Gnaeus looked at his list. "The ledger lists a male slave, purchased shortly before your father's death."

"I have no dealings with kitchen scum who clean." Paris's eyes narrowed. "Give me that." He ripped the scroll from the lawyer's hands. "Where, where is his name?"

Gnaeus cleared his throat again and pointed to a line on the ledger. "It's recorded here, Ferocianus, male slave, twenty-five years of age, health excellent, occupation, gladiator, purchased two months before your father's death."

"I know when he was purchased!" Paris shouted.

"Why would he buy a gladiator when he had started the library two months ago?" Sabina directed her question to Portia, but it came out louder than she intended.

Paris turned on her, puffing up. "You don't have to own a ludus to buy a gladiator. Ferocianus can train in any rented arena and still win prize money from his matches."

Sabina tipped her head. Was Ferocianus the key to Dionysius's change of attitude that Cassandra had related? Had Dionysius been planning the ludus all along behind everyone's back?

Paris confronted Gnaeus. "Father made a mistake. You can't free slaves that are newly purchased."

"Your father states all his slaves within the city's walls are to be freed. His farm slaves and other laborers are excluded, of course."

"Then categorize Ferocianus as a farm worker. I demand you exclude Ferocianus." Paris whipped the scroll around. It crackled as it unfurled. "He is the key to father's legacy."

Gnaeus's face began to turn red. "I don't have that authority to change his will."

Paris paced. "Ferocianus is an asset included in a business contract."

Gnaeus's jowls shook in tandem with his head bobs. "If you are referring to the ludus contract, Ferocianus's purchase preceded your father's signing of the contract. Legally, your father's will holds more weight than the recent business agreement." Gnaeus reached for the scroll.

"You don't understand. The contract depends on Ferocianus winning money."

"I understand perfectly," Gnaeus said. "You will have to find another fighter for your business venture."

"Tell that to my business partner Titus Mordax. Have you heard of him? A renowned gladiator, twenty-four kills without a single mark on himself, an unsurpassed fighter."

"Perhaps he could take Ferocianus's place in the arena," Gnaeus chuckled.

Paris's jaw flexed as he swung around on Gnaeus. "Mordax is the trainer."

Gnaeus held up his hands. "A bit of humor." His jowls stopped wobbling. His voice changed from consolatory to imperious. "Now, if you tell me where I can find this Ferocianus, I'd like to get measurements for his new clothing."

"Stop." Paris's face splotched a bright red, his blond hair the crowning glow to a flaming torch. "Buying Ferocianus was my idea. Father hadn't even heard of him. I found him. I purchased him. He's mine."

Gnaeus wobbled forward. "You said your father made the transaction."

"I won the auction bid," Paris said.

"Do you have a record of making the payment?" Gnaeus asked.

"Of course, Father kept the bill of sale," Paris said scornfully.

"I will look." Gnaeus walked over to a wooden box filled with papyrus sheets.

"Where did you get the money?" Ursula raised a skeptical eyebrow. "Don't say your race winnings."

Loukas leaned forward, his eyes intent. "Dio and I had many conversations about your gambling debts, young man."

Paris rocked from foot to foot. His expression shifted with each second that ticked by.

"Paris?" Ursula prodded.

"I didn't need money. At the auction, after I won the bid. Father guaranteed the payment with his signet ring."

"If your father hadn't heard about Ferocianus, why were you at the auction?" Sabina asked, confused. "When did he decide to buy him?"

Paris shuffled his feet, looking at the ceiling and then the floor.

"Ah." Loukas leaned toward Paris. "Dio didn't decide, did he, Paris? You took his ring without his permission."

"I borrowed it."

"No one borrows a signet ring." Ursula's voice was sharp and accusatory.

"How did you get his ring?" Sabina chanced another question, knowing this wasn't her place. "Cassandra said he never took it off."

"She was correct," Loukas said.

Paris scrunched his nose at Ursula. "Oh, he took it off. Quite often, in fact. When he and my stepmother were entangled in…"

"You slimy little snake," Ursula spat. "You stole it when Dio and I were making love."

"I had plenty of opportunities." Paris smirked.

"I wouldn't brag about that right now, Paris," Loukas warned.

"I didn't steal it. I told Father about the purchase and returned the ring immediately." Paris crossed his arms. "Father realized Ferocianus was an investment worth keeping—after we discussed it."

"Where is the ring now?" Sabina asked.

"It was destroyed and lost in the rubble." Ursula's voice was flat. "When they recovered Dio's body, his hands were crushed…unrecognizable."

"I found the receipt." Gnaeus waved a papyrus sheet he'd just pulled out. "It has your father's signature as the purchaser of the gladiator."

"I told you I signed it." Paris appeared unconcerned that he was confessing to forgery.

"The signature and your father's will stands as is. Ferocianus was your father's property and will stay on the manumission list. Unless Ferocianus refuses freedom and chooses to remain in servitude."

"I'll contest the will. Ferocianus has not served our family for the legally required time."

Gnaeus put a finger to his mouth, stood, and walked toward Paris, presenting the bill of sale. "You make a valid point a magistrate will consider."

Paris grabbed the papyrus receipt from Gnaeus's hand and glared at

Ursula. "Ferocianus is mine. You will not steal Father's dream. The law is on my side." Fuming, he clutched the papyrus and stalked from the room.

Gnaeus waved his hand. "Let us continue. I want to get home before dark."

Portia let out a defiant huff and rose. "I'm going to find Diana."

Sabina glanced toward Ursula, who had stepped between two arguing slaves, each clutching one sandal. Unable to catch Ursula's attention, Sabina shrugged and padded after Portia.

Paris had returned his father's ring accompanied by a costly bill-of-sale and Dionysius's signet guaranteed payment. The gladiator wasn't returnable. Cassandra said Dionysius was agitated around this time. Had building a ludus been the solution to his unexpected ownership of a prized gladiator? If so, it still didn't provide a clue to his and Cassandra's killer.

But a connection existed somewhere. And she would find it.

TWENTY-FOUR

D o you know where Diana's bedroom room is?" Sabina asked. "I believe it's off the Celestial Garden." Portia strolled toward the same peristyle garden where they had previously met Diana. "I had been friends with Diana's mother and continued to visit Diana and Paris after Dio and Ursula were married, until Ursula requested that I stop. I received an occasional dinner invitation from Dio, which kept me in touch with the children."

They strolled under the canopied portico protected from the late afternoon heat. Doors and hallways punctuated the walkway surrounding the interior garden with its fountains, fishponds, and arbor benches. The scalloped leaves of potted plants flanking the doorways softened the stark black and white geometric floor tiles.

An argument echoed from an open passageway as they neared the end of the garden. Raised voices, their strong emotion clear, even if the words weren't. Ahead, at the end of the hallway, Paris stood outside a door, arms planted firmly on his hips. Diana faced him, hands gripping each side of the door frame, barring his entrance. Neither sibling noticed their approach.

"Now, do you believe me?" Paris's voice radiated exasperation. "I just spoke to him. He wants you. He loves you. Look at him captive outside the house. It's not like he couldn't have other women who would appreciate his attention."

"I don't know." Diana's voice faltered.

"You were upset when you broke the marriage contract, accusing Otho of wanting your money. Now look what you've done. Mordax will sue us over your betrayal. Your childish tantrum has handed your dowry over to Otho's father."

Diana's hands dropped from the doorframe. Her voice was pleading and constricted. "I didn't betray anyone."

Paris leaned in, his face almost touching his sister's. His voice lowered. "I doubt I can find another suitor without your dowry to entice them."

Diana's shoulders slumped.

"Paris!" Portia skirted a sizeable potted palm and stormed toward the young man. "Stop threatening. Diana, don't listen to your brother."

Paris scowled at Portia over his shoulder but stepped back, raising his hands in surrender. "I don't want to argue."

Diana's voice faltered. "I'll ask Cassandra. She will know what to do."

"Cassandra lied to you, Diana." Paris huffed as if explaining to a child. "She told you Otho wanted your money, and you believed her. You're too gullible."

"Cassandra didn't say it was Otho. Next time, I won't assume." Diana looked miserable.

"There won't be a next time, Diana," Paris snapped back. "The witch has told her last lie."

Sabina's heart skipped a beat. "What do you mean told her last lie?" Sabina's thoughts returned to the room she had left barely an hour ago. Cassandra's body sprawled on the floor, the blood pooling around her head. Did Paris know? Why would he say that otherwise?

Paris spun around at Sabina's question. He shrugged. "Rumors, that's all. Slaves were gossiping like they always do."

"Gossiping about what?" Sabina knew slaves' gossip could fly across the city faster than her pigeons. Was it possible someone besides her, Amisi, and the murderer knew about Cassandra?

Paris opened his mouth as if to say more but clamped it shut, pushing past Portia and Sabina. He stopped before exiting the hallway and called. "You're running out of time, Diana."

"You're the one running out of time." Diana stepped out of her room. "Have you finished writing your funeral speech?"

His muffled response sounded something like, "Stop bothering me," before he disappeared.

Diana turned to Portia. "Paris is giving the main commemoration to honor Father. He puts everything off, and then it's too late." Diana bit her thumbnail. "Was Otho outside when you arrived?"

Sabina nodded. "He was waiting and watching you from across the street."

"He tried to talk to me today. I haven't communicated with him since I ended the engagement. Paris said I should speak to him."

"I don't think that's necessary or wise," Portia said.

"You heard what Paris said. I don't have much time." Diana's shoulders slumped. "What if Paris can't find someone for me to marry? What if Otho changes his mind?"

"You and Paris will have plenty of time to consider your options after your father's funeral," Portia said.

"Portia is giving good advice," Sabina said. "Rushing into a lifelong commitment is ill-advised." And in Sabina's case, ill-fated. Avoiding spinsterhood created a strong motivator, causing her to accept the older Xeno's marriage offer, disregarding Portia's warnings, her bishop Apollos, and her heart.

Portia led Diana into her bedroom. Sabina stood in the doorway watching the two women sitting on the bed, her thoughts jumping between Mordax's threat to sue over the broken betrothal, Cassandra's murder, and Paris's enigmatic comment.

Portia held Diana's hands. "I was sad to hear you were angry with your father before he died. I wondered if you'd want to talk about it?"

"I don't know what to say. His love was built on a lie. His apologies, presents, and hugs were to buy my forgiveness."

"Some hurts seem unforgivable, but your father is gone. Forgiving him is for your benefit. Your blame and anger reduce your joy." Portia repeated her advice, couched in her love.

Diana sniffed. "Portia, I'm so confused. One minute, I hate Father, and the next, I want to ask his advice about Otho, life, and even my poem. Now, I'll never know if he loved me."

"That is what you're telling yourself." Portia's voice radiated comfort. "But he told me he loved you with all his heart. He had no reason to lie to me." Portia wrapped Diana in her arms, pulling her close and stroking her hair.

Diana sniffled into Portia's shoulder. "I've been angry at him for so long. And now that he's dead, I can't stop." Diana pulled away, sitting straight. "He was so selfish."

"I don't disagree, but aren't we all selfish sometimes? Surely, you can name one good thing about your father."

Diana shrugged. "We played a game where he tried to make me laugh, and I tried not to." Diana's lips pursed into a half smile.

"Who won?"

"He made me giggle. Every time."

"One happy memory can start to change your thinking and your feelings…if you let it. You told Sabina he'd written you a letter."

Diana sniffled and wiped her nose. "I don't have to read it to know what he wrote. I'll just get mad at another apology."

"It sounds like he was attempting to heal the divide between you," Portia offered.

Sabina stepped into the room. "His letter might answer the feelings you're struggling with." And provide a clue into Dionysius's life and struggle before he died. He may have written about the person who wanted him dead.

"It might help with your poem," Portia coaxed.

"I'm going to burn it." Diana choked out a sob and started crying. Sabina stifled a moan, imagining her investigation dissolving in smoke.

Portia reached out and stroked Diana's arm. "There will come a time when you want to read what he wrote, when you're ready to forgive him. Remember, I'm here whenever you need me."

After several minutes, Diana's crying turned to quiet hiccups and deep breaths.

Sabina remembered her eight-year-old self, wrapped in the security of Portia's arms after Sabina's mother had died. She imagined the solace Portia had offered to so many suffering over the years. The spiritual gift of comfort was strong in her friend.

"I believe you asked me to help with your father's memorial," Portia said.

Diana tentatively reached for a wax tablet. "Women aren't allowed to speak at the funeral, but Paris is letting me read my poem at the cremation."

Sabina locked eyes with Portia, remembering Loukas's concerns about Diana's animosity toward Dio. How would Diana choose to memorialize her father?

Diana picked up the wax tablet lying on the bed and passed it to Portia with trembling hands. "I'd like you to read out loud. I want it to be perfect. I've erased and revised it a hundred times."

"I'm honored." Portia scanned the tablet and read:

"They say, what they like, let them say it, I don't care

"Go on, love me, it does you good."

Portia blinked, pausing thoughtfully. "It is succinct, direct, and… authentic," she critiqued solemnly.

Diana sucked in a deep breath and exhaled slowly. "Direct, I like that. I imagined it as if father were speaking."

Portia nodded. "I can envision him delivering this."

Diana turned to Sabina. "What do you think?"

Sabina hesitated, speechless. It was nothing like the poets Ovid, Homer, and Pindar, whom she had studied. Modern poets mimicked the old masters, their commissions based on how closely they imitated the age-old traditions. Sabina asked Portia to reread the lines. Sabina pinched her brows together while listening. "Original. Your father would know you wrote it to honor a unique man."

"Yes, that's it." Diana took the tablet back with a shy half-smile. "It's not sentimental or romantic. I know that wasn't my father."

Portia nodded. "Will you add more?"

"Would you help me?"

Portia smiled. "Of course."

Sabina excused herself. Neither woman noticed, head-to-head absorbed in their work. Now might be a good time to answer Ursula's summons. She wandered back toward the atrium.

She couldn't let Portia's emotional involvement with the family blind her to the deceptions swirling around this family. As duplicitous as Sabina felt, she had to focus on discovering the person with a motive to murder Dionysius and Cassandra.

Paris had said, *The witch has told her last lie.* Was there any other explanation other than the one swirling in her mind? How else could she interpret his statement except that he knew Cassandra was dead? If so, how did he know? Had Paris murdered her?

Was Diana truly unaware of Cassandra's murder? She hadn't questioned Paris's strange comment. Diana seemed an improbable suspect because of the murderer's timing and physical strength. But it became possible if an expendable suitor agreed to be her accomplice.

Sabina calculated the forty-five-minute walk from Cassandra's insula to Dionysius's house. One would have to climb the stairs and enter Cassandra's bedroom to see the body. She added the minutes. If a gossiping slave had discovered the body, it must have been shortly before Sabina and Amisi had arrived. It was unlikely, but possible, that they ran to Dionysius's home with the news. She needed to find out who else in the household knew about the murder.

Her father would be able to tell the time of death after examining the body.

Her father. Portia's words came unbidden. *Some hurts seem unforgivable. Forgiving your father is for your benefit. Blame and anger reduce your joy.* Was her condemnation of her father any different from Diana's? Did the original injustice matter if the result was the same, a lack of peace and broken families? What had Diana said? She had hated her father for so long that she couldn't stop.

Could one happy memory start to change her thinking and her feelings? Would she let it?

TWENTY-FIVE

The walkway tiles had absorbed the afternoon heat and now radiated it back. She passed a slave scooping water from the fountain and watering the plants. If she were lucky, most of the slaves would be available to question while Ursula and Dionysius's lawyer sorted out the future implications of their freedom.

Sabina scanned the atrium. Titos and Gnaeus stood heads together, holding the end of a scroll, scrutinizing the will. Ursula was gone. Sabina checked Loukas's alcove. Empty. The ranks of slaves had fallen out of line, milling around in restrained celebration. She heard bits of conversation but nothing about a murdered fortune teller.

Two women compared their identical new tunics. A toothless man with a wide grin tightened the stiff leather thongs of his new sandals. Others shuffled back and forth, looking baffled. Manumission and its exhilarating freedom to make life choices and open doors of possibilities weren't for everyone. Taking responsibility could be terrifying for those whose every decision had been made for them from birth.

For better or worse, most people here had never made a life-changing decision. Could they support themselves in an unforgiving city? Would they be able to find shelter? Afford clothing? Eat? Would today's distributed bread and tunics be the last they possessed?

Those with marketable talents, training, or physical health had limited opportunities to support themselves. If Dionysius's household needed their skills, they would be expected to perform the same duties as before but with pay. All newly freed servants were now bound as clients obligated to support the Dionysius family in return for their favors and support.

Titos was arguing with a gnarled, humpbacked older man. The elderly, or slaves with inadequate skills, had few options. They would starve on the streets of Ephesus or fall prey to worse situations. Sabina's grandparents had kept slaves when they became ill, disabled, or old. Her mother and father had continued the practice, and Roman custom supported it. What obligations would Paris's generosity, humanity, and finances accept?

But that was not her concern. She had other business with Titos.

No, Titos had not heard any gossip, rumors, or news that Ursula and Dio's fortune teller was dead. He was shocked. Was it true? How had he not been informed?

Sabina broke free, escaping Titos's nosey follow-up interrogation. She approached the two women trying out their new tunics. Their bored indifference to her questioning told her what she needed to know. After speaking to several more slaves and servants, Sabina found no one who had heard of a dead or murdered fortune teller. She believed them. All appeared bored or baffled by her questions. Not the reactions of people lying or hiding a secret.

Gnaeus, Dio's lawyer, flourished his quill across the scroll. "You may go." He addressed Titos. "I have all the required statements, minus one gladiator. I will follow up with Paris."

Sabina caught up to Titos. "Do you know where your mistress is? She wanted to speak to me." And I to her.

"My mistress has retired." He pointed to the room off the atrium where Sabina had first met Ursula. Sabina approached the door and heard voices. She raised her hand to knock and caught a muffled, "This has to be kept hidden."

Sabina pressed her ear against the door.

Ursula's voice reverberated through the door panels. "How was this leaked so quickly? We took pains to keep it a secret."

"It could have been anyone. People will begin speculating soon." It was Loukas. She froze, holding her breath.

"I'm worried. The timing couldn't be worse."

"Paris will use it against you. We have no defense."

Sabina's stomach churned. No defense for murder?

"May I help you?"

Sabina jerked her ear from the door and smacked into a glaring Titos.

"I'm just…" Sabina attempted a smile but managed only a grimace. She turned rapidly, fist raised, and rapped a quick thump before she poked her head in. Ursula and Loukas sat holding hands, expressing no embarrassment or remorse.

But then killers rarely expressed remorse and never embarrassment.

Ursula sat up and leaned forward. "Ah, Sabina, come, come." She let go of Loukas's hand and pointed to a seat. "I hope you have good news for me?"

"Good news?" Or news you already know. Sabina gritted her teeth to keep from lashing out at the lovers. Don't underestimate her, warned both her father and Portia. Had Ursula tricked her into spying on her stepchildren? And had Sabina's grave error in judgment led the murderer to Cassandra? Perhaps Sabina had shared something threatening with Ursula that had ended Cassandra's life? She would review her conversations when she could think clearly, which was impossible at the moment. After questioning the household slaves, she didn't believe gossip of the fortune teller's murder had randomly spread to this home an hour after Sabina had discovered the fortune teller dead.

The only way a family member could know of Cassandra's murder was if they were involved.

Visions of Cassandra's broken neck and blood-soaked hair spun through her thoughts. Poor timing? Kept hidden? Ursula's and Loukas's admissions had cleared Paris and Diana of suspicion. Would Ursula confess?

"I had hoped to speak to Cassandra. She wasn't available." Sabina choked the words out, watching Ursula.

"The fortune teller, why?" Ursula and Loukas looked at each other. Ursula frowned. "You said Cassandra shared her insights and was no longer relevant to Dio's murder. You told me she provided no help when you spoke to her the last time."

"I thought she was valuable to you." Sabina noted the flip of Ursula's wrist and Loukas's easy dismissal.

"She's gifted, but she is not the only one blessed by the gods," Ursula said.

Loukas turned to Sabina. "We were discussing Paris. He should not have run off when so many details needed to be decided. Dio's death means he is no longer without responsibilities." Loukas lied. That hadn't been the conversation Sabina had overheard.

"Did you speak to the petulant heir?" Ursula picked up a grape, inspected it, and returned it to the bowl. "Where's Titos? Have him throw these out. They're soft. Tell the cook she'll be out on the street if it happens again."

A chill ran through Sabina's body. Had Ursula disposed of Cassandra as easily? How did one learn to purge people from their lives like this? Or were humans born with that ability and had to learn compassion and restraint?

"Portia and I spoke to him." Sabina struggled to maintain a neutral expression and pretend she hadn't heard their exchange. *How was this found out so quickly? We took pains to keep it a secret.* A defense for murdering Cassandra? Watching the lovers made her stomach churn. "I have to go. It's late."

"Don't be ridiculous." Ursula's superior tone halted any disagreement. "You're here. You will stay."

"I will come back tomorrow." Sabina barely choked the words out before being assailed by an urgent need to get away from Ursula. She turned and ran out of the house.

She would be back, and her father would be with her.

TWENTY-SIX

When she arrived home, Felix informed her that her father was attending a dinner and would be home late. He would return tired and not receptive to the urgent plea burning in Sabina. Justice would have to wait until morning.

Amisi surprised her at her bedroom door and impatiently pulled her aside. "I saw Zarmig receive your note. I followed him to Cassandra's insula."

"You did what?" Sabina looked up sharply. Amisi had clearly recovered from the trauma of finding the body. "Did he see you?"

"Of course not," Amisi's smug self-confidence had returned in full.

It was best if her father didn't trace the anonymous tip to her. She would choose when to explain how she discovered the dead fortune teller and what she'd been doing there, without revealing Amisi's involvement.

Sabina quizzed her nurse until she grudgingly admitted Cassandra's facial mark was like that of the baby she had left to die. If Amisi knew more, she would not say. Sabina dismissed her for the night.

Sabina sat at the small table by her bed. Her carved ivory jewelry box, inherited from her mother, displayed shimmering gold bracelets, silver earrings, and pairs of brass shoulder clips for her stolas. She stared past her grandmother's copper ring, focusing on the limp curl of multi-colored cotton threads next to it, braided strands wrapped around her wrist twenty-eight years ago on the day she was born. Its elaborate pattern held a legacy passed down through generations of Amisi's female ancestors. Its creator recited an ancient incantation while braiding each colored thread. The black strand for fertility, the green for prosperity, the yellow beauty, and the red for health and longevity.

The fibers of a second braided circle drooped between Sabina's fingers. Its colors diminished and barely discernable. The black was faded to gray, the green to beige, the yellow almost white, and the red strands to pink. Sabina had torn this bracelet from Cassandra's lifeless wrist.

From the beginning of time, poor women had woven spells into talismans made of cheap cotton and flax, while wealthy women spun safeguards of silver, gold, and copper threads to guard their children against the perils of life and the certainties of death. But the braid of Amisi's Egyptian ancestors was unique, a specific pattern woven with each color and each protective incantation. With its diagonal crosses, the complex pattern braided over and under with vertical and horizontal stripes ended with two tiny carved wooden beads tying the individual threads together—identical to the bracelet nesting in Sabina's jewelry box.

The newborn talisman appeared to be proof that Cassandra had been born in this house, even though Amisi refused to admit she had made the charm.

Most adolescents outgrew these childhood charms and threw them away. Sabina knew she should have rid herself of the pagan talisman, but her mother had let her keep it, so she had stashed it away. Why Cassandra wore hers was easier to guess. It would be the only link to her origins, her past, and her mother. If her birth remained a mystery, a woven thread would always connect her to who she was and where she came from. Sabina tightened her fist around the strands, crushing them into a ball.

She couldn't talk to God about it. Not yet. The pain and anger churned, igniting a volatile mix. She could only rail at Him and the world's injustice. The events that led her to her sister and then took her away a second time felt unbearable. The prophets had argued with God. Moses and even Solomon had confronted God about the wisdom of His judgments, but Sabina didn't want to argue. She ached with a simple need for justice and perhaps revenge. At whom, she didn't know yet, but she promised herself she would find Cassandra's killer—starting with her obvious suspects, Ursula and Loukas. What did Cassandra know? Could she no longer be trusted to keep a secret? Could blackmail be a motive for her death? She initially suspected Paris with his knowledge of Cassandra's death. She'd changed her mind after overhearing Ursula and Loukas's near confession. Dionysius appeared more and more an obstacle to their adultery.

The couple's ties to the woman who had predicted Dio's death led Sabina to dismiss the dozens of Cassandra's other clients and her neighborhood criminals. She pushed away the depressing thought that she could be wrong.

She needed more information.

Unfortunately, her father forbade further involvement in Ursula's scheming. How could she get him to interrogate Ursula without alerting him to Cassandra's true identity? Did it matter now that she was dead?

She lay awake for hours planning and knowing nothing got by her father.

TWENTY-SEVEN

Sabina approached her father's office. A young boy neatly arranged several scrolls on a corner of a table. Her father retrieved a square scrap of papyrus from a cylinder smaller than her end finger. A report had arrived from some distant location on the leg of one of his pigeons.

"Sir." She cleared her throat. This may be her last chance...to what? Solve a murder? Free Yechiel? Leave her bedroom? "I heard Zarmig investigated the death of a fortune teller yesterday." A risk to be so direct, but after being awake half the night, she hadn't come up with anything subtle.

He didn't look up. She waited as he scrutinized the note. She counted the seconds until he finished, set it aside, and motioned for his assistant to leave. The young man placed a pen in its holder and backed out of the room.

"Are we talking about a particular fortune-teller?" her father asked.

"The fortune teller who predicted Dionysius's death."

"Who you believe is connected to Dionysius's murder?"

Sabina shuffled her feet but didn't break eye contact. Did she have enough proof to make the accusation she was about to make? "Maybe."

"She was involved in illegal activities. Why should I care about her death?"

Because she could be your daughter, Sabina bit back her sharp retort. "Don't you find the timing, only days after Dionysius's murder, suspicious? I do."

"How exactly did you hear about this murder?" He casually rolled the messenger cylinder between his fingers.

Was it time to tell him she had been in Cassandra's room shortly after the murder? That she and Amisi had missed the killer by an hour or two. Maybe not. "Paris, Dionysius's son, told me he heard about her death."

"Paris provided details?"

"Not exactly." Sabina bit her lower lip. "What did Zarmig find when he investigated?"

Her father arched an eyebrow and directed his full attention to her but didn't deny knowing about the murder scene. "Precious little. She was destitute, had no guild association, and had no family. We found some coins, which meant she wasn't robbed. Probably killed by a furious patron after delivering a disagreeable fortune."

"Cassandra never met clients in the morning—so I was told."

"Then your theory is one of the neighborhood criminals? And no one will testify against him."

"Him?"

Her father paused. "That we do know. It took strength for the brutal attack. The killer crushed her windpipe, broke her neck."

Sabina swallowed, remembering. She blinked back the tears welling in her eyes.

"Dionysius wasn't her only client in the family. Ursula was also."

He began gathering the loose scrolls. "I will not question the widow of one of the leading families in our illustrious city over the death of some street charlatan. Zarmig is waiting for me."

She couldn't let him leave. Sabina opened her mouth to protest.

He held up a staying finger. "I may stop by to offer my condolences on the death of Dionysius. You need to invent a better pretense for how you know. I never mentioned the time of the murder. I'm guessing Paris didn't either."

"No." Sabina took a deep breath. Her father had figured out the anonymous tipster. Why had she thought he wouldn't? "I visited her twice during my investigation."

"Do not call your pastime investigating. It's insulting."

She wouldn't let him bait her. Her chin trembled as she remembered the scene, the blood, her broken neck. She had to focus on her task—finding the killer. It was not the time to give him an excuse to end her search. "I was questioning Cassandra about Dionysius. I arrived at the sixth hour yesterday and found her dead. Blood from her fall was…"

"The killer slammed her head against the wall before he broke her neck."

"Dionysius's curse shall crush her bones," she murmured in a horrified whisper. Cassandra said her daemon didn't reveal her future, but she had foretold her own murder. Cassandra's spirit was a cruel master.

"What are you mumbling?"

Sabina could only stare at him. "When I found her, the blood was still fresh, though thickening. Within the hour, Paris knew Cassandra was dead."

Her father drummed his fingers. "Enough time for someone to discover her dead and have the gossip reach Paris. It is possible."

"But unlikely. Someone would have had to find her body before I arrived. Could Zarmig determine when she died?"

"From the drying blood, Zarmig estimated she had been dead two to four hours."

"Any of the family could have killed her or hired someone to. Paris was angry after Cassandra predicted Otho wanted Diana's money. Diana is having second thoughts about Otho and could have blamed Cassandra for ending her engagement. Ursula's anger had erupted once already when she stabbed Dionysius, and Loukas appears to be a pliable suitor. Even Titos might have stepped in to earn favor with his mistress. They all have motives."

"But you have no proof."

Sabina crossed her arms. Would her snooping count as evidence? "I overheard Ursula admit she was upset that some information she wanted kept secret had gotten out."

"That's it?" Her father's eyes widened. "Do you think I have nothing better to do than unleash Ursula's ire with unfounded accusations from you?"

Sabina didn't argue. "I told Ursula I was returning today. I could go with you." She held her breath. Would he refuse? Was her meddling in a real investigation not allowed?

"It appears I must find out who told Paris of Cassandra's death. And I can see no way to enter Ursula's home without speaking to her."

Sabina reasoned her father's answer was yes. He said nothing to her as she joined him, heading out the door to visit his former lover.

Titos showed Sabina and her father into a back room.

Ursula stretched languidly on a couch with Loukas lounging beside her, his eyes half-closed, opened suddenly alert.

"I see Sabina has persuaded you to take an interest in my plight," Ursula cooed, her tongue playing across her top lip.

Her father stiffened. "I have never known you to be in a plight."

Rarely had Sabina seen her father uncomfortable, and Ursula appeared to be enjoying every second of it.

"I've missed you, Catius. No one, not even Dio, could entertain me as you do." She reached out and ran a fingernail down his bare arm, leaving a white streak as he pulled his arm away. "Such stimulating conversations."

Her father coughed. "Paris heard a rumor yesterday."

Ursula sat up, and her body unfolded seductively. "I wouldn't believe everything Paris says."

"What rumor?" Loukas's expression turned serious.

"The death of Cassandra, the fortune teller," Sabina said.

Ursula looked between Sabina and her father. "Don't be ridiculous. I saw her the other day." All Ursula's playful taunting was gone. "Titos, what do you know of this? Why was I not informed of this gossip?"

Titos bobbed his head. "I heard it only this moment."

Loukas stroked his chin. "It is apparently not a rumor, which is why we enjoy Magistrate Sabinus's early morning visit."

Sabina's father addressed Ursula. "You didn't know that the fortune teller's body was found yesterday?"

"How would I if Titos didn't? We were busy with Dio's will. His lawyer was here all day. Death surrounds me." Ursula shuddered as if grasping an unfathomable idea.

It was difficult watching Loukas's and Ursula's reactions simultaneously. Sabina focused on Ursula. Genuine confusion or an act? Was this how a guilty person responded to being discovered? Sabina's father would be hard to fool, and Ursula would know it.

"How did she die?" Ursula asked.

"Someone broke her neck while strangling her," her father said.

"Barbarians." Ursula's gasp was barely audible. "Cassandra believed she was safe because people feared her curses. She said her daemon protected her."

Sabina prompted, "Perhaps you feared her daemon revealing your secrets."

The puzzlement on Ursula's face appeared genuine. "My secrets?"

"What are you suggesting?" Loukas leaned forward.

Sabina looked between Ursula's tired, kohl-rimmed eyes and Loukas's suspicious glare. "Yesterday, I overheard you saying there was something you needed to keep secret, and its discovery was inconvenient. Paris had just heard rumors of Cassandra's death."

"You were spying on me...on us." Ursula stiffened in outrage. "Why would the death of a fortune teller be inconvenient? Why would I care or want it kept secret?" Ursula's creased brow showed her bewilderment.

A tinge of doubt pricked Sabina.

Loukas was not in shock. He turned on Sabina. "You concluded that we were talking about Cassandra's death."

"No one else knew she was dead," Sabina said.

"Did I miss something?" Ursula huffed. "Are you accusing us of murder? Catius?"

Loukas burst from the couch and faced off with Sabina's father.

"And you went along with this farce? How dare you barge in with unfounded allegations. Titos, show Ursula's guests out." Loukas took a step forward, locking eyes with Sabina's father.

Sabina's father drew himself to his full height and glared back at Loukas.

Titos's gaze skittered between Loukas and Sabina's father. No one moved.

Ursula burst into laughter. "Oh, Catius, life is never dull with you. How delicious to think I am a murder suspect."

Her father's jaw flexed. "A simple explanation of what Sabina overheard will free us from inaccurate conclusions."

"We are not obliged to answer your insults," Loukas looked away.

"Oh, by the gods," Ursula stepped between the two men. "Catius dear, we were discussing a precarious investment."

"In Armenian carpets?" Sabina guessed. Marcus had enlisted many wealthy investors in his carpet venture.

Loukas smiled grimly. "Thankfully, no. I heard the ship's owner faked a shipwreck and his drowning, then absconded with the cargo. The authorities are looking for him."

"The authorities have found him." Her father's warning glare silenced Sabina. But it was unnecessary because she couldn't speak with her mind racing as fast as her heart. Amisi's rumors were true. Marcus was alive.

"Why were you trying to keep this investment secret?" Her father resumed control of the questioning.

Ursula and Loukas exchanged a glance. Ursula shrugged. "Tell him."

Loukas shifted uncomfortably. "The investment is legal, but it has developed at the inopportune week of Dio's funeral."

"It will have implications on Paris's lawsuit against me." Ursula squeezed Loukas's arm. "Loukas has been investing my money for years."

"She's doing quite well," Loukas said.

Sabina mentally rehearsed her question before blurting out another wrong conclusion. "Paris and Diana said you always asked your husband for money."

Ursula's eyes widened in mock surprise. "Don't all wives? With my money tied up, I relied on Dio to provide for my substantial daily expenses. He was generous, and now I am entitled to that same support as a grieving widow."

Minus the grieving. Sabina's thoughts weren't charitable. "That funding comes from Dio's will?"

"And why I hired you." Ursula shrugged. "Dio advised me to invest with Loukas what remained of my dowry after my last divorce. He's a magician with money. I built a healthy bank account. But I was not wealthy."

"Until now," Loukas added. "Last year, I combined a large portion of Dio's money with Ursula's in a joint venture with considerable risk—exploration of silver mines in Hispania. Dio could afford the risk and if it paid off, Ursula would become independently wealthy. You overheard us discussing yesterday's surveyors' exploratory reports from Hispania."

"The investment paid off?" Sabina asked.

"Oh yes, I no longer have to rely on Paris for my trinkets." Ursula wrapped a loose curl around a finger adorned with a sizeable amethyst ring.

"Wouldn't Paris be thrilled knowing his father's venture was successful?"

Loukas squeezed Ursula's hand. "That's the tricky part. It wasn't successful for Paris. I wrote the contract after Cassandra's prediction. Dio agreed to a partnership where should one partner die, the surviving investor would be the sole beneficiary of the mining investment."

"Dio agreed?" her father asked.

Ursula's mouth tightened, her features pinched. "At the time, Dio thought Cassandra's prediction was a joke. I did not. If Dio died, I didn't want my money controlled by Paris's whims of charity."

"The investment was death insurance," Loukas said.

Sabina's father frowned. "And now it looks as if you convinced Dio to invest his money and then killed him to reap the sole benefits of the investment. A convincing motive."

"And exactly what Paris is alleging—that I'm after the family money?" Ursula said. "Paris has no claim on the mines. But it will lend credibility to his accusations. I don't need his handouts, but I also don't want the social outcast for killing my husband for his money."

"The stigma will be the least of your problems if convicted of murder." Sabina's father raised an eyebrow.

"Had Dio not died, we would both have benefited. There are more profits than either of us could spend," Ursula said. "I had no reason to kill my husband."

"Unfortunately, there's no limit to human greed." Sabina's father looked grim. "Paris will sue. I would."

"Hence, the secret," Loukas said. "The longer we can hide the investment, the better. At least until after the funeral."

"We knew nothing of Cassandra's death," Ursula said. "Perhaps you should question Paris."

Ursula's composure was back. "Titos take Magistrate Sabinus to find Paris. Give him anything and everything he needs." She grabbed Sabina's father's hand. "Anything." She smiled.

Sabina doubted Ursula and Loukas would brazenly make up a story that could easily be disproven. Which meant they were telling the truth.

Her mistaken conclusion had been awkward. However, it had eliminated Ursula and Loukas as suspects in Cassandra's murder. She was making progress. Her father may not see it that way.

TWENTY-EIGHT

Titos led Sabina and her father toward the Celestial Garden, following the same walkway she had visited the day before with Portia. The morning sun hadn't breached the villa's walls, and the covered walkway shaded the mosaic tiles storing the cool of the previous night.

Sabina stopped her father before they entered the garden. "Has Marcus been arrested?"

"Now is not the time to talk about this." He directed a watchful gaze at Titos.

She touched his arm. "Is he being taken to Rome?" If so, she would never see him again.

"Not now," he raised his voice. Titos stopped and looked back curiously.

"I won't ask anything else. I promise," she whispered, removing her hand. Her father took a deep breath. "He will face trial in Ephesus."

"Thank you." She could have read her father's flicker of emotion as compassion if she didn't know him. Marcus had humiliated many wealthy and powerful men in Ephesus. Men who would seek revenge. She closed her eyes and prayed that Marcus had influential friends in Ephesus.

Titos gestured them forward and pointed into the garden where Diana had composed her poems. "The illustrious heir." He snorted, spun around, and hiked back the way they'd come.

Sabina stopped when her father did, taking in a cluster of three men. Paris stood at the center, gesturing in animated conversation. Otho stood at Paris's right side, although the third man had his back to her. There was no doubt who he was.

"Don't worry. I'm contesting the will." Paris's voice rose to a screech. His right hand braced against the bench's ebony trellis. In his left hand, a scroll flapped with each exclamation.

"I don't need to remind you that the gladiator is key to our contract," Otho said.

Sabina pointed. "That's Otho," she whispered to her father. "Ursula banned him from the house."

Diana was peeking from her bedroom door at the far end of the hallway. "Diana." Sabina raised a hand to wave. Diana jerked her head back, pulling her door almost closed.

Paris turned to face them, jerking his hand free from the trellis. "Ayii." He winced and picked out a thorn. "What are you doing here? Spying for my stepmother again?"

Sabina opened her mouth to reply, then closed it.

Paris bunched his fingers. "You thought I didn't know. I'm not stupid."

Her father's expression hardened, but he wasn't looking at Paris. He focused on the older and stockier of the men. "Mordax."

Mordax's expression wavered between a sneer and a smirk. He turned to his son. "Otho, may I introduce an old acquaintance, Eirenarch Catius Sabinus. And…" The ugly smile he turned on Sabina made her shiver. "Ursula's spy."

Her father stepped in front of her.

Otho nodded warily. "Eirenarch?"

"A magistrate. Finally," Paris blustered, seemingly oblivious to the tension between Mordax and her father. "I've been wondering when the city council would send someone to do something about my father's murderer. I heard you arrested Yechiel, the architect."

Her father turned to Paris. "I am investigating your father's death. We have arrested a suspect, and I am here to clear up a few details."

A small detail like Paris's alibi when Cassandra was murdered.

Mordax clapped his hands. "A matter that doesn't concern us. We will leave the magistrate to his duties." He narrowed his eyes at Paris. "I trust you will handle this misunderstanding with our gladiator."

Paris scrunched the scroll in his fist. "I have the money."

"Yes, for the original loan," Mordax's voice lowered and flicked the papyrus sheet. "But, as this contract states, that's not how interest works. It builds, it grows, it multiplies. I'm sure your guests aren't interested in the boring details of our agreement." Mordax squeezed Paris's shoulder until the young man grimaced. "I need to be clear that you understand the terms."

Her father stepped closer to Mordax. "Stealing from citizens again?" He growled.

Mordax released Paris but didn't back away. He glared, his face set like stone. "I see you're still the same pompous, self-righteous ass as before, Catius." Mordax pointed to the scroll. "This is a legal transaction, signed and sealed. I didn't force anyone to do anything."

"You have a way of lining your pockets with others' money." Her father's calm demeanor belied the steel in his voice.

"Unlike your master, the emperor." Mordax worked his jaw back and forth. "Who lines his bathtubs with the gold he taxes from his citizens, giving them a choice between starvation or selling their children into slavery? Don't judge me."

Mordax turned his back on her father and addressed Paris. "I'm meeting with a new architect to revise our plans this afternoon. We're expanding the training arena. I'll expect the funds to be available by next week." Mordax smacked Paris on the back, knocking him forward. Mordax's voice carried a tone of impatience. "Good to hear that you have the money." Mordax bumped into Sabina's father. "Out of my way, Catius. You're interrupting my day."

As Mordax and Otho pushed past, her father said, "I will be watching you."

The morning sun rose over the villa's walls, flooding the garden with light. Behind where Mordax had been standing, a tiny glint of light sparkled in the dirt of the trellis's potted vine. Sabina looked at the pot again, but Paris had shifted, blocking the sun. The glitter was gone. Was she so desperate to save Yechiel that she was imagining clues in piles of dirt?

Otho followed his father, looking back at Diana's door, where she had reappeared. He raised his voice. "The offer to sweeten the deal with your sister is still on the table." Otho grinned, winked, and blew a kiss. "I will be watching you." He turned and jogged after his father.

Paris slumped onto the bench. Diana crept out of her room and shuffled to her brother's side, her eyes narrowed, her face pale and full of questions. "What did Otho mean when he said the deal with your sister is still on the table?"

Paris's eyes flitted past her. "It was nothing, just an idea."

"An idea that sweetened what deal? Did you have an arrangement with Otho that involved me?"

"No, not really," Paris mumbled unconvincingly. "I accrued a bit of debt last year when I bet on a couple of chariot races. I wagered more than my allowance, so Otho lent me a bit to cover the losses."

"And small debts add up," Sabina's father said.

Paris took a deep breath, but his hands shook. "I had an unlucky year, and Otho and I explored my options." Paris rolled the loose scroll, not looking at Diana. "I mentioned you had money that could help."

"By money, do you mean my dowry?" Diana shot up from her chair.

"I wasn't serious," Paris said.

"Otho thought you were because he asked me to marry him. You bartered me to pay your gambling debts."

"You make the idea sound terrible," Paris said.

"Paris!" Diana screeched.

"The money would still have been yours," Paris said defensively.

"Under the control of her new husband," Sabina pointed out, imagining Diana under her father-in-law's thumb—an unpleasant thought.

Paris raised his hands. "You wanted to marry him. It's not like I did something wrong."

Diana's mouth dropped open. "Since when is lying and stealing your sister's dowry not wrong?"

"You're twisting my words," Paris stuttered. "I should never have admitted my mistake."

"You didn't admit it," Diana wailed. "And it wasn't a mistake. You were wrong, wrong, wrong. Did nothing pierce your conscience?"

"I intended to make us...you rich, richer by investing the money, which didn't happen." Paris ended on a defensive note.

"My brother plots against me and says it doesn't matter because he failed."

"Exactly. Nothing bad happened to you," Paris mumbled.

Diana leaned forward, her eyes intent. "Cassandra said someone wanted my money. It was you. Not Loukas or Ursula, not Otho. You need to apologize to me right now!"

Paris pinched his lips together. Then his shoulders sagged. "I only did it because I thought he would make you happy."

"At one time, I thought he would," Diana said sadly.

"I'm sorry," Paris opened his arms, and Diana crumpled into them.

Sabina almost felt sorry for the hapless Paris. It appeared his match-making skills weren't any better than his gambling luck. He might garner more sympathy if he'd own up to his poor choices.

Paris pulled away. "Thankfully, Mordax offered to step in and help."

Her father frowned. "Mordax makes a lucrative living by stepping in."

Paris held up the papyrus contract. "Father and Mordax agreed to cancel the debt in exchange for a share in the ludus."

"Is it possible that Mordax confronted your father with the growing interest and coerced him to sign," Sabina's father suggested.

Paris shook his head. "You don't understand. Father loved the idea of a ludus from the minute he overheard Otho and me discussing the lack of a local training facility. They drew up a contract when Father first considered a ludus. And if it hadn't been for Yechiel, Father would have signed before the interest became a problem."

Diana's gaze locked onto her brother. "Father would never be partners with freed slaves. Mordax and Otho work for us."

"They *are* working for us. But this way, Mordax has a personal stake in the success of the ludus, and we're debt-free. Once I get Ferocianus—"

"I'm tired of hearing about your stupid gladiator." Diana stomped her foot.

Sabina's father stepped between the siblings. "If you can, put your affections aside for a moment. I heard you reported the murder of the fortune teller, Cassandra, yesterday."

"Murder?" Diana slumped to her writing bench. "I didn't..."

"What does a dead fortune teller have to do with us?" Paris bristled.

"You tell me," Sabina's father pressed. "You were the first to know she died."

"Me? Oh, I see now." Paris glared at Sabina. "The spy brought you here for this...for the fortune teller?"

"You told me you'd heard the slaves gossiping about it," Sabina said.

"No, I didn't," Paris said.

Diana shot up from the bench, a warning in her voice. "Stop lying. I heard you."

"I said the witch," Paris mumbled.

Diana pursed her lips and crossed her arms.

"Fine. So, I heard some gossip." Paris challenged. "Why aren't you asking the slaves."

"We have. No one had heard of Cassandra's death," Sabina said.

Paris leaned forward. "They are lying to stay out of trouble."

"You were the only one with knowledge of the woman's death." Her father rubbed his chin. "According to my timeline, for that to happen, you must have been with her at the time of the murder."

"With her! I didn't leave the house yesterday. The slaves will vouch for..." Paris trailed off. "I don't know anything."

"You knew something yesterday," Sabina reminded him. "Either you were there, or someone told you."

"I stayed home. I didn't see anyone except for Otho," Paris said.

"Otho? Mordax's son, told you?" Her father's jaw flexed.

"Otho killed Cassandra?" Diana's voice quivered.

"No, no, I didn't say that." Paris turned to Diana. "Cassandra poisoned your mind against him. You loved Otho before that witch interfered. He wanted to talk to you, but you wouldn't listen. So, he went to Cassandra. He planned to pay her to tell you a fortune that would change your mind about marrying him."

"Cassandra would never lie for a bribe," Diana whispered, her voice hollow.

"You think that witch had scruples?" Paris laughed. "She lied to people for a living."

"And she won't be telling any more lies," Sabina said.

Paris's jaw quivered. "It's my father's murder you should be investigating, not that stupid woman's. It's Yechiel who is guilty. I insist on the death penalty. He's a Jew, you know."

"The courts and laws will determine Yechiel's punishment."

Paris waved an accusatory finger. "My father was one of Ephesus's leading citizens. Prosecuting his murder should be your only responsibility. I will ensure the city council hears of your misplaced priorities, Eirenarch Sabinus."

"Don't threaten me, boy." Her father growled, low and menacing. "I'm investigating the link between the fortune teller's murder and your father's. It appears to be Otho." Her father turned to leave. "I am prioritizing his interrogation as you requested."

"I did not request that." Paris grabbed her father's sleeve. "Otho and Mordax are my partners."

Her father wrenched his sleeve out of Paris's grip. "I suggest you seek legal advice on this business partner your father got you tangled up with. Knowing Mordax, it is already too late. And you," he jabbed his finger at Sabina, "return home."

Sabina winced, feeling the heat of embarrassment creeping into her cheeks. Leaving no doubt, he had had enough of her snooping in other people's affairs.

Her father turned and strode from the atrium. Sabina took a step to follow.

"Sabina." Diana furtively touched Sabina's hand, her eyes wide with a silent plea to stay.

Sabina looked between the two siblings. Paris glared at her, his fist clenching and crushing the contract's middle. "Didn't you hear the magistrate? Leave my house. I don't want you interfering in my affairs again."

Paris's rudeness made Sabina dig in. "I'm not sure Ursula will agree." After accusing Ursula of murder, she was ready to throw Sabina out as well, but Paris didn't know that.

Paris set his jaw but must have had enough confrontation for one day. He rolled his eyes and headed toward the bedroom hallway, then, changing his mind, whipped around and followed her father.

"Please don't judge Paris harshly," Diana pleaded, her voice weighted with sorrow. "Navigating father's death is difficult for all of us, especially Paris. He's doing his best."

"I heard your father planned for your oldest brother to take over as the paterfamilias."

Diana raised her head and nodded. "Paris wasn't prepared to be thrust into this role so soon. Is the magistrate your father?"

The abrupt question surprised Sabina, and a warning shiver tingled her back. "How did you know?"

"I'm a poet. I notice the small details of the world, and you and your father share an unusual blue eye color. I've never seen it before."

"That is all we have in common."

"I hoped you could ask him to help Paris. My brother can be irritating, and it turns people against him." Diana crossed her arms as if she were hugging herself. "I don't want to marry Otho, but that's not Paris's fault."

"Perhaps not, but he chose awful friends." Mordax had exploited the inexperienced young man and pulled Diana into his criminal schemes. It appeared both siblings were unprepared for life without their father.

Diana smiled sadly. "I won't disagree that Paris has horrible judgment."

"Mordax and Otho are expert manipulators." Sabina took her hand. "My father will question Otho about his involvement in Cassandra's murder. He believes he will find evidence linking Mordax to your father's death."

Diana's eyes widened. "My father and I shared many things. We appreciated music, art, literature, the sound of ocean waves." She smiled with the far-off look Sabina was beginning to recognize. "I thought about what you and Portia said yesterday. I read Father's letter."

"And?"

Diana raised her head, her forehead furrowed. "His message is baffling." Although they were alone, Diana moved closer to Sabina and whispered. "I need to show it to Portia. Would you come with me?"

"Right now?" Sabina looked nervously at where her father and Paris had gone. *You will not interfere in my family's affairs again.*

Diana shook her head meekly. "I can't leave until later this afternoon."

She wasn't surprised that Diana wanted someone with her venturing across the city, but she was unsure why Diana had asked her. Although with a murderer on the loose, perhaps she had no one else she trusted. What about Sabina's father's order to go home? He didn't specify when. On her way home, she could accompany Diana on a visit. Sabina took a deep breath. "I could meet you around the tenth hour. Outside your house."

"Thank you." Diana stared blankly at the vine, started to say something, then shook her head and hurried after Paris.

Left alone in the garden, Sabina drew a deep breath and followed Diana's gaze to the plant. It looked the same as when she had examined it four days ago. She had spent at least ten minutes waiting for Diana and admiring the exotic flowers and thorny stem. She had imagined replanting it in her bedroom garden. Nothing had sparkled. She slid closer, her gaze sweeping the garden for chance observers. Did this count as sneaking around in private spaces?

No dazzling clue leaped out to catch her eye. She bent over and quickly raked her fingers through the soil. She felt nothing but the grit of dirt under her fingernails. She dug deeper, the damp soil clinging in tiny clumps to her fingers. The pot was large, but the glinting object couldn't be buried deep if she'd seen it. Her fingers brushed against something round and solid.

"Ahem," Titos said behind her.

Sabina jumped and whipped around. "Eek, you frightened me."

"That is becoming a habit with you."

Sabina looked behind Titos but didn't see anyone else. "You're very good at sneaking up on people."

"Thank you." Titos looked from Sabina to the pot and frowned.

"I like to garden. I grow plants. This vine is rare." Sabina babbled. It wasn't rare, and she hoped Titos didn't recognize local fauna. "This soil makes it so...green."

"I know what soil does." Titos sniffed in disdain. "Master Paris gave instructions to escort you to the front door."

"Of course. Could you give me a minute to clean the dirt from my hands?" Sabina showed the black under the fingernails of her left hand.

"It's best if you leave now." Titos motioned her toward the exit, his gaze not wavering.

"Of course." Titos waited as Sabina edged in front of him. She glanced back once more at the pot.

Titos ushered her along the covered garden entrance, the short hallway, and back into the atrium. The few slaves in sight were chatting or lazily strolling through the atrium. The household had settled down since Sabina had witnessed the lawyer Gnaeus Gratus read Dionysius's decree to free the household slaves.

Not far from her in the middle of the atrium, Loukas reclined on a couch, chomping lazily away, a bowl resting on his lap. A brass drinking goblet and matching pitcher sat within short reach on a small table. Had the fox settled into his lair?

Paris stood glaring at Loukas. Diana close by his side as if in solidarity.

"Is my father's...I mean, my lawyer here?" Paris sounded out of breath. His bravado appeared shaken after his encounter with Mordax. Or perhaps confronting his father's confidant investment banker and stepmother's lover was awkward. "Order Gnaeus Gratus back here. I need his opinion." Paris's voice reverberated through the room.

Sabina slowed her steps to watch the drama.

"Ahem." Titos snapped his fingers and conducted her the final few steps to the front door. He then spun around and left without opening the door or ushering her out. She blinked in surprise, then smiled. He had escorted her to the front door precisely as Paris had ordered and not one step further—a subtle snub to the new master of the house.

She studied the door, then slipped behind a large pillar between the entryway and the atrium. The pillar gave her a hiding space to discreetly peek around for a view into the atrium and time to consider what to do with the item in her fist.

It had been an unconscious reaction to snatch the object out of the pot when panicked by Titos's unexpected appearance. Instinctively or impulsively, she had seized it without thinking. She wiped the soil residue from her left hand and transferred the round object from her right, sneaking a quick look while brushing off the dirt.

A man's ring oversized and heavy. Judging by its weight and luster, the ring had to be gold. Another glimpse confirmed that the engraved stone looked expensive. Not a ring a man would want to lose. So why was it in a pile of dirt?

Every slave and servant had access to that potted plant. Diana penned her poems there. Mordax and Otho met Paris there, and Ursula and Loukas passed it strolling through the garden.

Whose ring was it?

Cassandra's words flashed through her mind, Dio refused to remove his ring. Ursula declared that Dionysius's ring was destroyed in the collapse, which meant this ring wasn't related to the murder.

She couldn't leave the house with the ring. That would be stealing. She had to find a way to return it. Putting it back in the pot was not an option. She looked around for a spot where she could drop the ring. A place not too conspicuous but where it would be found and returned to its owner.

A household slave spotted her. She quickly slipped the ring into her tunic belt. The slave raised a questioning eyebrow, then shrugged and strolled back the way he'd come. The duties and discipline of enslavement were breaking down as freedom loomed.

Paris bellowed from the atrium.

She pressed against the pillar, moving to get an unobstructed view of the trio. They were consumed in conversation, but if they glanced toward the door, they would see her. She tried, unsuccessfully, to ignore the fact that she was eavesdropping, defying her father—and seriously contemplating stealing from the Antiochus family.

TWENTY-NINE

Paris brandished the contract in Loukas's face. "I need Gnaeus now," Paris yelled.

Loukas pushed Paris's hand away. "Your lawyer is consulting legal experts over your concerns about Ferocianus's manumission and will return tomorrow for the funeral. Rudely waving that in my face won't bring him back any quicker. Until then, I can give you a trustworthy opinion." Loukas popped a handful of something crunchy into his mouth.

"You're not a lawyer." Paris stepped back.

Did Paris's distrust and hatred for Ursula extend to Loukas? Sabina wasn't sure Ursula's lover was the best choice to look out for Dionysius's children.

"True. I am an investment banker. However, I have dealt with contracts and the law my entire life and usually come out on top." Loukas brushed his hands off on his tunic and held out his hand for the document.

Diana nudged Paris.

Paris looked at the contract and tapped it against his open palm. "I guess it can't hurt." He handed the papyrus to Loukas.

Loukas unrolled the contract and read. After a minute, he looked at Paris, his brow furrowed, his expression grim. "What is this?"

"It is the contract father signed before he died. It specifies the terms for the management and construction of the new ludus."

Loukas returned to scanning the document. His reaction alternated between eyebrow-raising and rubbing his chin. He set the contract on his lap. "This is not the contract Gnaeus and I drew up for the ludus last fall. Where did this come from?"

"I don't know," Paris said. "Perhaps it is the contract Mordax's lawyers drew up when Father and he first considered building the ludus."

The papyrus began to curl. Loukas flattened it with his hand. "This states a canceled debt in exchange for issuing Mordax twenty percent ownership in the ludus." Loukas raised his eyebrows. "What debt did your father owe?"

"It was Paris's gambling debt," Diana said.

"Paris's gambling debts are no secret," Loukas said. "Your father has been paying them off for years. What I don't understand is why he would make Mordax a partner as a way out of your debt."

"It wasn't a way out." Paris stabbed at the document with his finger. "Father saw an exceptional business opportunity. He obtained the most famous lanista in the empire and eliminated the debt at the same time."

"Twenty percent ownership is extremely generous." Loukas lowered the contract to his lap.

"Twenty percent was last year's share. Mordax required a bit more now with compounding interest and all." Paris reached for the contract.

Loukas pulled it back. "How much more?"

Paris pointed to a line in the contract. "A forty-nine, fifty-one split."

"You agreed to that?" Red splotches mottled Diana's face. "Who gets fifty-one percent?"

"I'm not stupid, Diana. I didn't sign away our family control. Besides, with Mordax training the gladiators, we will make barrels of money. Father knew we couldn't lose."

Loukas picked up the contract, mumbling words as he continued reading. "Your responsibility for the ludus is stated in rather general terms, including construction costs, materials, building maintenance, procuring talent, and support of said talent. By talent, I assume that means gladiators?"

Paris rolled his eyes. "Gladiators are the key to making money."

Loukas sucked in his breath. "There is a small addendum you signed...today?"

"Mordax just left," Diana said.

"It states a penalty should you fail to supply the agreed-upon talent." Loukas's gaze shot up. "An additional two percent of ownership transfers to Mordax, increasing Mordax's percentage to fifty-one percent."

Sabina covered her mouth to stifle her gasp.

"Paris?" Diana grabbed his arm.

He shook free from her grasp. "It is only if I can't supply Ferocianus. That's not going to happen."

Sabina wouldn't want to bet on Paris, and from Loukas's expression, neither would he. "Your father should have come to me, and you should have negotiated more favorable terms."

"I know what I signed." Paris pouted, sounding sullen. "It's not my fault. Father didn't sign the offer until after the interest had grown."

Diana's eyes widened. "Why would you agree to that? It jeopardizes father's legacy."

"It is Father I am thinking about. He can't be honored with inferior gladiators who lose."

And who die, Sabina shivered.

Paris stood straighter. "Which is why Ferocianus can't be set free. He is Father's legacy."

Diana spun to face Paris. "Ferocianus is not Father's legacy. I heard you and Father fighting after you bought him. Father didn't want a gladiator."

Paris glared at Diana. "You're wrong. We were not fighting."

"What do you call it?" Diana snapped back.

"We were arguing about how much Ferocianus cost. After Father calmed down, we discussed Ferocianus's earning potential. He was enthusiastic over the profits and said he regretted choosing the library."

Sabina recalled the date of Ferocianus's purchase. Was that when Dio began planning the ludus? Why hadn't he told Yechiel? Or had he, and Yechiel refused to listen?

"No." Diana shook her head. "It wasn't just about money. He talked about the Christians who don't believe in profiting from human suffering and death as entertainment?"

Ursula swept into the room, the nearly sheer black linen stola billowing behind her like a storm cloud. "What does Christian suffering have to do with Dio?"

"Nothing." Paris rolled his eyes contemptuously. "Diana overheard part of a conversation she didn't understand."

"I know what I heard." Diana crossed her arms, clamping her lips shut.

Paris took a deep breath. "We discussed the Christians," he enunciated slowly as if Diana was mentally unfit. "Not because he agreed with them. It was because their intolerance of the games could impact our profits."

Loukas snorted. "I don't see how. Christians are a small minority."

"Small but fanatical." Ursula sighed and placed a hand on Diana's arm. "They refuse to attend the games to honor our goddess, calling it cruel and murderous theater."

"I'm not excusing them." Diana's voice shook.

Paris nodded enthusiastically. "Normal people want to participate. The crowds are obsessed with the games."

Sabina couldn't disagree. At the last gladiatorial event she had attended, the crowd had erupted in a frenzy of blood lust, watching a man convicted of stealing bleeding to death from dozens of slashes and wounds. She had closed her eyes but couldn't block his agonizing screams or the crowd booing his final whimpers. When the gladiator pierced his heart, cheers exploded. She had not attended another event, but the tang of the arena's blood-soaked sand stayed with her.

"Why would your father agree with a cult that dishonors our goddess and provokes her punishments of drought, earthquakes, plague, and death on our great city?" Ursula looked briefly over Loukas's shoulder, glancing at the contract.

Loukas nodded. "Attendance at the games is one way authorities identify Christ's followers. If a neighbor witnesses a Christian's absence from the worship festivals, bringing them to trial is easier."

Sabina was thankful her father did not require her attendance. So far, his powerful position had shielded her, but she knew any church member, her bishop, or Portia could be dragged into the arena as a convicted criminal.

Loukas reached for his goblet. "Those zealots risk their lives rather than bow and offer a tiny pinch of incense at the emperor's altar. It makes no sense."

Paris nodded eagerly. "That's what father said. The narrow-minded entice the simple-minded away from the festivals and games."

Ursula turned to Diana. "I must agree with Paris. You misunderstood your father. He may not have believed in the existence of our lusty, unpredictable gods, but he would never tolerate a perfect God. What fun is that?" Ursula squeezed Loukas's shoulder.

Loukas chuckled.

"Now, what is this?" Ursula asked, taking the contract from Loukas.

"The contract with Titus Mordax," Loukas answered, his good humor gone.

"I don't know why you're bothered by this." Paris snatched the papyrus sheet from Ursula. "Father knew what he was doing."

"The question is, do you?" Loukas turned to stare at Paris, his expression stern, his voice hard. "Until Gnaeus determines these contractual obligations, you need to refrain from the family's usual spending."

"We certainly will not," Ursula said. "We have a funeral, and no expense shall be spared."

Paris lifted his chin. "Ferocianus will bring in all the money we need as soon as Mordax organizes more fights. You saw the interest at the exhibition, and people haven't even seen him slice into his opponents. He's amazing."

Loukas grabbed another handful of his snack and chomped. "That may be, but until Dio's will is settled, Diana's dowry is the only unencumbered money in your family."

Diana glared at her brother. "Don't you dare. That is my money."

Paris threw up his arms. "I know, I know, I wasn't…"

"What are you shouting about?" Ursula asked.

"Paris was bartering me to pay his gambling debts." Diana glared at

Paris, her fists balled. Even from where Sabina stood, she could see the red creeping from Diana's neck into her cheeks. Anger didn't become her.

"It was Mordax's plan, not mine, to forgive the loans," Paris grumbled. "And you threw a fit wanting to marry Otho," Paris smirked.

Ursula made a hex sign over her heart. "Thank the goddess we averted that disaster."

"You still want me to marry him—a murderer," Diana accused.

"Murderer?" Ursula grabbed Diana's arms. "Otho confessed to killing your father?"

"No." Diana pulled away, rubbing her arms. "Otho killed Cassandra."

"He did not say that. We don't know that." Paris's gaze skittered around the room. Sabina ducked around the pillar.

"So it was Otho who murdered Cassandra," Ursula said.

"Quit accusing my partner," Paris yelled.

"I believe I deserve an apology after Magistrate Sabinus's humiliating accusation." Ursula's voice dripped with satisfaction. "Even though it was rather exciting being a murder suspect."

Sabina almost felt sorry for her father. Apologizing to Ursula wouldn't be easy. But even if Ursula hadn't killed Cassandra, she was still a suspect in the death of her husband. She returned to her viewing position.

Diana clasped her hands. "Otho admitted to visiting Cassandra. The magistrate has gone to question him. Sabina said he would find Mordax and Otho entangled in Father's murder as well."

"Mordax and Father were on the verge of making a fortune," Paris shouted. "Why would Mordax kill him?"

"Why indeed?" Ursula quipped.

"I refuse to listen to this." Paris spun around and headed toward the door and toward Sabina.

She dodged around the pillar and ran, expecting someone to yell Stop, thief. The door banged closed behind her.

THIRTY

Sabina escaped unapprehended from the Antiochus family villa. Two blocks away, she bent over, panting for breath, slowing down; she walked another two blocks before stopping to examine the ring. The stone, an engraved garnet used to sign official documents, was valuable. A signet ring. She ruled out the slaves and servants immediately. And she had been ridiculed too often for her gardening oddity to believe any elite enjoyed digging in the dirt and had accidentally lost it. This ring couldn't have slipped off a finger unnoticed, even Dionysius's. The ring was a mystery.

Ignoring her guilty conscience, she tucked the band securely into her sash and strolled toward home, postponing any plans of how to return it or if she'd tell her father. She had several hours before meeting Diana and needed that time to strategize.

She reached an intersection and abruptly turned in the opposite direction of her house.

She needed information—trustworthy information. Who could she trust to answer her questions honestly without lying to protect themselves or someone else? With the death of Cassandra and expelled from Dio's house, her list of informants had dwindled to one.

Yechiel.

Carrying a valuable, priceless piece of jewelry to where she planned to go would not earn her praise from Zarmig for intelligence, but she didn't have time to drop it off at her house. Besides, its bulge rested nearly undetectable under her mantle.

The afternoon sun had peaked and begun its descent when she approached the prison. An older man and veil-wrapped woman exited the formidable fortress. The two glanced at her, and the woman spoke. The man adamantly shook his head and then shot Sabina a suspicious look before he marched toward her. The woman remained by the building.

Sabina tapped down her discomfort. He had every reason to be here. She did not.

"My niece would like to speak to you." Reuben nodded at the veiled Eunice across the street.

"I am surprised that she wants to. I need to apologize. I didn't know about my father..."

"We have a saying in our community." Reuben stared at her, his voice hard. "May God protect you from bad people and save you from the good ones. Come, we will speak privately where your father and his spies will not see us together."

Sabina followed Reuben and Eunice as they wound down streets and around corners, passing the same bakery twice. Nervously, she looked in the direction they'd come, unsure if she could find her way back to the jail.

She had assumed that Yechiel and Eunice lived in the Jewish quarter of the town, so she stopped in surprise when they reached a small plaza nowhere near the synagogue, its sparkling central fountain surrounded by two-story insulas. Insulas with solid foundations and walls freshly plastered since the last earthquake. The ground-level shops were modest. Their stone stoops swept clean, welcoming customers. Flower boxes ablaze with summer flora attracted a pleasant buzz.

They approached a sturdy doorway. It opened as if by a ghost, and Reuben stomped inside, followed by Eunice and Sabina. The cool of the darkened house enveloped her as an attendant closed the door silently behind them and vanished. Reuben led the way through the entryway, their steps echoing as they crossed into a small atrium.

Sabina blinked, adjusting from the sunlight outdoors to the shaded cool of the atrium. She didn't see or hear anyone else. With the owner and master in prison, even the water in the impluvium pool seemed to be in silent mourning.

Eunice stopped atop a mosaic of a pear tree laden with fruit and birds. She whirled around, tossing her veiled head covering back.

Sabina fought to keep the shock from her expression. This beautiful woman, so full of grace and poise the last time they'd met, had been transformed. The stress and strain of Yechiel's arrest had left her haggard with a waxy pall over her skin. The spark of hope Eunice had before Yechiel's attempted escape was stomped out by Roman boots.

Eunice squeezed her hands, then pulled back. "I do not blame you. I believe you did not mean to betray my husband."

Sabina nodded. "Thank you," she said, humbled by a trust she didn't deserve.

"Intentional or not, you led your father to him." Reuben's voice held the same blame that she felt for underestimating her father and Zarmig.

Sabina had vowed she wouldn't make that mistake again. "I can't undo what happened, but—"

Eunice waved her into silence. "Have you found Dionysius's killer?" Eunice's brown eyes appeared huge. The ravages of tears puffed the eyelids and turned the whites of her eyes into a spiderweb of red.

"Not yet, but…" But what? There were suspects, but not the evidence needed for an arrest. "I hope soon. I came to see if Yechiel could help me."

"We are out of time," Reuben said. "Yechiel is being transferred to Rome."

"Rome!" Sabina gasped. "How? Why?"

"Does it matter? No Jew arrives in Rome in shackles and returns alive."

"The authorities don't have enough evidence to put him on trial," Sabina said, her hope and confidence disappearing with Reuben's news.

"Since when does Emperor Domitian need proof to convict a Jew?" Reuben spat.

Or a Christian. Reuben was correct. When suspecting Jewish treason, evidence was immaterial. The stories of the horrible executions of two Jewish founders of Christianity, the apostle Peter's crucifixion upside down and Paul's beheading all for the crime of professing a belief. That deadly repercussions continued for others who believed in the resurrection of Christ and proclaimed Him Lord over Caesar. A warning fresh in the minds of believers after twenty-five years.

"When is he scheduled to be transported?" Sabina asked.

"It was to be today. The soldiers wait for a troop ship from Tarsus bound for Rome. It has been delayed," Reuben said.

Eunice picked absently at the shawl dropped across her shoulders. "He had hoped to hide the news from me, but I heard the guards talking when I brought him clean clothing." Her voice shook, her words barely audible as she looked with haunted eyes at Sabina. "My husband cannot go to Rome. He will be tortured."

"What she means is Yechiel will not be going to Rome." Reuben held out the coin that had lured Sabina into the murder investigation. "Because of this, we cannot risk a confession. Too many lives are at stake."

Eunice pulled her shawl tightly around her trembling body.

"We? The Brotherhood?" It was the name Yechiel had used to warn Sabina of the lethal consequences of being discovered with one of the coins. Coins minted in the Jerusalem temple before its destruction, and gold used to finance the first rebellion against Rome. The uprising that the current emperor's brother Titus had quelled. A revolution that had ignited Domitian's paranoia and ruthless determination to eliminate even the most innocuous of dealings if they hinted at a revival of a rebellion. Sabina stared at the coin, a revolt very much alive and resurging.

Eunice stared blankly, hopelessly at Sabina. "Yechiel awaits his next meal. I am to bring a mixture of broth, vegetables—and arsenic."

Sabina shuddered. "The same poison that killed his brother, Benjamin." She had watched the poison kill Benjamin. He had died quickly, but it had not been a painless death. "If the authorities do not suspect Yechiel's association with the Brotherhood, why would he confess to anything? If he could withstand—"

Reuben touched Eunice's hand. "I will deliver the soup." The older man's mouth sagged. His tone was full of sorrow. "Of all the men I know, Yechiel might be the one to withstand the emperor's brutal cruelty, but we cannot take the chance. This way we limit his suffering."

"And protect yourselves," Sabina said.

Eunice held Reuben's hand. "When my uncle was a teenager, a member of the Brotherhood rescued him from one such interrogation. The soldiers began by cutting into his face."

Reuben's bushy brows lowered, one corner of his mouth rising in a crooked smile, the other half fused in grizzled scar tissue. "I survived. The soldiers did not. I joined the Brotherhood as soon as I had healed. But I know the panic that overpowers the fiercest of loyalties. It is nothing to reveal one name, a location, or a date in exchange for not being blinded by a searing metal rod. In exchange for a swift death? Yechiel is only human."

"Yechiel knows too many Brotherhood secrets," Sabina said. A numbing sense of failure overpowered her. Roman justice made suicide his only option. Her father had not apprised her of his interrogation techniques. But the battle-hardened commander had rarely failed to extract information from enemy soldiers, traitors, and spies. If he failed early in his military career, it was because the captive died during the interview. In later years, Zarmig made sure that didn't happen. "What do you want me to do?"

"Nothing." Eunice collapsed in a chair. "You have already told us what we need to know. You have not found the murderer. Yechiel has no defense."

"I'm sorry." Sabina looked at the slight bump protruding from the center of Eunice's robe. The unborn child would never know its father—the wheels of Roman justice ground like a giant millstone. Once in motion, it pounded, crushed, and destroyed whoever fell under its charge. "I will ask my father—"

"You have done enough," Reuben silenced her, his tone biting. "We have very little time to spare Yechiel this injustice and brutal agony."

Sabina nodded. "It is not my injustice, but I will say nothing to my father. He will not know I came to your home."

Eunice looked confused. "My home?"

Reuben flicked his hand around the room. "We do not know who lives here. Nor do the owners know we are here. The Brotherhood arranges locations."

The door attendant appeared like a ghost at Sabina's side. She followed him out, glancing back once to see Eunice collapse into Reuben's arms, her sobs echoing off the empty atrium walls. Sabina had no hope to offer, but she still had one question that only Yechiel, a man with nothing to lose could truthfully answer. She looked at the sundial in the square and then asked the next passerby for directions to the jail.

She would have to hurry. Yechiel's time was running out.

Assuming he knew who owned the ring, she still had to find out who had hidden it and why. Even then, it may not be evidence pointing to the murderer or enough to convince her father. If convinced, he would then have to take it to the magisterial court, and by that time, Yechiel would either be poisoned or on a ship sailing toward his execution.

She had done her best to help Eunice and Yechiel and believed in Yechiel's innocence, but if Eunice were implicated, it would be disastrous for her and her unborn child. Eunice's confidence in her had radiated in her first smile. Eunice, a stranger, had believed Sabina could make a difference in a world that denigrated, disparaged, and belittled the talents of women.

She might be unable to help Yechiel, but that didn't mean she was stepping back or giving up.

She lined up, a lone woman blending into the crowd of lawyers, wives, children, and friends waiting to visit the inmates. A guard escorted her to the appropriate section of the jail. The stench of prison hit her long before the guard took her to Yechiel's cell. From experience, she had brought along a scarf that she held over her nose and mouth, stifling the smells of human sweat, blood, and waste. But she couldn't block out the din of the moans and screams of the prisoners and the insane housed here.

Yechiel crouched against the bars in the front corner of a crowded cell. His eyes, blackened from beatings, were closed, his neatly trimmed beard ragged and caked with dried blood. Where was the fresh tunic Eunice had brought him? Stolen? Confiscated? His circumstances were only going to get worse.

"Yechiel." She startled him with her greeting—another man, a stranger, crowded in. Yechiel stood and pushed him back.

Yechiel's eyes, mere slits, peered at her from swollen and bruised flesh. "I have nothing to say to you." His thin, haggard frame sagged, his arrogance and boldness gone.

"Surely, talking to someone would be a welcome diversion to this." She pointed to the stranger leering at her.

Yechiel grunted. "Why are you here?"

"Why do you think? I didn't mean to lead my father to you. I feel responsible for this." She waved her arm, taking in the dank, dark vault. "I'm trying to help."

The unknown man crowded in, pressing against the bars and making an obscene motion. "You can help me."

Yechiel pushed the man away and then glared at her. "Go," he ordered her. "This is no place for a woman."

She wanted nothing more than to leave here. The stink had permeated her scarf, and the jeers and cries of human misery had her nerves and heart pounding. "I have one question, and then I will leave." She had hoped to show him the ring, but with no privacy, she couldn't risk being caught with it. "Did you ever see Dionysius with his ring off?"

"His ring?" He looked behind her as if expecting Zarmig to burst through the door. "Your father is sending me to Rome for execution, and you ask me about jewelry."

"Eunice is afraid you won't get to Rome."

Yechiel's eyes flashed in understanding. "I've been told. Go home, Sabina. Stay out of my life." He picked a louse from his hair and flicked it away. His shoulders slumped.

"I can't. I was given a coin and pledged to answer its summons."

His laugh was stern, harsh. "You think too highly of yourself, woman. The coin has nothing to do with you. It's honor and obligation belong to my people."

"Truth and justice do not stop at religious boundaries. I promised Eunice that I would help her—help you."

"God has sent a way to end my misery," Yechiel said.

"You're a misery. You're a misery," the other man sang, creeping closer until Yechiel elbowed him. There was no space for the man to go, and he collided with a man crammed next to him.

Accustomed to Yechiel's prickly pride and self-assurance she was caught off-guard by his words of defeat. She spoke. "You do not know God's plans. When the Jews were carried away into captivity, the prophet Jeremiah reminded them that God would use their hardship to bring about His design. 'For I know what plans I have in mind for you, plans for well-being, not for bad things; so that you can have hope and a future. When you call to me and pray to me, I will listen to you.'"

"Do not lecture me from my scriptures." Yechiel stiffened. He stared at her, not blinking.

"They help me." She didn't want to argue. They were her scriptures, too, verses she recited whenever life became too hard.

If he were ordering her away, she would go. If he decided that suicide was the only way to save the Brotherhood, saving his life would be impossible. But she needed his help to find Cassandra's and Dionysius's killer. "The fortune teller Cassandra said that Dionysius never removed his ring. I found a ring. If it is Dionysius's signet, it was not destroyed in the accident."

"What is the significance of Dionysius's signet?" Yechiel's voice sounded tired.

"I don't know yet."

The other man cackled with sing-song laughter. "You don't know yet. You don't know yet."

"Shut up," Yechiel snarled.

The stranger stuck out his tongue.

She tried not to sound frustrated. "Did he wear the ring when he came to the work site?"

Yechiel closed his eyes, and she thought he would ignore her. When he opened them, he paused before saying, "I never saw him without it. His ring displayed his power and self-importance." Yechiel narrowed his eyes, and his slits appeared closed. "Dio was an arrogant and pretentious man."

Sabina choked back a retort, imagining Yechiel's pride clashing with a matching ego. She fingered the slight bulge in her belted sash. Could this be the Antiochus family signet? "I have a ring. Could you identify Dionysius's signet if you saw it?"

"Perhaps if I saw it." Yechiel's face tightened in warning. "Desperate people surround you. Do not reveal anything of value."

She nodded. "It has a red garnet carved with the head of the god Dionysius."

Yechiel nodded. "The god of wine is a common emblem."

Was she inventing a clue to Dionysius's murder because she had nothing else? Did it matter if it was Dionysius's ring? Or if he hid it while alive?

The guard escorted her down the prison hallway. The chorus of you don't know yet had started up again. Despondent, she turned toward Dionysius's house to meet Diana, wondering if she would see Yechiel again.

Not if the Brotherhood delivered his next meal.

THIRTY-ONE

Sabina hurried, half running, half fast walking, trying not to look conspicuous, as she hiked her mantle above her ankles. Returning to Dionysius's home, the scene of her crime, was a reckless idea. Whoever had hidden the ring could have discovered it missing and sent out an alarm. She would minimize her chance of being seen by waiting across the street until Diana came out of the house. But as Sabina arrived panting and breathless, Diana disappeared into her litter.

"Diana," Sabina shouted and waved, announcing herself to the neighborhood.

Diana peeked out, looking nervous. "Oh, I thought you'd changed your mind."

Sabina felt the pinch in her side as she scurried to the litter. "I'm sorry I'm late. I had an urgent errand to attend to."

Six slaves waited until Sabina was seated. Lifting it in one fluid motion, they rested the conveyance's two parallel poles on padded muscular shoulders. The men jogged in unison along the streets, carrying the two women toward the harbor and Portia's home.

Secure in the privacy of the litter's enclosed cubicle, Diana handed her a small papyrus roll. "Father's letter. At first, I thought he wrote me

263

a poem. But then I read the word *Christos.*" Diana pointed. "I couldn't understand why Father would write about a disgraced criminal."

Sabina unrolled it.

Then I heard a loud voice saying in heaven, "Now salvation, and strength, and the kingdom of our God, and the power of His Christ have come, for the accuser of our brethren, who accused them before our God day and night, has been cast down. And they overcame him by the blood of the Lamb and by the word of their testimony, and they did not love their lives to the death.

Sabina was just as mystified. She held a letter written by Dionysius, a pagan, describing the Christian beliefs of salvation, the kingdom of God, and the blood of the Lamb. She perused the letter again. "I recognize some Christian phrases." Sabina stopped and glanced at Diana to see her reaction. She remembered Diana's hostility and her vow to report any believers of the banned faith to the authorities.

Diana's features hardened. Her hands tightened, unclenched, then tightened again. "I knew it. This letter advocates a treasonous Christian kingdom. I could be arrested as a traitor. Why would Father give this to me?" Diana's splotchy spots were returning.

Why indeed? But more maddening was that Sabina did not understand Dionysius's message. A message cloaked in a coded language.

The litter jerked to a stop, tossing the women forward. Then started up again.

"It is difficult to read in here." Sabina rolled the letter up and handed it back to Diana. Surely, Portia was better equipped to navigate the treacherous seas of Diana's emotions and smooth out some of this confusion. "We are nearly there. I'm sure Portia can give some guidance."

They rode in silence, Sabina lost in thoughts of the last line of the letter: they did not love their lives to the death. It did indeed sound similar to the emperor's edicts against her faith and the martyrs' persecution, betrayals, and deaths.

The lurching stop snapped her from her reverie. When they disembarked, Portia's door servant informed them they had missed Portia by minutes.

Sabina returned to the litter. "Today is Tuesday. Portia distributes food to the widows of the church." Sabina bit her tongue at the word *church*, too late.

But Diana's brows drew together in bafflement. "What widows?"

Sabina scrunched her face. "Poo-or widows," she drew the word out, watching Diana's eyes narrow, realizing too late that this would make no sense to this wealthy patrician.

"The emperor and the city council feed the poor." Diana's statement echoed the elite view that Rome's welfare for widows and orphans was sufficient.

"Yes, they provide cheap grain, but it is not enough to live on, so the chur—Portia adds to it." Sabina hurried past the subject. "I know where we can find her. You'll have to leave the litter. The alleys are narrow in that part of town. We can walk. It's not far."

"Walk? Here, near the harbor? There are thieves. I am wearing costly gold jewelry."

"Bring your litter bearers."

Sabina had delivered food many times and knew the homes of the women who benefited from the congregation's assistance. Sabina, Diana, and the six slaves walked and found Portia exiting a doorway off a narrow alley.

Portia hefted two bags bulging with round balls the size of small apples or apricots and handed one bag to her servant Feya, who carried it to a stout young man she called Magnus.

"Hello, Portia, Feya." Sabina nodded to Magnus as he loaded a small hand cart.

He grunted and swung the cloth bag onto the cart laden with a large steaming kettle, bread baskets, and two tall earthenware amphoras with narrow necks. Sabina knew one was filled with olive oil, the other Feya's special beer.

"Sabina?" Portia emphasized her question with raised eyebrows. "Diana, what are you doing here?"

"You said I could come to you if I needed anything." Diana looked from the cart to Portia, her lips puckering in a frown. "I read Father's letter."

"I'm glad you didn't burn it." Portia bent over to plop her bag in the cart, straightened, and arched her back.

"I don't understand what he wrote." Diana huffed, shaking her head.

"Magnus, Feya, please finish the deliveries without me." Magnus and Feya curiously eyed Diana and the litter bearers, nodded, and padded off.

"Well, if it's a translation, we need Horace. My husband is fluent in multiple languages but is not home."

"No," Sabina broke in. "Diana meant her father's letter is puzzling. I believe you will find it interesting. But not out here." Neighbors were living on top of each other and could hear each other sneeze, snore, and recite suspicious messages.

"Euodia wouldn't mind if we use her house." Portia pointed to the door she'd just exited. "She is nearly blind and deaf. So, we needn't worry about confidentiality."

Diana shuddered. "I won't go in there. It is filthy. It reeks, I could get sick, a disease, lice."

"Euodia takes great pride in a clean home. But if you wish, you can wait until my duties are finished," Portia said. "I should be home before dark."

"Is there nowhere else? Father's funeral is tomorrow. I want to know what he said before he leaves us for the underworld."

Portia opened the door to the dusky hovel.

Diana bit her lip and wrapped her mantle around her nose before entering. "Argh."

Portia motioned the litter bearers to sit outside.

Sabina, Portia and Diana crowded into a room barely large enough for the small table, a stool, and a straw-stuffed mattress on the floor. But the packed dirt floor was swept, with no cobwebs or fly nests. Instead of an offending odor, Sabina breathed in a subtle hint of lemons and a tantalizing flora coming from a ball-shaped clay vase holding a fragrant multi-colored bouquet of lilies.

Portia yelled her request into the shriveled elderly woman's ear. "May we use your home for a short time?"

Euodia nodded enthusiastically with a toothless smile and offered a lone stool to her guests. Diana shook her head vehemently and pressed her back against the closed door while tugging her mantle tighter across her mouth and nose.

"Thank you," Sabina dropped onto the diminutive three-legged seat.

Euodia removed a cup hanging on a hook, then went to the rickety wooden table where two loaves of bread and a cracked pottery bowl sat brimming with velvety apricots. She reached for one of the rounded vessels next to the ripe fruit, but Portia covered the woman's wrinkled hand with hers and shook her head, mouthing *no thank you*.

She motioned for Euodia to sit. Euodia pushed the apricot bowl toward Sabina, then painstakingly lowered herself onto the straw mattress on the earthen floor, nodding and smiling at each of them.

Securely holding her face covering in place, Diana drew out the letter. She handed it to Portia, who carried it toward a brilliant rectangle of light streaming in from the gaps around a loosely hung back door. Portia pushed the door open, revealing a tiny strip of garden crammed between the neighboring insulas and bursting with lilies, roses, and poppies.

Sabina blinked at the bright light flooding the room.

Portia's lips mouthed the words as she read the scroll, her eyelids widening. Had Portia come to the same conclusion she had? Dionysius had written a letter containing Christian beliefs to his daughter. Portia stared at Sabina then back at the letter. A myriad of questions played out across her face.

"Do you know what he's saying?" Diana's words were muffled through her face covering.

Portia held the letter carefully as if it might break. "I have read this before."

Sabina jolted in surprise.

"When did my father show it to you?" Diana gasped.

"Your father did not write this."

"I know his handwriting," Diana insisted.

Portia looked at the letter again. "Perhaps, he copied it. I don't know how he got access to a private letter."

"Whose private letter?" Diana asked.

Portia tapped her fingernail on pursed lips, her expression serious. She spoke slowly, softly, as if weighing each word. "The author is a dear friend of mine."

Diana's brows knit together. "I don't understand. Sabina said this is Christian writing. Then your friend is…" Her voice faded to a stop.

"My friend is a believer in the Messiah Yeshua, Jesus Christ. We worship Christ as the one true God."

"We?" Diana looked from Portia to Sabina with a look of horror.

Sabina nodded warily. Perhaps Portia should have given more thought to the confession she just made. Portia had not heard Diana's contempt nor witnessed the venomous outburst toward Christians that Sabina had observed.

Diana's lip curled in disgust as her fingers fumbled behind her for the door latch. "You drink blood from human sacrifices?"

Portia shook her head, her voice calm, radiating the love she had demonstrated for Diana. "People ignorant of our faith spread many lies."

"You lied! To my father and me. I trusted you. I came to you for help." Diana pulled open the latch and turned to leave.

"I would never deceive you or your father. He knew about my faith."

Diana froze with her back to them. "I don't believe you. My father would never associate with traitors." She turned, flicking her hand at the letter. "Or spread your heathen propaganda. He would have reported you to the magistrates."

"He left you this letter. You want to know why. I can help if you'll let me. After that, you can decide what to do with the admission I entrust to you." Portia gestured to the door. "Perhaps you should close it."

Outside the door, the litter bearers lounged in various states of boredom. Diana slowly tugged the door shut.

Portia scanned the letter as she spoke. "The writer's name is John. He is almost one hundred years old. He was young when Jesus, our God, chose him to be His apostle. John and hundreds of others saw Jesus crucified and spent weeks with Jesus after He rose from the dead. Your letter is part of Christ's revelation to John while he was a prisoner on the island of Patmos."

"An escaped criminal?" Diana screeched.

"He was allowed to return home to Ephesus when he became ill. The authorities probably expected him to die. Domitian would not be pleased with John continuing his missionary work and writing this." Portia flattened the scroll. "It was not meant to be read outside our faith community."

"Your faith is outlawed. How did Father get this?"

"I don't know. Our church congregations have begun copying John's revelation for dissemination among Christian communities. But so far, only a few elders, scribes, and I have read it. I know of no pagans who have access to it."

"This makes no sense," Sabina said.

Portia shrugged. "It could have been stolen and circulated by someone seeking to harm the church or John. The authority of our apostles, both those dead and alive, is under attack."

Diana protested. "It is not your apostles who are under attack. This letter calls for a rebellion to cast Domitian from his throne, to take away his empire."

"Domitian's reign will end." Portia's eyes took on a faraway look. "But this battle is much greater than one emperor, country, and age."

"I don't believe you. You are lying to protect your friend. John writes that the accuser of your brethren will be overcome—with blood. Domitian has executed hundreds of Christians." Diana charged. "This letter incites a revolt to overthrow and murder our emperor."

"No. God's revelation to John describes a battle that crushes Satan's rebellion and ends Satan's enslavement of mankind," Portia explained.

"I do not know this Satan." Diana's voice vibrated with emotion. "And I am no one's slave."

"It is a victorious message. Satan, the father of evil, is defeated." Sabina repeated as much to herself as to Diana. After Portia clarified the message veiled within John's confusing language, the final line made sense.

"A victory?" Diana gaped at Sabina as if she'd lost her mind. "This message is declaring you traitors to our emperor. Father would never promote the overthrow of Rome, nor would he champion a Christian cause."

Portia's voice remained calm. "I agree your father wouldn't support either. When he gave you the letter, did he say anything to help explain?"

"No. He came to my room the night after his fight with Paris and asked if I'd read this letter. I told him no." Diana sucked in deep breaths as if struggling not to cry. "His final words were 'Remember, Diana, no one is worthy.' I cried after he left. I'd worked so hard to earn his love, his approval. How dare he tell me I wasn't worthy of it."

Portia glanced at Sabina then shook her head. "I think you misunderstood."

"What is there to understand? I didn't meet his expectations. He wished me the peace he had sought his whole life. And after destroying mine, he left." Diana's voice was bitter and unrelenting.

Sabina tried to make sense of the interaction the night before Dio's murder.

"Cassandra spoke of your father's turmoil." Sabina absentmindedly reached for an apricot, then put it back. "She said your father was searching, striving for something that would balance the scales of his life."

"Why would he care? My father wasn't truthful or just, moral or trustworthy. His heart wasn't pure."

"He was human. Our scripture says, all have turned away, they have together become corrupt; there is no one who does good, not even one," Portia said.

"That's not true." Diana scowled. "Socrates said, 'We cannot live better than in seeking to become better.' Father knew how hard I worked to be worthy. I constantly strive for a pure heart."

"This letter speaks of peace without striving or trusting in human efforts," Sabina pointed out.

Portia gestured to the bottom of the page. "The letter ends with the peace that passes all understanding. Sharing the letter could be his way of saying you no longer needed to prove yourself worthy—to yourself or him."

"He had no standing to judge me worthy or grant me peace."

"No, he didn't, but his letter reveals one who does have the authority." Portia handed over Dio's letter.

Diana crossed her arms, refusing it with a look of disgust. "You just quoted that no one is worthy," Diana said.

"There is one."

"Oh, I forgot." Diana's lips twisted into a sneering smile. "Your Christ God was born the perfect man. You know He is not the only one. Our gods and goddesses also came to earth disguised as mortals."

"Christ was not disguised. He was born mortal and died," Portia said.

Incredulity solidified on Diana's face. "That is the flaw in your argument and why no one will ever believe in your human God. Gods are eternal. They can't die. It is illogical."

Euodia grunted, her joints creaking as she levered herself from the bed mat. "My God died for me." She tottered over and grabbed the bowl, holding it out and offering Diana apricots. "My heart is washed pure with Christ's blood. I am worthy."

Diana pushed the bowl away. "I thought she couldn't hear."

Sabina and Portia looked at each other. "So did we."

"A poor beggar is worthy?" Diana jeered, shaking her head as if shaking Portia's words from her ears. "She has nothing a god would value."

"God values a generous heart," Portia said.

Euodia nodded and shuffled, smiling, holding the bowl out to Sabina and Portia.

Sabina scooped several apricots into her palm and nodded a thank you. "Your gods punish or reward based on whims, jealousies, and vengeance. Our God came to take man's punishment onto Himself, the final sacrifice, the payment required to buy humanity from the bondage of our accuser, Satan." She sank her teeth into the fleshy ripeness. Sweet tart juice squirted down her chin. She wiped it off.

"You believe your God sacrificed Himself." Diana wrapped the scarf around her face and pointed at Euodia. "For her?" She shook her head. "I didn't come here to be humiliated. If your God requires this," Diana shuddered, looking around the hovel, "groveling among the slums. My father would never have—never."

Portia stood. "Your father may not have believed, but he strove to learn, to understand."

A smiling Euodia took the lilies from the vase and thrust them toward a shaking Diana.

"Get away from me," Diana batted the flowers, sending them flying to the floor. Euodia bent down and picked them up. "None of this answers where my father got the letter and why he would jeopardize my life by giving it to me."

"After tomorrow's funeral, we will try to find out where your father got it," Portia said.

"I don't want you at the funeral. You are not the friend or the person I thought you were. Keep your hopeless, depressing God to yourself." Diana left, slamming the door. It banged closed, then slowly creaked open, swinging lopsidedly.

Euodia shuffled to latch it. "Not hopeless."

Sabina turned to Portia. "Your admission entrusts your life to Diana's silence." And mine as well.

"It is the risk we take every time we confess Christ as Lord." Portia looked down at the rolled scroll.

"I don't think Dio found peace. Cassandra said he left the last time in resignation."

Portia shook her head. "It's more likely that Dio's peace came when he committed to building the ludus. No more losing sleep deliberating which would bring him greater honor. I need to inform John immediately that his letter has been stolen and is likely on its way to Rome and Domitian."

Sabina headed for the door. "You said John has been planning to distribute copies of his revelation to the churches in the area. Perhaps a letter was intercepted. John could begin by questioning the couriers."

"This letter will heighten the emperor's paranoia. If he arrests John again, he will not survive."

The sun had set by the time they reached Portia's home. Portia insisted that Sabina ride home in her litter. Alone inside, she adjusted the cushions behind her back, pulled the ring out, and ran her fingers over the intricate detailing. Tiny inlaid silver leaves adorned the ring's band of gold. Silver prongs cradled a carnelian, a scarlet fire blazing in the heart of the stone. Two entwined grape vines were intricately engraved into the stone's surface. She wondered what her chances were of getting arrested.

She could not allow herself to be found with the ring, and the only way she could think to get rid of it was to give it to her father and face whatever retribution he would deliver.

He wasn't home when she crawled out of the litter. It had been an exhausting day, and the next day's funeral had arduous written all over it. She waited up until her eyes fluttered closed, but her father had not returned.

He did not tell her where he went at night, but the servants whispered about the increasing amount of time he spent with a certain widow named Octavia. When she could not stop yawning, she placed the ring in a small wooden box, set it on his desk, and collapsed into bed, sure she would have nightmares of Yechiel and Cassandra.

THIRTY-TWO

In the warmth of the early morning, the sheen of exertion glistened on Sabina's face and arms as she climbed the stairs to the rooftop. It'd been days since she'd had time to visit the pigeon loft, and her nerves showed it. From childhood, God spoke most clearly to her here among the cooing of the birds where she could be still and listen to His guidance.

Which she desperately needed.

Birds squawked and then settled back into their nests. Her father nurtured his selectively bred birds out of practical necessity. Sabina had adopted Cleopatra and Anthony, two albinos her father had rejected as inferior, spoiling them with love and attention.

Her pets fluttered from their partitioned-off nests, greeting her with non-stop cooing and pecking as she untied a bag of tasty oats and barley she used as rewards in their training. The pigeon keeper hadn't replaced today's straw, and the pungent, acrid droppings from over fifty pigeons hit her nostrils. The familiar smell wrapped her in a reassuring calm.

Sabina pushed aside a clump of soiled straw with her bare foot and knelt on the hardened clay floor.

Dear God, give me insight and wisdom to follow the path You've laid for me. Give Your angels charge over Yechiel, Eunice, and their unborn child. Save them and me from the evil seeking to destroy the truth You've

275

given to guide, sustain, and renew us. Please help me find Your truth and bring justice for Dionysius and Cassandra. In the name of—

She closed her eyes and pinched her lips together.

And provide me with patience and the heart of forgiveness for my father, in the name of Jesus Christ, Your Son, our Lord, Amen.

Her petition ended, and she extended her legs, letting the quiet rejuvenation soak in before attending the funeral procession that would last through the afternoon. In Ephesus, a leading citizen and patrician with the wealth of Dionysius Alexandros doesn't die in the prime of life every day. The festivities and pageantry would be an event to remember.

Cleo fluttered to Sabina's shoulder and nestled under her tangled cascade of russet hair. Sabina lifted Cleo, resting her in her palm and stroking the snow-white feathers of her pet, a squab she'd rescued before being fattened as a dinner entrée. Cleo's flashiness made her useless for her father's espionage needs.

"I'm sorry I've neglected you, but I had something important to do these last few days."

Cleo gently pecked at her ear.

"You don't believe me? I have more to do than shop for your dinner, and I have a cryptic letter to prove it. A secret Christian letter landed in the hands of a non-believer. No, he was a skeptic. And he was murdered."

Cleo fluttered down and stuck her head in the empty treat bag. She then looked up with a reproachful head bob.

"Well, you're wrong. I am helping find the killer so that Yechiel, an egotistical, rude, arrogant, but innocent man, can go free. But I am running into complications."

The door to the loft burst open, banging against the wall. Sabina jumped and scrambled to her feet. Dozens of pigeons burst from their roosts, wings clapping, and darted in panicked circles around the domed roof. Cleo and Anthony joined the fray.

Her father barged in with his usual inscrutable expression.

Sabina brushed mussed-up hair from her face. She hadn't expected her father to seek her out here. He visited the pigeon loft only when he needed to send a message, and he usually entrusted that task to his pigeon breeder and trainer.

He held out a small, unadorned wooden box. "What is this?"

She leaned forward and warily plucked the box from him. "A box for safekeeping."

"I don't mean the box. For the love of Zeus." He scowled.

She lifted the lid. "It is a ring." She picked up the gold circle, hefting it like she had when she first found it. "You were out late last night, so I put the ring in a box and left it for you. It's the emblem of the god Diony—"

He cut her off. "Why do you have it?" Her father snatched the ring and scrutinized the jeweled adornments.

"I found it hidden in a garden at Dionysius's house. Ursula told me Dionysius's signet ring had been destroyed the day of his murder. Crushed along with his body at the construction site."

"Ursula gave it to you?" He stopped examining the ring.

"Not exactly."

Her father's detached manner slipped as he shouted. "You stole Dionysius's signet?"

"According to Dionysius's family, the family signet doesn't exist." She bit her lip, and Cleo fluttered to her lap. She clutched the bird for encouragement. "I don't know if this ring is Dio's or not."

"What do you know?"

If it was Dio's ring, she had stolen the family signet, a priceless heirloom of one of the wealthiest families in Ephesus, a crime probably punishable by death. She avoided her father's smoldering glare. "If Dionysius wore this ring to the building site that morning, it could lead us to the murderer."

Her father raised an eyebrow. "This critical clue somehow found its way into our pigeon loft." He spoke each word as a threat.

She gulped, resisting the urge to point out that he brought it there.

He paced, the ring clutched in his fist. "I left Dio's house yesterday confident you understood your involvement with that family was over, finished. Is that what I communicated, or am I a babbling imbecile?"

"Well," Sabina hedged. Focusing on her disobedience didn't seem like a wise choice, nor did agreeing that he was an imbecile. "If you'd like to hear, I have worked out multiple scenarios of who could have hidden it." She took his silent glower as a go-ahead. "I have ruled out the family slaves unless someone ordered one to hide it, making them innocent of the murder."

"That leaves the entire family as suspects."

"They all have motives and access to the garden. The ring couldn't be hidden in a private room because a slave or servant would find it while cleaning. I'm sure the killer wanted to move it but had no opportunity. The plant provided an accessible and relatively secure hiding place for a short time."

"I hardly see how Ursula or Diana could have gone to the site and carried out the murder."

"They may have had accomplices, Loukas and Otho. Who also could have acted alone."

"The obvious explanation isn't always correct," her father mused. "Do not underestimate Mordax. He visited the house yesterday."

"Why would Mordax steal the ring and then hide it."

"Why would anyone risk taking it." He rubbed his jaw. "I have no choice but to return the ring and verify if the ring you stole is or is not the Antiochus family signet."

She held his gaze. "Did Otho admit to killing Cassandra?"

"He hasn't confessed, if that's what you're asking."

"But you suspect him?"

"He has incriminated himself with several statements, admitting specific details. Not just speculative gossip. Fortunately, the man doesn't have the criminal mind of his father."

"Did he admit to visiting Cassandra?"

"He acknowledged going for a reading as a pretext to bribe the fortune teller into convincing Diana to marry him. He said he left after she told his fortune."

"Diana said Cassandra would never take a bribe." Sabina wasn't sure she believed that.

"Refusing a bribe could be why Otho killed her."

"If you believe Otho killed her, he would have had the same motive for Dionysius's murder. His marriage to Diana."

Her father's face turned grim. "I'm convinced Mordax is involved. The timing of the newly signed contract and Dio's death are not coincidental."

"Mordax deceived Paris into signing away forty-nine percent of the family share of the ludus. If Paris doesn't uphold his contracted obligations, the majority control reverts to Mordax."

Her father nodded. "Then Otho's arrest came just in time."

"And you will charge him with Cassandra's murder?"

"First, we have a woman to visit."

"We?" She bit back a smile. He believed her.

"And you will be there to apologize if you are wrong." He turned and stomped down the stairs.

"I'm not wrong, sir. Remember, it's her husband's funeral today," she chimed out. He didn't respond. "Of course, he knew that." She nuzzled Cleo. "It's one of the biggest events of the year." Cleopatra pecked at Sabina's ear. "I'm sorry, I have to go. I'll tell you all about the funeral when I get back. I have a murder to solve."

Three hours later, with her hair and clothing in place, Sabina waited in the atrium to meet her father. She cornered Zarmig leaving her father's office, juggling a stack of scrolls with a cudgel strapped to his wrist.

She had not spoken to him after he had used her to capture Yechiel. She wanted to say he betrayed her, but she knew the rules of espionage taught to her by Zarmig himself. She had plotted her actions out and had been outwitted. Her father had ordered Zarmig to find Yechiel, and he did. It was her fault, her mistake, and blaming Zarmig was a petty gesture, but she couldn't help dumping some of her guilt on him.

Sabina raised her eyebrows at the cudgel.

"Funerals can get unruly. I may need to knock a few old women out of our way."

Sabina rolled her eyes. "I have a question."

"You're talking to me again? Am I forgiven?"

"No. Why is Yechiel being sent to Rome?" Zarmig could make amends for his part in Yechiel's betrayal.

Zarmig frowned at her around the side of the pile and kept walking. "I don't have time for this today."

"Yechiel doesn't have time at all. He's scheduled to be transported with troops leaving today."

Zarmig stopped. "How did you manage to come by privileged troop information?"

"I'm investigating Dionysius's murder."

"Right." Zarmig, infamous bodyguard, master spy, and assassin for her father, put down the ledgers with a heavy sigh. He captured several rolling scrolls, nudging them into formation. "Ephesus's prisons are full. This batch of prisoners has been scheduled for transfer for weeks. Someone added Yechiel to the inventory."

"Someone? A prisoner isn't randomly assigned to a troop transport ship."

"Now you are privy to the internal legal mechanisms of the city prisons?" He raised an eyebrow. "Do you have your own network of spies?"

"I don't have time for your jokes today." Sabina hated it when Zarmig ridiculed her.

"I was serious."

"An innocent man is being sent to Rome, condemned without a trial." She focused on his face, reading his expression.

Zarmig shrugged. "He can convince the judge in Rome of his innocence."

"He will die in Rome." Reuben's voice reverberated in her mind. Yechiel will not get to Rome.

"If that is what the Fates have decreed. Death awaits us all." The corner of his mouth twitched. That only happened when he lied. Zarmig knew something he wasn't sharing. But why? Her father had made it clear he didn't care enough about Yechiel to save him, let alone orchestrate an elaborate scheme to move him to Rome for execution. "Tell me."

"Tell you what?" Her father strode from around a corner.

"Your daughter asked why the impulsive Ursula fell in love with me long before you."

"Humph. The cart is waiting." Her father adjusted the folds of his toga. Had her father noted Zarmig's twitch as well?

They descended the front stairs to a waiting two-seated donkey cart. They would discard the conveyance before they got to the Antiochus villa. Spectators following the funeral procession to the agora would be crowding the streets. A groom handed the reins to Zarmig, then opened the side door to assist Sabina into the cart. The groom dropped his arm just as she braced against it to hop in. Support gone, she lost her balance and tumbled to her backside.

"Oww," she whined.

No one noticed.

Twirling his cudgel, Zarmig handed the reins back to the groom. A solid block of muscle barreled down on her father. She rose and brushed the street grime from her mantle.

"Mordax." Her father greeted and motioned Zarmig to stop his cudgel demonstration.

Mordax stopped a few feet from her father. "Release my son, Catius. You can't take your grudge against me out on Otho."

Her father strode past Mordax, heading toward the cart. Mordax grabbed his arm. Her father jerked to a stop. His jaw muscle tightened as he turned and stared at Mordax's hand. "Are you sure you want to do that?"

Zarmig stared impassively, but Sabina saw his stance widen, his hands caressing the wooden club.

Mordax dropped his arm. "I want him out of prison."

"You may file a complaint in my office tomorrow."

Sabina looked at her father, composed as always. She barely noticed his toga ripple with the tensing of his muscles.

"You arrested my son for no reason."

Zarmig laughed with a sense of disbelief. "Otho practically confessed to murder."

"He said you tricked him," Mordax spoke through clenched teeth.

She had no doubt her father had maneuvered Otho into revealing details he didn't realize implicated him. Trickery—or letting the criminal nail himself to a cross one admission at a time—was her father's and Zarmig's specialized skill.

Zarmig approached, the cudgel swinging at his side. "Otho admitted to calling on Cassandra. He attempted to bribe her to convince Diana to marry him. And when Cassandra resisted..." Zarmig raised the club and smacked it into his hand.

Mordax's glare switched from Zarmig to her father. "Otho may have lost his temper. That's not a crime, and there are worse vices."

"Like murder?" Her father's eyebrows arched in emphasis.

Mordax fixated on her father. "He admitted to being in the whore's rooms while she was alive. You can't prove he caused her death. Who knows how many other men the witch entertained that day?"

"He revealed information only the killer would know." Zarmig cracked the cudgel against his palm. "It's hard to entertain visitors with a broken neck."

Mordax bared his teeth, his eyes narrowing. "The witch told his fortune. The bones said he'd be arrested for a murder he didn't commit."

"You're lying." Heat flashed through Sabina. "Cassandra never used bones for her visions. She never told Otho's fortune."

"Bones or no bones," Mordax bullied. "She was a fraud who sold herself and her lies."

Sabina drew a long breath. "Her name was Cassandra, and she wasn't a prostitute."

"Stay out of this, Sabina." Her father motioned her into the cart.

Mordax flicked his gaze briefly over Sabina. "You're wasting your time. No one will pay for a lawyer to prosecute the death of a scabby piece of flesh."

"You don't know that." Sabina's chest tightened with anger.

"I said be quiet." Her father nodded to Zarmig, who took her arm, but she shook him off. Quietly shaking, she climbed stiffly into the cart and sat.

"You can ask Otho when he is freed." Mordax sneered. "The Rome you serve has laws against divination and putting spells on people. If Otho fixed her up, and I'm not saying he did, the magistrates will be thanking him for getting rid of useless vermin."

The horror of Mordax's words tore into the raw emotions of seeing Cassandra broken and covered in blood. Emotions she had repressed until now. Sabina stood, shaking in the cart.

Zarmig gave her a warning look.

She tried gritting her teeth. It didn't work. "My father will see Otho sentenced and executed in the arena you build. Cassandra will get justice."

"Your father?" Mordax narrowed his eyes and focused entirely on Sabina for the first time. "What makes you think your father wants justice? He wants revenge." Spittle shot from his mouth.

Her father's lips rose in an expression that was anything but a smile. "Justice is what separates humans from beasts."

Mordax threw back his head and laughed. "You and I, Catius, are the beasts. And the one who survives determines right and wrong, not some imaginary rules."

"Says the criminal who preys on the vulnerable," Zarmig grunted.

Her father smoothed out the spotless wool of his tunic. "Aristotle recognized the moral absolutes written in men's hearts. Ignoring them won't make them go away."

"I don't think Mordax has a heart," Zarmig said.

Mordax's eyes were bulging, his spittle spraying at every word. "You are self-righteous dogs. Lying, cheating, jealousy, greed, lust, it's all shifting shades of gray. Don't tell me you wouldn't look the other way if Otho were the son of a high and mighty senator."

"I'm not Otho's judge. Roman law will see him punished." Her father turned, motioning Zarmig to the cart. "Just because you've gotten away these years, do not think I haven't recorded your crimes. Even ones you have forgotten. And you and your son will pay for every one."

Mordax stepped closer, blocking their way. "I do not submit to your gods or your laws. No one determines my innocence or guilt." He spit on the ground. "That's what I think of Aristotle."

Growling, Zarmig pushed Mordax out of the way. Mordax crouched, bracing to strike, then rapidly flicked his gaze over Zarmig's tensing muscles, daring him to fight. Mordax stepped back, and Zarmig and her father walked past.

Zarmig took the reins from the groom, who climbed into the cart and sat at Sabina's feet.

Her father sat beside her on the cart's bench, musing loud enough for Mordax to hear, "Evil doesn't become good just because you deny it, Mordax. Lies don't become truth, hate isn't mistaken for love, and in my world, criminals don't go unpunished."

Mordax stepped in front of the donkey, blocking their departure. "It's not your world, Catius." He glared. "I'll do whatever it takes to keep Otho out of your grasp. Even if I must die in his place."

"You don't have enough lives to pay for your crimes, let alone his."

Zarmig snapped the reins, and the donkey brayed unmoving. The whip cracked above the beast's ears. Startled, it lurched forward. Mordax stumbled to the side. The image of a glaring Mordax regaining his balance receded with the donkey's clopping.

"He's right," Zarmig said over his shoulder. "No one will pay for a lawyer to prosecute Otho for the woman's death."

Sabina turned toward her father. "You said you would." Her father said nothing. "Then why were you talking about Aristotle's justice."

Her father adjusted his toga. "Mordax needs a jolting dose of fear. He's shown none for himself but might for his son."

Zarmig's mouth twitched as he snapped the reins again.

"You have no intention of prosecuting Otho for Cassandra's murder? You were goading Mordax?" Sabina understood the devastating undercurrents of her father and Mordax. "What about Dionysius's murderer?"

Her father paused. "I believe Mordax is linked to the murder, but he hides his tracks well. By killing the fortune teller, Otho gave us leverage over his father."

Cassandra wasn't just leverage. Was her father as callous as Mordax?

"Battle tactics," Zarmig said. "It is a two-pronged strategy. We squeeze Mordax at one end by arresting Otho. With Yechiel's arrest, pressure is off at that end, and an overconfident Mordax lets his guard down and escapes into the noose we have set."

"You're using Yechiel as bait to trap Mordax?" Sabina turned to her father, her mouth dropping.

"Bait is a rather strong word," Zarmig said.

"What happened to justice being the highest of all virtues?" Sabina said indignantly.

Her father didn't answer for a long moment. "Mordax's conviction is justice."

"Torturing an innocent man and sending him to prison isn't justice," she sputtered.

"Yechiel will be freed once we arrest Mordax," her father said.

The vision of Yechiel's poisoned breakfast sent a quiver of hopelessness through her body. The donkey slowed, Zarmig slapped the reins on its backside, and the plodding increased speed. "What about Otho?" Sabina pleaded.

"Mordax will secure his release," her father stated as if that explained everything. "The fortune teller was nobody, and Mordax has powerful connections on the city council."

"Bought and paid for with good money," said Zarmig. "But if Mordax is convicted of Dionysius's murder, every rich patrician in Ephesus will renounce any allegiance they have to him."

"No amount of bribery will get Mordax off," her father said.

"But Otho goes free?" Raising a quivering chin, Sabina drew in a deep breath. "Does Cassandra's death mean nothing to you? She was not a nobody. She was your daughter." She had not planned to say that. She had decided to follow Amisi's advice and keep her sister's search a secret, but he couldn't ignore her murder. She braced for her father's outrage, his excuses, his denials.

He cocked an eyebrow and looked at her with distaste, almost indifference, as if she were a worm in his peach. "I have one daughter. And she is one impertinence away from being thrown out of this cart."

Tears pooled. She blinked rapidly to stop them. Her father hated crying, hated it as a sign of weakness or, worse, manipulation. Hers was neither. The anger that fueled her tears flowed out as a silent plea for fairness. "Two innocent people suffered unjustly because you are obsessed with Mordax. Cassandra and now Yechiel will die." Long before he reaches Rome.

"Enough," her father shouted. "Stop the cart."

Zarmig glanced back with a you'll-never-learn shake of his head.

She didn't know if she was angrier at her father or herself. Feeling like a chastised eight-year-old, she glowered at her father. "Father never listens. He's taking his anger out on me because he knows I'm right about Mordax," she said to Zarmig as he helped her clamber down.

Zarmig slammed the door. "Your father's upset because he failed to stop you from making yourself a future target for Mordax's vindictive retaliation."

"Oh."

He leaped back, slapping the reins and leaving her red-faced, sniffling, and feeling very sorry for herself. She started walking to Dionysius's house.

She had been wrong to think the worst of her father. He was trying to protect her. Was she like Diana, basing her decision on childhood injustices? Portia said Satan uses our resentment to destroy our families, our relationships, and our joy. Bitterness certainly wasn't helping her cause. She stopped to shake a stone from her sandal.

If change starts with thanking God for His perpetual goodness, it wouldn't be easy.

THIRTY-THREE

Sabina had nearly caught up to the donkey cart, which had gotten snarled among the mob of funeral attendees. She arrived only minutes after her father and Zarmig, a small victory, but the sticky sweat prickling her face and back took away any urge to gloat.

She ignored Zarmig, stationed at the front door, raising her nose in a snub as she passed him.

Ursula stood opposite her father in the atrium. The two intently assessed each other.

"Catius, I am not in the mood nor have time for your apology. In case you haven't noticed, I am burying my husband today. It is the most significant public event of the year."

Her father held out the box. "Open it, please."

"Ooh, amends?" She took the plain wooden box. Sniffed disdainfully, then held it for him to take back. "I haven't decided your penance."

"It's not an apology," he said.

"Despite my irritation at you, I am intrigued." Ursula must have noticed her father's severe tone and stern expression. She opened the box. Her eyes widened, and her hand shook as she lifted the ring, her fist cupping it gently. "Where did you get this?" she whispered.

"Is it your husband's signet ring?"

Sabina watched Ursula's reaction closely.

Ursula nodded. Her chin trembled. "I asked where you found this. At the construction site?"

"The ring was found in your home," her father said.

She closed her fist around the ring. "Here? Who?" She glared at Sabina, her voice brittle. "You? I trusted you, and you betrayed me by spying on me and stealing." Her eyes blazed. "You are not like your father. He understands respect, loyalty, and integrity!"

Each accusation was like a slap. Sabina stepped back.

"Ursula, that's enough." Sabina's father's usual intimidation was absent, a courtesy perhaps, to their past relationship or consideration for the impending funeral. "You told Sabina the ring was destroyed."

"Now you're calling me a liar?" Her eyes flew open. "Or are you accusing me of murder…again?"

"The ring's reappearance is significant. I am asking you a question," Sabina's father said.

"I do not appreciate your little questioning game. I am under no obligation—today of all days. How dare you? It is my husband's funeral." Ursula's voice rose with each statement until she screamed the last one, her whole body shaking.

"Ursula, please. I'm sorry you are in mourning." Sabina would not apologize for her actions. "But we need an answer."

"You stay away from me." Ursula's gaze darted between the two of them. "This is not how to ensure I stay in Dio's will. You were supposed to prove my innocence."

Sabina tried again. "That's what I'm trying to do. We aren't accusing you. We need information about why this ring is in your home."

"I need Loukas," Ursula yelled. "Titos, get Loukas."

"Titos isn't here." Her father pointed out. "And we will be questioning Loukas as well."

"Of course, you're suspicious of Loukas because you're jealous of him. That's what this is all about."

Her father swore under his breath. "We are trying to find out who murdered your husband. If you didn't do it…"

"Of course, I didn't do it." Ursula screeched. "No, it's Loukas—you think Loukas killed Dio because he wanted me." Ursula stopped and licked her lips then smiled, her poise and self-confidence back in place. "Loukas would do anything for me. But he had no reason to kill Dio."

Sabina had never encountered such a swift reversal of mood. Portia had warned about Ursula's unpredictable emotions. "And the ring?"

"We assumed the ring had been crushed, like his beautiful hands. I have no idea how the ring got here." Ursula looked puzzled. "Paris ordered the workers to search for it when they cleared the blocks and devastation away. They didn't find it." She loosened her grasp on the ring. "Everyone believed it had been lost in the rubble."

"Not everyone," her father said. "We need to question Paris and Diana."

"Question me about what?" Diana strolled toward them, looking even more drab, dressed in funeral attire.

Ursula handed the ring to Diana. "Sabina found your father's signet."

"I thought it was destroyed." Diana glanced at the ring. "Did you find it at the construction site?"

"I found it in the garden. Near the bench where you write," Sabina said while studying Diana's reaction.

"Why would Father hide his ring in the garden?" Diana looked bewildered.

Ursula clicked her tongue. "You're normally a very intelligent woman. He wouldn't."

"I haven't thought about the ring. I had other things on my mind with Otho…." Diana blushed and trailed off before looking perplexed. "How did the ring get there?"

"That's what we want to ask you," Sabina's father said.

"I have no idea." Diana slipped the ring on and stared at it. "Maybe a slave stole it when removing debris from father's body." She spun it around on her finger. "It was foolish to hide it at the house."

"A slave wouldn't risk the death penalty." Ursula snorted. "I need to question Paris. Where is Titos? He needs to find Paris."

"Ursula, you cannot accuse my brother without proof." Diana faced Sabina. "You were supposed to be on our side."

"I'm not taking sides." Sabina understood the conflicting loyalties flitting across Diana's face. Diana had been angry at Paris earlier but not mad enough to side with her stepmother against him. And Paris held her future in his hands.

"Shouldn't we wait until after the funeral?" Diana said.

Sabina's father shook his head. "If Paris has an explanation. It will not take long."

"Titos," Ursula yelled. "Never mind. I'll find Paris myself." Ursula stormed away.

Sabina, her father, and a reluctant Diana followed Ursula through the atrium, onto the garden walkway, and toward Paris's and Diana's bedrooms. Zarmig trailed behind.

Sabina stopped. "Over there is where I found the ring." She pointed to the bench.

A rustling came from the spot, followed by a disembodied head floating through the dense shrubbery. Sabina screamed, and it disappeared.

Zarmig sprinted up.

"There," Sabina stammered, indicating a thick horsehair plume jiggling and bobbing in the air around the bench. The strange dance drew closer. An arm appeared, followed by a body with its back turned, wearing an ancient helmet topped with a large plume.

"Father's ghost?" Diana shrieked, gripping Ursula's arm.

Sabina's heart rate sped up. She stepped back, bumping into her father. I don't believe in ghosts.

The plumage fluttered enthusiastically, and Paris turned around, holding the wax death mask of Pelopidas Antiochus in one hand and brushing leaves and dirt from his costume with the other.

Sabina wasn't sure who gasped the loudest, Paris or her.

Paris pivoted to his left, then right, as if rehearsing an escape before the helmet slipped down over his eyes, pinning him in place. He nudged the helmet up with his free hand, smudging soil on his nose. "What? Have you never seen the uniform of a broad-stripe military tribune?"

Diana stalked up to him and smacked him on the shoulder. "Paris, you idiot. Your playacting scared me to death."

"I'm not playing, Diana. I'm wearing the uniform and mask for the funeral, representing our great-grandfather, a hero in the First Germanic Roman Legion." The white wool cloak draped over Paris's shoulder showed where moth-eaten holes had been repaired. Its distinguished purple stripe had faded over decades. The molded armor, crafted for a larger soldier, hung on Paris's smaller frame, making his movements stiff and jerky.

Diana turned to Sabina's father. "As children, my brothers played at fighting the German hordes at Long Bridges. Portraying our great-grandfather is Paris's dream come true."

Paris reverently placed the wax mask on the bench while he addressed Sabina's father. "If this is about Otho's unwarranted arrest, I don't have time for your apology. You can return tomorrow."

Sabina's father frowned. "Why does everyone think I'm apologizing?"

Diana held up the signet. "Look, we found Father's ring."

Paris's face turned red. "Where did you get that?" Paris snatched at it.

Diana lifted the ring from his reach. Paris's helmet slid down. He pushed it up. Fuming, he wrenched the helmet off and glared at his stepmother. "You sent Diana to spy on me."

Diana sucked in a breath. "How dare you accuse me."

Paris focused on his sister. "I'm sorry. I am just surprised to see that ring. Stunned."

"We all were." Sabina's father walked over to the potted vine, noting the upturned dirt and soil tossed onto the ground. "You need to explain why you were digging in the garden around this particular plant."

Paris brushed his hands together, smearing the dirt, not dislodging it. His eyes narrowed as he whipped around to Sabina. "You told him. You've been spying on me."

"I was investigat—" Sabina looked at her father, remembering him ridiculing her detective skills.

Paris appealed to Sabina's father. "As the head of the Antiochus family, the ring belongs to me. I don't see what the problem is."

Sabina's father cleared his throat, signaling Diana to hand him the ring. He held it up, examining the carving on the stone as if he'd never seen it. "You reported the ring destroyed after your father's death."

"Yes, the workers searched and didn't find it. You understand the site was chaotic, with splintered marble blocks and dust-covered debris everywhere. An object that small is easily lost."

"Yet here it is." Sabina pointed to the ring.

Diana's eyes widened. "You stole the ring from father's corpse?"

"No! I swear by the gods, no." Paris sounded panicked, his breathing audible and rapid. "I didn't take the ring. Father gave it to me."

"What?" Ursula snapped. "When?"

"That morning, when Father came to my room." Paris swallowed and rubbed his temples. Everyone waited while he paused. "He said he would be helping at the site that day, and he didn't want to lose the ring. When I decided not to go with him, he asked me to return the ring to his office."

"But you didn't return it," Sabina's father prodded.

Paris stammered. "I fell back to sleep. Then my steward woke me with the news that Father was dead, and I had to retrieve the body. I wasn't thinking about the ring."

"You forgot?" Ursula laughed mockingly.

"Yes, and when we found out Yechiel had killed him, I was angry. The ring didn't matter. I realized Yechiel must have written the note first luring Father to his death and then plotting to dislodge the beam to kill him."

Her father's mouth tightened, and his eyes sparked as they drilled into Paris. "What beam are we talking about?"

"The one that collapsed the arch." Paris sniffed as if questioning her father's intelligence—wrong tactic. Like a bull led by its nose, Sabina knew Paris's destination.

"The inspectors have not announced how or why the arch collapsed. Perhaps you could share your expertise with me." Her father's flat, neutral tone should have been a warning to Paris.

"I'm not the expert." Paris looked around as if trying to discover how he'd ended up at this dead-end. "Yechiel's the architect. He would know how to make an arch fall." Paris's voice regained some of his arrogance. "Isn't that why he was arrested?"

Sabina's father flexed his fingers without releasing Paris from his gaze. "There is a slight problem with his arrest. Witnesses agree Yechiel was praying in his synagogue at the time of the murder."

"Yechiel's lying." Paris snorted. "No one but slaves awake before dawn. No one worships that early."

"Jews do," Sabina said.

Paris stammered. "Then it must have been Agabus. He was there that morning."

"You are right, Agabus was there." Sabina's father examined the ring again, his gaze brushing over Paris as he handed the ring to Diana. "Still, the inspectors will be interested in how the signet ended up in your plant."

Ursula's mouth barely moved, her body rigid. "Dio would never have entrusted his ring to you."

"It was you Father didn't trust. He and I would run the ludus together after he divorced you." Paris clenched his fists before he turned to look at Sabina's father. "With Ursula and Loukas conspiring against me and Titos sneaking throughout the house, I could hardly leave the ring in my room for them to steal. I had to keep it safe from her." Paris pointed to Ursula.

Sabina's father nodded dispassionately.

"We will question Titos, your steward, the other household slaves, and servants to corroborate everyone's location and timeline that morning."

"My steward?" Paris blanched.

Her father nodded gravely. "There are occasional accidents while undergoing interrogation."

"You cannot torture my steward…he's old." Sweat droplets popped out on Paris's forehead.

Was Paris concerned for his steward? Had he developed a devoted relationship with the man since childhood, as Sabina had with Amisi? Or once freed, was Paris fearful his steward's loyalty was no longer guaranteed?

"Don't worry." Her father reassured Paris. "I promise your steward will stay alive long enough to reveal everything we need to confirm your innocence."

Paris was a novice at this game of snake and weasel. A game her father had learned from birth while growing up among Rome's social elites. A game he had refined in the military, interrogating spies on blood-soaked battlefields, and now perfected in the dens of secrecy, murder, and intrigue of modern Ephesus. Her father knew how to control Paris's concern for his steward or his fear. It didn't matter in the end.

"You don't need to question him." Paris blurted out. "I might have gone out earlier than I said.

Sabina sucked in a gulp of air. Her father displayed no emotion.

"Oh, Paris!" Diana's fist tightened on the ring, turning white. "What did you do?"

"Nothing," Paris hung his head. "That is the problem."

Before she'd been dumped out of the cart, Zarmig had explained the strategy of using Yechiel as bait. It had succeeded, just not in the way her father had expected. Paris, not Mordax, had felt overly confident after Yechiel's arrest. Her father would dig to the bottom of Paris's lies, especially if they pointed to his business partner, Mordax.

THIRTY-FOUR

Paris pressed his lips together, crossed his arms, and glared in turn at Sabina, her father, Zarmig, Diana, and Ursula. "Don't look at me like that."

"What happened that morning?" Sabina's father asked. "You obviously didn't fall back asleep."

Paris looked imploringly at his sister. "I wanted to. I had stayed out late that night, but Father insisted I accompany him to the building site. He woke my steward to get me dressed."

"Why didn't you tell us the truth?" Diana's eyes widened, filling with tears.

Paris's voice became hollow. "Because I was with him when the arch collapsed, and I couldn't save him. I felt guilty. I didn't want anyone to know I'd failed him, failed our family. I know I should have told someone."

Her father didn't blink. "Your father wore his ring to the building site."

Paris shrugged, avoiding her father's gaze. His lower lip quivered. "All the way there, Father talked about his big surprise for me. I got excited because I knew that he'd finally decided to build the ludus. When we arrived, he explained how he viewed us as the human keystones that would secure the glory of the Antiochus name. I kept yawning, and Father told

295

me to find a place to sit. I had barely taken a few steps when I heard a grating sound and spun around. The beam fell, and without the keystone to hold the other stones in place, the blocks tumbled. There was no time to scream a warning before the marble buried him. If I hadn't been half asleep, I could have reacted faster, perhaps pulled him to safety."

"Are you saying the supports collapsed at the precise moment your father stood under them?" Sabina was skeptical.

"It wasn't just a moment. Father stood under the arch a long time, going on and on about the weight of the blocks, their dimensions, and the physics of lifting thousands of pounds of marble with a pulley."

"You should have told me." Tears streaked down Diana's cheeks.

"I know. I feel terrible, but you don't know what it's like to be in shock." Paris held out his hands, imploring Diana. "I had just watched Father get crushed to death."

"And yet you had the composure to remove his ring." Sabina shuddered, imagining Dionysius's broken body.

"What? No—well, yes. I couldn't leave the ring for the workers to steal." Paris's lips tightened into a pout.

Diana covered her mouth. She looked ready to faint. "You dared touch his body with his ghost still present?"

"I was shaking and couldn't think. I was devastated. I heard the slapping sandals of the workers running to help. I know I should have stayed, but I couldn't help him. I barely stumbled home."

"Why bury the ring?" her father pressed.

"I told you. I had to keep it safe from her." Paris pointed to Ursula. "From everyone until the will was settled."

"But it wasn't safe from you." Ursula's mouth set in a firm line. "The signet gave you the authority to access Dio's money. How often have you used it to fund your betting?"

"No, I didn't use the ring for betting."

Sabina calculated the sequence of events. Paris pries the signet off his dead or dying father's finger. Add in time to report the accident and retrieve the body, then Mordax turns up with his letter. "When did you say your father signed the contract with Mordax?" she asked.

"I don't remember the exact date," Paris said. "I found the contract in his office after Mordax showed me his letter. What does that have to do with anything?"

Her father straightened. "We need to inspect the two letters written to Agabus and Mordax. I'll need Mordax's contract."

"Of course. Dio's lawyer is reviewing it," Ursula said.

"What are you talking about?" Paris screeched.

Sabina took a breath. "You admitted to forging your father's signature to buy Ferocianus. Someone else could have done the same. With the signet, whoever it was had the authority to verify forged documents. Perhaps the letters to Agabus and Mordax."

"No." Paris twitched. "Father wrote the letters. He sealed the contract. He and I were going to be partners. Why else would we go to the construction site? Obviously, he planned a future with Ferocianus and wanted to show me his vision for the ludus, the culminating tribute to his greatness, excellence, and worthiness."

Diana wiped her tears with the back of her hand. "Father told you that? That the ludus would be a tribute to him? To his worthiness?"

"His exact words." Paris nodded.

"Then why did Father tell me no one was worthy." Diana stole a glance at Sabina. "Something changed him. I read his letter yesterday. He wrote as if he had found peace with God. He wished that same peace for me."

"What's that supposed to mean?" Paris sneered.

Diana let her breath out slowly. "It means I was right about your argument. Father wouldn't let Ferocianus die so that you could make money. And you got angry. I heard him offer you God's peace when he left that night. Why would he say that to you? To us? He died before explaining his letter, but I think that was why he planned to free Ferocianus."

"Free him...no. Are you trying to destroy us?" Paris's body shook. "Father wanted his name celebrated with each of Ferocianus's victories."

"No, he didn't." Diana gave Paris an injured look.

Paris's body shook. "You don't understand what you're saying."

"I understand better than you know." Diana looked stricken. "The night before he died, I heard Father tell you what he had tried to tell me—that he was a Christian."

"Shut up!" Paris lunged toward her, but Sabina's father stepped in his way. Paris stepped back, and his voice dropped conspiratorially. "I saved Father's legacy. I saved us, Diana."

Sabina's father moved closer. "How did you save his legacy, Paris?"

"I don't have to…" Paris trembled, his pupils wide. "No one has to know."

"What did you argue about the night before he died?" Sabina asked. "The ring?"

"You know nothing," Paris jeered. "I told Father about Mordax's loan offer and how I could pay off my debt using Ferocianus's winnings."

"If he joined in partnership with Mordax," her father said.

Paris went on as if he hadn't heard. "Instead of praising me, Father told me there would be no winnings because he intended to free Ferocianus. Why? Why would he do that to me?"

"What happened, Paris?" Sabina's father's voice remained calm. "Did you decide to kill him that night after your argument? Or did you plan the murder at the building site the next morning?"

"No! I didn't plan anything. Father said he was saving me from making the mistakes he made, but life doesn't work that way. Not with men like Mordax." Paris laughed with a note of hysteria. "Tell them, Diana, how you hated Father's hypocrisy."

Diana opened her mouth, closed it, and then whispered. "No one likes being judged."

Paris scoffed. "He said he wanted to live like the Christian Christ, to be a better father." Paris laughed wildly. "This, from a man who had lived his life doing whatever he wanted. He answered to no one."

"Did he tell you he had become a believer in Christ?" Sabina asked. Her father glared at her but didn't intercede.

"Catius, stop this." Ursula narrowed her eyes. "Dio would never convert to that perverted religion. Admit it, Paris, you wanted your inheritance, and to get it, your father had to die."

"He intended to share his good news. Not just with Diana. He meant to confess to the world that he was a traitor. You see why I had to stop him."

Ursula's hands opened and closed several times. "I refuse to allow you to slander your father's name with this absurd defense."

Paris's gaze traveled from person to person. "He would have slandered himself and destroyed us all. I saved his reputation."

"Do you even recognize the truth?" Ursula's eyes flashed, her voice cutting. "Everyone knows what Dio was. No one will believe you."

"No one is going to find out." Paris held a finger to his lips. "We can't tell a soul. Shhh. One hint is all Domitian needs to confiscate our wealth. Father might as well have deposited it into the emperor's bank himself. Our family's reputation, our money." Paris pointed to the helmet and death mask, his voice ragged. "Our great-grandfather's heritage. Domitian would have stolen it all. He would have destroyed us, and I couldn't let Father do that."

"What did happen the morning you went to the building site?" Sabina asked.

"I went hoping that he had changed his mind about Ferocianus. I thought if I reminded him of the glory of the ludus, he might reconsider. Do you know what his big surprise was?"

Sabina shook her head.

"He wanted me to set the keystone. He explained how the winch would lift the stone in place—for the library," Paris said.

"Not the ludus?" Sabina asked.

"There was no ludus." Paris stared at the ground. "Father acted as if we had never discussed it, no fortunes to be made, no ecstatic fans, no glory for our family. Only money wasted on scrolls and expensive writings collected from around the world. He expected me to act excited while he dismantled my life. 'Paris, you will find your way'—after he destroyed my future. 'You will learn responsibility'—after he shattered my dream.

"One last time, I asked him not to free Ferocianus. He couldn't just say no. He had to preach that he'd been patient and had given me time to change my ways. Didn't I see this coming? If he had just shut up, I wouldn't have gotten angry. I wouldn't have turned the winch's handle," Paris explained calmly.

No one said anything.

Paris's detachment unnerved Sabina. Did he comprehend what he'd just admitted to?

Paris turned somber. "I am devastated at losing my father. I have nightmares of him looking at me. His eyes widened like he couldn't believe what was happening. When the beam squealed, he jumped, but it was too late. The first block hit him, burying him under the barrage. He didn't see that coming." Paris broke into a little giggle.

Sabina was the first to speak. "Your dream was restored with just enough time to write, seal, and deliver your forged letters to Mordax and Agabus."

"And you had the ring," Ursula said.

"I did it for Father. I couldn't let him destroy himself and our family. Now, no one will ever know. And instead of being reviled, the city will honor his memory, his life, and the Antiochus legacy our family has built upon for generations. I shall lead the procession as my great-grandfather who died defending the empire." Paris bent and grabbed the helmet in one hand and the mask in the other. "Grandfather passed the sacred torch of honor to my father and my father to me." Pumping his arms, Paris yelled, "To Rome, Ephesus, family." He rushed past them, stumbling through the garden toward the atrium and the entryway.

Zarmig ran after him. Her father turned to follow.

Ursula put a hand on his arm. "Catius, can't you wait? Paris is right about one thing. We must protect our family's honor. The city awaits Dio's funeral."

Sabina's father paused, then yelled for Zarmig to return.

"Thank you," Ursula kissed Sabina's father on the cheek. "Paris has no fear of the gods and the law. But he will not flee from his role as the dutiful heir."

"Paris's fear will return soon enough," Sabina's father said. "Dio's son has broken the only law that wouldn't pardon him for killing a

Christian. Romans will forgive the murder of our emperors quicker than patricide."

Ursula straightened her back. "I would appreciate it if you did not repeat Paris's malicious lies. Life with my darling Dio was challenging. But he did not turn against the gods and become a Christian."

Diana looked skeptical. "Then why did he free Ferocianus?"

Ursula wagged her finger at Diana. "If the gladiator is freed, it will be with all the other slaves granted manumission. There is nothing unusual about that. I don't want to hear another word of this Christian sacrilege against my husband."

"But the letter he wrote to me..." Diana said.

Ursula huffed. "A letter you admitted you did not understand. We will never know where he got the traitorous letter. I can testify that your father was steadfastly loyal to the emperor. And never spoke a Christian heresy to me."

Diana looked unsure. "Portia said that Father would never repent for his life of rebellion against God. She called it sin."

"Well, if Portia said it, it must be true." Ursula dusted her hands together as if the matter was settled. "Why would your father ask absolution for following his heart's desires? It would be admitting this dead Christ had authority over our lives." Covering her mouth, she reprimanded Diana. "The idea of eating human flesh makes my stomach turn. How dare Paris accuse your father of that savagery?"

"Someone told me that is a malicious rumor." Diana glanced at Sabina.

Ursula turned to leave, then stopped. "Catius, you must be extremely proud of your daughter. She found the ring, solved Dio's murder, and although the ending was unexpected, she kept me in Dio's will."

"Yes, she found the killer," her father said.

"That's all you have to say?" Ursula scolded. "She performed brilliantly."

"If you say so," he said.

"Don't flatter her so much." Ursula squeezed his arm.

Her father stared at Sabina, and she met his gaze. It was not his usual dismissive glance. Something had changed. Perhaps he saw her through Ursula's eyes. Or his perspective had shifted. Whatever it was, it was nice to be noticed, even if her stomach was turning flips.

"Dio's ghost has lingered here long enough." Ursula adjusted her mantle. "We cannot be late paying tribute to the love of my life. His honorable name shall be engraved above all the ludus doors and pillars. People shall proclaim his virtues for eternity."

"Just as Father desired." Diana nodded tentatively.

Ursula sniffed. "And tomorrow, we will begin finding you a new love match."

Diana didn't look back as she strolled out of the garden arm-in-arm with Ursula.

Sabina's father turned to Zarmig. "Follow Paris. Do not disrupt the funeral, but do not let him out of your sight."

Sabina turned to her father. "You knew Yechiel was innocent and didn't tell me? You must free Yechiel immediately."

Her father stretched his arms. "I imagine it is too late."

Sabina spun around. "Then I will go and—"

Her father raised his hand. "There is nothing you can do for him."

"But you can," she said.

Zarmig stepped forward. "I could go to the prison, and if the transport hasn't left for Rome…"

Her father shook his head. "You are watching Paris."

"Paris is presiding over the funeral. He's not going anywhere," Zarmig yawned. "Besides, I can't stomach another pretentious spectacle of the corrupt and decadent of Ephesus. I've had enough for one day."

Another of Zarmig's peace offerings? She held her breath.

"I see I face an insurrection. Never mind. I am attending the funeral. It was an opportunity to observe a certain brothel owner and his associates, but I will watch Paris until you return," he grumbled to Zarmig. "Get me a papyrus sheet, a pen, and ink."

Sabina opened her mouth to say thank you, but her father waved to her to be quiet.

Sabina's foot tapped as Zarmig scoured the near-empty house for writing materials.

Dear God, don't let it be too late to save Yechiel.

It seemed ages before Zarmig returned, and her father wrote and sealed Yechiel's release. Zarmig handed his cudgel to her father. "Watch out for the grandmas."

Had the ship already docked and loaded their prisoners, or as Eunice feared, was Yechiel's lifeless body being prepared for the grave, missing out on his life spent with his wife and child by mere hours or minutes?

Hurry Zarmig!

THIRTY-FIVE

Sabina and her father's pace slowed as they melded into the swell of enthused and giddy spectators. Paris had gotten a head start on them. Sabina jumped, trying to see a plume bobbing over the heads of the crowd. People crushed in around her. It was pointless. If Paris were here, they'd never find him.

Did her father regret agreeing to Ursula's plea? Did she, who could not be trusted, according to multiple sources, have an alternative motive for delaying Paris's arrest? The river of humanity was the perfect cover for an escape.

A block ahead, the melancholy throbbing of drums and wail of flute music drifted down from the front of the parade. The gloom in the air engulfed her. Dionysius was no longer an abstract celebrity or a mystery to be solved but a father, husband, and friend. She had solved his murder, yet Paris's confession had left an unsatisfactory void.

She moved in closer to her father. "Do you believe Paris murdered his father because Dionysius became a Christian?"

"Who knows? We surprised him, and he blurted out a rash confession. He had little time to think up a plausible excuse, and blaming Christianity is popular. His gambling debts and Mordax's claws sunk deep into the family fortune all point to the usual motive—money."

"Then Ursula was correct. Paris killed out of greed."

"I would bet on it. Even if Paris publicly accused his father of treason, it won't matter. Paris's crime is unpardonable."

A man in the crowd shoved Sabina and pushed ahead of them. Her father clouted his head with the cudgel. The man winced and staggered away, swearing, not recognizing them. Otho!

Mordax's influence had worked rapidly, as Zarmig had predicted. Her temper flared, knowing Otho would never answer for the death of Cassandra. Indignation rose against her father. Was his justice only for the rich and powerful? How dare he—she stopped mid-thought. Had she, like Diana, been angry at her father for so long that she couldn't stop? He was not responsible for Otho killing Cassandra nor for him walking free. Could she unchain herself from past pains? Portia said to start with one positive thought.

Her father had believed her after finding the ring. He had protected her from Mordax, defended her when Ursula called her a thief, and sent Zarmig to release Yechiel. The apostle Paul wrote, bear with one another; if anyone has a complaint against someone else, forgive him. Just as the Lord has forgiven you, so you must forgive. Isn't that what Christians do?

"Watch out!" Her father grabbed her before she was bowled over by two screeching women rolling on the ground.

"He don't want you." A middle-aged matron screamed, wrestling her younger blonde opponent and pinning her down. She jumped to her feet and elbowed her way through the crowd to her goal, a muscular gladiator at the center of the scuffle.

"That's Ferocianus." Sabina sucked in a surprised breath.

Ferocianus grasped the older woman's hand, kissed it, and waved goodbye to his devoted fans, who appeared far more interested in the living celebrity at the end of the funeral procession than the notable corpse at its beginning.

The gladiator joined a large contingent of Antiochus family slaves wearing skull caps, signifying their manumission.

"Apparently, Paris wasn't aware that the lawyer, Gnaeus Gratus, had authorized Dionysius's bequest to free Ferocianus," her father said.

"Paris's dream of riches appears blocked at every turn," she said.

Working their way to the front of the procession, they passed Dionysius's business associates, clients, and freedmen. They skirted a group of government and religious officials flaunting their influential positions and association with the famed deceased.

The wailing and howls of hired mourners, dressed in sackcloth and ashes, accompanied an assortment of Antiochus relatives, uncles, aunts, and distant cousins, arranged from least favored at the rear to most esteemed toward the front. Sabina thought she saw Portia, but lost sight of her when the Antiochus male hierarchy strolled by, wearing the death masks of their ancestors, a cult that Dionysius had newly joined.

At the front of the line, the grieving widow and Diana rode in an open litter.

Sabina gripped her father's arm. He tensed and rose on his toes. A swaggering Paris led the procession, wearing his great-grandfather's uniform, helmet, and mask.

Diana had been right. Paris would never miss playing the hero.

Eight men carried Dionysius's straw-stuffed corpse meticulously displayed on his carved couch. Reaching their destination, they lifted the couch and body onto the speaker's platform for all to see.

Ursula and Diana followed Paris as he ascended the steps, taking his place beside his father. He removed his mask, unrolled a scroll, and recited the family's history. Recounting decades of Antiochus civic service, offices held, and acts of valor, and highlighting the city projects the family had promoted and funded over the last century. An example for all listening to admire and emulate.

Ursula looked stricken but dignified. Diana sobbed. Many in the crowd wept, identifying with their grief. Sabina was sure the two women's emotions were much more complex.

"Citizens of Ephesus." Paris handed off the lengthy scroll. "My father, the great and honorable Dionysius Alexandros Antiochus, continues to serve the people even after his death. He has bequeathed to you a ludus guaranteeing our city's prominence throughout the empire." The crowd cheered, shouting their approval. Paris threw his head back and laughed. "All glory and honor to Rome, to Ephesus, and to my father."

A ludus sealed with Dionysius's dying breath and signed with the bloodshed of victims slaughtered by Mordax's trained and lethal gladiators. A ludus generating enormous profits amassed from citizens flocking to its gladiatorial spectacles.

Sabina's throat tightened. "Dionysius's dream of a library died with him."

Her father cradled the cudgel, his expression forbidding. "With or without Paris, the legacy remains doubtful. Mordax is sure to press his claim, and I'm sure has already mounted lawsuits."

"It seems like the entire city is here." Sabina had never seen the State Agora's spacious plaza filled. Scanning the crowd, she thought she saw a familiar face standing behind the crush of spectators. Surprised, she blinked, and he was gone.

She must have been mistaken. Why would Apollos, the bishop of her church, be at Dionysius's funeral? She peered at the cluster of people. A man blocking her line of sight stepped aside, and Apollos reappeared, gripping the arm of a hunched-over old man wearing a dark woolen cloak. When the man raised his head, she gasped. No. Her thoughts spun through dozens of situations but found no reason for either man to be here. To endanger themselves by attending the public funeral of a celebrated pagan.

A few spectators glanced at the two men. Was John's attempt at a disguise, a woolen cloak in the heat of the day, making him a curiosity? Or did they know who John was? She tensed. He had not been reticent about sharing his faith over the years.

Her father caught sight of the pair. "What are those fools doing?" His eyebrows drew together. "They have no business here?"

Sabina couldn't agree more. She slipped away, without answering her father, weaving her way to Apollos's side.

"Why are you here?" she whispered her father's question, but Apollos cupped his ear, unable to hear her. "Why are you here?" she spoke louder. Three people turned their way.

"We are here for Dionysius's funeral. Isn't that why you are here?" Apollos raised his eyebrows.

"Yes. No. Sort of." She didn't have time to explain her involvement. John looked baffled. "We were surprised to hear of his death."

"He seemed so vibrant and healthy the last time we saw him," Apollos said, and John nodded in agreement.

"What do you mean the last time you saw him? Where did you see Dionysius?" Not at the late-night parties of the wealthy and powerful. They wouldn't have bet at the circus races, and both were too old for gymnasium wrestling and boxing.

"His illness must have come on suddenly," Apollos said.

"He wasn't sick," Sabina said.

Apollos's face showed concern. "An accident then? We had not heard." Sabina leaned forward intently. "He was murdered."

"Murdered?" both men gasped.

"You didn't answer my question." What possible business did they have with Dionysius?

Apollos nudged Sabina. "I believe your father requires your assistance." Sabina looked up as her father barreled toward them, a glower seared into his face. People scuttled out of his path.

"I think we should go." Apollos half lifted the tottering John as they stumbled away, vanishing into the crowd.

Sabina swirled around just as her father grabbed her arm. "What are they doing here?" he hissed, his tone as unyielding as his grip.

She tried to pull away, but his hold tightened. She shuddered, feeling as if the entire agora were listening, but it was only because her brain had blocked out the commotion of the procession. The spectators turned to stone when her father hissed in her ear. "Ursula was wrong believing that you were clever. Every magistrate, official priest, priestess, and city council member is here. I'm sure the Roman governor is using this opportunity to observe and note any transgressions."

She remembered her father agreeing to attend the funeral to collect information. The year's social event had people to surveil, interactions to monitor, and vital gossip to collect.

"Flavius Fortunus is staring at us this very minute, which makes your last exchange one of the most thoughtless things you've done. And that says a lot."

"Flavius Fortunus?" She hadn't considered herself worthy of observation, but she was wrong. Sabina bowed her head trusting her father that his rival, the magistrate in charge of religious observance, had missed nothing. "I'm sorry."

"You invite our arrest? Your eccentric reputation will not shield us from association with one of the most despised men in the city."

"John?"

"The emperor's spies are here, and Domitian will not be made a laughingstock. John's freedom hangs by a thread, and whoever is with him when our emperor cuts the thread will plummet with him."

She didn't know whether to be shocked at being called eccentric or fearful for John. "But Domitian set John free. Does John know he's spied upon?"

"If he doesn't, he is more of a fool than you. Your apostle continues to jab a hornet's nest with his preaching and writings. This man you call a protecting shepherd put your life in jeopardy today."

"They were disguised," Sabina said weakly.

"They stuck out like two pomegranates on an olive tree." Her father's look of disdain mirrored her dismay. "You forget who you are."

Her father was right. With the entire city watching, she approached and questioned the leaders of a religious sect the emperor wanted stamped out, and Flavius Fortunus with his thirty-year hatred of her father, shared the emperor's goal.

Her conversation with Apollos and John could be all Flavius needed to destroy her family—her only recourse would be to publicly renounce Jesus Christ and worship Domitian, swearing her allegiance to the cult of the emperors and Artemis. And though she had grown up knowing this, she had openly and publicly broadcast her acquaintance with two church leaders.

Her father had every reason to be furious.

Paris ended his speech. "We consign the spirit of my father to the underworld." He descended the steps, and the family and couch bearers wound out of the agora and toward the Magnesium Gate.

"Stay by me," her father ordered as the crowd began to mill around.

The tombs lining the road into the city belonged to some of the oldest and most prominent families. An engraved marble bench announced the entrance to the Antiochus tomb, a circular vault large enough for a dinner party.

The crowd had thinned. The excitement of the parade, the eulogy, and the pageantry of the wealthy and powerful had subsided. Sabina had hoped Apollos and John had grown tired and, remembering their unpopularity, returned home. But they had joined the snaking line of people for Dio's last observance. Thankfully, far from her and her father.

Dionysius's final ceremony took place on a tall pyre near the tomb. His wasn't the only cremation that day. At least twenty fires spread out across the necropolis. The hired mourners' crying laments and the wails of the family and friends joined flute players' dirges. Diana stood to the side of the pyre and recited her poem. She held no wax tablet or written scroll as the words flowed, intermingled with her tears. She finished with a sob. Ursula stepped forward, and Diana collapsed against her. Her stepmother wrapped stiff arms around the younger woman, looking uncomfortable but nodding her approval.

Paris held a torch and ignited the kindling under the body. The flame grabbed by the swirling wind danced and rippled as it devoured the wood and body. Smoke billowed in a thick cloud, permeating Sabina's clothing and hair and burning her eyes. A sudden wind gust blew the twirling ashes and pungent fumes of burning flesh out to sea. The tears of the mourners flowed, washing the sting away. Ursula and Diana wept loudly and visibly.

Sabina hadn't noticed when her father had left. He'd moved behind Paris. Paris displayed a stoic calm as if wearing his own death mask. If he mourned, he kept it to himself. No flowing tears or cowardly appeals from Dio's indulged son.

She believed Paris had been provoked by his father pointing out his errors and flaws. A murder of passion. If Dionysius had offered a way out, would he only have encouraged Paris's addictions? Was this tragedy inevitable? Dionysius acknowledging Paris's crippling habits too late. Was Cassandra right that Dio's fate was set?

The guards unobtrusively encircled the scene. Paris would be running nowhere.

THIRTY-SIX

S abina brushed the dirt from the hem of her cotton tunic. With each step, the dark fabric was coated from the dust rising in puffs. Amisi trudged behind her, winding through this remote corner of the necropolis, far from the pretentious monuments, carved marble mausoleums, and towering statues Sabina had passed at Dionysius's funeral the day before.

Cassandra's burial would have no parade or historic eulogy. Still, the ceaseless business of death was the same, dozens of new funeral pyres glowed throughout the necropolis, their smoke curling serenely into the heavens, undisturbed on a calm morning.

The two women stopped at a mound of newly dug soil. Cassandra's grave overlooked a field of parched weeds, piled stones, and crudely carved wooden markers. Cassandra had not sought prominence and recognition during her life. Still, Sabina determined that her body would not be tossed into a pit of unknown orphans, widows, beggars, and thieves whose only connection to Ephesus was where their lives ended.

Organized funeral societies buried their guild members, bakers, fishermen, and other tradespeople, but none buried illicit fortune-tellers. Sabina had paid her entire savings to Cassandra the last time she'd seen her alive. She had pleaded with her father for money for a burial, knowing a cremation and an urn were too expensive. He had handed over the money he'd recovered from Cassandra's room after the murder. It had paid for this burial plot.

"She's in the ground. We can go now," Amisi decreed, glancing around nervously.

"I want to wait a bit longer." Sabina scanned the empty field. "I hoped someone would come." Her father couldn't have stopped her from posting an announcement of Cassandra's funeral. She'd prayed Cassandra had friends or patrons who remembered her and would attend, showing respect for the young woman.

Sabina fondled Cassandra's worn and faded charm bracelet, comparing the identical weave, colors, and thread to the one Sabina wore today. She kissed it and laid it on top of the grave. Her nurse looked away, refusing to acknowledge she had made it. But despite Amisi's fear of Sabina's father's wrath, Amisi had accompanied her here. Sabina was grateful.

"She's gone. Leave her be." Amisi started walking, then stopped suddenly as a party of men carrying a litter approached them.

Portia's litter.

Her friend's appearance was unexpected. Portia had participated in Dionysius's emotionally draining procession and funeral the day before. She'd be exhausted. Tears of appreciation welled in Sabina's eyes. The carriers lowered the conveyance, and Portia got out. Sabina's tension tethered to her grief and isolation melted away.

"Thank you for coming," Sabina welcomed her. Portia held back the curtain, and Apollos climbed out, followed by John. Sabina blinked in surprise.

Apollos opened his arms, hugged her, and gently held her at arm's length while searching her face. "Portia told me that you had found one of your sisters. Cassandra, am I correct?"

Sabina nodded, not able to voice the depressing end to her hopes. She wiped her tears.

Amisi snorted and whirled on Apollos. "It's your fault we're here today. You put Sabina in danger. If you had kept her sisters a secret…"

Sabina touched her nurse's arm. "Amisi, stop. I'm thankful Apollos broke his promise. I would never have known about Cassandra if he hadn't told me about Father's decision to expose the babies."

"And we'd all be better off if he'd kept his promise." Amisi glared at Apollos as if daring him to contradict her. "Otho could have killed Sabina along with that girl."

"Enough," Sabina rebuked gently, knowing Amisi's fervor stemmed from love and fear for her mistress. "I am safe, here by your side."

"Harumph." Amisi crossed her arms, obviously still aggravated, and stalked away to sit with the litter bearers.

Sabina turned to Apollos. "Do you remember when I told you I couldn't forgive my father?"

"Your father is a difficult man who has caused you much pain. He is accountable to God for his actions." Apollos put a hand on Sabina's shoulder. "Forgiving him is for your benefit."

Sabina nodded. "I dreamt of having parents who loved me, I desired to be married, and I fantasized about having sisters. I spent so much time feeling sorry for myself that I forgot to ask God what His plan was for me."

"And what is that?" John asked.

"I don't know. It is not easy entrusting my future to God."

John took a shaky step toward her. "Christ knows what you are doing. He has put in front of you an open door, and no one can shut it."

"Does that mean you have forgiven your father?" Portia asked.

"Yes, I am changing my thoughts. I want God's peace in my life."

"I am sorry you didn't have more time with your sister," Portia said.

"As am I." Sabina looked at the thin thread of her bracelet lying on the mound. "Ursula paid me for protecting her inheritance. I'm using the money for a stele to mark Cassandra's grave." Sabina hesitated. "She was not a believer."

Portia put her arm around Sabina. "You said she heard John speak in the agora,"

Sabina nodded. "Cassandra sought truth in many places."

"Then there is hope." Apollos inclined his head. "God promises if you keep seeking, you will find. Remember, only God knew Cassandra's heart."

Sabina spoke with a hope she hadn't felt since Cassandra's murder. "We could engrave *Seek, and you will find* on the stone." Tears blurred her vision. "Will you say a prayer?"

"Of course." John folded his hands and bowed his head. "How blessed are the poor in spirit! For the kingdom of heaven is theirs. How blessed are those who mourn! For they will be comforted. How blessed are those who hunger and thirst for righteousness! For they will be filled. Amen." John's legs trembled as he finished.

"You forgot my blessing," Sabina said. "How blessed are those who show mercy! For they will be shown mercy."

John smiled. "A beautiful promise. You asked a question at Dio's funeral. We should answer you before we go."

Sabina nodded. "Why were you there?"

"We came because Dio had contacted me after Portia referred him," Apollos said.

Portia's brow furrowed in puzzlement. "I didn't send him to you."

"I misspoke," Apollos said. "During one of your debates with Dio, you professed John's authority and knowledge as an apostle of Jesus. Dio came to my door demanding to know who had the wisdom, authority, and power to punish the world's wrongs. He was quite agitated."

"I remember that night." Portia wrinkled her nose. "We were discussing how courts hold convicted criminals accountable and demand restitution. It's no different when the evil one accuses us before God."

"Dio was confident that generously donating a library was restitution for his past and current wrongs." John spoke with the confidence and strength of a much younger man.

Portia surveyed the burning pyres in the distance. "After Cassandra's prediction, his legacy took on a greater significance. He wanted his life to matter, to count for something—failure wasn't a word Dio acknowledged."

John swayed but regained his balance. "As the library plans progressed, he began showing up and arguing with us weekly. Sometimes defiant, sometimes acquiescent, but always questioning who was the ultimate moral authority?"

"Who determined if his magnificent contribution wiped away his immoral acts, allowing him to be memorialized as a good Roman citizen worthy of his ancestors," Apollos said.

Sabina added. "Cassandra said he wanted to be the best person his money could buy."

Apollos stroked his chin. "He eventually asked his true question. Was gifting the library sufficient to influence what awaited him after death?"

"Dio never cared about the afterlife," Portia said.

"People don't want to think about it," Sabina said.

"He reasoned no one knows what happens after we die," Portia said. "So why worry."

Apollos looked at Portia. "You destroyed his ignorance and revealed his argument's logical flaw. You told him Christ had risen from the dead and He knows what happens after we die. Why do you think he argued so vehemently with you?"

Portia stared at the pile of newly turned dirt. "Because of the cracked wine goblet. He knew there is no one righteous, not even one."

Apollos frowned as his thoughts formed. "During Dio's last weeks, he was confronted with a failing. He recognized his actions, even the library couldn't repair it."

Portia inclined her head toward Apollos. "Diana's rejection."

Apollos nodded. "Diana was the tipping point. Then Paris's rebellion. Dio had no defense for his failings as a husband and father. His conscience would not allow him to ignore his disastrous relationships with his family."

Sabina squeezed in. "I don't understand. Cassandra said a week before Dionysius died, he seemed content. He wasn't anxious."

"His conversion took longer than a week. I should sit before I collapse." Apollos held out a steadying arm and helped John onto the ground. "Dio began to examine how his actions affected those he loved. The instability of his marriage, the destructiveness of Paris's gambling, and the hurt he'd caused by taking Diana's love for granted."

"What conversion?" Portia blurted with skepticism.

John held up his hand signaling to let him finish. "Dio's final decision came when he unexpectedly found himself the owner of Ferocianus. Dio was in the position to make a fortune from the death and human suffering in the arena, and no one would judge him for it. They would, in fact, praise him. He chose not to benefit from the opportunity and instead asked Christ to be Lord of his life."

"Are you telling me Dio suddenly became virtuous?" Portia shook her head in disbelief.

"Not virtuous, but humble." John grinned. "Our Lord only has flawed vessels to work with."

"I want to believe you." Portia sounded unconvinced. "I loved Dio, but his life was just so…wrong."

"I was skeptical as well." Apollos raised his hands. "Dio had ridiculed and rejected Christ's resurrection often in our discussions. But God changes hearts of stone. Dio freed Ferocianus, recommitted to Ursula, attempted to mend his relationship with Diana, and exercised some moral direction for Paris."

"His attempt was a letter to Diana," Portia said. "Wishing her God's peace that passes all understanding."

"Inner peace was God's first gift to Dio, and one he desperately wanted to share with Diana."

"Where did he get the letter?" Sabina asked.

"I gave it to him." John paused and took a deep breath before continuing. "Dio came to me when my scribe was copying my vision on Patmos detailing Christ's victory over Satan, our accuser, and Christ presenting His followers blameless before the judgment throne. That day, Dio acknowledged receiving God's gift of perfect holiness. He wanted to share the good news with his family and you, Portia."

"He did share it with his children." Sabina shuddered. "Diana rebuffed him, and a desperate Paris responded by turning the winch that sent the marble blocks tumbling. The consequence of Dio's good news was yesterday's funeral pyre burning into coals."

"After years of praying for him, I want to believe you." Portia looked ready to cry. "If what you say is true why didn't he tell me?"

"What if he did?" Sabina raised her eyebrows in thought. "What if you mistook Dionysius's thief on the cross for the wrong thief? What if he shared his good news as the thief who asked for mercy?"

Portia met Sabina's gaze. "God admitted the repentant thief into heaven the day he believed in the saving power of Jesus Christ."

Sabina nodded. "Casandra said Dio made a decision that would follow him to his grave."

Portia's eyes sparkled. "Then Dionysius's change of heart wasn't too late. I can look forward to debating with him again. In heaven."

"That is a heavenly discourse I shall respectfully abstain from," Apollos said. "But I will enjoy seeing Dio again."

"It has been a long two days," John's voice shook.

"We should go." Portia glanced at John with concern. "You need rest. And I need to process the miracle you just shared."

Apollos helped John to his feet and the four exchanged farewells.

"God's peace that passes all understanding be with you." Sabina kissed her friends.

"Peace be with you." Portia followed the men into the litter and closed the curtains.

"I thought they'd never leave." Amisi rejoined Sabina, then tensed, suspiciously eyeing two people standing outside the necropolis boundaries waiting for them.

The relief at seeing Yechiel and Eunice standing side-by-side left Sabina breathless. She hurried toward them, leaving a grumbling Amisi behind, then stopped abruptly, unsure of her reception. The last time she'd spoken to Eunice, Sabina had been unable to offer any assurance concerning Yechiel or the murderer.

Sabina approached tentatively. She tried not to stare at the gauntness and bruises marking Yechiel's face.

Zarmig had reported finding Yechiel's prison cell, but Yechiel was not inside, and no one seemed to know what had happened to him. A cackling man in the cell had repeated, "He's a dead man." Zarmig finally found a guard who remembered a group of prisoners had been transported to a troop ship docked in the harbor.

His dramatic account of Yechiel's rescue caused her father to raise his eyebrow more than once. Perhaps Zarmig hoped his embellishments would add to his act of apology. She was speaking to him again.

Eunice looked past Sabina and into the cemetery at the grave. "What was her name?"

"Cassandra."

Eunice held Yechiel's hand. "We cannot enter the graveyard. We will become unclean. But we wanted to recognize her for helping to save Yechiel. He said she directed you to the killer."

"The question I asked Yechiel in prison came from her. It pointed to Dionysius's ring and was crucial to Paris's arrest."

"And was key to Yechiel's freedom." Eunice's teary gaze fastened on her husband.

Sabina shuddered, "I was afraid I was too late. Zarmig said the transport ship was pulling away from the pier when he hauled you off."

"We had to jump. I was weak and missed the dock. Zarmig pulled me to safety, swearing your name the entire time."

"God's angels come in many forms," Eunice smiled.

"Zarmig an angel?" Sabina shook her head wryly. "I will need time to ponder that idea."

"Did Zarmig tell you Dionysius hadn't changed plans? He always intended to build your library."

"No." Yechiel grunted. "I wasn't in much shape for a discussion."

Sabina swallowed, remembering the poisoned food. "I am glad to see you are alive."

"I wasn't hungry." Yechiel's eyes looked haunted. "I will suffer consequences for my lack of appetite."

Eunice nodded hesitantly. "A friend reminded Yechiel that he answers to a higher authority than the Brotherhood. For I know the thoughts that I think toward you, says the LORD...to give you a future and a hope."

An open door? "It isn't easy trusting God when we are suffering."

Eunice closed her eyes as if sealing her tears in. Her eyelashes sparkled when they fluttered open. "The Brotherhood will realize Yehciel is more valuable to their cause alive." She held her hands protectively over her stomach.

Yechiel's expression remained solemn. "I am sorry Dio is dead. He was not a bad man. We Jews are a people of a covenant, set apart for obedience to God. The law of God is good and wise, teaching us to flee what harms our soul. For all his learning, Dio did not realize the hollowness of his wealth, power, and pleasure."

Sabina gazed at the funeral pyres burning in the distance. "Dionysius understood more than you realize." Now was not the time to explain Dio's conversion to Christianity.

"We will pray Dionysius and Cassandra find refuge for their souls." Eunice clasped Sabina's hands. "You solved the murder. I knew you could."

Yechiel shook his head. "You appear drawn to threats and dangers that most women—and men, would flee from."

Sabina's denial died before she could ask drawn by whom... Yechiel's higher authority?

"I thank God she is not like most women." Eunice winked at Sabina. "Where would we be if she had run away from our plight. And..." Eunice raised her eyebrows prompting her husband.

"Ahem." Yechiel cleared his throat. "Thank you for saving my life."

"Oh," Sabina stammered. "You're welcome." Yechiel's unexpected deference could not be mistaken for anything but sincerity.

"And..." Eunice elbowed her husband.

"Before we go," Yechiel said gravely, withdrawing a familiar cloth bag tied with a drawstring. He held it out to Sabina. "I will understand if you refuse it."

Sabina's eyes widened. "I don't understand." She didn't move.

"God answered my prayers." Eunice took the bag, offering it to Sabina. "If you ever need Yechiel's help, or mine, you will have this."

The treacherous coin appeared harmless, nestled in its simple woolen bag. Reuben had been tortured, Yechiel narrowly escaped poisoning, and millions had died for what this coin symbolized. It represented a threat but also symbolized their complete trust and gratitude.

An extreme risk or a precious gift?

Two sides of the coin—one deadly, the coin's secret could destroy their lives—the other side offered hope and had saved Yechiel's life.

Life was a series of choices, life versus death, risk against reward. Dionysius had faced that choice. He risked his life to spend eternity with the Messiah Yeshua, Jesus Christ.

On the scale of justice, his reward was priceless.

The bag lay innocently in Eunice's open palm. Danger or security. Which was God calling her toward? Either choice was one of faith.

Eunice smiled her lovely smile.

Sabina's fingers shook as she took the bag and fingered the coin, before tucking it securely in her belt.

What did her future hold? She took a deep breath, patted the coin, and prayed she was following God's will, not hers.

ONE

Sabina's eyes flicked open. She blinked, disoriented, awakened from a deep sleep. Something thumped outside her door, followed by a shattering noise.

"Fires of Zeus," a man swore. Torchlight flickered through the slats in her bedroom door, and his striped shadow rippled, rising like a ghost to the ceiling.

She held her breath, her racing heart jolting her fully awake. Her linen night tunic did nothing to stop her shivering.

The shadow shriveled, diminishing with the fading slap of sandals. After a minute of hearing only the rhythmic snoring of Amisi, her childhood nurse, asleep on a floor mat in an adjoining cubicle, she sat up. Staring into the dark, she slowly released her breath.

Quietly, she slipped from her bed, drawing Amisi's partitioning curtain closed—a useless defense against a thief or worse.

She crept to the door and leaned her ear against it. Nothing. She lifted the filigree iron latch and opened the door a crack. She peered up and down the covered walkway that encircled the interior courtyard. Moonlight reflected off the garden's small gurgling pool. Was he hiding in the eerie blackness of the sculpted shrubs? A cricket chirped. Nothing moved.

The intruder was gone.

She stepped out onto the damp mosaic tiles. To the right, a large ceramic vase lay in pieces. Its marble pedestal knocked askew.

Farther down the walkway to the right, the home's central atrium glowed, alive with oil lamps and candles, lit as if hosting a late-night dinner party. But no guests had been invited this evening. Or should she say, last evening? Surely, it was the early hours of a new day when everyone should be asleep. She had heard no alarm sound. Her trembling turned to prickles of curiosity.

At least a dozen household slaves and servants scurried back and forth across the atrium. A man wearing the official robe of a governor's lictor disappeared into her father's office.

What was happening?

Feeling her way back into the dark room, Sabina fumbled for the floor-length tunic she'd flung over a chair before bed and pulled it on. She gave up looking for her tossed sandals and hurried out the door, quietly securing it—and gasped in pain, jerking her foot up. Bending down, Sabina pulled a tiny ceramic shard from her heel.

The snoring stopped. She sucked in a breath and held it. Amisi, go back to sleep, Sabina willed. The last thing she needed was an argument over nosing into her father's magisterial affairs. Amisi wheezed, and her rumbled breathing resumed.

Sabina exhaled. A drop of blood had oozed from the wound. She dabbed it with the hem of her tunic. Fortunately, she hadn't stepped down hard. Tentatively, she edged around the broken vase and headed toward the beckoning lights.

Just as she stepped into the atrium, one of her father's guards came clomping down a stairway, nearly knocking her over. He rushed past her as if she wasn't there and sprinted toward her father's office. She turned to follow him, then paused. A lamp sputtered in a nook at the top of the dark stairwell leading to the rooftop pigeon loft. The pigeons would be sleeping unless—unless a message had arrived.

Her father had invested years establishing a complex roadway in the sky between their home in Ephesus and Rome, over fifteen hundred miles away. He was not alone in gathering and disseminating information this way, but she knew he was the best. His position as Eirenarch depended on it. Catching runaway slaves and ferreting out criminals, many among his fellow elites, made information more valuable than gold. More than a few of his informants were embedded within the custodians of power throughout the empire. A man needed every advantage to survive the cut-throat game of imperial politics, power, and fortune.

Tiptoeing up the stairs, she followed the light and peeked into the room at the top. Empty, except for the dozens of pigeons that delivered messages from Ephesus, Corinth, Athens, Caesarea, Rome, and places Sabina could only imagine. The birds came and went, arriving from her father's far-reaching network of spies.

Entering the loft, Cleopatra, her pet snow-white pigeon, greeted her with a welcoming coo and fluttered to Sabina's feet. Her mate, Anthony, blinked at her but stayed roosted, showing no curiosity or concern at the disruption in the household below. They were her third pair of Cleo and Anthonys. She'd received her first pair twenty years ago, when she was eight, the day after her mother had died. She looked around at the alert and flustered birds, noting several were asleep. Perhaps exhausted after flying hundreds of miles.

Several message bands lay on a table. Sabina picked up each one and looked inside the narrow cylinders. All were empty. She sighed, disappointed. The guard had obviously already delivered the message that had alerted the household. Confidential? Highly sensitive? Life threatening? The message that had sent a harried servant or guard crashing into her vase.

She tossed the messenger bands back with a sigh. She would probably never learn what they had contained, and she would be tired and crabby tomorrow, her curiosity unsatisfied with no way to discover the cause of tonight's excitement. She'd get no sympathy from Amisi for wasting a good night's sleep, but at least she had avoided a lecture about sticking her inquisitive female nose where it didn't belong. She wouldn't have to endure her father's ridicule at her irritating questions and disdain for his only daughter's willful behavior. She pushed the term *unloved* to the back of her mind.

Cleo flew, joining her at the table, and gently pecked at her hand. Sabina stroked the bird. "I love you too. Sorry, I don't have time to feed you a treat." At the word *treat* Anthony twisted his neck to look at her. "I have to get to bed. I don't have the luxury of sleeping all day like you." She pursed her lips, but her stern look didn't fool the birds. Anthony flew down to the table, joining his mate. Several other birds began cooing and ruffling their feathers. "Fine, but don't dare tell anyone I gave you a midnight snack." She removed the lid from a wooden box the breeder and trainer kept in the loft's corner. Dozens of flapping birds surrounded her, fluttering to the floor and bobbing their heads. Taking a handful of grain, she sat on the floor and scattered the feed around her. The beating wings dislodged a small piece of papyrus caught under the table.

She scooted toward the table and snatched it up. The disturbed birds clucked in annoyance.

The message was written in Greek, not the Latin of official magisterial business. She noted the time. It had arrived tonight. *A woman named Chloe was found murdered in the Nicomedian baths. Please advise. Leo*

The message wasn't in code, but it did contain information that was not explicitly written. No one went to public or private baths late at night. Either Chloe had gone earlier and never left, or something had compelled her there in the middle of the night.

Day or night, only a select few could afford the private baths of Nicomedian. Dozens of wealthy women died every day. Their passing was of no importance to the city leaders. But this woman was important enough to inform her father, a leading magistrate. Could it have been Chloe's death that caused the turmoil going on downstairs? Her murder?

Sabina had a childhood friend named Chloe. Their mothers were friends. In this city of two hundred and fifty thousand souls, there were hundreds if not thousands of women named Chloe and the last she'd heard, her Chloe had married and moved to Rome. She smiled at the thought of Chloe holding a baby surrounded by a jumble of children.

Sabina rose to her knees and petted Anthony and Cleo goodnight. They paid no attention as they jostled and pecked among the other pigeons for the remaining grain. She stood, the dull ache in her foot subsiding.

She reached the bottom of the stairs and counted ten people bustling about. A scribe bumped into her while juggling rolls of papyrus and a writing case containing pens and ink and trying to catch up to her father who was striding toward the door, wearing his official toga, accompanied by Zarmig, his bodyguard, confidant, and master spy.

Clutching the message, she wondered at the secrets it held. Secrets that had jolted a powerful magistrate awake.

Her father gestured to six of his guards to fall in line. "I won't be back until late tomorrow," he declared to no one specific.

Your prying nose is going to get bit off one day, Amisi's repeated warning pricked her memory. Sabina ran up and plucked at her father's sleeve. "Sir."

He shook her off and kept walking. "I don't have time for you, Sabina."

She let the stinging rebuke take its bite, then steeled herself. "I know about the murder."

He jerked to a stop, turning toward her. His stare hard, unreadable. "How?"

She swallowed, meekly holding up the paper. "I found the message."

Her father snapped his fingers, and the guard she'd seen running from the pigeon loft snatched the papyrus from her. "You will say nothing of this until I speak to the new governor." He strode to the door, followed by his retinue of guards and servants.

What murdered woman was significant enough to confer with the governor? She couldn't stop herself. "Do you know who killed Chloe?"

Her father stopped but didn't turn around. "Who?" He inclined his head to the guard who'd taken the note. The man murmured and handed her father the message to read.

He shook his head. "Go to bed, Sabina. Forget this." He crumpled the note and threw it on the floor. "Basil's daughter Chloe is of no importance. News arrived that the emperor has been assassinated." He lifted the hem of his toga and led his entourage out the door.

Sabina slumped on a bench, half in confusion and half in shock. Domitian was dead. Assassinated.

A slave padded past her, extinguishing the candles. Another circled the atrium, smothering the lamps' light. Yawning servants shuffled to their rooms. Their workday but a few hours away.

Sabina's eyes adjusted to the silver glow of the moonlight reflecting in the atrium's shallow pool until it disappeared, dipping below the roof's large opening, leaving her sitting in the dark.

She understood her father's urgency. He would be the first to hear the imperial news with his pigeons racing against the military relay of courier horses. His birds didn't need to arrange for river barges or depend on favorable winds to sail across the Aegean, but the arrival could be within hours of each other, leaving little time to forge the political allies needed to survive this transition.

After Nero's death twenty-seven years ago, the panic and bloody aftermath had nearly destroyed the empire. Four men vied for the highest honor on Earth. Within a year, three were dead, and Domitian's father, Vespasian, ruled. Domitian had no children and no heir and there were far too many eager to fuel political instability.

The newly arrived governor was an unknown. Who was he loyal to? Would he trust her father to aid in securing political allies? Could her father trust him? Because his position—their lives—depended on allegiance to those in power. Knowing who held the power was the trick.

She understood why her father had no time for Chloe. Her death would remain a mystery. The empire would turn its attention to finding a new ruler and hopefully averting a war. Shifting loyalties in a province unfamiliar to the governor could lead to unforeseen and deadly consequences for the province of Asia Minor, the metropolis of Ephesus, and the household of Eirenarch Catius Sabinus and his daughter Sabina.

And Chloe, the daughter of Basil, whose murder was of no importance, would be forgotten—unless.

Was her Chloe's father named Basil? Sabina searched her memory, but the name did not come to mind. Their mothers had chatted and smiled, while their daughters had played. Non-stop giggling had made Sabina's stomach muscles sore. After Sabina's mother's death, many friendships had slipped from her life. A sad nostalgia touched her heart. She hoped this wasn't her funny, light-hearted, and precocious friend.

She could easily put her mind to rest. No sense in grieving if her Chloe lived as a happily married mother in Rome.

Leo the informer's note was brief but not devoid of clues—the Nicomedian baths, for one. She could go there and ask Leo who the dead woman was. He would be awaiting directives from her father. Unless, not receiving an answer to his dispatch, he had resolved the incident, found the murderer, and gone home. Or given up and gone home.

Felix, one of her father's slaves, stumbled past, rubbing his eyes.

"Felix." Sabina stopped him.

Felix turned a wary look her way. "Mistress?"

"There has been a murder."

"Yes, the emperor," he said, sounding suspicious. "The master ordered us not to tell anyone, or we die."

"You aren't going to die." Sabina tried to sound dismissive, knowing her father did not make idle threats.

Felix was slowly shaking his head.

"I need you to accompany me to a different murder." A murder she couldn't forget.

If you enjoyed this book, will you consider sharing it with others?

- Please mention the book on Facebook, Instagram, Pinterest, or another social media site.

- Recommend this book to your small group, book club, and workplace.

- Head over to Facebook.com/CrossRiverMedia, 'Like' the page and post a comment as to what you enjoyed the most.

- Pick up a copy for someone you know who would be challenged or encouraged by this message.

- Write a review on your favorite book platform.

- To learn about our latest releases subscribe to our newsletter at CrossRiverMedia.com.

ABOUT THE AUTHOR

Liisa Eyerly is the author of two Christian mystery novels set in ancient Ephesus. She is a retired elementary teacher and school librarian but will never retire from inciting the thrill of reading in all ages.

She has lived in some of the most beautiful areas of the US. The passion for exploring new places and connecting with people began there and inspired her writing. Her publishing career started after getting married, teaching, raising three children, opening a small business, closing her small business, and finally getting serious about writing. She is a relentless questioner (a trait not appreciated by her husband) and a novice student of Christian apologetics. Her writing goals are to be entertaining, thought-provoking, and surprising.

Book discussion questions can be found at liisaeyerly.com/books.

If you would like to learn more about the Roman world that Sabina lived in or find book club and Bible study discussion guides for this book, you can visit Liisa's website at liisaeyerly.com

Many thanks to the excellent guides and teachers on my Turkiye "Seven Churches of Revelation Tour" offered by Tutkutours.com. Nothing beats walking in the footsteps of the Apostles for hands-on research.

Sinister forces are at work.
Who can she trust?

OBEDIENT
UNTO DEATH

More great historical fiction from
CrossRiverMedia.com

Roots Reawakened

Robbed of her family, Justine Davidson escapes to America to outrun her pain and loneliness. Penniless and homeless, she is pursued by two very different men. Justine's heart is torn between trusting a sovereign God and trusting in herself to avoid painful change. Will deception and the reigniting of an old passion bring Justine to the brink of hope or destruction?

Swept into Destiny

Maggie Gatlan may be a Southern belle on the outside but is a rebel on the inside. Ben McConnell is enchanted by Maggie's beauty and fiery spirit, but for him the South represents the injustice and deprivation he left behind in Ireland. As the country divides and Ben joins the Union, Maggie and Ben are forced to call each other enemies. Will their love survive or die on the battlefield of South against North?

Road to Deer Run

The year is 1777 and the war has already broken the heart of nineteen-year-old Mary Thomsen. Her brother was killed by the King's army, so when she stumbles across a wounded British soldier, she isn't sure if she should help him or let him die, cold and alone. Severely wounded, Daniel Lowe wonders if the young woman looking down at him is an angel or the enemy. Need and compassion bring them together, but will the bitterness of war keep them apart?

Wilted Dandelions

Rachael Rothburn just wants to be a missionary to the Native Americans out west, but the missionary alliance says she can't go unless she is married. When Dr. Jonathan Wheaton, another missionary hopeful, offers her a marriage of convenience, she quickly agrees. But she soon finds that his jealousy may be an even greater threat than the hostile Indians and raging rivers they face along the way.

Books that build battle-ready faith.

More great books from…
CrossRiverMedia.com

Ants Across the Page

This 1960s era story is told from the perspective of an undiagnosed dyslexic, motherless eleven-year-old boy, Luke, who tries to spruce up his father so he can win the heart of a woman they refer to as "the sarge" behind her back. In a nutshell, whether you're a kid whose letters move on the page, or an awkward man with tractor grease under his fingernails—there's always hope. Buy *Ants Across the Page* today and enjoy plenty of laugh-out-loud moments but keep the tissues handy too!

Surviving Carmelita

It was Josie's hands on the wheel, her foot on the pedal. Her fault. Now, sweet Carmelita will never see her fifth birthday. Where do you run when your world implodes and you can't function? Josie leaves her Chicago suburban home to stay with a cousin in Key West, unaware her journey is guided by an unseen hand and that a trailer park pastor, a battered horse, a pregnant teen, and a mysterious beachcomber might set her on the path toward redemption.

Love Final Sunrise

The lives of New Yorker Ruth Jessup and Amish-bred Joshua Stutzman collide as they battle wits against a psychopath and the New World Order. Suffering from amnesia, Ruth finds herself in a world without TVs, cell phones, or computers and if not for Joshua, Ruth would be lost and homeless. As the chaos of the biblical seven-year tribulation blankets the world, can Joshua's Amish ways help them survive the next three-and-a half years without the mark of the beast?

Claiming Her Inheritance

A shooting, a stampede, a snakebite… Sally Clark has received an inheritance of a lifetime, but first she has to survive living on the ranch in Montana. Chase Reynolds is astounded that his father has willed one-third of their ranch to a total stranger. Who is this woman and what hold did she have over his dad? What Sally and Chase discover is beyond their imagination and wields far greater consequences than the inheritance.

www.ingramcontent.com/pod-product-compliance
Lightning Source LLC
Chambersburg PA
CBHW072343020726
47506CB00004B/982